THE STONE MUST BREAK

THE STONE MUST BREAK

A Novel

Jean Lee Porter

iUniverse, Inc.
New York Lincoln Shanghai

The Stone Must Break

iUniverse books may be ordered through booksellers or by contacting:

iUniverse
2021 Pine Lake Road, Suite 100
Lincoln, NE 68512
www.iuniverse.com
1-800-Authors (1-800-288-4677)

ISBN: 978-0-595-45462-4 (pbk)
ISBN: 978-0-595-69743-4 (cloth)
ISBN: 978-0-595-89774-2 (ebk)

Printed in the United States of America

To my three sons Carl, David, and Marc, who believed in me and in *The Stone Must Break.*

Your pain is the breaking of the shell that
Encloses your understanding.
Even as the stone of the fruit must break,
That its heart may stand in the sun, must you know pain

—Kahlil Gibran, *The Prophet*

CHAPTER 1

❀

Thanksgiving afternoon, 1941, few automobiles raced along the California Bayshore Highway linking San Jose and San Francisco. Genevieve Carmel St. John, sitting in the back seat of the new Pontiac station wagon, stared glumly out the window. In her gray eyes, she attempted to conceal the agitation in her heart. Rainsqualls had passed, but the overcast winter sky, with rain predicted, only increased her anxiety.

She sighed and looked at the eastern side of the highway beyond the flat, colorless marsh. A constant wind pushed whitecaps across the enormous bay. Gulls dove at the water, skimming and racing the waves. Grabbing pieces of seaweed in their beaks from the crests of the waves, they carried their prizes in the wind. Then they dropped the weed and, shrieking, returned to the game.

The western side of the bay, with barren stretches of land, occasional groves of eucalyptus trees with leaves turned colorless in the wind, and sporadic dingy warehouses, loomed just as dull and boring.

"Dad," she blurted, "why can't we drive faster? Every car on the Bayshore is passing us. We'll be all day reaching San Francisco. It gets dark early now." She stole a glance at her father's face in the mirror.

At six foot two, Andrew St. John's erect body filled the driver's seat. He smiled. "You'll see your brother and Chet before the *Lurline* sails." He consoled her in his deep voice but continued to drive at the same steady pace.

She stared at his broad back in his gray overcoat, his crisp white hair curled out from under his gray Fedora. She wondered, with a sense of foreboding, what his reaction would be to her plans to leave home.

Her twenty-seven-year-old brother, Scott, sat beside their father. "Not bad! Brother Grant sailing to Hawaii on Thanksgiving Day."

Grant and the San Jose State College's Spartans football team sailed today on the *Lurline* to play in the big game December 13 against the University of Hawaii. The two men fell to discussing the Spartans' chances against the Hawaii team.

As much as Carmel cared for her older brother, Grant, and his friend Chet, they were not on her mind. She was not one bit concerned about missing the ship. If only her father and brother would stop talking about football so she could concentrate on her own objectives. Barely twenty years old, she was determined to move to San Francisco and live near Dr. Phillip Barron, the man she had vowed to love forever.

Andrew asked, "Daughter, why are you in such a bad mood? I thought you wanted to see your brother off with the team. Afterwards we'll have Thanksgiving dinner at the Palace Hotel with your aunt and uncle."

"Relax, little sister," Scott suggested. "We'll be there in no time. I like your new hat. You look swell."

She scowled at Scott. "Thank you."

He admired her for a moment and turned away.

Carmel had tucked her unruly shoulder-length black hair into a small burgundy wool hat with a pale blue feather. The hat sat at a rakish angle. Her matching burgundy wool coat accented her slender body.

Carmel's nose tilted when she smiled, giving her a spirited expression. Dimples added to her sauciness. Men found her expression enchanting and sensual. The highs and lows of her emotions were revealed in gray eyes as changeable as the clouds. She was blessed with a creamy English complexion. Her generous full lips suggested a petulant disposition. However, one found Carmel direct and forthright. She detested anyone who possessed a pouting nature.

The heated car with the windows closed, plus the smell of the men's lotion, stifled Carmel. Near panic at the thought that she might not persuade her father to allow her to move to San Francisco, she shivered.

Finally, at the sight of San Francisco's bustling waterfront, Carmel felt relief. Andrew drove to Pier 35 and found a place to park. She stepped out of the car, shut the door, and turned away from her father and brother to stare up at the city of San Francisco.

From the waterfront, Telegraph Hill soared above her. The white minaret of Coit Tower stood at the very top. Through the late afternoon she felt the tall, slim tower beckon to her. She inhaled deeply the bracing sea air blowing across San Francisco Bay.

Her thoughts turned to Phillip. She suspected Phillip thought of her only as the little kid growing up on the neighbor's ranch, running in and out of the house with his sister Laura, her best friend. Through the years Carmel had paid little attention to him.

Then last September she went next door to swim at Laura's pool. Phillip came home unexpectedly from the San Francisco hospital. He spent the entire afternoon with them beside the family's swimming pool. He teased her and laughed at her patience, insisting the new puppy, named Patti, learn to fetch the ball from the pool. They talked about the war coming. She learned he loved and adored his sister, liked big bands, and liked Frank Sinatra. Laura had said her brother intended to be the head surgeon of San Francisco's University of California Hospital. This news convinced Carmel she must live in San Francisco.

She simply had to move to San Francisco to be near him and do something to impress him. Since he liked big bands and music, and she had sung successfully with the college band, the thought occurred to her to find a job singing with a big band. Certainly this would impress him.

Her pulse quickened when she remembered Phillip's dark eyes and the penetrating look he had given her that afternoon by the pool. For a few hours, a man in red trunks with dark brown eyes and jet black hair had set her heart thumping and swept her away. She knew she would love Phillip Barron for the rest of her life. Carmel kept her feelings for Phillip a secret. She did not intend to tell anyone, especially Laura.

Inhaling the pungent air, she promised herself she would find a way to move to San Francisco and see Phillip again.

"Genevieve Carmel St. John." Her father's shout jostled her thoughts. "Stop lollygagging. Pay attention to what's going on here. Grant and Chet will arrive any minute."

Confident in her decision, Carmel moved to his side and took his arm. She smiled up at him. He was his usual dapper self in his Fedora, overcoat, and hand crafted black boots. His complexion was clear and tan, his blue eyes deep and discerning. Tiny capillaries, breaking on his cheeks, revealed the ravages of his beloved brandy. Still, he radiated robust good health.

Under the leaden sky, the waters of San Francisco Bay appeared choppy, the color of oyster shells. The Bay Bridge soared, a silver bird's wing to Oakland. The *Lurline*, with its pennants flying in the cold breeze, nestled against the pier like a great white birthday cake. Alongside the enormous ship, a small band of musicians played Hawaiian music.

Her father scrutinized the large crowd milling about. "Doesn't look as if Thanksgiving Day or the threat of rain kept families and fans of the Spartans from Pier 35." He grabbed Scott's arm. "Let's move closer to the docks. We're too far back. The boys will never find us in this mob. I know the team's here, probably aboard."

The three pushed through the mass of relatives toward the ship.

Carmel twisted the tassels on the collar of her burgundy wool coat. She sensed Scott staring at her and turned to look at him.

His eyebrows, darker than his thick blond hair, arched over wide, intelligent brown eyes. His skin had bronzed from long days spent in the orchards. She thought her brother, tall as their father, extremely handsome.

Scott had left his cane at home. Fifteen years earlier a drunken farmer pulled out in front of the car driven by their mother, Elizabeth Rose, killing her instantly and leaving Scott with a crushed left leg. Through four painful surgeries, months in bed, and his own resoluteness, he kept his leg. Now he walked with a limp.

Scott lowered his voice out of their father's earshot. "I know, little sister, when you twist the tassels on your coat collar, you're up to something."

Carmel stopped pulling on her tassels. "Dad, I think every conceivable contraption on wheels is here!"

Scott said in a harsh whisper, "Pretty face, bet I find out what you're up to before the days over."

Pungent aromas of roasted coffee from the nearby Hills Brothers factory filled the air, and cold, salty sea breezes carried the biting odor of lobsters cooking in steaming black pots.

She ignored him and asked, "Dad, don't you just love the smell of this place?"

Scott hissed, "Don't change the subject. What are you up to?"

She didn't answer, as it became necessary to step back from the enormous carts loaded with baggage being pulled and pushed toward the ship.

She asked, "Dad, did you ever think about living in San Francisco?"

Andrew grunted, "San Francisco is a great city to visit for business and such … oh, and to see your Aunt Lydia. City life is not for me."

"I think it would be a great place to live," Carmel muttered.

Her father heard her and frowned. "It might be for some gals, but not for my daughter. I hope you're not thinking of any such idea."

Carmel's heart sank. Her father was shrewd and she must not reveal her true feelings. Not at this moment. She didn't want anyone to know how much living in San Francisco meant to her.

Andrew suddenly asked, "How would you support yourself?" He laughed at such an impossible idea.

Carmel bit her lip. This wasn't going well at all. She wished she had never broached the subject.

"There's one thing for sure. No daughter of mine will be marching herself off to any big city. It's time to think about settling down in San Jose with one of the young men who keep coming around.

Carmel understood Andrew's plans for his family. Her brothers would assume the duties of the ranch, live there, and raise their families. She would marry a rancher, bear his children, and bring them all to visit on Sundays. Her heart pounded. The only person she ever intended to marry was Phillip.

Scott whispered to her, "So that's it. You want to leave the ranch?"

"Here come the Spartans' two best ball players!" shouted Andrew as the two young men with the intense vigor of young athletes nimbly sidestepped a heavy cart piled high with luggage.

Grant had inherited his father's romantic profile and tall, rugged figure. His curly hair was reddish gold in the sun, eyes the color of cinnamon. Full, sensuous lips hinted at a lustful nature.

Chet Whiting, Grant's best friend, was fair-haired with blue eyes. The twenty-two-year-old seniors had good looks and healthy bodies in common, but their temperaments were as different as night and day. Chet, slow to anger, thought before he spoke. Grant shadowboxed through life with his fists and jaw clenched.

Carmel saw Chet blush as he approached. She knew he had a crush on her. She beamed at her brother, Grant. He was so attractive that girls often begged her for an introduction.

Grant grabbed Carmel and swung her around in a whirl.

"Put me down."

"First, tell me what you want from Hawaii."

"Oh, pearls! Please. I love them."

"Okay. Pearls it'll be." He set her down.

"Are you coming aboard, Mr. St. John?" Chet asked. "I think the team's on board."

"Oh, no, Chet, we're going to meet my sister, Lydia, for an early Thanksgiving dinner. We're already late." He shook Chet's offered hand, "I hope you can keep that rambunctious son of mine out of trouble."

"I'll do my best, Mr. St. John."

As the band finished playing "Aloha Oe," there were two blasts from the ship's horn. Scott said, "Stay sober so you can watch for subs." He laughed, but his eyes were serious.

"That's not funny!" scolded Carmel.

"Mr. St. John, do you think we'll have a war with Japan?" Chet asked.

"Hell, no," piped up Grant. "The Japanese are now in Washington negotiating for peace. England and France are at war with Germany. That should be enough!"

Carmel nodded. "We don't ever need another war."

Chet asked again, "What do you think, Mr. St. John?"

"It doesn't look good to me, Chet. I don't trust the Japanese Government."

Carmel took her brother's hand. "Grant, when will you be home?"

"I'll be here to fill your Christmas stocking with pearls." Grant laughed and looked at his father, "Thanks, Dad, for seeing us off."

Andrew felt their exuberance. His voice was gruff. "Take care of yourselves." He shook hands and then patted Grant on the shoulder.

"Give me a kiss, my angel." Grant kissed Carmel.

"Watch out for those Hawaiian gals. I hear they're lookers," Scott gripped Grant's hand.

"That's exactly what I'm goin' to do."

Chet shook hands with Andrew and Scott. He picked up the suitcases and grinned at Carmel. She grinned back. He blushed and stammered, "We better get on the boat, Grant, I mean ship."

The green hills of Berkeley had become dark shadows rimming the distant bay. Beside the huge illuminated ship, three small tugs waited to push it away from the dock and into the bay.

Carmel, Andrew, and Scott silently watched the young men stride toward the ship, climb the ramp, and disappear.

Suddenly everything in the bay turned black except for the rim of lights on Alcatraz and the distant, twinkling lights of Berkeley. The red spires of the towering Golden Gate Bridge had disappeared.

Wordless, the St. Johns returned to their car.

Andrew paused to look up at San Francisco. "Some families have already turned on their Christmas lights."

Scott said. "Ye gods, Dad, let's get Thanksgiving over before we start on Christmas."

Carmel whispered to the lights of the city, "I'll be back, San Francisco. You just wait and see. Nothing in the whole wide world will stop me. I'll figure out some way to come back to you and Phillip."

The three family members stood at the entrance of the elegant Garden Court. The men's hats and topcoats checked they waited to be seated.

Secure in her decision to live in San Francisco, Carmel was swept by a sense of independence. How and when this move would come about she didn't know. But for the moment she relished having Thanksgiving dinner with her family in the Palace Hotel.

"I never tire of this wonderful room," Andrew admitted. "It radiates all the charm and sophistication of San Francisco."

The thought crossed Carmel's mind she might someday spend many hours in this famous hotel. She stared at the magnificent room.

A glass roof forty feet high crowned the beautiful Garden Court. Twelve crystal chandeliers glittered and twinkled above their heads. Elegant table settings, snowy linens, sparkling china, crystal, and gleaming silver added to the beauty of the room. Gold and purple jewel tones of the carpet repeated in the centerpieces of tiger lilies, cattails, and purple liatrias.

The captain led them past a dais in the center of the room where two violinists and a cellist entertained.

Andrew's sister, Lydia, and her husband, Russell Bannister, were seated at the table.

Carmel leaned down to kiss her adored aunt. "Auntie, you look lovely."

Lydia Bannister was forty-five years old, five feet six inches tall, with unlined skin and clear blue eyes. A navy pancake hat sat atop her red hair. She smiled at her niece. "Thank you."

Uncle Russell stood to greet the family. Silver softened the edges of his raven hair. His Roman nose, set in a narrow and handsome face, gave him a hawkish appearance. Trim in a charcoal suit, three-button vest, and a silk red tie, he generated the dash of a retired colonel. He kissed Carmel's cheek. "It's good to see all of you." A Texas drawl slowed his words. He shook hands with Andrew and Scott and then settled into his chair.

"I would guess Grant's on the high seas by now," Russell said. "He'll have a lot to tell us when he gets back. Hope his team wins."

Andrew nodded. "If they do, he'll be even harder to live with."

Carmel perused the menu. "Wonder if having Thanksgiving aboard a ship is as good as ours?"

Scott teased, "Better not order everything. I don't want a fat sister."

"No one diets on Thanksgiving," Lydia insisted.

Carmel smiled at her aunt. "Auntie, that's a problem you'll never have." She acknowledged Lydia's slim body in her navy blue suit with white ruching framing the neck.

Russell turned to Andrew, "I'll order the champagne as my contribution to dinner." He signaled the waiter. "Andrew, we don't seem to tempt you to spend time at our place."

Lydia added, "Yes, brother dear, with all of our bedrooms, you would be no trouble at all."

"I know. Every year I promise myself I'll visit," Andrew acknowledged. "The ranch seems to take every minute of my time."

"We have so many exciting things to do in San Francisco. You didn't even show up last year for the 1939 World Exposition on Treasure Island."

Andrew, ignoring her remark, looked around at the large room. "I've never seen so many service men in San Francisco at one time."

"Part of that's due to the draft," Russell said. "There's a sense of restlessness in the air. Can't you feel it? By the way, pilot training jumped from five hundred a year to thirty-three thousand. Don't tell me we're not gearing up for something."

Carmel interrupted the two men. "Let's not talk about the world situation. It's too depressing."

"Yes," Lydia agreed. "Let's enjoy ourselves. We see so little of our family."

Andrew persisted, his voice impatient. "Russell, you're right. What's Hitler doing to the low countries? We have to decide how distant we can remain. How about the alliance Japan signed with Germany and Italy? How about that, eh?"

"That's what I'm talking about," Russell answered. "The situations are becoming more intense every day. Just listen to Ed Murrow."

"Navy Secretary Knox says war's inevitable with the Japanese," Scott chimed in. "I read yesterday some Japanese paper says if the Japs can't get oil from us and the East Indies by ordinary means, they'd take extraordinary means. Their country cannot exist without it."

Russell's brow furrowed. "I'm very, very concerned about Europe. What's Germany doing? What incredible guts the British have displayed. Imagine four hundred thousand men waiting on a Dunkirk beach, scrambling into any kind of a boat to cross the channel with Germans firing at them. They figured maybe twenty thousand or thirty thousand would make it. I guess three hundred thousand made it. Amazing!"

The waiter arrived with the champagne. He arranged the bucket of ice on a stand beside Russell and presented the bottle of Moet for his approval. The group watched silently as the waiter expertly opened the bottle, placed stemmed glasses before each person, and filled the fine crystal.

They lifted their glasses. Lydia gushed, "To the family, and a Happy Thanksgiving."

They all sipped champagne.

Andrew said, "I think Roosevelt is smart with this Lend-lease program, sending military goods and equipment to Britain."

Carmel whispered to her aunt, "They just won't quit talking about war! Why won't men do what you ask them to?"

Lydia gave her niece a knowing look. "They will, if they want something."

"How about those Merchant Marines on the North Sea?" Andrew asked. "They can carry cargoes without destroyers convoying them across the North Atlantic. Why? Because now they're armed."

"So technically we're already at war with Germany," Scott said.

"Son, our president has one hell of a job. Churchill has probably told him the British can't survive without our help. The American people are dead set against going to war. Since Britain needs equipment and has no money, Roosevelt must convince Congress to help the Allies *save* democracy." He shook his head.

Scott cast a grim look at his father. "We're going to war. It's inevitable."

Lydia cried, "All right, that's enough. We're having a dinner here, not a war council."

"Sorry. I guess I should cheer up." Scott cleared his throat. "Hey! We're probably sitting where Caruso sat."

His father held up his hand. "No, no. We're sitting where the carriages in the 1890s were driven into the building from the street and turned around to go out again. All these floors above were open balconies where people walked and watched the promenade below." Andrew took another sip of champagne. "This entire hotel, all six hundred rooms, was rebuilt after the 1906 quake." His enthusiasm rose. "During the quake, Caruso ran up and down the halls weeping, or so I heard."

Carmel listening, said, "What a wonderful place to live." She looked up from her chilled lobster on ice straight into the eyes of a man sitting at the next table. Her smile froze.

Flanked by two other well-dressed men, the man's black eyes drew hers like a magnet. He was broad shouldered with thick black hair shaping his groomed head. Heavy eyebrows over his well-spaced eyes gave him a brooding look. She gasped! He must be at least thirty years old. She felt a flash in her mind, warning her to be careful. Careful of what? The man meant nothing to her. She averted her eyes.

"Genevieve Carmel." Her father interrupted her thoughts. "We've decided to enjoy a traditional Thanksgiving dinner with all the trimmings. Do you agree?"

Carmel nodded to everyone. "That sounds great."

Halfway through the meal, Lydia surprised her. "Would you like to live in San Francisco?"

A miracle, Carmel thought. My darling aunt has brought my problem to the surface. "I'd love it."

Lydia studied Carmel. "I thought you were happy at San Jose State?"

"I've changed my mind."

"Do you know *what* you want to do?" Her father's voice sounded testy.

"Yes, I do. I want to be a singer."

"She does have an exceptional voice, Dad." Scott turned to his sister. "Where would you like to sing?"

"With dance bands in a hotel." Looking around the room, she waved her arm. "Just like this one."

"This is ridiculous. Spend your nights with men ogling you?" Andrew's voice rose. "That'll be the day my daughter does that."

"Dad, you make it sound preposterous." Scott grinned at Carmel. "I bet you'd knock 'em dead."

Lydia's eyes twinkled. "Why don't you come and live with us? Give yourself the chance to find out. Andrew, there's only one place that offers real opportunity, and that's a large city like San Francisco. Besides, we would enjoy having Carmel live with us."

"Just a minute, dear sister. You're jumping the gun here. I may be a rancher in a quiet valley, but I know one thing. My daughter should be thinking about choosing a husband, not moving to a city where everyone is a stranger."

"Oh, Dad, I'm not ready to think of marriage. I want to do something that's me. My music is *me*."

Scott winked at Carmel. "Why don't you strike a bargain, Dad? Give her six months to see how she does? What harm is there in it?"

Carmel could have kissed her brother.

Andrew exploded. "You folks are ganging up on me. And you, Lydia, my own sister, grinning like a Cheshire cat, trying to steal my daughter."

Andrew looked at Carmel, her skin luminous in the reflected light of the chandeliers and her beautiful gray eyes pleading with him to let her go. He lowered his voice. "How do you feel, daughter? I didn't know you wanted this so much. Enough to leave home?"

"Yes, but I did know I wanted it so much."

She could not believe this conversation. Her gaze fastened on the man at the next table. Their eyes locked. She could feel herself getting warm. Why is he upsetting me? She tried to concentrate on the words at the table.

Fortunately, the three men stood and left the dining room.

"Dear brother, I'll watch her like a mother hen. Make sure she meets all the right people. By the way, we know some lovely young men at the Presidio."

Russell grinned, adding his hearty support. "Happiness is our beautiful niece coming to live with us."

"Happiness for me is seeing my daughter happy." Andrew slammed his fist on the table, disturbing the china and crystal. "All right, six months."

"Oh, thank you, Father."

Andrew raised his glass. "Let's have a toast to Carmel's success."

She raised her glass. For one tiny moment, she felt a sharp twinge of guilt at wanting to leave her father. Unshed tears brightened her eyes.

CHAPTER 2

Doctor Phillip Barron, alerted to three accident cases, strode swiftly and silently on crepe-soled shoes down the wide hospital corridor toward the emergency room.

Phillip, six feet, three inches tall, slender, and just past his thirty-second birthday, had inherited his mother's fair skin and aquiline nose. His abundant black hair, jet colored eyes, and square jaw came from his father's side.

He grew up on his family's one-hundred-acre ranch in San Jose, with doting parents and a loving younger sister, Laura. He loved and respected his parents, and at an early age decided to follow in his father's footsteps and become a surgeon.

Medical school had been easy for Phillip, as he had a fascination for medical science. Surgery had remained a challenge, and his ambition was to be one of the best. He grew up admiring his father, but he planned that once he became a doctor he would remain in a large hospital. To practice in his father's medical clinic would confine him, might even smother him.

Phillip was an agreeable host and houseguest, but somehow women read more into his graciousness than he meant. A natural charmer with good looks, Phillip attracted women. They often flirted with him, hoping to penetrate his male ego. Men sought his approval but inwardly resented his indifference and lack of warmth.

Nurse Ryan waited outside the emergency room. "Automobile accidents. I think they were racing."

Phillip pushed through the swinging doors. He felt comfortable with Ryan, a capable nurse who knew her job. He thought her damned attractive in her slim nurse's uniform, blonde hair tucked up under her white nurse's cap, and blue eyes, which were clearly flirting with him.

From the beginning of his internship at the hospital, he made a solemn oath never to date the nurses. A workplace romance would complicate his life. When he desired companionship, San Francisco socialites were always available.

In the brightly lit emergency room, each of the three gurneys held a still body. Phillip judged they couldn't be more than seventeen or eighteen. The emergency staff waited for orders. He leaned over the first boy, whose eyes were closed and his face pale. Phillip asked for his blood pressure.

The emergency nurse informed him, "Seventy-four over forty-eight."

"Get him into X-ray. Prep for surgery. Start the IV."

The second boy cried out, "Oh, help me. Please help me."

Phillip examined the patient. He noted the youth was bleeding internally. "X-ray him. He'll need blood."

The young man continued to moan as two nurses wheeled the gurney to X-ray.

A medic stood by the third gurney. "They thought this boy was gone, but they picked him up and brought him here just in case."

Phillip looked at the body of the handsome teenager and thought it a tragic waste. Regretfully, he pulled a sheet over the young face and left the room to scrub.

Surgery finished at dawn. The young patient was wheeled into intensive care. An internist advised Phillip that the boy with the internal injuries remain under observation.

Phillip learned the boy's parents had been in the waiting room all night. He crossed the corridor to the silent room. In his usual courteous, professional manner, he informed them their boy's chances for recovery were better than average.

He left them for coffee and entered the doctors' staff room.

Doctor Larry Marsh, holding a cup of coffee, smiled when he saw Phillip. Larry stood five feet nine and rail thin, with auburn hair and alert blue eyes set deep in a ruddy face. He always seemed to need a haircut.

"Up all night again, Phillip. If you'd break down and marry one of those socialites pursuing you, you wouldn't have to spend the night standing up." Larry and Phillip had been friends since Stanford and medical school. He understood that Phillip's cool detachment covered up a perfectionist's mind. If Phillip was critical of others, he was doubly critical of himself.

Phillip welcomed Larry's friendship and candor. He sank into a chair. "Marry? Not yet, my friend, not yet."

"Are you seeing Sylvia at Christmas?"

"I'll be seeing her New Year's Eve. I plan to drive to San Jose to see the family for Christmas Eve and return on Christmas Day, maybe in time to see Sylvia." Phillip ran his fingers through his dark hair.

Sylvia Lacey, a petite blonde, lived on Nob Hill. She had attended Bryn Mawr College and after graduation had come home to her rightful place in San Francisco's social life. As a dedicated member of the Junior League, she regularly attended Monday lunches at the St. Francis Hotel, often returning Friday afternoon to the hotel's tea dances. She was the only child of her millionaire banker father, Alec Clemens.

Sylvia's cousin, Tom, introduced Phillip and Sylvia during a St. Francis Yacht Club dance. Friends were accustomed to seeing them together. Phillip found the relationship convenient, nothing more.

"Where're you spending Christmas?" Phillip asked.

"The folks are having Christmas at home. I'll run over for dinner."

Larry's home was a small house in the Avenues. His folks sacrificed for years to help him with tuition at Stanford and medical school. Phillip knew he planned to repay them someday.

"Does your father still talk to you about joining his clinic in San Jose?" Larry asked.

"Nah. He's beginning to understand I need the pace of a large hospital."

Phillip rubbed his chin. "I need to get rid of this stubble." He rose and started for the door. "Have a great Christmas dinner, and give my regards to your folks."

"Same to you, my friend. Have you heard from the draft?"

Phillip said over his shoulder as he left the room, "No, but I know some of the guys are signing up. Personally, I think they're jumping the gun. Seems to me we won't have to worry about the draft for a while."

CHAPTER 3

❀

Four days had passed since Carmel's conversation with her family at the Palace Hotel. She had promised to meet Laura at the Joss House to have their fortunes told by the Chinese priest.

Carmel was late. She maneuvered her father's station wagon through the crowded streets of downtown San Jose. A fine morning mist fell on the city and the traffic moved slowly.

Due to heavy rains, the 1941 Thanksgiving parade had been delayed for three Saturdays. People joked about building an ark. Finally, despite the bad weather, the committee decided to go ahead with the celebration. The streets were filled with happy Christmas shoppers, some under umbrellas. Men in uniform joined the crowded sidewalks to watch the parade.

The place of worship named the Joss House was built in 1888. When San Jose boasted the second largest Chinese settlement in the United States, San Francisco's Chinatown was the only rival. For fifty years, Chinese men and women had used the two-story brick structure. In the 1890s, the Tong Wars were planned behind its bullet proof walls and barred doors.

Despite a violent past, Chinatown was no longer dangerous. However, it was a frightening place for a girl alone on a wet, rainy afternoon. Carmel's throat tightened. Her father would not approve of her going to the Joss House in Chinatown, much less having her fortune told.

Maybe it wasn't a good idea to have the Chinese priest tell her fortune in front of Laura. What would she do if the priest revealed her love for Phillip?

Carmel found a place to park on Fourth Street. The mist had turned into a heavy rain. Damn! She asked herself. Why did I forget to bring a scarf to tie around my head? She ducked against the rain as she hurried toward the Joss House.

She crossed St. James Park, where a vigilante mob once had brought their families to watch the lynching of two men. The mob then stripped the tree of its bark and sold it as souvenirs. Carmel shuddered.

She found Laura, shivering in her raincoat, at the top of the steps of the Joss House, sheltered by the narrow overhang of the roof.

Laura's thick blonde curls fell around skin the color of soft apricots. A tiny spray of freckles crossed her cheeks. She scowled at Carmel. "Where have you been?"

"Have you been here long? I'm sorry. The parade traffic was terrible."

"I thought you might not come." Laura looked worried. "I'm afraid to go in alone."

"I told you I'd be here." Carmel pushed open the massive double doors. "Come on."

The heavy acrid smell of incense smoke from hundreds of candles burned their eyes. The young women waited to accustom themselves to this darkened house of worship.

Rows of well-worn wooden benches filled the room. At the far end, a short Chinese man, his shriveled face a map of brown wrinkles, stood before an altar as if waiting for them. He smiled and then bowed. They stepped closer. Carmel noticed the altar sat on a blue satin embroidered cloth covered with dust. A large Chinese god in cardinal red was recessed above the altar and also covered with dust.

The little priest, whose yellow satin robe had dark stains on it, moved quietly. He poured red wine into two cups and graciously offered a cup to each girl. He bowed. "You drink sacred wine." He bowed again. "You come for Chinese fortune?"

The girls nodded in unison. Carmel hoped the cups were not dusty. They drank the small amount of bitter wine and handed him the empty cups. The old man returned the cups to the altar, slowly lit two candles, and placed them in holders.

Carmel rummaged in her purse. The priest shook his head. "Later, you pay. Two dollar in brass bowl." He turned, picked up some pear-shaped pieces of wood, and tossed them on the altar. Carmel watched them roll against the Chinese god.

The old man squinted at Carmel. He began in a singsong voice. "Fires cover the earth … fires change life … winds change life … you cross dried lake before you find happiness. Your first baby, a boy."

"I don't want to know about babies. I want to know about marriage," Carmel muttered.

He ignored her. "You move far away." His head bowed low. "You sing many songs. You smile outside. Many, many tears inside. You strong lady. Climb many steps before sunshine. That's all. Next lady."

The priest peered at Laura. "You more quiet. Different lady. You gentle. Winds bring one fire … dark days … later climb to sunshine … that all, lady." He backed away from them.

Laura walked toward the door ahead of Carmel. They dropped their dollars into the brass bowl on a table by the door.

The heavy door closed behind them. "Well, that was sure a waste of time," Carmel said. "The old fool, what did he mean far away?"

Laura laughed. "I guess that's what you get when you have your future told. I don't think we're supposed to know. What about me? Winds bring fire. What did that mean? Boy, did he smell! I'm glad to be out of there."

"Let's get a Coke. I have something to tell you."

The rain clouds had moved on. They walked a block to a small restaurant on the outskirts of Chinatown.

There were no customers in the tiny restaurant. Carmel looked around. "Better keep your coat on; it's cold in here. I'm going to have coffee instead of a Coke."

A young Chinese girl seated them and took their order. On a juke box in the back of the restaurant they heard Sinatra singing "I'll Never Smile Again."

Laura asked, "Well, Carmel, how long do I have to wait?"

"You know I'm moving to San Francisco?" Carmel wanted to see if her words would get a reaction.

"Yes, you told me that after you went to see Grant leave." Laura sounded impatient.

"I think it's very odd that the old Chinese would tell me about singing many songs." Carmel paused. "Because that's exactly what I'm going to do."

"What?"

"Find a job so I can sing. Nothing is going to stop me."

"I'll admit you were really good when you sang with Sammy's band. But you amaze me, Carmel. You've never had to come up with money for anything. Think about rent, food, and clothes." Laura stared at her friend. "You're so set on running away. To top it off, you're going all the way to San Francisco. My father says there's going to be a war. We can't avoid it. If there is, your father will make you come home. What's happened to you? I've never seen you so determined."

Carmel wanted to scream, "I'm madly in love with your brother. I have to live in San Francisco." She felt disappointment at her friend's lack of enthusiasm. "I thought you would understand more than anyone. I'm not going to stay in San Jose forever. I really want to live in San Francisco. A war won't stop me from singing. How could it affect my life? Besides, did I tell you I'll live with my aunt and uncle?"

"Yes, you told me."

The waitress served their coffee.

Carmel's plan to be a vocalist began when Sammy Gumm led the college band that played for the San Jose State dances. She teased Sammy, saying he must be related to Judy Garland, since they had the same last name. Carmel begged him to let her sing. Sammy liked her and one night gave her a chance. She knew the words to the popular songs and had no problem with the tempo of the band. Sammy said she was a natural.

He invited her to sing two more times during the Saturday night dances. She was nervous singing the first time, but the crowd liked her and she began to relax. This led to her wondering if she might earn her living as a singer.

She still couldn't believe her aunt and uncle offered her a place to live. Everything was happening so fast.

Carmel thought Laura had absolutely no adventure, no desire to change her life. "Would you like to live in the city?"

"Have you forgotten I'm going to be a nurse? I'm already in the nurses' program at San Jose State. Honestly! You know how Scott and I feel about each other. We do plan to marry some day."

"Yes, I know." Carmel felt a twinge of guilt. She was not thinking about her brother. Sometime ago, the two families accepted that Scott and Laura would fulfill their destiny and marry. Suddenly, she reached across the table, taking both of Laura's hands in hers. "No matter what happens we'll always be friends." Carmel and Laura had been friends since babyhood, running in and out of each other's homes. Both girls were tomboys and challenged each other climbing the walnut trees. They spent hours in the Barron's pool, went to the movies, or finagled someone to take them to Santa Cruz and the beach.

"Yes," Laura said, "we've shared a lot of good times."

Laura squeezed Carmel's hand and smiled. "When are you going to the city?"

"Sunday morning, December 7. Dad'll be in church." She didn't want her father to take her. He would only start to fuss. "Could you take me to the train? I've called Aunt Lydia and she's expecting me."

"I wanted to tell you not to go." Laura forced herself to smile. "Yes, I'll take you."

"Then I'll see you Sunday." Carmel gulped down her coffee. "Look outside. It's starting to rain again let's leave. I've a lot to do."

Laura said softly, "I hope the glamorous life of San Francisco doesn't change you too much."

Carmel, already at the door of the restaurant, promised, "It won't."

CHAPTER 4

The pepper trees James Andrew planted years ago lined the long gravel drive-way leading to the house. Mexican workers had dynamited the hills in back of the Almaden cemetery and hauled the black rock by wagon to build a rock wall across the front of the property. A rich green lawn stretched from the wall to the house. One hundred acres of walnut and cherry trees extended behind the house and barns. Spring produced blossoms of heavenly aroma; anyone who came near felt he entered paradise.

Three generations of St. Johns had added their diverse designs to the already unconventional structure. Tudor chimneys, painted white, rose out of the solid brick walls. Andrew had added a Spanish wing with enormous rooms, English paned windows, tile floors, and heavy beams. This lack of planning added a distinct and individual charm to the house.

The morning rains kept Andrew at work in his office. The eucalyptus log fire in the hearth snapped and crackled, adding a pleasant aroma to the room.

Bruno, the mastiff, and Howard, the golden retriever, slept in front of the fireplace.

The fire cast a warm glow on the rosewood-paneled walls. A large cherry wood desk and two comfortable leather chairs filled a corner of the room. Book filled shelves lined one wall.

Photographs of the old and new ranch houses, young orchards, and Grant and Scott on horseback hung on the walls. There was a favorite oil painting of his wife, Elizabeth Rose, a slight smile turning up the corners of her lips. His parents' somber faces looked out of duplicate silver frames on the opposite side of the desk. A large ash tray held remains of Bull Durham cigarettes.

Though he protested over the rosewood-paneled walls and a thick Oriental carpet, Elizabeth Rose triumphed. She insisted he needed beauty and comfort.

Sitting at his desk, Andrew wore his usual attire of riding boots and jodhpurs. He knew his sons laughed when he stomped around the property, calling him C. B. DeMille, after the famous movie director. He didn't care. As far as he was concerned, the famous movie director copied him.

Scott appeared at the open door. "May I have a word with you, Dad?"

At his father's nod to enter, Scott sat down in one of the soft leather chairs.

The expression on Scott's face was enough to warn Andrew that his son had something on his mind. "For some time, Dad, I've been wondering what to do with my life. And as you know, our growing season this year produced one of the largest fruit and vegetable packs for the canneries."

"Yes, go on, son."

"That's helped me decide. Dad, I want to figure out how to freeze food, package it, sell it, and even ship it out of the country."

"And what happens to Rancho Costalotta?" Andrew's father's name for the ranch was an inside joke for the family members.

"Dad, I'm serious. This is your ranch; I want to do something for myself."

Andrew took his time to roll his favorite Bull Durham cigarette. Finally, he lit it and blew out a cloud of smoke.

"Scott, this is the home and future of all the people here. I've told you before. You know our history."

Scott sighed and sat back.

"After," he added, "your Irish great-grandfather, James Andrew, orphaned at eighteen years of age, his home destroyed, left South Carolina with a wagon train and migrated to the Santa Clara Valley. Before he could buy land, he picked fruit for three years. This is hard-won land, Son."

Scott leaned forward to interrupt his father.

Andrew held up his hand for Scott to listen. "Grandfather James went to Mexico, found Rosita and Jose, and offered them a home in San Jose to live and work his land." He took a drag on his cigarette and blew smoke. "James promised them a permanent home. I intend to keep that promise. Their children, Juan and Pedro, were born here. I will not hear of you leaving." His voice rose. "I thought you went to Stanford to learn something? Do you have any idea how much money is needed for your ideas? What about your experience? This is a harebrained idea, almost as bad as some of the ideas your brother gets."

"But, Dad, I want to try on my own."

"I'm trying to make a point here, Scott. I wanted you to stay in college at Stanford and study agriculture, but you wouldn't. You stayed just two years! Stanford was good enough for me. Good enough for me to meet your mother."

"Dad, I know all that. I've learned a lot about the crops. I know how enterprising Grandfather James Andrew was. He planted cherry and walnut trees for the future. How he planted strawberries between the trees and marketed them while waiting for them to mature. I promise you, I'm just as enterprising. Besides, I know people in Watsonville who will help me get started."

"It'll take hundreds of thousands of dollars." Andrew had been suspicious for some time knew that his son was thinking about something, but he had no idea it was such an impossible scheme. "I don't think you can manage your enterprise alone. You need partners, at least someone who can handle the machinery."

Scott stopped him. "I can do it! I tell you I've learned a lot working in the cannery."

"But that's not all, son. You'll need laborers to get the product out of the fields." He shook his head. "It isn't possible."

"I'll find men to work. I know how to get along with these people." Scott had spent many hours out in the sun working in the orchards with the Mexicans, whom he considered his friends. At night, he often sat in the large kitchen, laughing and singing their songs.

He gritted his teeth. "This subject is not over." He stood and left the room, his lameness obvious.

Andrew watched Scott limp away. Memories flashed of the little boy in the hospital bed who cried for his mother. Scott, with his serious brown eyes and taffy hair, looked like Elizabeth Rose. He admired his son's courage, but leaving the ranch was out of the question. Scott was right—the conversation was not over.

Later that afternoon, Andrew waited by the fire for his daughter and thought about his family. He kept to himself his thoughts of a coming war. By hook or crook America would soon be at war. Carmel seemed determined to leave. He wondered if her move to San Francisco was a good idea. When his sister Lydia sided with Carmel and offered to watch over her, he had felt trapped.

The winter skies were dark by the time Carmel returned. Andrew surprised her at the front door.

"Are you waiting for me?" She smiled as she took off her raincoat.

"I've been sitting by the fire. Let's have coffee, shall we? I've asked Anna to send Lupe with a tray of goodies. I promise not to spoil our dinner."

Carmel hung her raincoat in the hall closet under the stairway. The carpeted steps led upstairs to five large bedrooms. In the center of the polished tile entry hall, a walnut pedestal table held garden-fresh flowers bursting from a heavy jade vase.

She stared for a moment, saying good-bye to this beautiful home.

Oriental rugs covered the glistening hardwood floor of the forty-foot living room. A baby grand piano occupied one corner. The enormous overstuffed couch and chairs provided comfort. A field-rock fireplace covered one wall. Beamed ceilings added grandeur to the imposing rooms.

The waxed terra-cotta floors of the large sun-filled dining room had withstood the scuffing of boots by three generations of St. Johns pushing away from the table to resume their chores in the orchards. Red and gold draperies covered the floor-to-ceiling windows. A massive mahogany dining table and sideboard held Elizabeth Rose's inheritance of ornately carved silver candlesticks, sparkling crystal, and an antique silver coffee service.

Double doors opened onto a twenty-foot sheltered walkway to the kitchen where Anna and Rosita prepared meals. Food was rushed from the kitchen in silver chafing dishes to the long sideboard.

Pictures of California art, oaks in golden fields, and vistas of orchards in full bloom hung in gold frames on the paneled walls.

She joined her father in the living room. Andrew had moved chairs closer to the coffee table and the fire. "Dad, how handsome you look in your white wool cardigan."

"You gave it to me last Christmas, Carmel. Remember?"

"Yes, I do."

Bruno and Howard lay in their favorite place before the fire. Their chins rested on their paws. Brown eyes followed every move Andrew made.

"Ah, Lupe, thank you. Put the tray here." He motioned to the coffee table. The silver tray held a pot of fresh coffee, cups, and saucers. A plate of teacakes with a dab of icing and fresh scones emitted a delicious cinnamon scent.

"We should do this more often, Genevieve Carmel."

"When you use my full name, Dad, I know this could be a serious conversation. Well, it's a perfect time for a tea party before the fire."

"We better do it now, because you won't be here much longer. You seem so hell bent for a life in the big city."

"Oh, Dad, I'm not going to another planet. San Francisco isn't so far away. You can come and visit."

"You know I seldom leave the ranch." Andrew took a scone and a teacake and placed them on his plate. "I hoped this would always be your home and you'd settle down here."

"Dad, this *is* my home, but I want to see what I can accomplish in the city."

"I thought I might teach you about the orchards so you could take over one day, if need be."

"What about Scott?"

"I think you're not surprised Scott wants to move to Watsonville and learn the frozen food business. He wants to have his own cannery. He's not interested in growing things; just wants to put them in cans. Ha!" Andrew grimaced. "But getting financing will be something else."

"And Grant?"

Andrew shrugged. "Grant would be a mercenary if he could. Perhaps he was born fifty years too late?" He took a bite of his scone and a gulp of coffee. "My apparent heir is not interested in the ranch or its future. Grant has built a wall around himself and resents anyone, especially his family, intruding."

"You spoiled Grant."

"I suppose I have."

Carmel placed her coffee cup down on the tray, rose from her chair, and moved over to the fire. For a moment, she stared at the blue and yellow flames before she spoke. "Dad, I don't feel this is a life for me. I love this ranch, but …"

"Don't say anymore. Yes, you do love this place, but you don't know how much. Not yet. This is hard-won St. John land. Your grandfather, James Andrew, went through hell to own this land." He sighed and looked into the fire.

"Your mother loved this place and wanted to live here forever. Your grandmother planted the wisteria that climbs around the porch posts and the pink and red camellias under the sycamore tree."

He chuckled and sipped his coffee. "I remember growing up—if there was danger of frost, your grandparents and I worked all night." He paused. "And we *still* light smudge pots." He began to tell Carmel an often-repeated tale.

"Your grandparents worked so hard, Carmel, so hard. They reached their sixties before I persuaded them to take their first vacation, a week aboard a large riverboat on the Columbia River. The drunken captain did not see the steam boiler overheating."

His voice trembled. Andrew was talking about yesterday because his daughter was leaving. Carmel listened.

"As you know, no one survived, including the captain, his passengers, and the ship. Your grandparents were never found. Only their trunks washed ashore. I was thirty-nine years old. I guess I blamed myself for their trip—and their deaths."

"It wasn't your fault, Father. Is that when you took Mother to Europe?"

"Yes. It was a trip we both needed."

Andrew laughed suddenly. "I always said your grandfather, James Andrew St. John, was a non-violent man. But one time his brandy got the best of him. When the house was finally ready, he was drunk. Your grandmother refused to move into the remodeled house until he sobered up. Your grandfather picked up his gun, the one he used to scare the Kingfisher from diving into his pools to steal his fish, and shot out the new light fixtures in the house."

Carmel joined his laughter. "I wish I'd known him."

"He would have been proud of you. As Andrew stood, he put his arm around Carmel's shoulder. They watched the fire and listened to the wind beat the rain against the windows.

He kissed her on the cheek, "My sweet daughter. I'll be here and you'll come back someday. You'll see."

CHAPTER 5

❀

Sunday morning, December 7, 1941, dawned without a cloud in the sky. With a crystal-clear day to start her new life, nothing could go wrong.

She hummed as she packed. Since Laura promised to drive her to the railroad station, she had persuaded her father not to miss the morning service at the Presbyterian Church.

Anna walked into Carmel's room, her arms full of freshly laundered clothes. "I hope you take care of your things. Don't be a burden to your aunt. Hand wash sweaters. Skirts go to cleaners."

Carmel thought, for a woman in her forties, Anna was still slim figured and carried herself proudly. Anna's face, with her wide cheekbones, beautiful dark eyes, and raven black hair always in neat braids around her head, indicated her Spanish heritage. Her skirts reached the floor, and her blouses, freshly laundered, were white or pastel colors, some with embroidery on the neckline. Long silver earrings touched her shoulders.

No one knew too much about Anna. Years ago, Benito and Rosita's son, Juan, had gone to Mexico City to see the sights. There he met Anna, married her, and brought her back to San Jose to live on the ranch. When Juan died suddenly from a burst appendix, Anna had remained on the ranch. The men respected her and the young ones were in awe of her.

Carmel was five years old, Grant nearly six years, and Scott almost twelve when their mother Elizabeth Rose was killed. Anna quietly accepted the responsibilities of Andrew's children and household.

As a young child, Carmel followed Anna around the ranch asking questions. She delighted in helping Anna gather rose petals from the garden and dry them on trays in the sun to capture their sweet essence. She helped put the potpourris in sachet bags and hang them in the closets. Carmel loved Anna and was careful not to lose her respect.

When Carmel grew older, Anna taught her to roast a chicken until it was golden brown and bake fish in a wine sauce. To chop cilantro, squeeze the lemon and add herbs from the garden. Carmel even supervised a lamb barbecue for her father. Anna told Carmel when she married, if her husband could cook, they would enjoy sharing their talents. If he couldn't, she could teach him. Carmel laughed—as if she would marry a man who cooked.

Now Anna fussed about, not waiting for an answer. "Do you expect to take three suitcases? Are you going to take these dirty brown and white oxfords?" Anna began to fold clothes slowly, stacking them into neat piles on the bed. "Remember, act like a lady. Just 'cause your father treat you like a fairy princess and you wrap him around your little finger don't mean you don't have to mind your manners. Don't be taking your Aunt Lydia's house servants for granted, asking them to do things for you. Once in a while offer to help your Aunt Lydia. Make me proud of you."

Carmel felt herself bristle. "Oh, Anna, stop fussing. I won't forget anything you've taught me."

Carmel heard the dogs barking and suspected Laura had arrived. Her fingers shook as she fastened the heavy suitcases.

She threw her arms around Anna. "I'll be home at Christmas." She felt herself choking. "And everything will be the same."

Anna hugged her, fighting back tears.

When Carmel went downstairs, Jose and Pedro put the small bag and three suitcases in the back seat of Laura's convertible.

"*Buenos tardes*, Carmel. Come back Christmas. *Buena suerte. Adios.*"

The dogs barking added to the excitement. Carmel shouted, "Good-bye. Hush, Bruno, Howard. You be good dogs." She slid into the passenger seat.

Laura had admiration in her eyes, "My, Carmel, you're really dressed up. You look keen."

Carmel felt that her yellow wool dress, brown wool coat, brown alligator pumps, and matching bag made her look grown up. A yellow felt hat perched over her left eye. "Thank you, Laura."

She turned and waved to the group by the door. There was a tiny stab of guilt. She was thankful her father wasn't there.

The railroad station was across downtown San Jose. Strangers entering the city often remarked it reminded them of a small Midwestern town. The large elm trees arched over the wide streets and shut out the hot California sun.

Laura drove her 1939 Chevy convertible through the empty San Jose streets.

Carmel had thought on this special day of leaving that there would be something unusual going on, but there wasn't. It was just an ordinary Sunday morning in a half-awake little California town.

Laura's voice was soft. "It's going to be awful with you gone."

Carmel looked at her friend in her pink shirt, plaid skirt, and scuffed saddle oxfords. Carmel had to admit she felt quite sophisticated. "Come and visit me. Aunt Lydia will put you up."

"You know I can't leave. Mother would never stand for it."

Carmel suspected Laura used her mother as an excuse. Scott was the real reason she would not leave.

Laura smiled. "Why don't you look up Phillip?"

The remark surprised Carmel. She quickly searched Laura's face. She saw nothing to make her suspect Laura knew anything about her feelings.

Carmel planned to be on the train leaving at noon. It would arrive in San Francisco by three thirty, and she'd find a taxi to her aunt's house.

The two-story red brick South Pacific Station with its red tile roof came into view. Pepper, pine, and palm trees lined the parking lot in front of the building.

Laura drove to the station entrance and stopped at the curb. "You get out here and let the porter take your things. I'll park and come find you."

There were few people around the station. A porter appeared, lifted the suitcases out of the car onto the cart, and took them to be checked.

Inside the nearly deserted orange and blue tile station, Carmel bought her ticket and arranged for her bags to be picked up. She discovered her palms were damp. I'm really going, she thought. I didn't think I might be nervous.

Laura returned as the departure time for Carmel's train thundered over the loudspeaker. The two girls walked through the arcade toward the train.

"For heaven's sake, Laura, you act like I'm going to the moon. Come see me soon. Maybe you can come at semester break." She hummed a few bars of "I'll Be Home For Christmas."

"You're so happy today I don't think anything in the world could affect you."

The girls hugged each other and Carmel walked down the ramp to the train. She turned and waved.

For an instant, Carmel felt a twinge of remorse for leaving her friend in San Jose while she was headed for an exciting new life in San Francisco.

She boarded the train and found a seat by the window. She put her overnight bag on the rack above and settled down on the dark green seat. The railroad car smelled of cigar smoke, but she didn't mind; she liked cigar smoke. She thought the noon train might be empty.

A Chinese family—mother, father, and two little boys—sat down on the seat in front of her. The boys, Carmel thought, must be about six and four years old. They stood up on the seat and stared at her. Their black eyes were without expression, and then the older one smiled. Carmel smiled back. Their mother said something to them. They turned around and sat down.

The train pulled out of the station and picked up speed, railroad cars rocking back and forth. Warehouses of the Southern Pacific yards flew by.

Carmel listened to the whistle as the train passed pepper trees and towering eucalyptus trees with the Pacific Coast Range Mountains in the background. She thought, Phillip will be surprised when I tell him I'm living in San Francisco. How to let him know might be a problem. She wished she could call and simply say, "I want to see you," but if she called him and he rejected her ... it was a risk too big to take. There had to be another way.

The conductor, in his navy wool uniform, reached for her ticket, punched it, and handed it back. "Did you hear the news? The United States is at war. Pearl Harbor was bombed. The Japanese bombed Hawaii."

Bombed Hawaii! That's where her brother was. How could this be happening? Where did her brother say he would stay in Hawaii? How far away was Pearl Harbor? Everyone said there was a war coming, but not now. Not when her new life was starting. Had the world gone mad? Questions were tearing at her mind.

Then another thought entered her mind. What will happen to Phillip? He's a doctor. Will he leave San Francisco and go to war?

The train slowed to a stop. "Palo Alto," the conductor called.

Carmel saw people waiting in clusters on either side of the brick and stucco station. They moved toward the train. In the distance through the acres of trees rose large turreted buildings with the buff colored walls and red tile roofs of Stanford University. Her father had wanted Grant to go there. If Grant had attended the university, he wouldn't be in Hawaii now. She wondered if her father was thinking the same thing.

The seats filled and the train rolled on.

"Is this seat taken?"

A young man, tall and thin, stood in the aisle looking down at her. His blue shirt matched his eyes. He wore a brown jacket. Taking off his dark brown hat, he revealed abundant brown hair.

"No." Carmel moved closer to the window to make room for him.

He put his hat on the rack above them. "I wasn't going to the city today, but the news … there may not be any taxis running."

"What do you mean?"

"The report is the Japanese may be on their way to bomb San Francisco."

Carmel shivered in her brown coat.

"I didn't mean to frighten you. It was thoughtless of me." Then he quickly added, "I'm Jerry Cassidy."

Carmel hesitated a moment, but she saw the concern in his eyes. "My name is Carmel St. John."

She stared out the window as the train came to a stop in Menlo Park. She thought about friendly Mr. Kato, the Japanese man who delivered the brightly colored goldfish in the ten-gallon metal milk cans to the house. Twice a year he put fish into their garden pools. He was a little man, and his bowed legs bent even more under the weight of the heavy cans. He always wore a smile on his lips over big yellow teeth, but no expression in his black eyes. She asked herself, did he know about Pearl Harbor? Turning to Jerry, she said, "My brother is there. He just sailed on the *Lurline* with the San Jose State football team."

More people boarded the train. No one spoke, the expressions on their faces grave. The warm and sunny Sunday that promised to be so enjoyable became ugly. The seated passengers turned toward each other and talked quietly or stared straight ahead, lost in their own thoughts.

Two men entered the car, searching each passenger's face. It was obvious they had authority to be there. Dressed in gray suits and gray hats, the men stopped at the Chinese couple sitting in front of Carmel. She saw one of the men lean over and show them a badge. The boys began to cry. People stared at the scene.

Carmel felt her heart beat faster. Something about the scene frightened her.

The older boy jumped away from his parents' arms and ran up the aisle of the train, crying, "I'm no God-damn Jap." He screamed as he ran into the conductor's legs. The conductor instantly scooped the boy up into his arms. The man in the gray suit turned crimson at his mistake. Carmel heard him apologize to the couple. He walked rapidly away. The conductor returned the frightened boy to his parents.

Jerry shifted in his seat. "It's really unfortunate when the FBI doesn't know the difference between a Chinese and Japanese."

Carmel wondered, what will happen to us? She felt stunned and worried. A feeling of quiet urgency grew among the passengers. People just wanted to get where they were going.

She looked out at the blue sky and wondered if enemy planes were coming.

Jerry asked, "I'm not trying to pry, but is someone picking you up at the station? It'll probably be getting dark."

"No. I'm arriving earlier than planned, and I don't want to bother my relatives, so I'll have to find a taxi."

"My intentions were not to upset you. I'll find a taxi. Maybe we can share one." He felt her tense up. "I'm going straight to my job at the Chez Paree if it's open tonight. I play piano there."

She had noticed his hands. They looked clean and strong. He really was quite handsome.

She looked at him. He smiled at her. She liked his directness. "That's very nice of you. I'm going to Chestnut Street on Russian Hill. Is that on your way?"

"That will be close enough. As a matter of fact, nothing is far in San Francisco. You can cross the whole city in an hour, if the traffic's right."

"Redwood City," called the conductor.

Carmel could see the words "Weather Best by Government Test" on the arched sign over the main street.

"How long have you been playing piano at the Chez Paree?" She was beginning to feel more relaxed with him.

"Two years. What do you do?"

"I'm a singer." It was the first time Carmel had told a stranger she was a singer. She waited for a reaction.

"You are? Where have you sung?"

"I sang with my college dance band."

"That's great. Do you have a job now?"

"No. I have to look for one."

He looked at her perfect complexion and huge gray eyes. "You're so pretty; you'll do all right."

The worried lines on Carmel's face relaxed. "Thank you. I hope you're right."

The Chinese boys were standing, leaning on the back of their seats, and staring at Jerry and her. Carmel grinned back at them. Their mother said something and they sat down.

The Tanforan Race Track appeared on the right, and then the bay appeared. A train passed them, going south with a blur of lights and people.

She asked, "Doesn't the enemy always bomb the railroads?"

"Yes, railroad yards, ships." They passed the Southern Pacific roundhouse. Schlage Lock came and went.

Carmel's mind sank; her body grew heavy. Is this what fear did to you? She wasn't sure she was ready for San Francisco. Maybe it was the wrong time for her to be here.

The train entered a tunnel. The lights remained on. The loud roar made the two children hold their hands over their ears.

"San Francisco," called the conductor. The train roared through Tunnel Number Two, in seconds, Number Three and Four. It slowed rounding a curve. Carmel saw hundreds of Southern Pacific tracks crossing each other. Passengers gathered packages and put on their coats.

"Carmel, do you have any other baggage?" Jerry lifted her bag off the rack.

"No. A trunk and suitcases are being picked up later." She pulled on short white gloves. The train stopped and passengers left the car.

Carmel and Jerry departed from the train and walked toward the station. The metal roof extended to the tracks. It shut off the remaining light of the winter afternoon. Past four o'clock, the effect was gloomy.

Service men walked by them, intent on their destinations. Parents carried children, some of them crying. Redcaps pushed luggage wagons and baggage carts. Steam rose from under the huge black engine. Jerry took hold of Carmel's arm, guiding her quickly into the high vaulted station. They crossed the marble floors through the great station, with its fake Spanish facade and detailed grillwork. Carmel felt grateful for his presence.

Outside the taxis lined the curb waiting for customers. Jerry hailed a taxi, opened the door for her to get in, put the bag in the trunk, and climbed in beside her.

Carmel said to the driver, "Please take me to 1100 Chestnut, near Hyde."

The driver, barely waiting for Carmel to finish her request, moved into traffic. "Have you heard the news? Pearl Harbor has been bombed. The Japs did it. Hickam Field is burning. Those Japs ain't got no manners, starting a war on Sunday."

"Manners!" Jerry shot back. "Hells bells, we were in the middle of negotiations. Aren't some of their ambassadors in Washington now?"

Carmel instructed the driver. "Please, drive up Powell Street."

As the taxi crossed Market Street and turned up Powell, Carmel was astounded. In four blocks, there were barely eight people on Powell Street. The San Francisco cable cars ran from Market Street up Powell past the St. Francis Hotel to Fisherman's Wharf. The street usually bustled with people catching the cable car, visiting the hotels and restaurants. Were people afraid? A person could roll a bowling ball down the middle of the street and not hit a soul.

On the corners, Christmas lights blinked and shimmered in the late afternoon. Union Square blazed with lights. How lovely it was, but it was somehow ominous without people. Christmas needs people, she thought.

The taxi turned west on Geary past the Curran and Geary Theater, where Katherine Cornell was playing in the *Doctor's Dilemma*.

Jerry said, "Maybe I could help get you a job."

"You better hear me sing first."

"I'm going to try and help you."

The taxi reached Chestnut Street and started up the hill. The driver looked for the number.

Carmel said, "This is the house."

The driver stopped the taxi in front of a three-story Victorian. He got out of the cab, opened the trunk, lifted her bag out, and sat it on the sidewalk.

Jerry held the taxi door open. "May I call you if I find something for you?"

Carmel felt drained. A day of supreme happiness had given way to numbness, confusion, and fright. I don't know what's going to happen next, she thought. Making an effort to sound grateful, she said, "Yes, you may call me. Uncle Russell's last name is Bannister. He's in the phone book. I think it's an Ordway number. Thank you for sharing the cab." She reached in her purse for change.

"No, let me. I'll call." He climbed back into the cab.

Carmel picked up her small bag, turned, and faced the house.

CHAPTER 6

A small brick courtyard, walled and almost hidden with pink and red hedge roses, fronted Aunt Lydia's and Uncle Russell's home. The pale pink house, mainly of Italianate design, had been built for a carriage maker and was grandiose with its fluted columns and portico porch roof.

Carmel looked up at this elegant structure with its slanted, squared bay windows rising to the third floor and the French mansard roof. She felt goose bumps rise on her arms. This impressive, beautiful house would be her new home.

She felt a slight breeze from the bay as she climbed the steps. When she rang the bell, a tall, slim man in his fifties opened the door. His eyes and hair were the color of pewter and his complexion nut brown. She wondered how anyone could be so tan in December. He wore his houseman uniform, a white jacket and black trousers.

Madison had been with her aunt and uncle since before she was born. He smiled broadly. "Hello, Miss Carmel. Mrs. Lydia and Colonel Russell will be glad to see you."

Russell and Lydia's feelings for Madison extended past the employer and employee relationship. Madison had spent twenty years serving Lydia and Russell before he met and married Helen, an excellent cook. She was asked to join the household. Now, both Madison and Helen were an accepted part of the family.

"Oh, Madison, I'll certainly be glad to see them." She stepped into the wide hall with its parquet floor and curved staircase. How she admired this house. A massive Chinese teak couch sat against one wall. Vases as tall as Carmel sat on the polished floors, holding exotic floral arrangements. The house smelled of lemon oil, camphor, and places far away.

A radio and voices sounded from the back of the house. She suddenly felt glad to be in San Francisco; her feelings of anxiety began to ease

Madison said, "Your aunt and uncle are in the morning room. Shall I tell them you're here?"

"No, Madison. Thank you. I'll go myself."

"I'll put your case in your room. Shall I take your coat and purse?"

Carmel took off her coat and handed it to him. She put her gloves in the purse and snapped it shut, taking it with her. "Thank you."

Carmel walked toward the end of the long hall. The morning room was on the north side of the house with windows on three sides of the room. The windows caught the early morning light and the late afternoon sunsets over the Pacific.

Uncle Russell saw her and rose from his chair. His black cashmere sweater, white shirt, and gray slacks were, as always, meticulous. He leaned down and hugged her. In his soft Texas drawl he said, "My dear, welcome, welcome. We're so happy to see you. Have you heard the news?"

"Yes, I heard on the train."

She turned to her aunt, who was coming toward her followed by two black dachshunds, Heidi and Hilda, dancing at her heels. Lydia's red hair was swept up in a pompadour. She wore a black-and-white checked wool dress. Ruby earrings caught the light and flashed as she moved.

Lydia hugged her niece. "So glad you're here. The news is so shocking. Grant is there and we have so many friends in Honolulu. We're very concerned."

Russell motioned with his hand to be quiet as he resumed listening to the small radio. "What are they saying? It's from New York."

The commentator continued: "The Tokyo station, which normally broadcasts Domei News dispatches on the air at 1:40 Pacific Time, today said, 'Sorry to keep you waiting for so long a time, but there is no news right now.'"

They stood in silence. Carmel looked around at the deep green rug and comfortable rattan furniture. Pictures of Singapore and Hong Kong and watercolors of San Francisco hung on the walls. Green and yellow draperies framed windows that looked out on a garden full of bottlebrush covered in red blooms. All was so tranquil; it was difficult to comprehend that thousands of miles away American blood was spilling.

Through the tall windows she could see San Francisco Bay. The dusky streaks of the remaining sunset had disappeared. Night was beginning to cover the city.

Uncle Russell cleared his throat. "Would you like something to eat?"

"No, I'm not hungry. Thank you."

Aunt Lydia said, "My, my. I'm so rattled I forgot to ask how you got here. We were going to meet you."

"I took a cab with a nice man I met on the train."

"What? A stranger. Carmel, we have to be so careful these days. It's not like it used to be. San Francisco's filling up with riffraff."

"Oh, Auntie, don't worry. He's a piano player." She didn't mention he'd offered to help her or that she had told him it was all right to call.

"Let me take you to your room so you can get settled. I put you in the bedroom on the north side of the house, where you can see the bay." Lydia moved toward the front of the house. "You stay here, Russell. Listen to the news. I want to know if they're going to bomb San Francisco."

They climbed the stairs. "And where is your luggage, Carmel? I forgot to ask."

"I have my overnight bag. The trunk and three suitcases are at the railroad station."

"Madison will take care of picking up your things."

Heidi and Hilda followed them. "I don't know what I can do to stop these sillies from climbing stairs." Lydia turned and the dogs stood motionless. "You are bad girls. Climbing stairs is not good for your little backs." They waited only a minute and, relieved the scolding was over, scampered behind Lydia.

She stopped before a closed door at the end of the long hall, opened it, and the dogs dashed ahead of them into the room. "You enjoyed this room so much, I thought I'd put you here again. You have your own bathroom."

"You're very good to me, Auntie."

The bedroom was large. Four windows faced the bay. The walls were Persian blue. A mahogany bed with an enormous carved headboard filled half the room. The gold silk bedspread matched the silk draperies at the windows. A mahogany chest of drawers and a small secretary stood against the wall. Chairs covered in blue velvet faced the windows. A small table with a vase of pale yellow and white roses sat between them. A beige wool carpet covered the floor. Above the fireplace hung a mirror framed in gold.

Carmel said, "What girl wouldn't be happy in this beautiful room." She hugged her aunt. "I'll try not to be a burden to you and uncle."

Lydia, touched by the hug, said, "When things settle down I'll invite some people for you to meet." Her aunt turned at the door, "I must return downstairs. I'm so worried about everything. I hardly know what to plan. Dinner is at eight, but it's after five now. Come down when you like and join us."

Carmel nodded. "I'll wash up and join you now."

Carmel's Aunt Lydia had fallen in love early in her life with young Captain Russell Bannister. They met in Texas, his birthplace, and in three months were married. He rose to the rank of colonel, serving in Europe and Asia. They lived a happy and fulfilled life.

Fifteen years before retiring, they bought the house in San Francisco. The house bulged with paintings, furniture, and sculpture acquired from their travels. Lydia kept her home immaculate with the help of Madison and Helen.

Carmel was fascinated by her aunt. She never knew what to expect. Lydia's mind zigzagged down some strange detours, moving from one subject to another, dazzling everyone listening to her chatter. She was often compared to a bird darting down a path, realizing too late she had gone too far. She would recover gracefully and then repeat the same pattern.

Lydia tried to stay aware of current events but invariably got her numbers and zeros in the wrong place. Her occasional lack of logic in her conversation bewildered her listeners but also intrigued them.

She was devoted to Hilda and Heidi. They pranced constantly about her heels. Russell frequently accused her of paying more attention to her dogs than to him. Lydia would just wave a chiffon handkerchief doused heavily with Chanel No. 5 and laugh the subject away.

Carmel's thoughts were interrupted by the sudden blast of a siren, which sent her out of the room and down the stairs. She entered the morning room. "What on Earth?"

Her aunt and uncle were pulling the heavy draperies across the large windows. Russell yelled, "It's a blackout signaling us to turn off the lights. Carmel, please return to your room and close your draperies so that not a bit of light gets through. I'll explain when you come back and join us. Be sure your lights are out."

Carmel ran upstairs to do as she was told and returned in a few minutes.

Lydia had been rushing around the house with the dogs close behind. She was breathing hard. "Russell, tell us what the radio said. I hate that sound." The sirens continued to shriek.

"Planes are approaching. The Golden Gate Bridge and Bay Bridge are under twenty-four-hour guard. I guess they're stopping drivers. Come on! Let's get every window covered. Madison! Helen!" he called. Russell hesitated. "It seems enemy planes have been sighted approaching San Francisco. Mayor Rossi has declared San Francisco in a state of emergency."

Helen appeared instantly. Carmel saw she was still plump and younger looking than her fifty years. Her usually smiling face was serious. She looked at Carmel. "Hello, miss. Yes, sir. Colonel Bannister, I've already started. My, my! What a noise." She scurried from the room.

Carmel called to her. "I'll come and help you."

Lydia said, "Guess I'll get yards of black from the City of Paris to cover these windows if this keeps up." She left the room to shut the heavy burgundy draperies in the living room. Heidi and Hilda ran before her, their toenails clicking on the polished floors.

With the job completed, Carmel, her aunt, and her uncle returned to the morning room to listen to the radio. With a single table lamp burning, the morning room might have been cozy except for the screaming sirens.

Russell looked at his watch. "The sirens started at five and it's now five twenty. Not bad considering we're amateurs."

The phone rang. Russell picked it up. "Yes, I know. It's probably orders. Yes, I'll let you know." He put the phone down. "That's Bob Cook, a retired major. He thinks it's a hoax."

Madison came into the room and asked, "Couldn't the Japanese planes that bombed Honolulu ... couldn't they fly over here?"

"I was wondering the same thing. They would have to take off from a carrier at some point." Russell said.

Lydia said, "I want to see what's happening. Let's turn off the light and look out."

The sirens had started their alert again. Russell immediately turned off the lamp and reached to pull the long draperies away from the window. The four stared at the city. In the moonlight, they could see Coit Tower in the distance like a white finger pointing to the sky. A red haze lit the downtown. They could easily make out San Francisco's skyline.

"The city sure isn't hidden. I bet someone's ass pays for that," Russell said grimly as he covered the windows.

Lydia turned the light back on.

Carmel watched her relatives. Relief swept over her. She was impressed with her uncle's calmness and suspected it came from his long experience in the army. Carmel strained to hear airplanes. "How can anyone hear anything but sirens?"

Lydia replied, "Let's have a drink for Carmel's first evening here. Besides I need one."

Russell agreed. "Good idea. Madison, get Helen and join us. I'll do the fixings. I won't take no for an answer. We're all in this together."

Russell served each one a martini. Raising his glass, he said, "Here's to General MacArthur."

Carmel thought, I'm standing in a room toasting a General MacArthur, someone I have never thought about in my whole life.

As the sirens bleated, the five of them listened, consumed with their own thoughts. They drank in silence. Madison and Helen finished their drinks and went back to the kitchen.

Abruptly, the strident sirens stopped.

Russell looked at his watch. "It's almost seven; lasted almost an hour. That's the 'all clear'; should sound for only two minutes."

"Well, that's a relief. Let's have dinner. I think it's ready, though it's a little early tonight." Lydia walked toward the dining room. She frowned. "Carmel, under other circumstances, dinner would be a celebration to welcome you to San Francisco. I feel bad about that."

"Don't worry about it, Auntie."

The dining room had a vaulted ceiling, soft apricot walls, thick carpets, and commodious chairs surrounding the polished table. Lydia had placed golden and black tiger lilies in the center of the mahogany table. "Oh, Aunt Lydia, the setting is beautiful."

In spite of everyone's effort, dinner was nearly a disaster. Uncle Russell was called to the phone every few minutes. Each time he brought bad news back to the table.

"The tube to Alameda Island with its Naval Air Station and the Naval Supply Depot is closed."

Lydia looked down at the fresh red snapper on her plate and sighed. "I so wanted Carmel to have an enjoyable dinner her first night in San Francisco."

"It is, Auntie. It's excellent."

Russell said quietly, "Lydia, Carmel is not a completely dense human being. She's fully aware of the circumstances."

Uncle Russell's eyes were unusually bright, but his voice revealed the strain of answering the calls from his army friends "Lydia, I may have to get into this fight. Could you manage alone?"

"I don't know."

Carmel thought Lydia might have a total collapse if Russell was recalled.

Looking at the half-empty plates, he suggested, "Let's have our coffee in the morning room."

"Uncle, how will I know if Grant is all right? How will we hear from him?"

Her uncle guided them into the morning room, his voice reassuring. "Didn't you say the team was staying at the Moana Hotel? That's quite a distance from Pearl Harbor."

"I hope they're at the hotel, not running around the island." Lydia said. "I'm sure your father will hear something soon."

The phone rang. "I'll answer it." Russell left the room.

Madison returned and asked Carmel. "Would you like sponge cake with peach ice cream?"

"No, thank you, Madison, just coffee." Carmel, feeling tired, sat down on one of the comfortable chairs near the fireplace.

She thought Lydia, sitting opposite her, was showing signs of strain. She looked up at Russell's face as he entered the room. "What's happened?"

"The President will speak to the joint session of Congress. It'll be broadcast at nine thirty in the morning."

Carmel asked, "What does that mean?" She remembered the conductor said war had been declared. Apparently, he was wrong.

"The President has to ask Congress to declare war."

"What? Is that a problem?" asked Lydia.

"It could be. Congress members are not all in Washington at this time. The majority will win."

Lydia turned to Carmel. "Dear, I imagine you're exhausted. We should go to bed and try to sleep tonight. What do you think?" She stood up, and the sleeping dogs were instantly awake, eyes bright, ready to play.

"Oh, Auntie, I agree. It's been quite a night." She gave her aunt a kiss.

Uncle Russell got to his feet and kissed Carmel. "You picked a helluva day to move to the city. I hope you can manage to sleep well."

Carmel said, "Thank you. I'm sure I will. Good night."

Once in bed, her mind raced with questions. Was this really the time to leave San Jose? Did she bring worry to her father and distress Anna? What about Grant? Was he all right? Where was he? Was she a burden to her aunt and uncle's busy life? What about Phillip? Yes, what about Phillip? Too many questions she couldn't answer. In the dark, she stared at the ceiling.

CHAPTER 7

Carmel woke early. With the heavy drapes closed, the room was silent. Then she remembered. The war!

She got up and went to the window, opened the drapes, and stared at the city. Yes, it was still there. Dawn was only a faint light behind the tall dark buildings silhouetted against the sky. A fine gray mist hung over the skyline. She remembered last night. The night had been frightening with the threat of Japanese planes bombing San Francisco. In one day, her whole world was turned upside down.

Would her father insist she return home? Was it only yesterday morning that she thought everything good was beginning to happen? And now … Oh, Phillip! He didn't even know she was in San Francisco. Her spirits sank. Was she a foolish girl crying for the moon?

She heard household noises coming from downstairs. Carmel pressed her lips, "I'm not going home. I will get a job and figure out how to see Phillip." She went to shower.

Dressed in a pink sweater and skirt, she went down stairs to breakfast.

Her aunt and uncle sat at the breakfast table reading newspapers. Hilda and Heidi got up from under Lydia's chair. They wiggled over to receive their morning welcome.

The dogs delighted her. Carmel laughed, "Okay. Okay! Good morning. I'll rub your tummies after breakfast."

Everything seemed so normal. The table was set with bright yellow dishes. Yellow tulips were the centerpiece. Her aunt wore a pale blue wool dress and cardigan. Carmel sat down.

Helen brought orange juice and poured her a cup of hot coffee.

Lydia held up the front page of the *Chronicle*. "Look at this. The Final Morning Extra."

U.S. AT WAR!
PARATROOPS LAND IN PHILIPPINES!
AMERICA AT WAR! MAN, WOMAN, and CHILD. UNITE.

Russell took the front page away from Lydia. He read, "General Ryan said, 'A strong squadron was detected approaching the Golden Gate. It was not an air test but the real thing. Some of them got near the Golden Gate and turned southwest.'" He continued, "General De Witt said he made a full report to Washington. Seems he thinks they were on reconnaissance from an aircraft carrier somewhere off shore. Boy!" Russell bellowed. "Is the general steamed. Nearly all the neon lights downtown were on."

Lydia said, "Well, they did turn off the lights on the Golden Gate Bridge and Bay Bridge. Four women and a boy slept in the Twin Peak's Tunnel all night, wrapped in blankets. I guess they were petrified."

Russell got up to answer the ringing phone. "Oh, Carmel, your father called. He said he went to San Jose this morning. People are so nervous that if anyone popped a paper bag, they would jump down a manhole. He has heard nothing from Grant. He asked if you want to come home." Russell gave her a steady look. "Wanted to know what we knew about the Japanese planes."

"Thanks, Uncle. No. I do not want to go home. If they're fine, they don't need me." She began to eat the eggs and bacon Helen had set before her.

Russell returned to the table.

Lydia poured coffee into her cup. "Russell, Mayor Rossi said for us to stay off the phone."

"That's during a blackout, Lydia. There'll be a meeting tomorrow. They want to talk to me about Civil Defense."

Russell refilled his coffee cup. "Well, it seems a highway patrol radio picked up the call on shortwave and notified Harrington, the manager of the bridges. Harrington ordered the bridge lights out and all navigation lights out. Then he found out after an hour the report wasn't valid and ordered them back on. People crossing the bridge had to sit there in the dark till the all clear. A sentry on guard on the Golden Gate Bridge shot a woman in the back while she was in the car. Her husband didn't hear the order to stop. Imagine how *he* feels."

The two women listened intently.

Russell continued, "Last night was bedlam. The police rushed up and down the streets instructing people to turn their lights out."

"Have we declared war?" asked Carmel.

"The President has to get Congress to vote in favor of it. As I told you last night, at this time of the year Congressmen aren't around. It might be a tough task getting them there. The President will be speaking this morning at nine thirty. We'll find out."

Finished with breakfast Carmel went upstairs, but was soon back. "Aunt Lydia, do you mind if I wait to unpack? I don't seem to know what I'm doing."

"Your things will wait for you. Have another cup of coffee."

President Roosevelt spoke to the nation. "Yesterday, the seventh of December, is a date that will live in infamy. I have asked the United States Congress to declare a state of war to exist between the United States and Japan. As commander-in-chief of the army and navy, I have directed that all measures be taken for our defense. No matter how long it may take us to overcome this premeditated invasion, the American people in their righteous might will win through to absolute victory."

During the long day the household listened to the news reporter say that the raid had taken a heavy toll. Starting at 8:10 a.m. Honolulu time, witnesses say fifty planes attacked Hickam Field, three miles northwest of Honolulu. The attack lasted one hour and a half. Most of the fifty planes flew high. A few flew under a hundred feet. We shot down only two. One hundred and four were dead and three hundred wounded. There was no confirmation on how many ships were destroyed, as some were still burning.

Something was happening every second. The reporter announced the Golden Gate and Bay bridges were under twenty-four-hour guard with posted sentries.

In California, all leaves and furloughs of the Eleventh, Twelfth, and Thirteenth Squadrons had been canceled. All Army Air Corp bombers and fighters stood ready, on alert.

Secretary of State Hull came on the air and stated that while meeting with the Japanese ambassadors, he never saw a document so crowded with falsehoods and distortions.

Reports in Washington, D.C., said citizens got in their cars and just drove around so they could listen to the radio.

Carmel sat beside her aunt in the morning room. She watched Lydia knit and smoke constantly. Carmel felt useless.

Lydia said to no one in particular, "Thousands of men and women registered at the firehouses. In Oakland, four hundred signed up for Civil Defense in one day."

No wonder there were few people on Powell Street, Carmel thought.

Carmel's luggage arrived. Russell helped Madison make two trips up the stairs to her room with the trunk and suitcases.

Returning, Russell asked, "Did you hear what the fire department ordered? They will sound the air raid alarms for three blasts. A steady sound indicates 'all clear.'"

"Russell, we *are* listening. The mayor said not to go crazy, to use your horse sense, to stay home, stay calm, and stay away from windows. Above all, put out the lights." Lydia's tone was very manner of fact.

Russell nodded, "Good girl. That is just what we will do. The stock market may close. Local shortwave ham radios are ordered off the air. Signals can be picked up from the enemy. California needs ten thousand men eighteen to sixty years old to sign up for State Guard for one year if they are not subject to military call." He stood and suddenly said, "Girls, I'm going down to my active duty station."

"Yes, dear, I expected you to do that." Lydia listened for a moment. "Did you hear that? The Japanese announced they now control the Pacific. Their war bases stretch out ten thousand miles across the Pacific. And twenty-five thousand Japanese live on this California Coast. I'd like to know who thought the news was another Mars hoax. Ha!" She reached for a cigarette.

Carmel asked, "Uncle Russell, are you going downtown to the active duty station now?"

"Yes, I'll feel much better if I crawl into the mouth of the lion." He gave her a salute and left. They heard the front door open and close.

Carmel sighed. "I guess the least I can do is try to unpack."

"Take your time, dear. I'll just stay here and listen to the news."

"I'll probably be right back to listen, too."

CHAPTER 8

Four air alerts during the night made sleep impossible. Carmel's bedside clock read 6:00 a.m. She groaned and decided to get up. She showered, slipped on a white sweater and brown wool skirt, brushed her hair, and went downstairs.

Her aunt and uncle were seated at the breakfast table. She kissed Lydia and sat. "Good morning, or is it?" Her aunt wore a housecoat printed with brightly colored parrots. She looked tired.

"Good morning, Carmel. After last night, your guess is as good as mine."

"Morning, Uncle Russell. What's the latest news?" She poured herself a glass of orange juice.

Russell, in a conservative brown suit, held up the front page of the *San Francisco Chronicle*.

JAPANESE PLANES NEAR SAN FRANCISCO.

"It seems," her uncle read, "that General De Witt, Commanding General of the Fourth Army here, was informed that a squadron of airplanes believed to be the enemy were sighted off the Golden Gate. With radios ordered off the air so the enemy couldn't tune into our radio beams, he ordered another blackout." Russell folded the paper to read it easier. "To quote him, we were 'insane, idiotic, and foolish.' So get this." Russell read, "'Last night there were enemy planes over this community. They were enemy planes! Japanese planes. You hear that signal? TURN OUT YOUR LIGHTS.'"

Lydia smoothed jam on her toast. "Did you hear the motors fly over? I did."

Russell nodded. "The army notifies the police and the police tell the Civil Defense.

Lydia interrupted. "Someone said there were dogfights in the air."

Helen brought in a large platter of ham and scrambled eggs.

"Thank you, Helen," said Russell. He helped himself, handed the platter to Carmel, and continued, "They insisted flares were dropped from the planes, but it turned out to be the blue lights flashing on top of the trolleys. I think we're going to hear a lot of unconfirmed news before we really know what is going on." Russell paused. "I'll probably find out the scoop at the meeting."

"What meeting?" Carmel asked, serving herself ham and eggs.

"Russell's going to a Civil Defense meeting today. Mrs. Roosevelt and Mayor LaGuardia from New York City will be at the meeting tomorrow." Lydia added, "Russell, I wish you would tell me why I can't go. I would love to meet Mrs. Roosevelt."

"It's very simple. You're not in Civil Defense. The meeting is closed to heads of Civil Defense. There'll be fire and police chiefs from all over the bay at Mayor LaGuardia's request. He'll be there, and then he's off to Los Angeles to set up more defenses."

Carmel sensed Russell's respect for the mayor of New York.

"Well, I want you to remember everything that happens, especially what she's wearing."

"You told me you would be very busy helping the Volunteers of the Red Cross."

"That's true. We're swamped with women wanting to sign up. I read the women's clubs are organizing classes. Carmel, are you interested?"

Carmel was not ready for this. It was premature to commit to any women's volunteer group. "What're they doing, Auntie?"

"They run errands, wrap packages, fold bandages, answer telephones, pick up and deliver military personnel. The California Club, Danish American Club, Mills Club, Child Health Care—the list goes on and on—all wonderfully involved." She almost sang the words.

Russell asked, "Are the radios back on? They were ordered off last night. We're supposed to listen and find out what to do in an air raid, in case a bomb lands near us."

"Oh, My God … Russell, I'm not listening to that! You can tell us later. I'm going downtown to the Red Cross headquarters to offer my services. Did you know the Red Cross is called the Mother of the World? Carmel, would you like to come with me?"

"No, Auntie. Thank you, but I've plenty to do here."

"The President's speaking this morning. I want to hear what he says." Russell left the room. In a few minutes, he was back. Carmel was drinking her second cup of coffee.

"The President has declared war. It took only one hour for Congress to vote. The President said they were waiting to hear from Berlin, to see what our relations would be. Don't tell me we have to fight those Germans again."

Carmel tried to concentrate on what her uncle was saying. It was the start of her third day in San Francisco. All anyone talked about was the war. She was anxious for her brother and the men in Hawaii, but what could she do for them? Her aunt was determined Carmel join some ladies' group to help with the war effort. Carmel wanted to avoid any commitment. Finding a job came first. Somehow she had to let Phillip know she was in San Francisco.

Carmel returned to her room. Lydia gave her liner paper scented with roses to put on the bottom of the dresser drawers. It was time consuming to fold, cut, and fit the paper. Anna would have a conniption if she knew how carelessly Carmel tossed in her underwear, slips, and stockings.

She hung up blouses and dresses and wondered if her clothes were too girlish for San Francisco. She found a place for shoes and bags in the back of the closet.

On the dresser, she put a silver framed picture of her father with Bruno and Howard. She placed her brush and comb beside them.

In the enormous bathroom, a blue rug covered the floor. Thick white towels were stacked on a lacy white chair. The blue shower curtain over the tub had white gulls swooping across it. Carmel put her two bottles of cologne, Chanel No. 5 and Chantilly inside a closed cabinet door to preserve the scent.

She wondered if Grant might return home by Christmas. And there was Christmas to think about. Her father had given her money the night before she left. She could manage until she found a job. One thing at a time, she told herself.

That night during dinner Lydia made an announcement. "I'm going to rip out the flower beds and replace them with vegetables. We were instructed to visit a farm and learn how to garden, can them, and raise poultry."

Russell said, "Lydia, we are *not* raising chickens in the middle of San Francisco. Those friends of yours do get carried away. Gardening I approve of, but trust me, canning would be a master challenge for you."

Carmel was only half listening until she heard her aunt's reply. "Well, the hospitals are way ahead of us. The doctors and their staffs have special telephone lines directly to the Red Cross. A large parking lot has been cleared to handle victims of air raids and bombings."

Russell asked, "Don't you remember when San Francisco ridiculed the medical defenses because they were preparing plans on how to handle earthquakes, fires, and epidemics?"

"Well, yes, I remember something about it. It looks like they're already prepared. They have eleven aid stations set up. Grace Cathedral's one of them."

The phone rang. Helen came to the door and said, "It's for you, Miss Carmel."

Carmel answered and heard her father's voice. "Carmel, have you been thinking about coming home?"

"No, Dad, I'm going to look for a job here."

"Don't you go volunteering for any service like your crazy brother."

"What do mean? Which brother?"

"Grant's going to stay in Honolulu. He'll work with the police department."

"Is he all right?"

"Yes," he said. "Chet left Hawaii by ship and will be home around Christmas to tell us everything. I want you home at least a week before Christmas. The Barrons are doing their usual and coming over for Christmas Eve, for music and holiday cheer. San Jose's in an uproar trying to set up their registrations and committees. How about those blackouts? That city's filling up with foreigners. Don't be a burden to your aunt and uncle. There's nothing worse than a retired colonel who wants to get into the fight." He burst into song, "Ta-ra-ra-boom-tee-aY." He chuckled. "Thank goodness Scott's still here." Abruptly, he said, "Let me talk to your uncle."

She called, "Uncle Russell, my dad wants to talk to you." She came back to the table. "Auntie, would you mind if I called Laura?"

"Of course not. By the way, sometime this week let's go see *The Maltese Falcon* with Humphrey Bogart and Mary Astor. The second feature's some RAF bombing of Germany. The theater put in rocking chair loges. I'd like to try them. They're brand new, and I hear very comfortable."

Russell re-entered the room. "Indeed, you will not! Not with Japanese planes flying around and bombs falling. Your brother just asked me not to let Carmel do anything foolish, and you suggest this!" He left the room shaking his head disgustedly.

Lydia rolled her blue eyes skyward.

That evening Carmel called Laura. If she had to wait much longer to hear about Phillip, she'd scream. All that talk about the doctors and what they were doing for San Francisco made her nervous. Did that involve Phillip?

Laura asked so many questions. "What about the airplanes? Have you seen any? What did you do during the blackouts? Some of our friends at school are talking about joining one of the services. And did you know Mickey Rooney is going to marry Ava Gardner?"

Through all of this she didn't give Carmel a chance to respond. Finally, Carmel said, "For heaven's sake, Laura, who cares?" Mickey might be newsworthy, but who is Ava Gardner?"

"Oh, and Phillip called. He's terribly busy, but he wants me to come to the city and have dinner with him. He said to bring you."

Carmel could have kissed her.

"When?"

"He said he'd call. He's going to try to come home for Christmas Eve."

Suddenly Carmel felt alive. That was all she needed, knowing she would be seeing him. He had asked her to join them, actually mentioned her name. Oh, life was too delicious. She barely listened to her friend before they said good-bye.

Later that evening, Russell, Lydia, and Carmel sat in the morning room to hear the news and have their after dinner coffee. Lydia said, "I believe you are feeling better, Carmel. Talking to your friend Laura was a good idea."

"Auntie, I should go home. I have to do my Christmas shopping and I want to decorate the house for Christmas."

"Well, my dear, that sounds sensible to me. Russell and I will be here for Christmas. There's too much going on with his Civil Defense and my Red Cross to leave here."

Russell added, "I don't think you'll be looking for a job until Christmas is over. Always a bad idea at Christmas. Better to start fresh at the beginning of the year."

Lydia said, "I read the *Lurline* and the *Mariposa*, the ships we sailed on to Hawaii, have been painted gray and become military transports for hundreds of men."

Russell added, "Bill Cousins, the assistant manager at the St. Francis Hotel, told me hotel rooms are at a premium. In order to supply sleeping chambers, they added extra compartments to their banquet and sales rooms. The jewelry shop in the lobby was remolded into small cubicles, each with a bed. A stay of three days is permitted unless they're on official military business. He said several of the servicemen occupy a three-room suite, remain after the midnight curfew to drink, and entertain the women they beguile to enter the room. He says no one seems to sleep."

"Sounds like men who expect they'll not return. I guess I don't blame them." Lydia got up. "I'm turning in early. I slept so little last night." The dogs were on their feet. "Come on, girls." She gave Carmel a kiss on the top of her head. "It's so lovely to have you here, Carmel."

"Thank you. I'll trot on up to bed, too. Good night, Uncle."

Knowing she would be seeing Phillip at Christmas, Carmel went happily to bed.

CHAPTER 9

✿

"Are Red Cross classes starting this morning, Auntie?"

"Yes, I'm looking forward to them," Lydia said. She was seated at the breakfast table elegantly clad in a simple gray dress and jacket.

Russell sat beside Lydia reading the front page of the *San Francisco Chronicle.*

Carmel saw the headline:

JAPS SINK 2 GREAT BRITISH WARSHIPS

Her uncle began to read aloud. "'The HMS *Prince of Wales*, 35,000 tons, and the *Repulse*, 32,000 tons, were both sunk off the coast of Singapore by Japanese aircraft. They believe there are 2000 survivors.' Call them survivors! Those poor bastards will be Japanese prisoners. I remember what the Japanese did at Nanking."

Lydia gasped, "Oh, my God. That was inhuman."

"What was "The Rape of Nanking?" Carmel asked.

Russell said. "The Rape of Nanking occurred in 1937. The Japanese army raped and murdered the Chinese women, mutilated their bodies, and threw the body parts into the streets. They tied Chinese men together and killed them along with the children."

Lydia said, "We're not going to talk about that in front of Carmel."

"Aunt Lydia, you don't have to keep things from me. I am almost twenty-one, you know. Uncle Russell, isn't the *Prince of Wales* the ship where President Roosevelt and Prime Minister Churchill signed the Atlantic Charter?"

"Yes, Carmel. I didn't know you were such a history buff." He chuckled.

"You're not the only one in this house who reads the newspaper."

Lydia said, "I'm concerned about the two alerts we had last night. I wonder when we'll be able to feel safe and get some sleep."

"As long as the army thinks there's a need for alerts, we'll just have to be notified. The President said news would not be good for a while but to prepare for worse news. He also said, 'We're going to win this war, and we'll win the peace that follows'. As a rule, the Japs don't tell the truth, so it's probably not as bad as it sounds."

Lydia insisted, "I keep thinking about our friends in the islands and the Philippines. Don't suppose we'll know anything for a while."

Carmel finished her breakfast. The phone rang as she got up from the table. "I'll answer. Might be Dad." A strange voice said, "Hi, Carmel. This is Jerry Cassidy, remember me? I met you on the train."

"Of course I remember. How're you?"

"Fine, just fine. San Francisco's been going through a lot of changes since we last saw each other."

"That is certainly true."

"The reason I'm calling, I have news. The girl singer at the Chez Paree is leaving. Her husband is in the service, and he wants her to live with his folks in the Midwest. She'll stay here through Christmas. The Chez Paree will be looking for a singer. Why don't you audition?"

Audition, she thought, so soon! I haven't touched the piano or sung one note since I arrived.

He felt her hesitate. "Well, we can make it after Christmas, if you like. I can call you."

"Thank you, Jerry. I'll hear from you after Christmas." She wished him a happy holiday and hung up.

What kind of place is the Chez Paree? Obviously, she thought, a French nightclub, maybe even on the naughty side. Life was becoming interesting.

Russell announced, "I'm off to be with Eleanor Roosevelt and Mayor LaGuardia."

"And I'm off to the Red Cross. Don't forget, Russell, to memorize what she's wearing."

After her aunt and uncle left the house, Carmel went to the baby grand piano in the living room. She opened the piano bench and found it full of sheet music.

She selected a few songs and sat down at the piano. She found "Deep Purple" and enjoyed playing the familiar melody. Her aunt loved Cole Porter's music and had a collection of songs from his musical comedies. Carmel sang several. "What Is This Thing Called Love" was the first. The last song she sang, Jerome Kern's "Smoke Gets in Your Eyes," was one of her favorites.

Lydia, I've already told you what she wore." Russell said, exasperated. "Now here are more important things you should know."

"Oh, all right."

"My dear, I'm trying to tell you." Russell stood as he carved generous pieces of roast pork. "The room was packed. Mrs. Roosevelt was most gracious and, I might add, extremely patient. She asked how many air raid wardens we had trained. I had to tell her none. So embarrassing. We are to prepare for an emergency, know our doctors' telephone numbers, the emergency hospital closest to us, and, most important, keep a bucket of sand close by."

"Whatever for?" Lydia asked.

Carmel wasn't sure if her uncle was teasing. "I guess they're expecting bombs?"

Russell finished carving and sat down. "The fire chief, Brennan, wanted to know how we can train people to put out incendiary bombs when we don't have any equipment. Mrs. Roosevelt said anyone could carry a bucket of sand and put out the fire—even children in London were doing it."

Lydia asked, "What did he say?"

"He repeated the question, insisting he had no equipment." Russell took a sip of wine. "Mrs. Roosevelt repeated the instructions, said not to put any water on the fire bomb but a small drizzle from the hose, and then use a bucket of sand on the fire. Stubborn Chief Brennan repeated he had no equipment and sat down. Dummy!"

Lydia and Carmel joined Russell in the laughter.

"I think you both look like Christmas tree ornaments," Russell said, referring to Carmel's green wool dress and Lydia's red wool dress.

"Since I'm going to San Jose in the morning and your house looks so festive, I thought I'd dress up a bit," Carmel said.

"Yes, it does look nice. Putting the tree in the hall makes the whole house smell good. Madison and Helen decorated the house this morning and finished hanging the wreaths. Where were you all day?" Lydia asked.

"I had to see the Christmas tree at the City of Paris. The four-story tree this year is gorgeous. Each year the decorators outdo themselves. Oh, did you know sand bags are piled along the front of the telephone company?"

"Yes, Carmel, other buildings are going to do the same." Russell added, "Mayor LaGuardia mentioned it."

"Oh, what did he say? I think that man's so cute," Lydia said, listening intently for the reply.

"Mayor LaGuardia said we should meet every morning and get organized. The Civil Defense has to have many more members. He wasn't very cute when he said it. I think he's upset with the people of San Francisco. He had three interpreters in three languages to get the message across." Russell's voice became grim. "We're to train firefighters, train air-raid wardens, train messengers—train, train. We are not prepared. And is own city, New York, is not prepared.

"He also said don't sit in the dark in an air raid. Turn out the lights, but sit in the one room that has the lights on and blackout curtains. Also, to get on the floor if a bomb falls. He's disgusted with us, I think."

"But no bombs have fallen," Carmel said.

Lydia said, "I know the paper stated we have to stop using blue paper to cover our car headlights. Just turn them off."

Carmel added, "I heard three people were killed last night."

Russell answered, "Two! A passenger car ran into a taxi diver. Both drivers were killed in the blackout. I guess some poor woman panicked and jumped out the window. She was frightened during the air raid."

"Let's hear some good news—please, Russell," Lydia insisted

"Okay. How about the *China Clipper* making it home. It's the only plane that flies internationally. The newspaper said the pilot, Captain Hamilton, while on Wake Island watched from a drainpipe while the Japanese bombed Wake with no return firepower from us. There were about nine Japanese planes. They riddled the *China Clipper*.

"After the Japanese left, Captain Hamilton got the Pan Am crew and took off. The crew heard Pearl was being bombed when they were 450 miles from Honolulu. They had dumped fuel so they could reach landing weight on Wake. From then on, that trip must have been hell, not knowing if a Japanese plane would come out of the blue. Seventy-two hours without sleep. They knew San Francisco was blacked out and were nervous about enemy planes that might shoot them. They finally landed on Treasure Island. That is some kind of a captain."

"We'll probably hear a lot of stories about brave men," Lydia said. "The suggestion was made to put plywood on our windows. Russell, what do you think?"

"That's crazy, Lydia. These windows are large. Just continue to use the black flannel or whatever you're using."

Carmel listened to the conversation, hating the confusion the war scare brought to San Francisco.

Russell offered, "Well, Mayor LaGuardia said it was going to be a long war, but we would win."

"When I think of the young men that have to face this awful war for maybe months … oh, please God, I hope not for years …" Lydia's voice trailed off.

At Russell's suggestion, the family agreed to retire early. It had been a long day for each one of them. The hope of a good night's sleep was on their minds.

CHAPTER 10

Carmel returned home to Costalotta and assumed her customary job of decorating the house. She worked all morning with the green pines Pedro had cut and brought her. Her usual task of arranging bouquets of boughs with red ribbons and tying them to the stairway brought a sense of familiarity and reassurance, settling her scattered feelings.

The Christmas tree Anna decorated in the corner of the living room touched the ceiling. Long strands of Christmas tinsel hanging from its branches shimmered with reflected firelight.

"Looks like Christmas around here," Scott said. He watched Carmel standing on the ladder tying ribbon to the boughs along the stair rail. "Want me to hold the ladder?

"No, I'm fine."

Scott watched his sister for a moment. "You're awfully quiet this morning for a girl who's about to change her life. You're usually singing while you work."

"I was thinking about Grant. This is the first time in my life he won't be home for Christmas. I wonder why he decided to stay in Hawaii."

"Chet arrives in San Francisco today. I guess a lot of the team came back. Chet's coming over and we'll find out what our brother's doing."

"So much has happened since Thanksgiving dinner at the Palace. Will he be here tonight?"

Andrew heard her. "I spoke to his folks. He'll spend Christmas Eve with them and see us in the morning. The Barrons will be here tonight for carols and some Christmas cheer. Phillip's coming down from the hospital."

At the mention of Phillip's name, Carmel flinched and almost fell off the ladder.

Scott rushed over to steady the ladder. "Do you *have* to do this? You better get down before you break your neck."

"This has always been *my* job, and I can't do it and wear gloves. If the boughs are cut too early, they will dry out and—"

Scott backed away from the ladder, "All right, all right."

Andrew went to the front door and opened it. "Listen to that rain. I hope this downpour doesn't slow the boy's arrival from the city."

Scott asked, "What time is this shindig? I've got some wrapping to do."

"The Barrons are expected around seven," Andrew answered.

They listened to the pounding rain on the terrace roof. The sky had darkened, casting a wintry gloom over the three of them.

Andrew shut the door. "Scott, why don't you turn the radio on? Let's have some music. While you're at it, turn on the Christmas lights. Let me help you, Carmel. What can I do?"

She smiled at him. "No thanks, Dad. Why don't you sit and relax?"

Scott plugged in the Christmas lights and turned on the radio. Bing Crosby singing "Jingle Bells" filled the room.

Carmel said, "Scott, hand me some of those boughs by your feet."

He handed her the boughs. "Sis, are you staying for New Year's Eve?"

"No, I'm planning on going back as soon as I can. I want to get settled."

She climbed down from the ladder and surveyed her work. "I did my customary excellent job."

"I suppose you'll be climbing this ladder when you're old and gray?" Scott said.

Carmel laughed. "If I am, I'll buy a new ladder. This ladder should be named Atlas, it's so old. I don't know how Anna managed to hang all these blackout curtains and stand on this old thing. Aunt Lydia couldn't do it. She'd have Uncle Russell climb the ladder."

They all laughed at the thought of Russell climbing a ladder.

During the long afternoon, the wind died down but the rain continued its relentless pounding.

Carmel looked forward to the evening. Christmas Eve was a holiday tradition for the two families, which shared a long-time custom of giving and receiving gifts to be opened on Christmas Day.

She took her time to dress in her floor-length red velvet gown. Draped to accent her small waist, the gown had a low and flattering neckline. The gold earrings she wore were Aunt Lydia's Christmas gift.

She dabbed Chantilly behind her ears and onto a piece of cotton she put between her breasts. Finished, she looked at herself in the mirror. The rich burgundy accented her creamy complexion and made her eyes sparkle. She hoped Phillip would think her desirable.

It was a relief when she heard the shouts of "Merry Christmas," followed by Harold, Cynthia, and Laura's arrival. They entered through the newly hung blackout drapes accompanied by the yapping dogs.

Andrew, elegant in his black tuxedo and red Christmas vest, greeted them at the door, "Howdy and Merry Christmas."

Scott took their raincoats. Harold and Laura gave their brightly colored packages to Lupe to put under the tree. Their voices echoed, "Merry Christmas, everyone."

Harold Barron gripped Andrew's hand and then Scott's. "Happy Holidays to you both."

Carmel thought the men looked courtly in their tuxedos. They beamed when she told them, "You all look like movie stars."

Andrew said, "Scott, do something about these dogs."

Scott laughed, "Dad, they think this party is for them. Come Howard, Bruno." He opened the front door and the dogs raced out. He returned to Laura and leaned down to give her a light kiss. "Merry Christmas."

"Merry Christmas, Scott."

Carmel saw Laura's eyes light up, full of love for Scott. "Laura your yellow silk dress shines like gold."

"Thank you," Laura said. "You look gorgeous in that red velvet. I'm so glad something lured you home. Scott says you're going back tomorrow." She looked wistful. "We never see each other."

Carmel hugged her friend. "Come to the city and spend a couple of days. We can catch up if you can get away from him." She looked at Scott and laughed. The two friends joined the guests.

The families found places to sit near the fire.

Andrew enjoyed being host. If a guest preferred, he planned to serve hot buttered rum and eggnog from the ornate silver bowl on the table. Carmel saw his disappointment when Cynthia was the only one to ask for eggnog while the others drank champagne.

Carmel sat opposite Cynthia Barron. Cynthia was a comfort to be around with her easy manner and soft voice. Carmel observed that her eyes were the same color as Phillip's.

"It's always lovely to be here, "Cynthia said. "Do you have any idea what kind of employment you'll seek, Carmel?" Cynthia asked.

Laura sitting beside Scott said, "Oh, Mother, there're so many jobs in San Francisco now that the war has started. A girl can write her own ticket." She sat beside Scott.

"Write your own ticket? What a peculiar way to express yourself? Where do you get some of your expressions?" Cynthia, smiling at Carmel, asked, "I understand you're living with your Aunt Lydia?"

Carmel's answer was lost when the dogs outside commenced their wild barking. Pedro shouted at them. She heard Phillip's voice as he greeted Pedro. Her heart began to thump. Her velvet felt too warm. She held her breath as the front door opened.

Phillip pushed through the drapes. His energy radiated throughout the room. He handed his raincoat to Anna and with long strides crossed the length of the room to the group by the fire.

Andrew rose to greet him. They shook hands. "Glad you made it safely."

Phillip reached for Scott's hand. "Forgive me for being so late. I couldn't get away from the hospital."

He kissed Cynthia on the cheek. "You look beautiful tonight, Mother."

His father got up and Phillip shook his hand. "Hello, Dad."

His father said, "I was afraid you wouldn't make it. You're so engrossed in your life in the city.

Cynthia said, "And you seem to have more and more reasons to stay away."

"I agree I've missed too many Christmas Eves," Phillip replied.

Laura slipped her arm through her brother's. Phillip leaned down to kiss her cheek, "You pretty thing, breaking all the boys' hearts?"

Scott snapped, "Hey, old boy. I resent that remark 'breaking other men's hearts'! She's my gal."

"We all know that," Phillip said with a smile.

Carmel waited for Phillip, tall and handsome in his navy suit, to acknowledge her. The moment their eyes met, chills ran across her body.

"Well, Carmel, how long has it been since we've seen each other?"

She wanted to ask how he could forget last August. She was sure he noticed the flush she felt and saw her pulse thumping. "It's good to have you join us," she mumbled.

Andrew asked, "Phillip, how about hot buttered rum?"

"Sounds great."

Phillip joined his mother on the couch.

Cynthia asked, "How is San Francisco reacting to the war?"

"Well, the mayor seems pretty upset. He's threatening to put people in jail if they don't pay attention to the blackouts. Cars are running into each other, mainly at the intersections. The police seem pretty nervous. Some of the guards on the Bay Bridge took potshots at the painters working on the bridge. It's just mild hysteria." He took a swallow of the drink Andrew brought him. "That's just what the doctor ordered." He chuckled.

Anna announced dinner. "Oh's" and "ah's" followed the first glimpse of the dining room. The blazing fire in the hearth and candles were the only light in the room. A red damask tablecloth draped the long table. In the center of the table were three silver candelabras. Sterling silver and sparkling crystal reflected the candle light.

On the sideboard, ornate silver salvers held a sumptuous Christmas dinner with all the trimmings. The room glowed in the firelight and candles. Guests, warm from the Champagne, were relaxed.

Cynthia asked, "Carmel, did you have time to put this entire meal together? It's delicious."

"Oh, no. Anna prepared our feast."

Carmel watching Phillip. He teased his sister Laura a great deal. Carmel felt he made an extra effort to pay attention to his mother. Did he know something about the war he wasn't telling? He acted as if he wasn't going to see them for a while. She felt the whole family was trying to keep things as normal as possible. This might be the last family gathering for some time.

Don't borrow trouble, she thought. Enjoy the moment. Except for Grant, all the people she loved most were gathered at this table.

Anna proudly served her chocolate Yule log. She accepted the applause for the dinner and dessert and then disappeared into the kitchen.

When everyone finished their dessert, Andrew said, "Let's have some carols."

Scott groaned, "I'm too full to sing one note."

Harold laughed. "He's right. I'll just listen."

"Oh, come on. We only do this once a year," Andrew said.

"Okay, okay, I'll sing," Harold said.

Andrew laughed. "Coffee and cognac in the front room, everyone."

The group followed Andrew into the living room.

"You play the piano, Carmel, while we catch our breath," Andrew suggested. Carmel went to the open piano and sat down. "I'll play a selection I love."

Anna served the cognac and coffee from the wheeled bar while Carmel played Beethoven's "Moonlight Sonata."

The finish brought applause.

"You play beautifully, Carmel. I hope you continue to play," Cynthia said.

Carmel said, "Thank you. Now let's sing some carols. Here's one." Carmel began, "It Came upon the Midnight Clear." Her father and Scott approached the piano and stood behind her. Carmel's clear soprano blended beautifully with her father's bass and her brother's tenor. Afterwards they sang, "Joy to the World" and "Deck the Halls."

Andrew bragged, "I think we're pretty good. Come on, Harold, Phillip, Cynthia. Get in on this." Both father and son joined them at the piano.

"I can't carry a tune in a rain barrel," she said, laughing at the old cliché.

Laura sat beside Carmel. She turned the pages and joined with a strong alto. After three more carols, ending with "Silent Night," Carmel's father protested, "That's enough for me." He sank into the couch and said, "Scott, please refresh the drinks."

Scott said, "Carmel, since you're planning on earning your living as a singer, why not sing something for us?

As Carmel sang and played, her tension lifted. She gave everyone a radiant smile. "Here's one I especially like."

She turned back to focus on the music. Singing "Smoke Gets in Your Eyes," she was no longer a young girl. Her voice, warm and vibrant, caressed the notes and filled the room. When she finished her audience was quiet for a moment. Then they applauded and asked for more. She wanted to lift up the mood of the room and decided to sing a more popular song, "All the Things You Are."

Carmel felt Phillip watching and listening to her sing. The feeling lifted her spirits. Her graceful fingers flew over the keys.

When she finished, Phillip joined in the applause and said, "I had no idea you had such a voice. You seem able to handle it any way you like." His eyes looked deep into hers.

"Thank you. I enjoy singing." At last, she thought, Phillip sees me.

Laura said, "There's a lot you don't know. She's living in San Francisco."

"What! When did you move to the city?" Phillip asked.

"She's living with her aunt and uncle and plans to get a job."

Scott added, "She's going to get a job singing with a dance band."

"Oh, how exciting," Cynthia cried. "Well, we wish you all the luck in the world. Harold, I think we better brave that storm outside and start for home."

Laura laughed. "You make it sound like we live miles away, not next door."

Harold rose with his wife. "A beautiful evening. Thank you, Carmel. You're truly blessed." He smiled at her and gave her a quick kiss on the cheek. He turned to Phillip. "Son, how long will you be with us?"

"I'll have to leave sometime tomorrow afternoon."

Scott limped to get their coats. "Chet'll be here in the morning to tell us what happened in Hawaii."

"Is Grant with him?" asked Cynthia.

Scott answered, "Grant's already volunteered to stay there, but we don't know any more than that."

Scott kissed Laura lightly on the lips; they smiled at each other.

Everyone was leaving. Carmel heard her father ask Phillip, "Would you give Carmel a lift tomorrow afternoon on your return to the city?" She held her breath. Everything in room stood still, her heart, the people in the room …

Phillip turned to her. "Carmel, I'll be happy to give you a lift to the city."

Carmel muttered a quiet, "Thank you."

"I'll pick you up around four o'clock."

"I'll be ready when you are," she replied, her heart pounding.

"Good nights" and "Merry Christmases" filled the air as the Barrons left. Christmas Eve 1941 had ended. The open door finally allowed Howard and Bruno, panting and tails wagging, to dash into the room.

"Goodnight all," Scott called to Andrew and Carmel as he made his way to bed.

"Come on," Andrew said to the dogs, "upstairs to bed." They slept on the floor in his room. Andrew banked the fire and unplugged the Christmas lights.

Carmel started to pick up the brandy glasses from the table.

"No, daughter, you go to bed. Lupe will take care of this in the morning."

"I am tired." She placed the brandy glasses back on the table. Then she turned to hug her father and give him a kiss. They wished each other Merry Christmas and good night.

Once in bed, Carmel tried to gather her thoughts. The drive to San Francisco was over an hour. All that time, she'd be alone with Phillip.

Oh, no! she thought. What on Earth will we talk about?

CHAPTER 11

Christmas Day 1941 was one of the longest days of Carmel's life. The family was up early to distribute gifts among themselves and to others living on Costalotta. Carmel smiled mechanically and carried on desultory conversations but afterwards remembered nothing she said.

Her thoughts were riveted on Phillip and their drive to San Francisco. Her hands were damp; her heart kept thumping way too hard. Once she thought in a panic, Suppose he changes his mind and leaves without me? Hoping fresh air would calm her nerves, she found a jacket in the hall closet, put it on, and went outside.

Last night's heavy rain had finally stopped. She wondered again what it would be like sitting beside Phillip in the car.

She heard Chet talking to the dogs and went to welcome him. He looked healthy but tired. It was like having Grant come home. She forgot his bashfulness, gave him a quick hug, and led him into the house

Scott admired Chet's blue jacket. "Did you get it for Christmas?"

"Yes, but I won't be wearing it long. I'll be changing it for a uniform a lot sooner than I thought."

Andrew grabbed Chet's elbow. "Let me take your jacket and come and sit on the couch. We're having coffee and Christmas cookies. Or anything you like to drink." He took Chet's jacket, hung it on the back of a chair, and directed him into the living room. "We want to hear everything. It's good of you to take time for us, especially on Christmas Day."

Chet sat on the couch, while the family found places to sit. A tray on the coffee table held a plate of cookies and a coffee service.

"I wanted to be here," Chet said. "I'll have coffee and a cookie." Carmel handed him a large cup of coffee. He refused the cream and sugar and reached for an oatmeal cookie. He took a bite and drank some coffee before he began to talk.

"We were docked by noon yesterday in San Francisco, and immigration put us right through. The buses were waiting to bring us to San Jose. In the beginning, we went to San Pedro from here, and the next day started the six-day trip to Hawaii."

Scott sat across from him. "Were you at all worried during your crossing? I mean, you were on open sea for a long time."

"There was a lot of joking about seeing periscopes in the water. We probably had submarines on our minds. Did you know the coaches were going to cancel our trip two weeks before we left? I think we were probably a little worried; we just didn't discuss any possibilities of danger.

"We landed in Hawaii on the third, and on the night of the sixth we went to a big doings with the University of Hawaii. We were supposed to be in our hotel by midnight, but a lot of us didn't get in until three or four in the morning." He looked sheepishly at Andrew.

"It didn't matter much, because we didn't know we weren't going to be playing football anyway. On the following day, the seventh, we were scheduled to have a trip around the island with a group of Hawaii University girls in two or three buses and lots of food. It was just a special sightseeing trip planned for us."

Scott asked, "Were you guys all together at the hotel?"

"Yes, at the Moana Hotel. It's right on the beach. That morning we had gone down to breakfast early; we wanted to be out by seven to start the day. We were just eating our breakfast and looking out the big plate glass windows over the channel. We could see a ship out there zigzagging, whipping back and forth, doing all kinds of maneuvers."

Andrew interrupted, "What kind of ship?"

"Well, it was one of ours, a merchant ship, and we thought it was on maneuvers because the ships had been put on alert when we arrived. There was water spurting up here and then over there." Chet was waving his arms. "So we didn't think anything of it. Then, after breakfast, we walked out in front of the hotel, and a police officer drove up and told us the Japs were bombing Pearl Harbor. Needless to say, the trip was off." He took a gulp of coffee.

"We went up to the roof of the hotel to watch and could see a dive bomber coming in over Pearl and the smoke boiling up from Hickam Field, and we stood there and watched it. We didn't have any place to run. We weren't in any danger and there was no damage in town except for our own antiaircraft shells that went up and came down and didn't explode. There were two holes in the street within two blocks of the hotel."

"They went up and came down?" Carmel asked.

"Our antiaircraft shells were exploding, all right. They went up like twenty feet in the air, all the way up and all the way down. We were *really* disorganized."

He shook his head. "There was no question about it. The only damage in town, in lives taken, was from these shells that didn't explode when they came down and then exploded when they hit. We were a little edgy because, as I say, we didn't have anything to do. In fact, some of us decided that there was no need to let all that food for the tour go to waste." He laughed. "After it all subsided, we got the pineapple juice, chicken, pies, and all the trimmings and went down to the park and had ourselves a picnic." He looked sheepish.

"I guess a bunch of guys would do that," Carmel said.

"Did you realize we were at war?" Andrew asked.

"Oh, yes, but what were we going to do about it? The *Lurline* had left immediately for the mainland. We were stranded."

No one noticed his empty coffee cup. "They just left you?" asked Scott.

"They didn't notify you?" Andrew asked, concerned.

"Things were getting hectic, sir. Army vehicles were busting up and down the streets about 65 mph and seeming to go nowhere. It was five in the afternoon on the seventh and we didn't know what to do. The football team and the coach were milling around. We didn't know if the Japanese were coming back. The military had finally got some barbed wire along Waikiki beach, and they had a few fifty-caliber machine guns and a couple of antipersonnel guns set up. It took all day to do that, and then that night everybody was apprehensive. The blackouts were severe. Everybody had to be off the street at six o'clock."

"Were they prepared for a blackout?" Scott asked.

"No. There were no lights allowed."

"Did they *have* a blackout?" Carmel questioned.

"Not then—by the time we left they had blacked out the windows, and they blacked out headlights on automobiles, leaving just a little slot with a hood over it. People without authority had to run with absolutely no headlights."

Andrew asked, "What did the boys want to do? Did they want to come home?"

"Well, no one knew what they wanted to do at that stage of the game. Grant and I decided that we would go down and ask the police department if we could volunteer for some special duty. There were rumors that parachutists were landing in the mountains on the island and that there were transports landing on the other side of the island, the windward side. They were just rumors, but we didn't know that."

Andrew broke in: "Had it occurred to you before you left San Jose that you would go into the service? I think that was the last thing on Grant's mind."

"No. Some of the boys got their call from the draft, but it was delayed so they could make the trip."

"Better have a fresh cup," Carmel said, pouring more coffee.

Chet continued, "Well, to make a long story short, nine of us went down to the police department to volunteer and they issued us armbands, helmets, riot guns, and gas masks. We were told to patrol with regular officers. Grant and I were on duty at midnight, so we went back to the hotel and decided to take a little nap. Just before we were to leave for the police department, we heard a fifty-caliber machine gun chattering away, and I don't mind telling you I was scared to death. It was right outside the hotel on the beach. We finally learned the noise was a dory broken away from its mooring. We sunk it with a fifty-caliber machine gun." He laughed and shook his head.

Scott joined the group's laughter. "Did you know Tiny, your coach, called the athletic director here and let us know you all were okay?"

"Yes, we knew. Frankly, we didn't know how and when we could get home. Some of the fellows were sent to guard the power plants and water plants. Grant and I were with a Korean officer who could have gotten us in serious trouble with his sawed-off shotgun and a bunch of buckshot. He was so nervous and jumpy. If we had spotted a tilt light on the pinball machine in the back of the store, he was ready to shoot the plate glass window out.

There was shooting all night long. Out in the basin, the military were shooting at goats and even at the officers who went to investigate the shooting."

Carmel was beginning to wonder what effect all this news about Grant would have on her father. "Where were the Hawaiian people?"

"They were all indoors. It was illegal to have a radio on or any type of broadcast, and if anyone lit a match on the porch or anywhere, they were fined two hundred dollars. Martial law was declared, and boy it was tough! Only the military could be on the streets. They were shooting all over town all night long."

Andrew asked, "Did the Hawaiians have guns?"

"No, only the military, sir. As a matter of fact, at about four in the morning we were downtown on River Street, and we heard planes coming over and I thought they were coming back—the Japs, I mean—and we were firing at these planes. There's a marine base right out of Honolulu, and the tracer fire in the air was tremendous. It was like a Fourth of July celebration. A wave of B-17s was coming in. Then we found out that the planes were our planes. Thank the Lord we didn't shoot any down. They landed somewhere near Hickam."

Andrew, totally absorbed in Chet's story, asked, "Had you boys been deputized?"

"We were sworn in as special officers, sir. Oh, yes, as a matter of fact, Grant and I rode the next night in a patrol car with an officer called Sing Chang. For some reason neon lights had a way of snapping on, and we rode around shooting out the neon bulbs. I can see the Studebaker sign still full of buckshot." Remembering, he shook his head.

"When's Grant coming home?" Andrew asked.

"I don't think he'll be coming for a while. Grant has a job over there, sir."

Surprised, Scott asked, "Doing what?"

"After eight days they needed officers so badly they offered us a job on the regular force. Grant had to take a test and now goes to school eight hours a day and pounds a beat at night for another eight hours. He'll have to buy his uniform and a .38 revolver. I was going to do it, too, but on the eighteenth we had to move out of the hotel and in two hours we were given notice to board ship. I was broke. I landed with forty dollars in my pocket, which I spent in the first two days. I decided to come back. We came back steerage and had to wear life jackets day and night. It was quite a difference from the *Lurline*. There were a lot of wounded and burn victims aboard. We offered to help as much as possible." He sighed.

Andrew changed the subject. "I know you young men will never forget this trip. It sounds to me like your team was there when they were needed." He smiled at Chet. "How much will Grant earn?"

"For now, a hundred and six dollars a month."

"Can't get into much trouble with that kind of money." Andrew stood up. "Well, I guess he'll be there for a while." He put his empty cup on the tray.

Chet volunteered, "Honolulu is a beautiful place to live."

"Yes, when there's no war. I've got a fool for a son," Andrew said.

Chet stood up. "I should be leaving."

"Did you boys see Hickam Field or Pearl Harbor?" Scott wondered.

"No, we had no authority to go there. We sure heard all the news, though. Unbelievable—the *Arizona* sank with all aboard lost."

Andrew put his arm around Chet's shoulder. "It was generous of you to share your Christmas Day with us and tell us what happened."

"Glad to do it, sir. I hope I've remembered everything." He turned to Carmel. "I hear you moved to San Francisco."

Carmel, listening to Chet, had forgotten for a few minutes how interminable the waiting had been. "Yes, I'm going back today." She heard the clock chime three thirty and realized departure was only half an hour away. "It was thoughtful for you to come and tell us what happened over there. I'll excuse myself."

She hurried up the stairs to her room. Anna followed her.

"Anna, will you please find the green sweater Dad gave me for Christmas?" Carmel was pulling on a green corduroy skirt. "I'll never be ready in time." She felt desperate. She had waited all day, and now, when it was time to leave, she wasn't ready.

"Yes, you will." Anna found the sweater under some empty Christmas boxes. "I'll have to get this room to rights after you've gone."

Wrinkles be damned! Carmel thought as she pushed clothes into the large suitcase.

"Here, here—let me do this. Find your coat and gloves. I'm sure glad you're living with your Aunt Lydia. I can imagine what your place would look like if you were alone."

"Well, that's exactly what I'm going to do as soon as I get a job—get a place of my own. Too many people are telling me what to do."

"Your father won't like that one bit, and I'm not too happy to hear it either," Anna grumbled.

"Phillip's here," Scott called from downstairs.

Carmel threw her arms around Anna and said." "I'll surprise you sometime and do everything right."

Anna hugged her and said, "I'll settle for half."

Carmel started for the door, hoping her heart wouldn't jump out of her body.

CHAPTER 12

Carmel settled herself beside Phillip in his midnight blue Chevy coupe. She felt sophisticated in her black coat with the black Persian lamb collar and matching hat.

Phillip gave a glance to the back seat of the packed car. "I don't believe we could put one more thing in this car." As he steered out of the driveway, he laughed. "With your luggage and Christmas presents for your aunt and uncle, and my suitcase and presents, the little car is full. To top it off, my mother always sends a batch of cookies and fruitcake for my staff."

They rode in silence, crossing the streets of San Jose. Sitting beside him in the winter darkness, she detected the faint apricot odor of his cologne. Each time he shifted gears she felt his elbow touch her thigh. Thrilled by this contact, she wished she could see his eyes and flirt with him now that they were alone. In an hour, he would leave her. She had so little time.

As Phillip turned onto the Bay Shore Highway, he asked, "Did Chet come to the house?"

"Yes. He was at the house for at least two hours. He left just before you came."

"How many members of the football team stayed in Hawaii?" Phillip shifted gears to pass a huge semi-truck.

A picture of Grant's handsome smiling face suddenly appeared in her mind. Maybe Grant had made the wrong decision. The war was changing so many lives.

"Carmel!"

"Yes!"

"I asked how many of the football team stayed in Hawaii?"

"Nine." Relieved to have something to talk about she told him what happened to Chet and the team on December 7.

"Chet said the *Lurline* left them immediately. I guess everyone was thrown off balance. Some of the boys joined the police department. But Chet decided to return. Grant stayed and joined the military police."

"If I know Grant, he'll do well. That boy has a lot going for him. But I've always thought, of the two, Scott was exceptionally mature for his age."

"They are different, aren't they?"

"I would imagine all that surgery on his knee and the pain forced him to accept life and what it offered."

The Bay Shore Highway curled along the shore, north towards San Francisco. As they neared the city, heavy fog covered the ground. It was necessary to slow the speed of the car and drive with dimmers on.

He continued, "I'll admit I was surprised when I heard you sing last night. It takes guts to move to San Francisco and look for work in the profession you have chosen. If the right person hears you, Carmel, you might become a huge success. Where did you learn to sing?"

"Frankly, I haven't had any lessons. I sing with records. I love Ginny Simms, Ella Fitzgerald, and Sarah Vaughan."

"They're all great. However, I'm surprised your father agreed to your move to the city."

"Because my aunt and uncle invited me to live with them until I can find work. I've met a piano player who said he'd try and help me find a job." Now why did she tell him that? She changed the subject.

"What about you? Will you go into the service?"

"We're waiting to see what doctors will be inducted. Our hospital is equipped for any emergency. We just bought three new ambulances.

"Aren't you head of the orthopedic department?"

"Not yet."

"Do you like being in a large hospital?"

"Very much."

"Does your dad want you to practice in his clinic?"

"Yes, he does, Carmel, but he also knows I like the experience I'm receiving in a large hospital. Every day is different. I'm learning, learning."

"If you enter the service is there a chance you will be stationed in the Pacific?" She resisted the urge to tell him she didn't want him to leave just as she moved to San Francisco.

"I'll go whenever they need me."

"You don't approve of my moving to San Francisco, do you?" she challenged him.

"It's just that you seem young to leave home and go to one of the largest cities in the world, particularly during a war. Have you thought about the fact it's a city that will be changing so fast? Do you realize San Francisco will be a city of embarkation and disembarkation, filled with servicemen from every walk of life?"

"I guess I hadn't thought of it quite like that. But I'm almost twenty-one years old and very capable, and I can certainly take care of myself," she answered tartly.

He laughed. "I bet you can."

They arrived in San Francisco and drove up the hill to Chestnut. Carmel fretted. They would be at her aunt's house any minute. Carmel wondered with a kind of desperation when and how to see him. They hadn't talked enough. She wanted him to want to see her again. She had hoped to be entertaining and provocative, and now it was too late.

He said, "I suppose now Laura will get itchy feet. She'll want to follow you here."

Perfect, Carmel thought. With Laura here, there'd be all kinds of excuses to see him. "I wish she would come for a visit, at least."

The thick ground fog, curling in from the bay, made it difficult to see. "Here's the street. It's the second house from the corner," she announced.

Phillip found the curb in front of the house. He carried her bags from the car and set them on the porch.

She stood at the door among her bundles, muddling over how to say goodbye. "I really appreciate you driving me to San Francisco. I know you're in a hurry. If you like, you may say hello to my aunt and uncle another time."

"Another time would be fine. It's no problem to bring you—glad to help out. I wish you good luck finding a job." He stood on the porch looking down at her. In the distance, foghorns were the only sounds in the night.

Carmel wasn't aware of how small and vulnerable she appeared, her face lovely in the half light. The essence of fresh mint drifted up to him. Phillip reached for her. His arms slid across her back, pulling her close. His mouth touched hers, his lips warm and gentle, moving slowly, insisting, and exploring her lips.

Carmel gave herself without resistance. He had strong arms in which she could stay forever. She yielded her body to his.

Suddenly, Phillip pushed her away from him. Holding her by her forearms, he studied her face for a moment. "I'm sorry. I didn't mean ..." He backed away. "Take care of yourself." He walked down the porch steps and climbed into the Chevy.

Stunned, she watched the red tails lights disappear into the fog. Bitter tears stung her eyes. Take care of herself, indeed!

Carmel unlocked the front door, sensing she was alone. She carried her luggage into the hall and found the note on the table.

Carmel, welcome back. We have gone to church for the Christmas program. Helen and Madison, too. See you in the morning. The dogs are shut up in the back. Love, Aunt Lydia.

Carmel was relieved she didn't have to talk to anyone. However, once in bed, sleep eluded her. She thought about how warm and searching his lips were. No one had ever made her feel so totally alive. She didn't try or want him to stop. Remembering the strength and smell of him, she trembled deliciously in the dark.

CHAPTER 13

New Year's Eve newspapers and radio announcers advised the citizens of San Francisco to celebrate at home. The pubic was relieved to learn the Highway Patrol officers carried rifles in their patrol cars if a paratrooper should drop out of the sky. However, citizens of the old guard suggested the city was filling up with rabble.

New Year's Eve found Lydia, Russell, and Carmel sharing a bottle of champagne in the morning room.

They had rolled up the rug and Carmel watched her aunt and uncle dance to the music of a Guy Lombardo broadcast from the Rainbow Room in New York. Russell wore his red cardigan and red bowtie. Lydia, elegant in her shiny black and silver evening dress, glided in his arms.

Carmel enjoyed watching her aunt and uncle's devotion to each other. The music changed to a fox trot and her uncle asked her to dance.

They floated around the room. "Uncle Russell, you're a wonderful dancer."

"Thank you, but only when I have a good partner." He swung too wide and bumped the coffee table.

Lydia laughed. "Feeling rambunctious, are we, dear?"

"You're right," Russell said, reaching for his pocket handkerchief. He wiped his face and looked at his watch. "We have nine minutes. I'll open another bottle of champagne. First, I'll get Madison and Helen to join us."

Lydia wondered, "Carmel, do you have any resolutions?"

"I'm too superstitious to make resolutions."

"They're secret," Lydia agreed. "I don't blame you."

Madison and Helen walked into the room, followed by Russell. He filled their glasses and they toasted the New Year. When Lombardo's orchestra played "Auld Lang Syne," they all sang the words. Before saying good night, everyone exchanged best wishes for the coming year.

Carmel hugged her aunt and uncle and thanked them for supporting her move to San Francisco.

In her room, Carmel admitted she had only one resolution—to see Phillip. Unnerved by a sudden twinge of jealousy, she wondered whether he was celebrating and with whom?

The following Friday afternoon, Carmel sat in a taxi on her way to meet Jerry at the Chez Paree for her audition. A soaking winter rain the night before had left the streets wet. Traffic inched along. The sidewalks were crowded with people carrying umbrellas.

Her throat felt dry at the thought of asking someone for a job, much less singing for him. She gripped her umbrella so hard she saw the streaks on her palm.

She tried to calm her thoughts. She had better pick something slow so she would have enough breath. She made herself stop worrying. Think of Jerry. He had made all this possible.

"Embraceable You" popped into her head. That was the song to sing.

She leaned toward the driver and peered through the window at the traffic ahead. "Driver, you're going against the traffic. You can let me out at the corner. I'll walk."

The driver stopped at the corner. "Here you are, lady. Seventy-five cents." He didn't bother to open the door, just put out his hand. She gave him a dollar and got out of the taxi.

The street was teeming with traffic as she waited to cross Geary Street. The wind blew her skirts, and a taxi full of sailors whistled and grinned as they passed. One yelled, "Hubba-hubba." She ignored them.

The Chez Paree was a block down Mason Street. She struggled to hold her skirts against the wind. She knew her hair would be an absolute mess.

When she reached the club, she found Jerry waiting outside. In her nervousness, Carmel missed the gaudy signs advertising full-length bodies wearing scanty two-piece outfits.

"Have I kept you waiting? Am I late?" she asked, breathless from the walk. Her cheeks glowed. The soft yellow scarf around her throat made her eyes look huge and dark.

"No. Don't worry," he said. "You don't have an appointment."

Carmel raised questioning eyes to him. "How will I know what to do? I—"

Jerry interrupted, "Charlie is always here this time of day. He's the manager, and I thought you'd just come on over to the piano. I'll ask you to sing something while I'm fooling around on the piano."

He took her by the arm and guided her through the black double doors and then through heavy blackout curtains into a small room. They proceeded down a long stairway to the floor below. She saw the chipped green paint on the walls.

At the bottom of the stairs, they entered a large room. Carmel's eyes adjusted to the dim light. On the left side of the room, she saw a bar that ran the length of the room. Across the dance floor on a raised stage an upright piano stood. Small tables held chairs turned upside down. The dark room reeked of stale tobacco smoke and aged wood, the musty smell of a cavern never exposed to daylight or fresh air.

A man stood back of the bar, lining up bottles.

"Charlie. I want you to meet Carmel St. John. She's a singer."

Carmel thought Charlie's skin had the pasty look of a man who stayed out of the sun. His dark, beady eyes were as hard as stones in his coarse features. The clothes on his short body appeared worn for several days.

Charlie was interested. "Let's see what you look like. Take off your coat." He rolled his cigar to the other side of his mouth.

Carmel stared at Jerry. He nodded and smiled. "Here, give me your coat."

Charlie's bluntness startled Carmel, but she did as Jerry said. With a weak smile, she removed her coat and handed it to Jerry. Carmel was glad she wore her green wool. In her effort to be simple, the princess lines, instead, drew attention to her small waist and ample bosom.

He shifted his cigar again and ran his tongue over his thick lips. His gaze started at her feet and continued up to her eyes.

She shuddered, but Jerry encouraged her. "Come over to the piano." He led her around the forest of tables and chairs toward the small stage.

Charlie came from behind the bar and seated himself on a stool. "Maybe she don't need to sing. Can she dance? Raise your skirt, honey. Let's see your legs."

Jerry seated himself at the piano and ignored the remark. "What do you want to sing, Carmel?"

Jerry looked at her intently. Carmel hesitated. She wanted to grab her coat and leave this awful place and its smell. Her voice was low. "Embraceable You."

"What key?" Jerry played some chords with his right hand.

"E flat." Carmel moved closer to the piano.

Jerry's introduction and the sight of his strong hands on the keyboard gave her confidence. With her back half-turned away from the room and Charlie, she sang. Her voice was quiet at first and then, as her confidence grew, it filled the spaces in the room with her amber tones as she caressed the words. When she was through, the man with the broom had stopped to listen, and his clapping was the only sound.

Jerry stared at her. "Gosh, gal, you can sing."

Charlie stood up. "Hey, kid, can you handle a mike?"

Carmel, thrilled by Jerry's compliment, smiled. "Yes."

"We need you tomorrow night. Be here at eight thirty. Wear something sexy." Charlie stared at her breasts.

"Can you make it?" The expression on Jerry's face begged her to say "yes."

Carmel nodded. Could she make it? All the king's men and the horses they rode couldn't stop her. "I'll be here."

Jerry reached for her coat. "Come on, let me show you around."

Charlie continued to leer at Carmel.

Jerry led her to a stairway back of the stage. Carmel stood for a minute. "Aren't there any lights back here?"

"I'm sorry. I forgot you don't know your way around." He disappeared for a minute and bright lights snapped on. "This is where you'll change, with the other girls."

"Are they singers, too?"

"No. You're the only singer. They dance." Jerry grinned. "Don't pay any attention to Charlie. He always wants to see girls' legs."

Still uneasy, Carmel was far from being convinced.

"Here's your dressing room."

Carmel stared at the long, narrow room with green paint peeling off the walls. There were three mirrored makeup tables with open boxes of powder and cans of cold cream on them. She could smell the faint odor of Tabu perfume. In the middle of the room, a long rack held a line of brightly colored costumes. Bits of paper and empty Coca-Cola bottles covered the floor near the wastebasket, as if the plan was to miss the basket.

"Do they all dress in the same room?" Carmel picked up a blue feather off the floor.

Jerry watched her face. "Yes. The gals are real nice. You'll get along fine. One's your age. You're twenty-one, aren't you?"

Ignoring his question, she asked, "How many girls work here?"

"Three. Maggie—she's your age—Elka, and Tempest Storm."

"Tempest Storm? What does she do?"

Jerry ran his fingers inside his collar. "She's an artistic dancer. You'll like her. Come on, Carmel. Let's get out of here. If you like, we can find a place and have some coffee, maybe decide what you want to sing?" He walked over to switch off the lights.

They made their way back down the long hall into the big room. Charlie wasn't there. Carmel stopped abruptly. "Jerry, am I working in a strip joint?"

Jerry managed a rueful grin. "It's not really a strip joint. It's a club, and the girls don't actually strip, but they do bumps and grinds. Remember, you wanted to be a singer. You have to start somewhere."

Her thoughts raced. My God! Bumps and grinds! How would she tell Aunt Lydia? How would her father react? Would he understand? A strip joint. She could just hear him howl. More importantly, what would Phillip think? This job certainly wasn't wearing a long dress and standing in front of a big band.

After dinner, Carmel joined her aunt in the library. "Russell had gone to arrange the schedules for the Civil Defense volunteers.

The fire Madison lit in the small marble fireplace added a warm glow to the room. Brass Stiffel table lamps gleamed in the firelight. The deep reds in the Oriental rug added to the rich colors in the room. Bookcases lined one wall. Framed pictures of President Roosevelt and General MacArthur, with his ubiquitous corncob pipe, hung on the wall. Lydia's collection of Chinese porcelain was displayed in a glass case against one wall.

This was Carmel's favorite room. Two Queen Anne wing chairs faced each other by the fireplace. Carmel sank into one of them, facing Lydia in the opposite chair. Heidi and Hilda slept close to her feet.

Lydia reached into a full basket on the floor and picked up brightly colored knitting yarn. She wore a soft gray dress with a pale orange silk scarf around her neck. She reminded Carmel of a small gray finch. Lydia's fingers flew over the yarn as she knitted.

Carmel waited. I should just blurt it out, she thought. Get it over with. Her throat felt dry as she said, "Aunt Lydia, I start a job tomorrow night."

Aunt Lydia's eyes seemed very blue to Carmel. "A job? So soon? Where, my dear?"

"At a French club, the Chez Paree." She wasn't exactly telling a lie if she left things out, was she?

"How fortunate. You'll be able to practice your French. How did this happen so fast? Should we have your Uncle Russell check the place out?"

"Oh, no, I promise I'll tell you if there is any trouble. Do you remember before Christmas the man I met on the train? He plays piano at this club and said if an opportunity came about, he would try to help me. The singer in the club is leaving. Her husband went overseas, and she's living with her husband's parents in the Midwest. Jerry Cassidy—that's his name—called me to audition and I did, and they hired me ... I mean, they offered me a job singing and I accepted."

"Will you sing with a band?"

"No, there'll be four musicians."

"Well, that sounds exciting. Do you work every night?"

"I think four or five."

"What time do you have to be there?"

"A little after eight."

"We'll have to arrange an early dinner for you."

"Oh, no. No dinner, please. I'll eat later. I don't want to be any trouble. As a matter of fact, as soon as possible, I plan to find my own apartment."

"Humph ... that's not likely." Lydia frowned. "It was difficult enough to find a place to live before this war started, and now there'll be even more problems with all the servicemen and their families coming here." She extended her yarn with her hand. "I never in my life thought I'd be sitting here and knitting for soldiers again. World War One was supposed to end all of this." She looked directly at Carmel. "You certainly found a job fast. Have you thought how you'll get home at night?"

Carmel hadn't thought that far. "I'll take a taxi home," she said.

Aunt Lydia seemed satisfied. "Where did I put my cigarettes?" She searched her lap.

"Here they are, under your feet." Carmel rose, picked up the pack of Lucky Strikes, and laid them on the small table. "Auntie, please excuse me. I'm going to bed. It's been a long day for me." She kissed her aunt.

"Thank you. Sleep well, my dear."

CHAPTER 14

The following evening Carmel packed a small valise with her pearl gray formal, artificial deep red silk flowers, and gray satin slippers with tiny high heels. She included a small silk purse with powder, lipstick, and mascara.

As she waited for the taxi, she wondered how many evenings she would be able to afford a cab. It was high time she found out what her salary would be.

With streetlights blacked out and automobiles allowed only a single slit of light over their headlights, Carmel saw little on the way to the Chez Paree. As the driver turned from Van Ness onto Geary, they heard the screech of tires. The cab stopped abruptly.

"Shit. The idiot almost hit us. I'm sorry, miss. Are you all right?" The driver looked back at her. "I'm trying to drive as slow as I can."

"Driver, don't worry about it. I'm fine." Anxious about her singing, she hardly noticed the near miss.

The trip took longer than she planned. She arrived at the Chez Paree intent on the performance ahead. Again, she overlooked the half-nude girls advertised on the billboards outside the entrance.

Once inside, she looked through the partly open blackout curtains. The bar overflowed with servicemen, mostly sailors, some already drunk. The only way to get to the dressing rooms at the back was to pass through the bar. She promised herself to arrive earlier in the future.

She raced past the bar to the stage and through the faded curtain, ignoring the catcalls. "Hey, girlie, where you running to in such a hurry? Hubba-hubba."

She found the dressing room door. Not sure what to expect, she took a deep breath and pushed open the door.

"Hi, I'm Elka," said a tiny, perfectly shaped Dresden doll with huge blue eyes. "You're the new singer, *ja*?"

"Yes, I'm Carmel."

Elka shouted, "*Frauleins*, make room for our new singer. Carmel, meet Queenie."

Queenie, with hair as black as coal, acknowledged Carmel by extending her hand. Carmel felt her strong handshake. She said, "I'll take your bag, kiddo." Queenie dropped Carmel's valise on a wooden chair. "You dress next to me."

A voice behind her said, "I'm Maggie." Carmel saw a pretty girl with red hair and soft brown eyes smiling at her.

Carmel couldn't help but stare at a woman who stood with one leg up on a chair, shaving her legs. She wore pink underpants and a bra. She dropped her leg and looked at Carmel. "I'm Tempest Storm." She spoke in a low voice, with a southern drawl.

"Yeah, she's a tempest in a storm," Queenie laughed.

Carmel thought Tempest Storm had the tiniest waist and the largest bosom she had ever seen. Her perfect skin was smooth and very white. Abundant auburn hair fell below her shoulders. She had deep-set blue eyes behind thick, dark lashes. "You can hang your clothes there," she said, pointing toward the rack.

"Queenie," Tempest said, "I'd appreciate it if you would stop hanging your clothes on my rack."

Queenie sniffed. "Miss High and Mighty has top billing and top *everything*." She glared at Tempest and grabbed an armful of clothes from the rack.

Maggie said, "Queenie, ya love to start trouble. Kid, where'd ya work before?" She pulled on a short blue satin skirt over her slim hips.

Carmel hesitated, and then decided to tell the truth. "I haven't, unless you count singing with college bands."

Maggie said, "That's okay, kiddo. We won't hold it against ya." She pinned on a blue ostrich feathered headdress.

Elka, the Dresden doll, smiled at Carmel. "Jerry says you're swell."

The door burst open. An emaciated man in dark trousers and a soiled white shirt stared at Carmel. His features were sharp, and there was a deathly pallor to his colorless skin. "Okay, youse dames, it's ten minutes 'til show time. Who's the new broad?"

Carmel, with her dress half off, crouched behind a chair to hide her semi-nakedness. What an awful man, she thought, to come bursting in the room calling her a broad.

"For an old guy," Queenie said, "you'd think you never seen a woman before. Carmel, this vermin's called 'Stickman.'" Queenie pushed him out of the doorway. "Get outta here."

Elka protested. "*Liebchen,* he's harmless. Don't be afraid. He just likes to stare."

"Oh, yeah? I dare you to give him a chance." Queenie lit a cigarette.

Carmel shuddered. She dropped the gray silk dress over her head and looked for a dressing table to freshen her makeup.

Tempest said, "Here, you can use the table next to me."

Carmel sank down on the chair beside Tempest and began to comb her dark hair. The chattering of the women in the small room, the odors of body powder mixed with a heavy scent of Tabu, the lacquer the girls used on their hair, combined with cigarette smoke, seemed to assail her all at once. A faint feeling of nausea swept over her.

She heard the loud laughter of the customers coming from the bar. She shook her head—if she wanted to sing, why did it have to be in a place like this? Everything was moving too fast for her.

There was a light tap on the door. Jerry opened the door and peeked in.

Elka said, "Come in, Jerry. We're dressed." She stepped away from the door. Carmel sensed Elka liked Jerry.

Jerry entered the room. His gaze found Carmel. "I'm glad you're here." He announced to all, "I need to talk to the new chanteuse." He looked down at Carmel. "I thought I'd tell you tonight's lineup. What'd you decide to sing?"

Carmel could have hugged him. "Should I sing 'Embraceable You' again?"

Queenie raised her eyebrows. "You mean ya ain't decided what to sing?"

"Not really," Carmel said.

Elka cautioned Queenie, "*Nien,* the poor kid's scared enough. Don't add to it."

Jerry answered Carmel's question. "You did a great job. Later I'll pick out a number for the eleven o'clock show. Remember, after the ladies do their number, you're on. I'll give you an eight-bar introduction. The musicians know you're new and they'll follow you. You'll be swell." Jerry patted her shoulder and left the room.

Maggie, Elka, and Queenie followed him out.

"Miss Storm, I guess I seem like a rank amateur to you," Carmel said, pinning the magenta flowers into her hair.

"Honey, please call me Tempest."

"When do you go on?"

"I do a specialty act." Tempest fastened a chiffon pink skirt over her sequined G-string. "Honey, when I first started, someone gave me good advice. Pick out one person in the audience and pretend you know him. Just do the show like he's your lover." She rubbed more rouge on her cheeks.

"Thanks, Tempest, I'll try that." Carmel returned to her makeup. She was fascinated by Tempest's G-string, never having seen one before—it covered enough of a girl's body to avoid arrest. With Tempest's soft southern voice, long pink nails, and ladylike manners, Carmel would never guess Tempest to be a stripper—at least what she imagined strippers to be.

She could tell the girls were on by the music and raucous noise from the bar. To think I have to do this twice a night, she thought. I hope I survive through the first show.

The girls returned to the dressing room.

Queenie teased Maggie. "What did you say to keep that good-looking marine off the stage? He only wanted to pull your skirt off."

"I asked if he wanted to see my grand opening."

"What did he do?"

"He fainted or pretended to and fell off the stage."

All the girls shrieked with laughter.

Jerry entered. "Come on, Carmel." He took her to the door of the stage.

"Stickman" wore a black jacket, and with his hair plastered down he looked more cadaverous than ever. He grabbed her hand, led her over to the mike, and introduced her. "Ladies and gents, straight from Nob Hill, Miss Carmel St. John."

Carmel heard catcalls and a sprinkling of applause.

Jerry sat at the piano, a bass player stood beside him, and a saxophone player sat beside the drummer.

Jerry began the introduction of "Embraceable You." Carmel couldn't see past the bright lights for a minute. Then she saw the sea of uniforms and faces. The men grinned up at her whistling and catcalling. She looked over at Jerry, who smiled to reassure her. When Carmel came on stage in her long simple dress, the whistles and catcalls stopped.

Carmel began to sing. They settled down and listened.

To her surprise, Carmel relaxed. Her voice grew louder and more confident. Holding the mike with both hands, she found a sailor with shining blue eyes. She sang to him. When she finished the song, the men yelled, clapped, stamped, and wanted more. Carmel walked off stage. Happiness, surprise, and relief welled up inside her.

She returned to the dressing room and passed Tempest, who was wearing clouds of chiffon. The beat of the drums indicated Tempest's type of dancing. Carmel decided to catch her act later.

She opened the door to the dressing room and was greeted by the three girls. "Wow! Hubba-hubba ... you're swell." Maggie grabbed her arm. "I never heard a gang of guys shut up for nobody."

Carmel said, "Maybe they didn't know what to expect."

"Well, they do now, *liebchen*." Elka winked at her.

Carmel waited for Jerry to see her after Tempest's number was finished.

Jerry came back stage, "What did I tell you? The men loved you." He laughed. "Let's do a jump tune. Do you sing 'All of Me'?"

Carmel nodded her head.

At the eleven o'clock show, the sailor was still in his seat. She sang to him.

For the last show the crowd was larger and noisier, but they listened when she sang.

Later, Jerry explained there was a midnight curfew for men and women in uniform. He asked her to wait for the end of the show at eleven-thirty. He would see her home.

As they waited for the taxi, Jerry said, "You're on your way, little gal. Those guys could eat you up. How would you know those young men who sat out there in the dark are from small towns and cities all over the United States. Some are dazzled with the choices of where to drink and brawl in the tawdry nightclubs. Women appear before them half dressed in feathers and satins. This is San Francisco, Carmel, one of the wildest cities in the world. In a single block in the Tenderloin there's forty bars. Service men are shipping out to God knows where and might not come back. Those men sat glassy eyed and excited, probably feeling a little guilty. You reminded them of the girl or the sister they had left behind. That's the reason they shut up."

"But those bawdy girls."

"Only Maggie gets carried away. They're not too bad. Don't worry—you won't be at the Chez forever."

"It's good of you to see me home. It's going to be expensive to take a cab every night."

"I forgot to tell you your salary's sixty dollars a week." He saw her face light up.

"That news will make it easier to explain my hours to Aunt Lydia."

CHAPTER 15

Carmel wondered why Elka was rushing her across Broadway at Kearny Street in North Beach. Elka mentioned she had a surprise for Carmel.

The streets were very dark. Past midnight, few cars were on the street. However, the sidewalks of North Beach bustled with people looking as if they'd spent the night searching for a good time. Now, because of the midnight curfew, many of them, especially servicemen, hurried to get off the streets. Some had their arms around girls, who giggled as they disappeared into buildings and cars.

Carmel sensed that for some men, San Francisco was where their world ended. It was the place to give it all they could—to clap the last clap of hands, down the last cold beer, love the last woman, triumphantly cry the last hurrah. She felt uneasy, an outsider watching man's struggle to experience all of life perhaps for the last time, a desperate personal struggle that was not appropriate for her to witness.

Elka led her through the blackout curtains of Vanessie's restaurant.

Elka said, "*Liebchen*, follow me."

She followed Elka down the narrow aisle of the burgundy and gold carpet. To her left, she passed booths crowded with customers. On her right, men and women sat at a long counter, watching with fascination as chefs prepared enormous amounts of Italian food.

She saw no men in uniform. They had disappeared with the curfew. These customers acted as if they intended to stay for the night. Carmel heard music coming from the bar on the left.

At the back of the restaurant were six large banquettes upholstered in red leather. A gold mirror in a diamond pattern covered the wall behind them.

Four people sat around a table covered in white linen. Elka stopped at the table.

"Hello, Caesar. Meet my friend, Carmel."

Goosebumps moved across Carmel's back. She was startled to recognize the good-looking man who had stared at her on Thanksgiving Day at the Palace Hotel.

His black eyes bored into hers. "Give the gals some room." His voice was low.

Carmel didn't doubt he remembered her. She wondered why on Earth Elka had brought her here.

There was a shuffling sound as the group made room for Carmel and Elka.

"My sister, Marlena." Elka pointed to a Dresden doll duplicate of herself.

Carmel noticed how close Marlena sat to Caesar. She nodded. "Hello." Was meeting Marlena the surprise?

Elka introduced her to the other men. "Dancer, say hi to Carmel."

"Pleased to meetcha." Yellow teeth flashed in a narrow face marred with deep acne scars and framed by thin dark hair. His eyes passed over her. He didn't get up.

Elka continued, "Jake, meet Carmel."

Jake remained seated and darted a look at Carmel. "Hi, kid." His pointed nose and small waxed mustache reminded Carmel of a mouse.

Carmel squeezed into the small space. She was bewildered but made an effort to look pleasant and interested in what they were saying. She turned to Elka. "What a surprise. I had no idea you had a beautiful twin sister."

"Marlena's the girl in the fishbowl."

"Fishbowl? Where?"

Dancer laughed. "Where'd you get this broad?"

Elka frowned at Dancer. "Three sixty-five Market Club. She moves nude in the fishbowl. It's done with mirrors. She lies on her back and no one can see anything."

"Yeah, some night she's gonna slip and show a teat. Kaput!" Jake smacked his hands together.

"That's enough," Caesar said.

A waiter in a white jacket began to put silverware, glasses of water, and white napkins in front of each person. He placed a large basket of sourdough French bread in front of Caesar.

"Let's have some fresh coffee all around. Her too." Caesar nodded at Carmel.

The waiter bowed, "Yes, sir, Mr. Almato."

Now Carmel knew his last name. He must be in his late thirties, she decided. Instinctively, she knew it could be risky to refuse him. Everyone had a cup and saucer in front of him or her. She said, "Thank you."

Marlena stared at Carmel. "You're the new singer at the Chez? My sister told me."

The waiter brought her a cup of coffee and poured fresh coffee for the others.

Dancer immediately passed a flask around.

Elka took it and poured some dark liquid into Carmel's cup of coffee. She explained, "We can't buy liquor after midnight."

The waiter returned carrying a large bowl of spaghetti and meatballs. He set plates in front of each person. Carmel didn't feel hungry.

"Help yourself, kid." Dancer piled food on his plate and began to shove it into his mouth.

Carmel sipped her coffee with the liquor in it. The drink burned her throat. She didn't know which was worse, the coffee or the liquor.

Two men stopped in front of the table. Caesar admonished, "You're early."

Jake growled, "You know better than ta come early and bother the boss when he's eatin'." He got up and went over to stand in front of the intruders.

Carmel heard one of the men. "Sorry, Jake. We forgot."

Suddenly, Jake put the palm of his hand up and thumped each one of their foreheads viciously.

Ouch, Carmel thought, that must hurt.

"Knock it off, Jake. We have a guest." Caesar continued to stare at Carmel.

The two men left holding their injured heads.

To escape Caesar's penetrating stare, Carmel looked around the restaurant. On the back wall was a large mural of a donkey in a vineyard carrying baskets full of grapes strapped to his back.

She wondered how long she had to stay. The noise in the restaurant increased as the place filled with people.

Many of the patrons knew Caesar. They stopped at the table to say hello. Caesar nodded but didn't say anything until a short, muscular man with dark hair and an Italian accent approached. "Good evening, Mr. Almato. Good ta see you. If there's anything you need?"

"Everything's okay, Joe."

The man gave Carmel a penetrating look. She knew she would be remembered.

Elka said, "He's the owner, Joe Venezia. We come here lots."

"Hi, beautiful."

Carmel heard a familiar voice and was relieved to see Jerry.

"Hello, Caesar." Jerry acknowledged the group with a nod. "I've just finished breakfast. I'm headed home. Carmel, can I get you a taxi?"

"Yes, I really should be going. It's late for me." Carmel stood.

Again, none of the men got up. "Yeah, nice to meetcha." Dancer and Jake echoed their goodnights.

Carmel nodded to Elka and Marlena. "Thanks for the drink." Caesar's black eyes continued to stare at her.

Elka said, "Jerry, show her the waterfall."

Jerry guided Carmel down the aisle of the restaurant. "Let's take a quick look." They went into the bar. "Hey, Mike, turn on the rain for my friend."

"Sure, Jerry." Mike moved easily to the end of the bar.

Carmel saw a large mural on the wall behind the bar. She recognized the Venetian scene of San Marco's piazza. Rain began to fall across the picture. The sounds of water quieted the noisy crowd.

"Why, it's beautiful," Carmel said softly. The night hadn't been a waste after all.

The rain fell for three minutes. Jerry took her arm. "Let's go."

Once outside the restaurant, he asked, "How did you get with that crowd?"

"Elka wanted me to meet her sister."

As they settled into the cab, Jerry asked, "Do you know who Caesar is?" He paused. "It's rumored he runs the black market, among other things."

"I don't think I want to know what he does." As if to avoid the danger, she pulled her coat tighter around her.

"Have you thought about singing elsewhere?"

"Some, but I'm not sure how."

"It's time the guys at the Musicians Union knew about you."

In the dim light of the car, he looked at her. "Carmel, I'm going to make it my number-one priority to help you."

"Sounds wonderful to me. I'm so lucky to have you for a friend." Carmel meant every word. Trust was a wonderful feeling.

CHAPTER 16

The first week of February, Carmel sat at the piano, struggling to learn the song "I Don't Want to Walk without You," a popular Harry James recording. She had been singing at the Chez Paree for two weeks, and though her work didn't demand a large repertoire, she felt she had to keep learning new songs.

The phone rang. Carmel answered and heard Laura's voice. "Guess what?" She sounded excited and did not wait for an answer. "I'm coming to the city. Phillip is taking us to dinner."

Carmel's heart started to race. Relieved her friend couldn't see her face, she tried to sound casual. "When's this event?"

"It's next Monday. That's your night off, isn't it?"

"Yes."

"Since the tire rationing, Dad won't let me drive unless it's really necessary. I'll come up on the train, catch a cab, and meet you at Phillip's. Won't it be fun?"

"Slow down. Where does your brother live?"

"Nine twelve Parnassus Avenue, apartment 2. Write it down. Got to run. I'll see you at six o'clock Monday at his place."

Carmel hung up. For a moment, she lost herself remembering his dark eyes peering into hers. Again, what would she say? She knew she was overreacting, but making a good impression on Phillip was the most important thought in her head. Thank goodness Laura's enthusiasm would get her through the evening.

Later that afternoon, Carmel welcomed the fact she had promised to help her aunt at the Bundles for Britain Volunteers, an organization formed in 1940 to send food and clothing to needy friends or relatives in England.

Working with the ladies in the basement of the YWCA, she listened to their laughing chatter. In the atmosphere of good will, Carmel managed for a few hours to forget her anxiety.

Monday morning dawned gray and wet. Rain continued on and off all day.

Laura telephoned late in the afternoon. In a hoarse voice she said, "Carmel, I won't be able to join you tonight."

"You sound terrible."

"I know. I have a sore throat. I would have called sooner, but I fell asleep. I'm sorry I won't be there. Will you call Phillip? I tried him at the hospital and at home, but he's out."

"Yes, I'll take care of it. The weather's awful here. Maybe it's a good idea you're not coming tonight. Stay in bed."

"I am. Oh, please tell Phillip how disappointed I am."

"Yes, I will."

"Good-bye."

"Bye."

Carmel put down the phone. What now? She felt frustration yet relief. With Monday night off, she should get some much needed rest. Who was she kidding? She wanted to see Phillip! She hadn't seen him since Christmas, when he had kissed her. This was her chance to see him alone. Carmel plotted. A kaleidoscope of thoughts tumbled in her head. It would be a mistake to call Phillip and tell him his sister wasn't able to come to the city. He might cancel dinner. She couldn't let that happen. She went to take a shower.

After her shower, she splashed cologne over her body, dressed in her prettiest brassiere and panties, and snapped on her garter belt. She pulled on her last pair of silk stockings.

She brushed her hair to a shine. After a light touch of Dorothy Gray powder on her face, she brushed mascara to the tips of her lashes, ran a blue-gray shadow along her lids, and added Tangee's coral lipstick to her lips. She slid on a white lacy slip and stepped into her wool dress, buttoning the tiny buttons down the front. An inspection in the floor-length mirror revealed she needed sparkle. Her small aquamarine tourmaline earrings were perfect.

Once downstairs, she saw that it hadn't stopped raining. Old or not, her worn raincoat would have to do. She slipped it on and stepped onto the porch to wait for her cab. She felt a quiet excitement, as if she was about to do something illegal.

The taxi driver found Phillip's flat easily. She discovered his name among the four listed residents and rang the buzzer. Almost immediately, his broad frame filled the doorway. "Hi, Carmel." He seemed glad to see her. "Come on in." He pushed aside the blackout curtain for her to enter. "I'll take your coat."

She always thought a man appealing when he wore a white shirt open at the throat with the long sleeves cuffed back. It made his wrists appear strong. He wore dark brown slacks and brown loafers.

"May I fix you a drink?"

Carmel wondered if he could see her pulse pounding. "Thank you, I'll have whatever you're drinking."

"Two martinis coming up." As he headed for the kitchen, he called over his shoulder. "Have a seat. Make yourself comfortable."

She gazed around the room. A large couch faced the fireplace, where a fire burned brightly. There was a tan leather chair beside a table holding a reading lamp and books. There was room for a combination radio and record player, and books lined one wall. "Deep Purple" played on the radio. In the small but adequate dining room, she saw a table set for three. Carmel sat down on the couch.

Phillip returned with their drinks and sat in the chair opposite her.

"Cheers." He raised his glass to her and sipped. "Not bad."

"Cheers." The martini tasted good. Carmel said what her uncle always said, "Dry and perfect."

"You look like the world is treating you well." Phillip was looking at her. Her dark hair, slightly damp from the rain, curled around her face. Her skin glowed in the firelight. With deep gray eyes, she stared back at him.

"Yes, it is."

"We can relax a minute. I'm not on call tonight, so I'll enjoy this evening. It's so grim out I thought I'd show off for you girls and prepare dinner myself." He looked at his watch.

Carmel opened her mouth to tell him his sister wasn't coming, but Phillip interrupted. "Carmel, did you find a job singing?"

"Yes."

"Where?"

She hesitated a moment. "At the Chez Paree."

"The one on Mason?"

"Yes."

He frowned slightly. "Doesn't Tempest Storm work there? The woman who the newspapers say insured her breasts with Lloyds of London for fifty thousand dollars?"

Carmel thought of Tempest with her soft southern voice. "Yes, that's true. She's very helpful to me, not at all like her publicity."

"Very interesting. I hear the place fills up with servicemen."

"Aren't most places full of servicemen?"

"Yes, I would guess you're right." A timer rang. Phillip rose with his martini and went to the kitchen. "I wonder where my sister is."

Carmel joined him. "She's not coming. I'm sorry I forgot to tell you. She has a sore throat."

"I'm disappointed, but if she has a sore throat it's a good idea she didn't come out in this weather."

He leaned over and opened the oven door. "Let's see what my chicken is doing. Ah, she's doing nicely. Would you like another drink?"

"Not really. You go ahead."

"I'll wait, too. We're having a bottle of wine for dinner."

"Let me help." She placed her empty glass on the kitchen counter.

"There's nothing to do. Oh, you can take Laura's place off the table."

Blue candles stood in silver candlesticks on a white tablecloth. Pale blue napkins, wine glasses, and individual wooden salad bowls rested beside each white plate. Carmel removed the extra place setting and carried it into the kitchen.

Phillip handed her a basket of bread. "Do you like sourdough French bread?"

"Doesn't everyone in San Francisco?" She placed the basket on the table. "These Foolish Things" played on the radio. She hummed under her breath, "remind me of you."

Phillip took a bottle of wine from the refrigerator, opened it, and set it on the table. He removed the roasted chicken from the oven and placed it on a platter. Baked potatoes were added with snow peas and salad from the refrigerator, and everything was put on the table. They sat down opposite each other.

"How impressive this looks, and smells yummy. I know your sister would love this."

"I hope you enjoy it."

The strains of "Clare d'Lune" came on the radio. She asked, "Do you like Debussy?"

"Oh, indeed. You must remember I grew up listening to Mom's monthly musicals at the house."

"I remember. Laura told me your mother isn't having her musicals these days."

"She stopped a long time ago. I think her arthritis causes a lot of discomfort. I'm sure you'll like this Chardonnay." He poured wine in Carmel's glass and then his own.

Carmel watched him carve the chicken and place some on her plate. Suddenly she felt hungry.

"Now, tell me about your job." Phillip said. "I like listening to you talk."

"What do you want to know?"

"Does your family know where you sing?"

"They know I sing in a nightclub of sorts." She took a bite of chicken. "Phillip, you are a good cook. This is delicious."

"Thank you." Phillip studied her over the rim of his wine glass. "I don't believe they know what the Chez Paree actually is. I heard there have been fights, and at one time the military police thought they would close it down."

"That's not been true since I've been there." If only he knew how the place quieted down when she sang. If she told him, he might think she was bragging. "I like the dancers very much, and Jerry has helped me a lot with my music."

"Who's Jerry?"

"He's the piano player who arranged the audition for me."

"Maybe he didn't do you any favor," Phillip commented dryly.

She could see he didn't really understand anything about the direction her life was taking. Without Jerry, she wouldn't have a job. "I feel lucky to have met him." A cold feeling of dread swept over her. She couldn't bear Phillip's disapproval.

"I think it's great you're living with your aunt and uncle. You're protected there. Frankly, I'm quite happy my sister stays in San Jose."

Carmel nodded. "I believe she really wants to be a nurse. You said once the world will always need nurses."

"Ha! Trapped by my own words, and I meant it." He sipped his wine. "Carmel, this is such a new life for you, leaving home and San Jose. I'm impressed you managed a job so quickly. What do you hope to accomplish with your singing?"

She could hardly tell him she wanted him to notice her and pay attention to her. "Well, to sing with a dance band, and from there, who knows?"

"I wish you good luck and success. You know your father will want you home someday."

"Yes, he mentions it, but I have to prove something to myself before I would go back to San Jose."

He grinned. "I would guess you're leaving a lot of broken hearted beaus behind in San Jose."

"No one serious, yet."

"Well, my sister has Scott—or Scott has Laura—and your father has Anna."

"What do you mean my father has Anna?"

"Oh, come now, Carmel, she's loved by all of you. Anna's a beautiful woman, and I believe your father enjoys Anna's companionship."

His eyes had been full of laughter. Now they were serious as he looked back at her.

Although Carmel resented his remarks, she herself had wondered more than once about her father and Anna. Maybe Phillip was right, but it was really none of his business.

"It's true, we all love Anna." Carmel took a sip of wine. She had to know. "What about you, Phillip. Will you be leaving for the service?"

"I don't think so—not for a while—but I'm in the navy. I could receive orders anytime. The war's accelerating and I have a feeling the situation could change rapidly. With General MacArthur fighting in the Philippines, it'll be some time before we know the results of that battle. Of course, gas rationing has meant huge changes for us all. We're told there are a lot more shortages we'll have to get used to. For sure they'll ration tires, white shirts, food, and probably shoes."

"My uncle said San Francisco has taken to the war like a kid with a new sled and fresh snow on a hill."

He joined in her laughter. "I believe your uncle has hit the nail on the head. Our old San Francisco is changing so fast. When the war began, we were not considered an industrial state. Now Kaiser and Bechtel, both engineering firms, have begun to meet the demand of war by building ships. The shipyards need women and men and they have come by the thousands to San Francisco. Many feel the Depression is over."

"I hate this war—and they say we haven't even begun to fight, that Germany has to be beaten first, then the Pacific."

"Yes, I've heard that statement. If that's true, it may mean a long war for the whole world. I don't want to depress you, Carmel." He folded his napkin and placed it on the table. "Have you thought of singing at the hospitals?"

"Yes, but Jerry said we must work out a routine first. He'll accompany me on the piano, and we'll put something together for the future."

"I heard the most improbable song on the Hit Parade. Something about 'Let's put the axe to the Axis. We're going to find the fellow in yellow, and beat him red white and blue.'" They both laughed at the silly lyrics. He continued, "Carmel, I admired the way you interpreted the songs you sang for us at Christmas."

"Why, thank you." A compliment, she thought, at last.

"We're having hot apple pie. I bought it at the bakery."

"If you don't mind, I'd rather not have any dessert. Coffee, if you have some?"

"Sure thing." He rose. "Let's have our coffee by the fire."

She helped clear the table. Phillip brought the tray with a coffee pot, cups, and saucers. He placed the tray on the small table and sat down beside her on the couch.

"Do you take sugar or cream?"

"Neither, thank you, just black."

The coffee was hot and tasted good to Carmel. The room felt comfortable with the table lamp turned low and the glow of the fire. The room was quiet. She realized he had turned the radio off. They were silent staring at the fire. The burning wood snapped and cracked. She heard the steady beat of rain on a drainpipe outside the windows. Occasionally, a car passed the building, climbing the hill on Parnassus.

Phillip placed another log on the fire. She watched his tall, muscular body move easily, the angular planes of his face lit by the firelight. His handsome profile, set in a determined expression, gave Carmel little information about his thoughts.

Phillip turned from the fire. "Would you like more coffee?"

Not waiting for an answer, he moved toward her, took her empty cup, and set it on the table. He reached for her hand and pulled her toward him.

For just a moment Carmel remembered her resolve of prudence and caution, but only for a moment. She caught a glimpse of dark eyes before his mouth sought hers. His insisting warm lips stirred her, demanding a response. Carmel clung to him, returning his fervor. He searched her mouth with his tongue. Phillip murmured against her mouth, "Do you want me to stop?"

Carmel answered by searching for his mouth with her own. His hunger brought desires that flooded her thoughts and body.

Phillip kissed her gently, taking his time. His lips left her mouth and traveled to her ear lobes and neck. His hand cupped her breast. She trembled as strong arms forced her to lie on the couch.

Her gray eyes held his as his mouth closed down on hers. Carmel placed her arms around his neck and ran her hands over his back and arms. She gave herself to him, returning his kisses with a fervor that made him gasp. He unbuttoned her dress, revealing the swell of her breasts. He began to kiss her throat, then the hollow between her breasts.

Suddenly, he sat up and pulled her up beside him. He smoothed her tousled hair away from her face. "This is not the time. You're so damn beautiful—I about lost control." Then he gathered her in his arms and held her close. Silent for a moment, she felt their hearts beating against each other. He said, "You're a lovely vixen."

"Oh, Phillip." She nuzzled her face into his neck, taking the warmth and feel of him with her to remember.

The sound of the rain beating on the drain reminded her it was time to leave. Feeling embarrassed she pushed away from his arms and kept her head down. She wasn't sure she wanted to see his face, to see his expression.

He said, "It's getting late. We better say good night. If you want to use the bathroom, when you're ready, I'll take you home."

Suddenly, she didn't want him to tell her good night in a cab. She looked at him. "Oh, please, with gas rationing … just call me a cab. I'll be ready in a minute." She left the room to fix her face and comb her hair.

When she returned, Phillip said, "The cab's here. I'll take you to it." He had her coat in his hand and held it as she put it on. "Thank you for coming," Phillip smiled.

Carmel couldn't answer.

They hurried out to the curb. Phillip gave directions to the driver and paid him. He leaned in the open door. "Good night, Carmel." He paused as if to say more but he didn't.

"Good night, Phillip." She tried to sound casual, as the cab pulled away.

Settled in the cab, she wondered what had happened to all her resolves. She was the lady who was going to be in control … that was how she would impress him. Well, she had impressed him all right. She had been heedless and encouraged him. She would not have stopped him, and he knew it. Tears of frustration filled her eyes. Where would it all end? Every plan she had made was ruined. She clenched her fist in the darkness.

She wanted him so much for all of these months. She hadn't thought about the consequences of making love or how she would feel. It had happened so fast. She didn't believe Phillip had planned to kiss her. And he had been the one to stop them. What an idiot she was She wanted to erase it all, the whole evening. She made impatient swipes at the tears on her cheeks.

CHAPTER 17

Chen, Caesar's houseman, shuffled across the deep gold carpet in his master's bedroom. It was 10:00 a.m. He pulled the heavy, dark blue drapes away from the windows. Brilliant sunlight from the San Francisco bay lit the room.

Caesar took the robe Chen handed him. "Beautiful day, Mister Caesar." Chen bowed low.

"Yes, Chen, the sun is blinding." He entered the bathroom. "I won't work out this morning." He followed a strict daily regimen with body weights and a massage afterwards to keep his body lean and muscular. "The black jacket will be fine with my gray slacks. Bring my orange juice while I shave." He couldn't be late for his eleven o'clock appointment. He had important business this morning.

Caesar finished his shave and stepped into the shower. He let the hot water spray over his body and planned his day. Last night at Vanessie's he had heard there might be interference in receiving and shipping on the docks. Someone was trying to control and plug his market. He knew it wasn't the Chinese. He had made a point of staying out of Chinatown, away from their opium and gambling, but the black market was his. He laughed. No one slipped by Caesar Almato. He would visit his friend the mayor. It wouldn't hurt to tighten the knot of friendship. A morning visit to his office would be a reminder.

In spite of going to sleep at six this morning, he felt great.

Out of the shower, he grabbed a towel and rubbed his wet head vigorously. "Chen, are the boys here?"

"Yes, sir." Chen handed him a cup of hot coffee.

Caesar entered his elaborate dressing room. Closets lined both sides and full-length mirrors covered one wall. He opened a drawer and selected a monogrammed shirt, his tie, and a matching maroon handkerchief for the breast pocket of his black jacket. With polished black shoes, he was ready for his day.

He walked into his large living room, whose floor-to-ceiling windows covered three walls. He saw Jake and Dancer waiting for him.

"Hi, Sammy." Caesar stopped in front of a large Cancun parrot sitting on a perch. The red and blue parrot cocked his head and started to sing the song Caesar taught him, "Somebody Loves Me." Caesar laughed.

Each of the five large birdcages along the wall held a single bird or more. Caesar asked, "Has everyone had breakfast?" Cockatoos, finches, and parrots cackled and screeched.

While he filled the feeders in the cages with birdseed, he carried on a continuous conversation. The birds turned somersaults, shrieked, rang bells, and scolded him.

Finished with their feeding, Caesar started toward the door. "Let's move it."

Jake and Dancer, relieved to see their boss in a good mood, crossed the room ahead of him. Dancer turned before he opened the door. "Where we goin', boss?"

"We are goin', as you put it, to city hall."

Caesar was 4F and tried to hide it. Only those close to him knew he was deaf in his left ear. When he was eleven years old, his friend Jimmy Crossetti, playing with Jimmy's father's rifle, had pulled the trigger of the loaded gun. Caesar carried the scar where the bullet creased his ear. He learned to read lips.

When Caesar was ten years old, his father got a job on the San Francisco docks with the teamsters. The family moved into a two-bedroom flat. For his mom and dad this was a move up from the big rooms above a bar in China Beach. Caesar continued to sleep with his younger brother, John. They bathed in the same bath water; he hated it.

When the night wasn't too damp with cold and fog, Caesar sat in the dark on the fire escape. He would stare up at Nob Hill and vow he would live there someday.

He got a job washing dishes in the kitchen of the Flor d' Italia. Big Al had a special table in the back of the restaurant for the local racketeers. When they sat with Big Al eating spaghetti and drinking wine, Caesar observed how the men dressed. "I saw their gun holsters under their coats," he bragged to little John, who was four years younger and idolized Caesar.

Caesar didn't like school, but his father made sure he attended. "Do you want to end up like me, on the docks?"

"Yeah, Dad, I do. I like working on the docks. I like the ships."

His father cuffed him on the ear. "No you don't. You're goin' ta get someplace. Not live like me. Some mornings it's so goddamn cold down on the docks I can hardly move." He rubbed his knees with his hands.

"You're right, Dad. I won't end up like you." My old man works too hard, he thought, and what does he have to show for it? A dump. The faucets in the apartment don't work most of the time. There's never any hot water. No matter how hard Mom tries, she can't keep the old rugs and furniture clean. Everything in the place looks shabby.

Caesar was sixteen when his father died. Lifting a load onto the ship, he didn't moved fast enough when one of the cables slipped. Caesar consoled his mother. "It was fast, Mama. He didn't know what hit him."

That night, he told John, "I'm going down to that goddamn dock and get a job."

"You'll have to quit school. Mom won't like it."

"Someone has to go to work. I'll make more money working than Mom. Besides, I can go to night school." Both boys knew he wouldn't return to school.

The next day Caesar put on a clean shirt and went to see Louie.

Louie sat behind his desk and looked at Caesar. "I didn't know Al Almato had such a good-looking kid. How old are you, kid?"

Caesar didn't like being called a kid. "I'm almost seventeen. I'm strong and can do anything you want."

"I'm not in the market for anyone right now. Why don't you go over to the Teamsters Union?"

Caesar stopped him. "They won't hire me. They'll say I'm too young. I really need a job. I thought since my father ..." He stopped. He thought, I sound like I'm begging.

Louie knew everything he said was right. "Okay, okay. Why don't I put you in the warehouse? Stay out of sight for a while. I don't want to get into trouble with some of the union guys."

Caesar grinned. He watched Louie's mouth. Though he hadn't heard every word, he knew he had a job. He started to thank Louie.

Louie waved him aside. "See you at four. Be on time. If you work out, you'll have to join the union."

Caesar reported on time the next morning. He worked hard, stacking crates, cartons, and containers. As the weeks passed, his body became strong and muscular from the heavy work. The men liked him, and his job went smoothly. Eventually, Louie managed to secure a union card for Caesar.

Working on the docks was exciting. The slips were always filled with ships. Their massive steel bodies came into docks high in the water. Stevedores swung nets heavy with cargo into their holds and the water line disappeared.

Dice games were rampant at lunchtime. The men bet on anything and everything—the time the fog would lift or the time of arrival or departure of a ship.

Caesar's black eyes absorbed everything. He kept to himself and the men became used to his silences. Louie found he liked the young man.

One evening in the Far East Restaurant in Chinatown, Caesar watched the gambling and betting most of the night. Since it was already three o'clock in the morning, he decided to go to the warehouse and wait until his shift began. He was asleep on top of some cardboard cartons when he heard the large warehouse door grind open. From his spot, he saw two men carry three large wooden crates into Louie's office. They picked up two large containers inside the warehouse and put them into their truck parked out in front. In a few minutes, Louie arrived and went into his office. The heavy doors ground shut.

In a few days, Louie called Caesar into his office and said he had an errand for him. Some sixth sense told Caesar that Louie knew he had been in the warehouse.

Louie saw Caesar had ambition with brains to back it up. "I like you kid. You keep your mouth shut and I'll see you make more money than you ever dreamed possible."

Caesar learned the black market in San Francisco was an organized business. Louie knew the cargo on each incoming ship and what was in demand. The price of shoes from Italy, Venetian glass, fur coats, and, most important, how quickly it could be obtained.

One day he told Caesar he didn't think of himself as a thief. He simply saw his business as an exchange of one item for another. Caesar's responsibilities increased. Louis shared his knowledge with Caesar and taught him who he could trust to remove contraband faster than anyone and make it disappear into the catacombs of the black market.

Caesar liked where he was going and worked hard. His photographic mind remembered everything and everyone. Eventually he moved into a larger apartment in North Beach. At this rate, Nob Hill was just over the rise.

When he offered to find his mother a more comfortable apartment in a nicer neighborhood, his mother wouldn't move. She liked the neighborhood. Her friends were close by.

Often he stood on the docks and watched the planes from the Alameda Air Base soar over the water. His deafness and 4F status had kept him from his secret dream to become a pilot. Sometimes a small plane flew under the Golden Gate Bridge. Caesar laughed at their daring.

Once John asked, "Why do you keep birds in cages, locked up so they can't fly?"

"They were locked up when I got them. I'm only taking care of them."

John had his own answers about Caesar and the birds. Caesar had confided in him about wanting to be a pilot.

Louie began to turn his heisting business over to Caesar. When the Japanese bombed Pearl Harbor, Caesar was thirty-two years old. The business moved from clothes to cigarettes, white shirts, booze, meat, and tires.

Caesar encouraged John to become a CPA. Then Caesar persuaded Louie to hire him. It was good to have another member of the family in the business.

Some time before, embarrassed at his lack of education, Caesar started night school. But he felt older than the other students and stopped going. The owner of the newsstand at Market and Kearny liked him and introduced him to books. As a result, Caesar became an avaricious reader, reading anything and everything that came on the book market.

Caesar insisted on being different. Sometimes he drove a white convertible in the winter with the top down. He looked handsome in anything he wore. In restaurants, the socialites flirted with him from across the room. He ignored them.

Marlena had style, independence, and raw sex. That was what he liked about her. He was determined to acquire all life offered—beautiful women, dinners in the classy hotels and restaurants, jazz in the Fillmore district, and a house on top of the hill.

The city of San Francisco stimulated and excited him. His business added risk to the excitement—it was a life that breathed twenty-four hours a day. Money. Gambling. It was magic. His blood moved. The undercurrent, intoxicating and challenging, made him feel alive. The uncertainty? He was never uncertain. There was a future in gambling. He confided in no one.

Caesar began to formulate an idea in his mind. He recognized business would change after the war. It might be time to own a club for himself. He traveled to Reno and Las Vegas looking for a possible location. He decided to name his first club the Royal Flush. Maybe in the future he would consider buying two or three small clubs and work toward owning a bigger one. It was like having a family.

Now, as he rode toward city hall, his mind was on business—serious business with city hall. Caesar intended to be only generous enough to see his contacts confirmed, protected, and irrevocably under his control.

CHAPTER 18

Each time Carmel recalled her passionate evening with Phillip and their love-making, she felt a sinking feeling in her stomach. In one minute, her emotions careened from ecstatic to desolate. She had experienced heaven, to remember she was in hell. There was no way to know when she would see him, much less spend another evening with him. Tears filled her eyes when she realized it was possible that evening would never repeat itself. Hadn't she resolved not to see him again? But with the thought of his dark eyes looking at her, his half amused smile, the old familiar ache returned.

She wondered when Phillip would be receiving his orders. What then? Thank God she had work to keep her from fretting about him.

The following evening, Carmel arrived before the first show to find the bar already full. She made her way as rapidly as possible through the raucous crowd to the dressing rooms. By now, dodging their wild grabs was a nightly occurrence.

Surprised to see no one in the dressing room, she hung up her coat and put her purse away. The place was a mess, as usual. She picked up empty Coca-Cola bottles and placed them in a box under the sink, cleaned out ashtrays, took clothes off the chairs, and hung them up. Trying to bring any kind of order to the dingy place was an act of futility.

She felt uneasy. The quiet without the chattering girls was spooky. She wondered where they were.

Carmel decided she might as well get dressed for the evening performance. She took off her blouse and skirt, hanging them both on a wall hook, and put on her flowered robe. She sat down in front of the mirror to begin her stage makeup.

The noises from the bar seemed to become louder. She hadn't heard anyone come into the room. Suddenly, a hand moved fast as lightning across her shoulder and grabbed down for her breast. Carmel screamed. Behind her, Stickman's face stared in the mirror.

She rose and whirled to face him, clutching her robe about her. "How dare you!"

The slight man reached for her again, but with the strength of a brute. He bared his teeth, animal like. She beat her fists against him, trying to wrench away from his grip.

He hissed at her. "You know you want me to feel your tits, girlie. You wear them low dresses." He pinched her breast.

Carmel felt herself panic. It was so noisy at the bar she knew no one would hear her scream. Stickman pushed her back against the makeup table. She frantically grabbed behind her for something to hit him with. Her wrapper fell open. His mouth agape, he tried to lick her breasts with his tongue. Carmel recoiled from the feel of his skin against hers. Wild energy flooded through her as she fought madly to push him away.

"Struggle all you want. No one's comin'."

Carmel's hand closed around the handle of a silver-tipped mirror. She gripped it and swung with all of her strength against his temple. Stickman reeled from the impact of the heavy mirror, as he attempted to ward off her blows with his hands. His forehead trickled blood.

He muttered, "I never knowed you was such a little tiger." He reached for her again.

Her body surged with adrenaline; she gasped as she hit him for the second time on the temple, making him cringe.

"What the hell's going on here?" It was Jerry.

Stickman pulled a handkerchief from his pocket and held it to his forehead. The blood seeped through.

"What's going on here? You better answer me, Stickman." Jerry glared at him.

"She tried to kill me," he whined. "Look, blood."

"Are you all right, Carmel?"

"I am now."

"Get out. If you ever touch her again, I'll kill you."

Stickman, holding the handkerchief to his bleeding head, left the room.

Jerry said, "My God, Carmel, I'm so sorry this happened."

Carmel pulled her robe tightly about her exposed breasts. "Where is every-one?"

"You didn't work last night, so you didn't know the gals decided to skip the first show here to put on a show for the boys in the hospital."

"Suppose you hadn't come back. I was so angry I could have ..." She shuddered at the thought that she might have killed him.

The blood drained from Carmel's face. Jerry put his arm around her. It was a relief to let her head fall on his shoulder.

"Are you okay? Can you sing?"

"I can sing. I think I'd better look for another job." Her trembling began to stop.

"I'll help you. Go to the Musicians Union. Get a list of local bandleaders. They always need singers. Go tomorrow."

Carmel promised she would.

Soon the girls returned, excited about performing at the hospital. They giggled, teasing each other over the night's events. Tempest had performed a simple waltz in flowing robes.

Carmel pulled herself together and sang that night as if nothing had happened. She decided not tell the girls about Stickman's attack. Just thinking about the nightmare made her shudder.

Later Jerry called a cab for her. He said he would tell Charlie she would not be back. There should be no trouble. Carmel wondered what would happen next. Hadn't she just thanked the Lord for a job? And now she didn't have one.

However, she trusted Jerry. Now with her experience at the Chez Paree, short lived as it was, she could honestly say she was a singer. She would call the Musicians Union tomorrow.

CHAPTER 19

Lydia followed Carmel into the hall. The Dachshunds played at their feet, growling and biting each other. She asked, "What is so important for you to go out in this squall?"

"Oh, Auntie, you call every storm a squall. This is not a bad storm. The weatherman said it would be over soon." Carmel pulled on her raincoat and gloves. "I have some papers to pick up. I've called a taxi." She kissed her aunt.

Lydia didn't press Carmel. "All right. Don't get wet and catch cold."

Carmel wasn't ready to tell her aunt she was looking for a new job. She went out the door and stood on the porch. Lydia was right; it was pouring.

She opened her umbrella and hurried to the taxi waiting at the curb. She put the dripping umbrella on the floor. "The Musicians Union, please."

The cab entered the downtown area of San Francisco. Carmel was amazed to see the streets filled with automobiles and taxis. With the shortage of gas and tires, she thought people had stopped driving.

Due to the heavy downpour, the honking and screeching of brakes was deafening. The cab driver let her off in front of the Musicians Union at 230 Jones Street.

She entered the large reception hall, which smelled of cigar smoke. Several men stood near the front desk and she heard some of their conversation.

"Yeah, you'll be lucky if the draft board lets you stay here another week," a man said.

"You either wait for the greeting letter or you volunteer," another said.

"I heard half the musicians in town are on their way," the first man said.

Carmel stopped in front of the sullen face behind the desk, a bald man who wore thick-rimmed glasses. His gravel voice greeted her. "Yes, miss?"

"Hello, I called earlier. Someone told me to stop at the desk for names of local band leaders."

"That was me. Yeah, I got 'em here. Are you the singer? Carmel ... uh ..."

"Yes, I'm the singer, Carmel St. John."

He thumbed through a pile of papers and handed her a sheet. Carmel glanced at the list of names on it. "I appreciate you doing this for me."

"I added telephone numbers for you."

"Thank you. What's your name?"

"Just call me Ed." He took off his glasses and stared at her. "Good luck ta you. If you sing like you look, you'll have no problems." He winked at her.

Carmel walked out to the street. No rain. She paused and filled her lungs with fresh air. Already she felt better. Holding the list of names of the local bandleaders, she was eager to contact them. If I have the guts to sing at the Chez Paree, she thought, I can sing anywhere. The prospect of singing before a crowd of dancers was certainly better than singing before the noisy animals that expected women to take their clothes off.

Carmel caught a glimpse of herself in the store windows. She saw a girl with a cloud of dark hair swirling around her head, a brilliant scarf of greens and yellows at her throat, and a smile of happiness. Suddenly, she wanted to talk to Jerry. He'd know just who she should contact for a job.

She entered a drugstore on the corner and found a pay phone. Dropping a nickel into the slot, she waited impatiently for him to answer.

Jerry sounded sleepy but glad to hear from her. "Sure, I'll get dressed and come talk to you. I worked late last night on my scripts."

Carmel started to apologize.

"Stop," Jerry said. "I'll meet you at Fosters on Jones across from the Musicians Union in a half hour. I'll have breakfast there."

"Thanks, Jerry. I have to get some stockings. See you in a half hour."

Finding stockings had become a big problem. Available stockings were generally cotton and ugly. Silk was being used for parachutes.

Carmel was lucky. The saleslady at the City of Paris had put aside two pairs of rayons. Her eyes sparkled behind glasses when she shared the news with Carmel, "Betty Grable just auctioned nylons at a war bond rally for forty thousand dollars a pair."

Carmel laughed and agreed the information was important. She hurried out the side door of the City of Paris onto Stockton Street. At the corner of Jones and O'Farrell, the wind lifted her skirts. She grabbed at them. Her closed umbrella had become a nuisance.

She smiled at Ron, the flower vendor on the corner. His flower stand was bursting with fresh spring flowers. He handed her a yellow rosebud. Carmel stuck it in the lapel of her raincoat.

When she entered Fosters, Jerry was waiting at a small table. The large restaurant with tile floors and cafeteria-style service was full of people. Carmel heard the clatter of dishes and conversations.

Jerry stood to greet her. "This is a musicians' hang out that's open all night. Give me your raincoat and umbrella. Can I get you anything?" He took her things and hung them on a hook.

"Just coffee, please," she said, sitting down.

Jerry went to the counter and brought back breakfast for himself and coffee for her.

"Your decision to leave the Chez is a good one." He smiled. "You seem to be sparkling this morning. Show me your list."

He took the paper she offered and glanced at the names. "Hey, some of these fellows are swell for you."

Carmel watched Jerry while he read the list. "Please go ahead and mark the ones I should call."

"Well, Phi Vero is very good. Sal Carson, likewise. Al Wallace has one of the best casual bands in the city. He works a lot of highbrow society dances, definitely in your class."

"What if they have a singer?" She took a sip of coffee.

"You have to run that risk. They'll probably let you sing one night to see how you do."

"Maybe I expect too much, too soon."

"Nobody makes it without some risk. Nobody," he repeated.

"To be able to sing and be paid for it is truly mind boggling."

"Carmel, if my hunch is right, I think you'll get what you want. Let me share something with you. This city's jumpin'. Any musician that's in town is working. A lot of musicians have gone into the service or are about to. People want to listen to music and forget the war. This town's wide open. We have a mayor who doesn't threaten to change things. We're supposed to have a curfew at midnight, but there's always a club open. The Fillmore district's rockin'. You can drink and jam till dawn in the after-hour joints. The uptown clubs are full of people who love to dance and be entertained—"

Carmel interrupted him. "I'm realizing how little I know about San Francisco's nightlife."

Finishing his breakfast, he reached into his pocket for a cigarette, lit it, and inhaled. He blew smoke away from her. His expression became serious. "You have an opportunity to make people happy, Carmel. They listen to you. You can hold an audience like a storyteller. Haven't you noticed how people congregate around the bandstands to listen to the ballads? It doesn't make any difference if it's Kay Kayser with Harry Babbit or Jo Stafford and the Pied Pipers. It seems there are two kinds of audiences now. They either stand in front of the band or go nuts dancing. Jitterbugging. Ha! I believe the movies and bandleaders and their bands set the mood for us. The rumor is that Benny Goodman saved the San Francisco Fair in '39."

"How's that?"

"People thought with the New York World's Fair going on, ours wasn't much. Besides people were still feeling the pinch of the Depression. Anyhow, Benny Goodman's band was so great that we were waiting for him, word got around, and the people started coming to the fair. I think the kids listening to Goodman's music on the radio in the East, which actually played here three hours earlier, did the trick. He had a built-in audience waiting for him." Jerry took a drag on his cigarette and blew smoke. "Do you know that the radio has probably influenced our interest in music more than anything? Every show on radio has its own band."

"Are you saying I should aim for singing on the radio?"

"Don't think about that yet. Get busy and let these guys know you're available. Start to learn songs. If you know 'The Last Time I Saw Paris,' sing it. You've got the voice for it. I have to leave. I'm due at the club to rehearse, not that it does much good." They stood. "If you want me to help you set the keys for your songs, call me."

"Thanks for meeting me, Jerry. You've helped me so much. I'm sure my aunt and uncle won't mind if we use the piano at the house. I'll start calling some of these bandleaders."

Jerry followed her out to the sidewalk. "This is a tough town to get ahead as a singer. But with luck and hard work and your passion to succeed, I think you'll make it."

A huge smile lit Carmel's face, deepening her dimples. "I'm a lucky girl to have your help. I couldn't do it without you."

Jerry put his hat on his head. "We'll see, we'll see. I figure I'll always be around to help you." He grinned and walked away.

CHAPTER 20

"Auntie, Auntie!" Carmel entered the front door of the house. "Where are you?"

"I'm in the library." Her voice sounded muffled.

Carmel found Lydia standing on her head, her arms folded, her legs propped against the wall, her toes barely touching the flowered wallpaper.

Carmel leaned over, trying to peer into her aunt's face.

"You don't have to do that. I can hear you well enough. Why all the shouting?"

"Oh, Aunt Lydia, Jerry is making it possible for me to meet the most wonderful bandleaders. I'll be able to sing in the hotels."

"Is that what you want?"

"To dress up and sing with a really big band in San Francisco? Of course! That's what I've been hoping for. I don't have a job yet, but I will." Carmel waltzed around the room, arms raised over her head, her skirts and petticoats rippled, showing silken slim legs.

"Calm down," Lydia laughed. "You better learn to stand on your head. It's excellent for the nerves."

"Is that why you stand on your head? For your nerves?"

"Yes." Lydia moved and her skirt fell over her face, revealing pale pink underwear pulled over a garter belt and stockings. "Oh, dear. I guess I've had enough." Her voice muffled again as she moved to let her feet touch the floor. She sat up. "Is my face red?"

"Just a little pink. It's very becoming."

"Supposed to be a temporary facelift. You should try it sometime. If you like, I'll have my yoga instructor teach you."

Lydia stood up and went to the table, picked out a cigarette from a pack, and lit it. She inhaled deeply before she blew the smoke out of her mouth and sank into an upholstered chair. Carmel wondered if her aunt thought yoga and smoking were compatible.

"I need your advice, Auntie. I can come back some other time."

"No, now's fine."

Carmel paced around the room as she talked. "I've decided I need at least six long dresses to start with. I really don't know how much work I'll have in the beginning ..."

"Clothes have become very expensive, my dear. I know."

"With Dad not wanting me here in the first place, he isn't the ideal one to ask for money."

"I would be happy to help you."

"Thank you, Auntie. You're sweet. But I have to do this on my own. I've been thinking I might go over to Nellie Caffney's and I. Magnin's. Try on some long dresses to see how I look. Would that be terribly dishonest?"

"Then have a dressmaker copy them? I don't really see what would be wrong. Plenty of customers try on clothes they don't buy. Who knows? You may be Nellie Caffney's best customer someday. Your biggest problem might be to find the right materials."

"I love silk. It feels as if I am holding on to air. Silk just floats around my body. But isn't all available silk being used for parachutes?"

"That's what we hear. Let me lend you the money for materials. You can pay me back whenever you can afford to, if that will make you feel better."

"If I take the loan, Auntie, it'll be strictly business. Could you come with me today? Let's go try on long dresses."

"I'd love to. Just let me change my clothes. Maybe later we'll have time for tea at the St. Francis."

The women rushed upstairs to change.

Carmel was grateful to her aunt. Now she could focus on her career. She felt almost a desperate need to find something to do to prevent thinking about Phillip. Every time the phone rang she hoped it would be him. One minute all she wanted was to talk to him; with her next breath, she never wanted to hear from him again.

Carmel added a brown jacket to her beige blouse and skirt. She knotted a soft green and white scarf for extra color. A brown wide-brimmed hat gave her the look of the San Francisco sophisticate. She hummed to herself as she went downstairs to meet her aunt.

Lydia waited by the front door in an emerald green wool coat, white gloves, white turban, and gold earrings.

"You look elegant, Auntie, but then you always do."

"Thank you, child. Let's take the Hyde Street cable car."

The day shimmered in the warm sunshine. A light breeze blew across their faces as they walked the short distance to board the cable car at Chestnut and Hyde.

War Bond advertisements were plastered on the outside of the cable car. Navy, Marine, and Army posters encouraged enlistment, Uncle Sam's finger pointing at potential recruits. Inside, caricatures in black and white of Hitler, Mussolini, and Tojo stared back at the passengers.

Carmel and Lydia stepped off the cable car at Powell Street in front of the St. Francis Hotel. The city streets teemed with servicemen and expensively dressed ladies, many of them in furs and hats. Flags of the Allies floated from the flag poles high above the hotel.

Lydia said, "Let's come back here for tea."

The entrance to Nellie Gaffney's was the next stop on Powell Street. The quiet shop was a domain of refinement, a noticeable contrast from the noise on the street. The salesgirl, who spoke in a low, well-modulated voice, seated them on chairs covered in rose silk. After a brief consultation, she disappeared and returned with a selection of long dresses for their inspection.

Carmel tried on three. They fit perfectly, but their colors did not appeal to her. It wasn't difficult to tell the salesgirl she would have to think it over.

Afterwards they crossed Union Square and headed for I. Magnin's. On the corner of Geary and Stockton streets, the flower stand overflowed with every glorious color of the rainbow. The aroma of fresh flowers enchanted them. The vendor smiled and waved a small bouquet of glistening violets at them.

Lydia waved back. "Oh, it's sheer heaven to see the flowers. It wouldn't be San Francisco without them."

Four young ladies in white satin coats and satin berets stood on the corner selling War Bonds. Lydia explained, "Those girls are from I. Magnin's. They're models."

"They're so attractive; they're perfect for the job."

I. Magnin's elegant store catered to the carriage trade. The dark gray building with Roman columns stood on the corner of Geary and Grant. Large windows advertised elegant, stylish fashions.

Once inside Lydia looked up at the soaring ceiling. "This building always makes me feel we've been plunked down in the middle of Paris. Carmel, why not pick out brighter colors this time."

When they entered the salon, a petite saleslady greeted Lydia. "Mrs. Bannister, it's lovely to see you. What can we show you today?"

"Hello. Today we're shopping for my niece, Carmel."

They were seated on a comfortable green velvet couch. Carmel was asked about her size, where she planned to wear the dresses, and her favorite colors.

Carmel fell in love with four long dresses, all in vibrant colors and terribly expensive. She promised herself someday she would come back and buy one. They thanked the sales girl and left.

Their heads bursting with ideas, they decided to cancel visiting Livingston Brothers. Besides, it was time for tea.

Back at the St. Francis, as they waited to be seated in the Mural Room, Lydia told Carmel, "I don't know what orchestra is playing here at night. It could be Harry Owens or Freddie Martin. Look, here comes Ernst Gloor."

Carmel saw a serious-faced man coming toward them.

"He's Swiss and the absolute major majordomo," Lydia continued. "He decides who's important and rates customers by where he seats them. The tables by the door are the most prized."

Ernst nodded at Lydia. "It's nice to see you, Mrs. Bannister." He seated them close to the door.

An assortment of tiny sandwiches and small cakes were placed before them. Lovely bone china held pots of delicious tea with choices of cream or lemon. Four musicians on the bandstand played classical music in the background. "This is luscious," Carmel said, biting into a small cucumber sandwich.

"The seven huge murals covering the walls portray the old world bringing gifts to California. The bare-shouldered goddess on the wall represented California. The model for the goddess is rumored to be a prominent socialite, but no one's telling who." Lydia arched her eyebrows and smiled.

"They have a fascinating custom here in the hotel since 1938," Lydia continued. "Every day, a man named Arnold collects the silver change—dollars, quarters, dimes, any silver—and washes it all, polishes it. Then he returns the silver to the cash register. The washing keeps our white gloves clean." She picked up one of her white gloves and waved it in the air to show Carmel.

"Auntie, you look as fresh as when you left the house. I'm exhausted."

Lydia sipped her tea. "Stand on your head, my dear! Remember, I didn't have to try on clothes; I just sat and watched. Carmel, you do look divine in simple dresses."

"Thank you, Auntie."

"I have a Chinese friend who's a seamstress. I think I'll give her a call and see if she's available."

"Right now, if I had to hem a tea towel, I wouldn't know where to begin."

"Then let's finish our tea and go home. We'll take a cab."

CHAPTER 21

Though it was noon in San Francisco, due to the heavy coastal fog, the February sun remained hidden for three days. The winter day was overcast, the air damp and cold. People shivered and felt chilled.

Caesar sat in his San Francisco waterfront office staring out the windows. Men were loading a cargo ship with army trucks and tanks, but his mind did not focus on the scene before him. He sipped coffee as he went over in his mind how he could manage to see her again.

Caesar's good mood was due to the fact, while dining at Vanessie's, he met Carmel. What a stroke of luck! Now he knew her name and where she worked. He was surprised she had a job at the Chez Paree. This was the woman he had seen at the Palace Hotel. Never had a woman possessed his mind as she had. It wasn't just her looks that affected him. A quiet determination surrounded her. She emitted the air of a winner.

Instinctively, he would treat her differently from any woman he had known. He had to think about how to approach her. Carmel would refuse him if he asked her out in the usual way. It would have to be original.

Days went by and he had no answer. He laughed at himself. He usually solved his problems, but he had no solution to this one. Maybe she'll come into Vanessie's again. He would have to think of something soon or go nuts.

Carmel thought she might pinch herself. She was actually on her way to sing in a famous hotel. Her first call for work came in February when the bandleader, Larry Fields, called to say his vocalist was unexpectedly ill and would she fill in.

He instructed Carmel to use the Geary Street entrance to the St. Francis Hotel. "Come to the Colonial Ballroom. The band starts at nine o'clock; please be early."

She climbed the few marble steps to the spacious lobby and wondered if she would feel out of place crossing it in her long dress. She walked on a deep-piled crimson carpet. She reminded herself this was where heads of state, royalty, military, and theatrical luminaries had walked. Men in every branch of the service filled the room. Some gathered in small groups, smiling and laughing. A well-dressed dowager passed, nuzzling a small dog against her face. Two bellboys followed her, pushing a cart piled high with luggage.

Carmel heard the music of an orchestra coming from the celebrated Mural Room, where she and her aunt had taken tea. She looked for the famed magenta master clock, the popular place for men and women to meet their dates. Sure enough, two young ladies waited under the clock with expectant expressions on their faces.

Carmel felt the excitement generated by the comings and goings in the hotel lobby. Everyone acted as if it was party time, not the middle of a war.

Why should she feel uncomfortable, she thought, when a man wearing a white turban stood nearby? A small woman stood next to him wrapped in a golden sari.

Mr. Fields had told her the ballroom was on the mezzanine. She waited at the elevator. Three Air Force lieutenants held out their arms as if to grab her and then laughed at her indignation.

On the mezzanine, she stopped at the entrance of the Colonial Ballroom. She stared at the breathtaking scene. Gold fluted columns reached a ceiling three stories high. The mural behind the band covered the entire wall. In the scene, white-wigged gentlemen bowed over hands of ladies in hoop skirts. They appeared to walk down steps to enter the dance floor.

Edging the large dance floor were small tables covered in pink and red linens, with center bouquets of red tulips.

Musicians in tuxedos milled about the bandstand unpacking and tuning their instruments. How elegant they looked. This was what she had hoped for, to sing with a first-class band. She said a silent prayer. Please, help me sing well.

She went over to the stage, where a slim, blond-haired man, about her age, sat on a bench in front of the piano. She looked up at him and smiled into friendly blue eyes. "I'm supposed to see you first ... I mean, the piano player. I'm Carmel St. John."

"My name is Carl. You can come up on the stage there." He pointed to steps at the side of the bandstand. "Larry is backstage. I'll get him."

Carmel climbed the steps and stood by the piano. Some of the musicians smiled while others continued to set their music on the stands in front of them.

Larry Fields came onto the stage. He was deeply tanned with soft brown eyes. He wore a red satin vest with his tuxedo. His curly white hair was trimmed close to his head.

"Hi, Carmel. I like it when a vocalist is early. We can set up your songs." He turned to the band. "Okay, guys, this is Carmel St. John. Watch your manners." He chuckled. "I always threaten them when a pretty new singer arrives. They're really harmless." He extended his arm. "Here, give me your coat and I'll put it back stage. Put your purse inside the pocket. It looks small enough." He made her feel welcome, and she liked him instantly.

"This is a Valentine dance and a real swell crowd. Your dress is perfect." He took her coat and went through the door.

He referred to her red silk dress with the tiny white hearts. Ruffles bordered the low-cut bodice and accented her waist. Her mother's diamond earrings sparkled in her ears.

Carl began to separate the piles of music on either side of the piano. "Did you bring your stock sheets?"

Carmel had no idea what he meant. "No. Should I have?"

Carl gave her a hard look. "This your first gig?"

Gig? Stock? Words she had never heard. "Not exactly," she replied, hoping gig meant job. "I've been working with a small combo."

"Larry likes ballads. Since we're playing for a Valentine dance, there'll be plenty of schmaltz." He saw the small blue notebook in her hand. "I bet that has your list of songs. Let's see."

He glanced at the pages. "Well, it seems you have learned quite a few."

Larry came over. "Got it all worked out? Carl, this is an uptown group tonight. It's an old San Francisco crowd. By the way, Carmel, there's a chair for you." He pointed to the chair in the curve of the baby grand piano. He turned to the band. "Let's shake it up. Ready, boys?" He waved a short baton.

Carmel sat down on the chair by the piano and listened to the band play "Heartaches." The room began to fill with women in evening gowns, jewels sparkling. Some wore red to celebrate Valentine's Day. Many men wore tuxedos and a few were in officer's uniforms.

She hoped a smile on her face would hide her nervousness. She tried to stop the trembling in her legs. Her anxiety mounted when she got up to sing before the microphone. Carl winked at her before he led her into the introduction of "I've Heard That Song Before." She concentrated on the words of the song. She heard the big band sound behind her and felt lucky she wasn't ahead or behind the music, grateful her mouth wasn't the least bit dry. Instead, when the song ended, she was thrilled to have sung with a ten-piece band.

Larry gave her a nod of approval and the dancers applauded her. Relieved, she smiled at the audience and returned to her chair.

The band was popular and the dancers loved Larry's style. Carmel had watched other singers with swing bands bounce and tap their feet to the rhythm of the music. She felt that was the thing to do.

When it was time for a break, Carl came to her. "Carmel, confess. You didn't think you'd make it, did you?" He chuckled.

Carmel wasn't going to tell him how really scared she was.

"You've got a damn good voice. The guys feel the same."

At his words, a feeling of happiness flooded through her. The whole evening exhilarated her. She was singing and she loved so to sing. The dancers in the beautiful room were having a marvelous time. She sang during every set, the four hours sailing by. The musicians smiled their approval and obviously appreciated her work. During the evening, Larry let her know he would be sure to call on her again.

At midnight, the lights in the room were dimmed and Carmel sang "Dream." She thought, what a difference from the Chez Paree. No whistles and stamping of feet, no banging on the backs of chairs. These dancers held each other in their arms and moved smoothly around the room. At the end of a song, they applauded.

She begged silently, Please God. Don't let my bubble burst.

CHAPTER 22

Finished with her dental appointment, Carmel entered the elevator on the fifth floor of the Medical Arts Building on Post Street. A lone man was in the car. He turned toward her and she recognized Caesar. She was as startled as he was.

Overwhelmed by his closeness in the elevator, she barely managed to say "hello."

"Is it possible we meet so soon? Perhaps you don't remember me."

Carmel, appalled at the rush of blood to her head, said, "Yes, I remember you. Caesar, right?"

"You flatter me." White teeth flashed as he grinned at her.

The elevator descended to the first floor. The doors slid open. They could see through the glass doors into the street and the pouring rain.

"I have my car. May I give you a ride?" Black eyes stared into hers.

Carmel hesitated. She opened her mouth to decline. On the other hand, if she refused, he might think he had upset her. And besides, it was raining very hard.

"Yes. Thank you."

She saw a large black Cadillac parked by the curb and recognized Jake at the wheel. He sighted Caesar and jumped out of the car. Though he was short, he opened an umbrella and managed to hold it above their heads until they reached the car.

Once in the luxury of the car, Carmel felt grateful she didn't have to wait for a cab. Caesar asked her address and repeated it to Jake. In the closeness of the darkened limousine, she was aware of his masculinity, and instead of relaxing she felt uneasy. For some irritating reason he disturbed her as he had at the Palace Hotel.

Caesar watched her. "I hear you left the Chez Paree?"

"Yes, I left a short time ago."

"Are you singing?"

"Yes, with dance bands. We play for private parties or events."

"I'd like to hear you sing sometime. Do you mind if I smoke?" She shook her head.

He reached in his inside coat pocket, produced a silver cigarette case, opened it, and offered her a cigarette.

"No, I don't smoke." Carmel wished he wouldn't ask her any questions. She didn't want him to know anything about her.

He lit his cigarette and exhaled. "Please, I would like very much to see you. Perhaps we could have dinner … sometime." Black eyes stared at her.

"No, no, that's impossible," she heard herself say, grabbing for any excuse. "I'm engaged."

"Is the fortunate man in the service?"

"That's really none of your concern."

"Leaving a beautiful lady must have been very hard for your fiancé. You must be lonely."

"No, I'm not lonely." Carmel wanted to get out of the car and escape from this man.

"May I call you?"

Carmel ignored his question as they pulled up to the curb in front of the house.

"Thank you very much." Jake held an umbrella over her head as she quickly got out of the car.

Once inside the house, Carmel closed the door and leaned against it. She had a feeling she came very near to stepping into a bottomless pit. Frightened and disturbed, but somehow thrilled, she shivered.

CHAPTER 23

Carmel liked Elka the first time they met at the Chez Paree and wanted to remain her friend. She found Elka's stories of her life in Germany fascinating. Elka had agreed to meet Carmel for lunch in Bernstein's Fish Grotto on Powell Street. The front of the famous restaurant, shaped like the prow of a ship, jutted out onto the sidewalk. The prow contained a tank of brightly colored fish. Ships' lanterns and pilots' wheels hung on the beige walls of the restaurant along with large lifelike tuna and marlin staring down at the clientele. Pictures of San Francisco Bay and the waterfront were scattered among the nautical objects. A second-floor balcony with tables and chairs served more patrons. The restaurant was full of customers and noisy chatter.

Joe Bernstein, nicknamed the Silver Fox due to his abundant head of white hair, was an inveterate gambler. When he saw the two attractive women, he walked over to their table with a twinkle in his brown eyes. "Bet you can't guess how many fish are in the tank?"

Carmel wondered how he could prove the number. She stared at the dizzying colors flashing in the big tank. "Seven hundred and forty three," she said.

"That's right. You win a free lunch." Both girls laughed at the joke. Joe went back to greeting customers.

The girls ordered large bowls of clam chowder and coffee for later.

Carmel encouraged Elka. "Please tell me more about your life. Germany seems so far away."

Elka began to speak in her soft German accent as if she related a story about another girl in another time and place. "We live in three-story red brick house. Iron gates at entrance and beautiful gardens with fountains and iron statues of deer. My mother's mama and papa live with us. They spend time in gardens tending roses, grape arbors, and small apple orchard. My grandfather, a dentist when a young man, used portable foot driven drill. He travel sometime five miles to see patient."

Their lunch arrived. "My father, dentist too, use first floor for office with many patients. Sometime he teaches at the university, so I never see. Our family lived on top two floors," she began to eat her soup.

"I imagine your house was beautiful."

"Each family member has his own bedroom and sitting room. We meet for meals and family pleasure. Home is always filled with music and laughter. Our musician friends stay after large dinners and entertain. My mother teaches cook to make our favorite dishes. Our live-in servants' are like family."

"I do love hearing about your life. Where did you go to school?"

"Tutors come to house for lessons. Marlena hated it. She wanted private school. She fuss and fuss at Mama till Papa tell her to stop. Marlena was trouble most of the time. Terrible flirt, once caused problem with gardener."

"My father speaks five languages. We are German, Russian, French, Latvian, and we are Jews." Her voice dropped. "Soldiers marched by house every day. One of Papa's friend and patient was Gestapo. Papa didn't worry about safety. He trusted German friend who said we would be warned in time. I find out from grandparents."

"My grandparents tell us stories and read Grimm's Fairy Tales."

"Where are they now?" Carmel had finished her lunch.

Elka looked at her friend for a long moment and said, "*Liebchen*, if you finished, we go sit in Union Square in sun, then I tell you."

Carmel and Elka thanked Joe Bernstein for their lunch and promised they would come back soon. They walked a block up Powell Street to the square. Servicemen crowded the sidewalks.

A naval officer wearing a doctor's ensignia passed, the sight stabbing at Carmel's heart. Where was Phillip? What was he doing? How long would it be before she would see him? She remained silent walking with her friend.

Union Square, a two-acre plaza, was framed by department stores and the St. Francis Hotel. Below it was an underground parking garage. Admiral Dewey's memorial statue stood in the middle of the square with four cement walkways crossing it, leading to the surrounding streets. Palm trees and graceful Irish yews added beauty to the formal garden.

Ladies wearing hats and gloves, with shopping bags at their feet, sat on metal benches deep in conversation.

Carmel and Elka found a bench and sat near a woman feeding pigeons. They watched two small children laugh at a mime, imitating a man walking on a tightrope. He pretended to fall off the imaginary rope. The children's nannies stood near, laughing. Carmel looked across at the St. Francis Hotel and the clear sky above. "Did you ever feel you could eat this air with a spoon?"

Elka smiled back at her. "It's a beautiful San Francisco day. We're lucky, to enjoy."

Carmel studied her friend, a breeze ruffling her short blonde hair. "Is remembering too personal? You don't have to continue." Carmel saw Elka's eyes darken while she remained silent. "Elka, you don't have to …"

"No, *liebchen*, don't stop me. I want to tell. We were seventeen. Mama and Papa go to wedding for weekend. That night my grandparents wake Marlena and me, tell us, "Hurry, dress warm." We don't lock doors. We pack baby buggies, walk to train. Later I find dental gold sewed in hem of clothes. My grandparents give us passports to our cousin. People everywhere, wait for crowded trains. Some hang outside, too weak. I hear they drop and drown in river. My cousin stayed with us till we board ship in Hamburg. I never see my grandparents or Mama or Papa. I pray every night I see my family sometime."

"Oh, Elka, I'm so sorry."

"We board ship. Long time ago, Papa worked out plans. My cousin said other cousin would meet us on Ellis Island and travel to San Francisco. The captain is good. He send steward to watch us. I was afraid. I cry every night." She tried to smile at Carmel.

"You have your sister," Carmel offered.

"*Nien*, Marlena never talk about past. It's over for her."

Carmel winced at Elka's words. She had suspected Marlena would take care of herself first.

Elka continued, "Our tutors taught us to tap dance. Marlena said fire tutor if tutor didn't teach us. That why I learn Chez Paree dances. Marlena tell 365 Club she showgirl in Germany. She said they never check. Now, Marlena come home with fur jackets, jewelry, and even money." Elka shook her head and rose to leave. "It late and I work tonight."

"That's right. I don't work on Mondays. Elka, I appreciate you for sharing so much of your life with me. When I talk to you, I feel nothing has ever happened to me."

"You're a good friend. *Auf Wiedersehen*."

Carmel watched Elka walk away thinking about the many losses her friend had suffered. But for some reason, Carmel felt a sense of foreboding about

Elka's future. An undercurrent she couldn't understand or name stayed with her.

CHAPTER 24

On March 1, 1942, Phillip received orders to board the *Solace,* a United States naval hospital ship, in Hawaii.

Dr. Larry Marsh, tall like Phillip, stood in the kitchen of Phillip's San Francisco apartment, watching him mix martinis. Both doctors were off duty, relaxing in short-sleeved shirts.

Larry said, "You seem happy about your orders."

Phillip saw the concern in his friend's blue eyes. "Actually, I think I am. I know I'd rather be on a ship than stuck in an island hospital." He handed Larry his martini. "Here's to a short war. How about you? Have you received any word?" Rumors had been flying around the hospital for weeks, and each doctor wondered when he would receive his orders.

"Nothing so far. Do you realize how fast those Japs are moving across the Pacific? They've captured Guam and Wake. Christmas Day they took Hong Kong. Now they're in Singapore." Larry smiled wryly. "I don't see any short war."

"There's one consolation. Japan's thought her attack on Pearl Harbor she would capture the island chains in the South Pacific. But as devastating as the attack was in sinking so many of our battleships, our four carriers were at sea, not at Pearl Harbor." Phillip sipped his drink. "That's our consolation."

Larry followed Phillip into the small living room. He seated himself in one of the comfortable upholstered chairs opposite Phillip. "How much time before you leave?"

"One week." Phillip groaned. "I have referred my patients and subleased this apartment." He paused and looked at Larry. "I have to go to San Jose and see my parents."

And, he thought, there is Sylvia, glamorous, shining Sylvia. He knew she'd be relieved to know his orders arrived. "I'll take Sylvia to dinner. I'd better call her."

He asked himself, will I see Carmel when I go home? I'm not ready for a serious relationship. Carmel, with her dark hair and gray eyes, too wise for her own good, might become too important.

He looked around the room. "It'll take me a couple of days to get packed up."

"Well, packing books is not my forte, but I'll help you with the paper work at the hospital if you want."

"Thanks, Larry."

Even though the surgery schedule was heavy, Phillip managed within the week to reschedule his patients and store his furniture. He planned to sell his car after he returned from San Jose. To sublet was easy. Places to live were at a premium.

Carmel checked her face in the mirror. She looked pale but presentable. Her father had invited the Barrons to dinner, and she and Anna worked all after-noon to prepare the meal.

When all was ready, Anna sent her to dress for dinner. Carmel dressed in a simple blue silk dress, with a single strand of pearls and pearl earrings. She prayed to have the chance to speak to Phillip alone and arrange to see him later. If Laura hadn't let it slip in a telephone conversation that Phillip was coming to San Jose to say good-bye, she might never have seen him before he left.

Four weeks had passed since the romantic evening in his apartment. She had spent sleepless nights remembering how his body felt against hers, remembering the words they exchanged. Tonight, when she thought of him, her apprehension was as crippling as the worst kind of stage fright.

She heard a car in the driveway and knew the Barrons had arrived. She listened for a moment. The rain had begun again. Every time the Barrons came to dinner, she thought, it rains. The dogs barked as people entered the house, laughing and festive. Carmel left her room to greet her guests.

As she entered the hall, she heard her father tell Lupe to take Harold's and Cynthia's coats.

"Andrew," Cynthia said cheerfully, "it's so good of you to have all of us for dinner, especially on such short notice."

Andrew shook Harold's extended hand. "You look beautiful in that color, Cynthia. Is that called *mauve*?" He chuckled.

Cynthia smiled at Andrew's attempt at humor.

Andrew continued, "It's possible, my dear. I wouldn't have seen Phillip if I hadn't invited you here for dinner. You see, there was a motive in my invitation."

They followed him into the large, comfortable living room. The polished parquet floors glowed from the blazing fire in the hearth at the end of the room.

Carmel hugged Cynthia, who said, "How lovely to see you."

Andrew answered, "Yes, for me too. I'm delighted at my daughter's unexpected arrival. Where is that handsome son of yours?"

Harold led Cynthia to the couch. "He's bringing his sister. They're right behind us."

At that moment, Phillip and Laura stepped through the open doorway. Carmel saw the raindrops glistening on Phillip's navy topcoat. She smiled at Laura.

Lupe took their coats. Phillip wore his lieutenant commander's uniform with the gold doctor's insignia on his blouse. Phillip and Carmel looked at each other. She felt her breath stop while his energy leaped at her. "You're looking splendid, Phillip.

"And you're looking beautiful." She saw his brown eyes darken a moment as he held her warm hands.

"Thank you."

"Carmel, I know this dinner was unexpected," Laura said. "I bet you've worked all afternoon."

"No, Laura. Anna, Lupe, and I enjoyed the chance to cook together." She beamed at Laura and realized how much she missed her friend.

Laura walked toward Scott and took his hand. "Where've you been all day?"

Carmel didn't hear Scott's answer. She could feel Phillip watching her and felt attractive in her silk dress.

Phillip turned to his father. "I appreciate you folks make it easy for me to see all of you before I leave." He grasped his hand.

"Well, son, we're damn glad you could get home."

Phillip went to his mother, who sat on the couch. He bent down to gaze into her brown eyes. "How are you?" He laid his cheek against hers.

"I'm fine, just fine." Cynthia, Carmel thought, seemed more fragile than she remembered.

Bruno and Howard had followed Phillip and Laura into the room. They were wagging wet tails and sniffing greetings to the guests. Andrew called Lupe to take the dogs out of the room.

Phillip walked over to Andrew and shook his hand. Andrew wore a green wool shirt with a flowered ascot tied around his throat. "You certainly look festive on this damp night."

"A little extra cheer never hurts. Phillip, if I remember, you drink martinis?"

"Right."

"We wouldn't miss saying good-bye to you, old man," said a smiling Scott. He wore a sporty wool shirt.

Harold turned to Carmel. "My, my dear, how is it possible for you to look prettier every time I see you?"

"Please sit, we have time for a drink before dinner."Andrew said. "Come on over folks. Who would like a drink?"

Andrew served martinis to his guests and sat down.

Cynthia looked at her son in his uniform and sighed.

Harold heard the sigh and asked Phillip, "Tell me, son, do you know anything about your orders?"

Phillip had joined his mother and father on the couch. He took a sip of his martini. "Well, I think I can tell you this without letting the cat out of the bag. I'm to board a hospital ship, the USS *Solace*, somewhere in Hawaii."

Cynthia wondered, "Are there many hospital ships?"

"I believe this is the only one at the moment."

"What are her facilities?" Harold asked.

"She's a converted cruise ship. We'll be able to provide care for most patients. Severe cases …" he hesitated, "will have to be taken to the shore hospitals." He took a sip of his drink.

Andrew said, "I guess we'll have fewer and fewer opportunities to know where you are, eh, Phillip?"

"Well, as a matter of fact, I got this idea from another doctor. I'm going to leave a list of girls' names with you, and each name will tell you which island I'm near, on, or where I'm headed." He reached out for his mother's hand.

His father responded, "A great idea, son."

Anna came to the door and signaled Carmel. Carmel said, "Dinner is ready. Please, bring your drinks with you."

A fire crackled in the dining room fireplace. The heavy brocaded drapes were pulled, and rain beating against the windows could be heard. The sense of coziness added to the charm of the room.

"It's a lovely table," Cynthia said, referring to the bowl of yellow roses in the center of the table with candles in tall silver candelabras.

When Harold saw the rack of lamb, he said, "Someone gave up a lot of red points."

Andrew said, "No red ration stamps needed to buy this lamb. It came from our larder, butchered this year."

The lamb was served with new potatoes and fresh vegetables from the garden. The proper wines were served, and Anna and Carmel kept the plates replenished. Carmel made an effort to see the conversations were cheerful, even though they referred to blackouts, rationing, and which one of their friends had been drafted. But Phillip, sitting at the table in his uniform, reminded everyone that this dinner and this evening was the last one for some time.

"Carmel," Phillip asked, "did you leave the Chez Paree as you had planned?"

She wished her feeling of slight embarresment would go away. He acted as if everything remained the same. She definitely did not feel that way. "Actually, I left after two weeks."

She looked at Phillip, who grinned at her. He knew she hadn't told the family about the Chez Paree. Damn him!

He sat calmly, questioning her brother. "Scott, Laura tells me you're interested in freezing food for the future?

"Those little cases of food in refrigerators don't come close to what I have planned."

"What's that?" Phillip asked.

"I see great storehouses of frozen food."

Andrew raised his voice. "Here we go again."

There was an awkward pause. Scott said acidly, "Let's skip this discussion." He reached for his glass of wine.

Cynthia asked, "Carmel, where are you singing?"

"When band leaders need a vocalist, they call me."

"My, my, you are brave!" Cynthia said. "Just think how many songs you have to learn. Do you know 'The Last Time I Saw Paris' and 'All the Things You Are'?"

"As a matter of fact, I do. I'll sing them for you sometime, specially."

Cynthia mouthed at Carmel, "Thank you."

Andrew asked, "How about after dinner?"

Everyone in the room voiced the same opinion. Carmel nodded. "Okay. I'll sing after dinner."

Harold said, "I guess you know, Phillip, your sister is enrolled in nursing school."

"She asked me once about it, but I didn't realize she was serious. Good for you, Laura." Phillip raised his wineglass to her.

"Your opinion has always been important to me. With the gas shortage, I'll have to take the bus into San Jose State every day. I don't mind, though."

"I think you'll make a wonderful, caring nurse—let alone a pretty one," said Harold.

Everyone listened to Harold and Phillip discuss the Rockefeller Institute discovering the RH factor in blood and what it could mean to the world. Both doctors were excited about the results.

Carmel listened, but her mind was on Phillip.

He exuded a sense of command, and his uniform added even more authority. She wondered if he was uncomfortable and talked just to keep his family from asking any questions about the war. She gripped her hands under the table. It was almost time for him to leave. She dreaded saying good-bye.

After coffee and dessert of cheesecake, Andrew suggested brandy in the living room.

Harold said, "No brandy, but if Carmel will sing the song about Paris. Then we must be leaving."

They joined Carmel in the living room.

The group watched and listened to the voice of a beautiful woman tell the story of her unfortunate and tragic farewell to Paris, a city she loved. The words and scene reminded them of the seriousness of the war. When the song ended, there was no applause. They were all too moved by Carmel's singing.

Cynthia said, "Carmel, never, never stop singing."

Phillip sat against the wall away from the group and watched Carmel while she sang. When she finished, she barely heard the word, "Remarkable."

Harold said, "Thank you, Carmel. I've never heard that beautiful song sung any better." "Andrew, it's been a special evening."

Phillip said, "I have to start back to the city." He looked at his parents. "Dad and Mother, I think the rain has stopped. I can spend a few more minutes with you if I drive you back to the house. Laura can drive your car home."

Lupe brought their coats.

Cynthia hugged Carmel. "You're quite a cook, Carmel. Dinner was excellent. With your beautiful voice, you have many talents."

Carmel had an unflagging respect for Laura's mother. "Thank you."

"Phillip, my one and only brother, take care of yourself." Laura said.

Phillip laughed. "My one and only sister, take care of yourself." He hugged her.

Andrew shook Phillip's hand. "Safe sailing, and all that goes with it."

"Thank you, sir."

"Thank you for having my family over," Phillip said. She felt his lips brush her cheek. He whispered in her ear. "Time escaped me. I'll call you before I leave."

She didn't respond. She wanted to kiss him, hold on to him, but the front door opened, the night air flowed in, and the guests were gone.

Scott and Laura joined Andrew for coffee and to sit near the replenished fire.

Carmel wandered to the piano and began to play the mournful notes of "Moonlight Sonata." Phillip was actually leaving for the war. Even worse, he might not return. What was he thinking while she sang? Will he keep his word and call?

CHAPTER 25

"Oh, Phillip," Sylvia said, "let's go see whose band it is." She laughed up at him. Her blue eyes sparkled. She wore a peach silk dress with a full skirt cut low in the front to reveal her creamy breasts.

They were in the hall of the Palace Hotel and heard the music from the Gold Ballroom. Phillip shook his head. "No, I don't think that's a good idea. We'll go to the Drake and dance." The expensive bottle of champagne at dinner in the Garden Court gave her a sense of daring.

"No, darling, this is our last night together! I want to dance, now. Listen to that music." She swung away from him, pulling him to the entrance of the ballroom.

"Okay, okay. We'll take a quick look, but that's all. I have a hunch it's a private dance."

They approached the wide doors to see a room full of marine officers in dress uniforms and ladies in ball gowns.

"Look at them," Sylvia said, not giving up. "I guess we can't go in since you're not a marine."

At that moment, two drunken young officers swept past them and entered the dance floor, almost knocking Phillip and Sylvia down.

Phillip looked into the darkened hallway and was shocked to see Carmel clutching her torn blouse, her breasts exposed.

Carmel, stunned to see Phillip, whirled away to escape into the darkness. Angry tears of frustration filled her eyes. Carmel's mind reeled with recriminations. He would think she had provoked those marines. Oh, God, now she would lose him for sure. Damn this war. Phillip, who is that beautiful woman hanging on to you? Carmel's heels clicked on the wooden floor as she hurried toward the ladies' room. Carmel held her hands over the torn blouse as she rushed past two waiters, who jumped aside.

Sylvia spoke first. "I swear, it takes all kinds of women to get a man. What do you suppose she was doing?

"I know that girl and I know her family. I saw the look on her face. I do not believe she deliberately provoked those two men." He floundered.

"She's very beautiful. What's her name?"

"Carmel St. John."

"How do you know her?"

"She's a friend of my sister's. They grew up together."

"She sure was in a panic."

"Wouldn't you be if your clothes were half torn off?"

"Oh, she'll be okay." Impatient, she said, "Let's go to the Drake now."

Carmel had disappeared. Phillip shrugged. "Let me get your coat."

Ribbon, the attendant in the ladies' rest room, gasped when she saw Carmel enter the room. "What happened to you?"

"Help me turn this blouse around. Do you have any pins? You could pin the back up if I turn it around. Thank goodness it's too big for me." She hoped the dark green taffeta would hide the pins.

The women worked quickly. Carmel was grateful to Ribbon for remaining silent.

Ribbon found several small pins and joined the torn edges together, hiding them in the material. Carmel looked at herself in the mirror. Her eyes were huge and dark in her white face. Perspiration lined her upper lip. She rubbed lipstick on her cheeks to bring back some color, dampened her fingers, and smoothed her hair with her hands.

Carmel admitted to herself that she was almost frightened out of her mind at the way those marines had looked at her. The larger officer was drunk and stank of whisky. "Let me see those big teats, baby. I want to know if they're real." The other officer hadn't waited. He reached for her blouse at the neck and ripped it open to the waist. Her brassier barely covered her breasts.

His buddy said, "Jesus, they're real."

At this moment, his companion saw Phillip and Sylvia in the hall. "Let's get outta here!"

Carmel's color came back to her face and with it her reassurance. She shouldn't have spoken to the marines on her way to the ladies' room. She only said, "Hello," but it was enough for them to follow her into the dark hall.

Ribbon's black face showed honest concern. "Honey, you got ta be careful, even when you is in a big hotel, maybe even more so. There're lots of crazies now and they is drinkin' and nowhere is safe. A lot of these guys is not comin' back, and they don't give a damn."

"I promise it will never happen again." Carmel glanced at her small watch. "I must hurry. I have to sing the next set. Thanks, Ribbon."

Carmel wondered if that wrong turn into a darkened hallway marked a wrong turn in her life with Phillip.

In the Starlite Room on the top floor of the Drake Hotel, Phillip and Sylvia danced. Heavy blackout curtains hung on the windows circling the beautiful room, hiding the spectacular views of the city. The music from the band was marvelous, the dance floor crowded with people celebrating.

Sylvia flirted and snuggled up to him on the dance floor. Phillip remained charming and impersonal. She chatted to old friends that this was Phillip's last night to celebrate. He would be leaving that week.

"Why are you telling people I'm leaving, Sylvia? We're told over and over again not to talk about plans or schedules of any kind at any time. *Sealed lips will not sink ships.*" He reminded her of the wartime slogan seen on Merchant Marines placards all over San Francisco.

Friends wanted to buy them drinks and continue the evening, but Phillip said he had an early morning call and it was time to take Sylvia home.

Phillip didn't linger over passionate kisses. He left Sylvia at her door, promising he would write.

CHAPTER 26

In Pearl Harbor on a gray, windy day, Phillip stood on a Captain's gig headed for the hospital ship *Solace*. The trip from shore to the ship atop the whitecaps was a bumpy one. Phillip climbed the steep ladder to board the *Solace* and saluted the colors and the officer of the day.

"Lieutenant Commander Phillip Barron. I request permission to come aboard."

"Permission granted, sir."

The ensign, looking young and scrubbed in his whites, said, "Welcome aboard, sir! This way, sir."

The *Solace* lay at anchor. Before the war, she had been an 8,900-ton passenger liner. Her commission as a hospital ship came in August 1940. The white ship had a broad green band painted around her hull and large red crosses on either side of her stack. Phillip noticed with satisfaction how scrubbed and spotless the ship appeared. Following the ensign, Phillip avoided the sight of the damaged harbor and the oil slick from the tragedy of only eight days before.

The ship was getting underway by the time he reached his quarters. A slim officer was unpacking. When the officer stood, Phillip saw they were the same height. Blue eyes stared at him over a wide smile.

As if reading Phillip's mind, the officer said, "Makes you wonder how two grown men can share such small quarters. Will Nickerson. My friends call me Nickers. Here, let me." Nickers lifted Phillip's gear onto the lower bunk opposite his.

"Phillip Barron." The men shook hands. He sat down on the bunk. "Yes, this'll do fine."

"I think most of the medical personnel are coming in from University of Pennsylvania Hospital. That where you're from?" Nickers leaned on the bulkhead and offered Phillip a cigarette from a pack of Lucky Strikes.

"No, thanks." Phillip shook his head. "I'm from the University of California Hospital in San Francisco."

"I hail from Children's Hospital in Los Angeles. This old gal," he patted the bulkhead, "may not look like much, but she's already seen duty here at Pearl."

"How many doctors aboard? Do you know?"

"I think there're about ten. Dr. Pearlman's the CO." He glanced down at his watch. "It's almost chow time. Let's go. I'll introduce you."

On the way to mess Nickers explained, "The doctors and nurses have their own quarters on the top deck. All medical facilities cover the lower deck, including our mess and ward, which is separated from the crew's galley."

They entered the officers' mess. Phillip was introduced to Captain Pearlman, who reached across a table covered with white linen and clasped Phillip's hand in a strong grip. "Welcome aboard. Excuse me, Dr. Barron, for starting my lunch. Supplies are aboard and I need to authorize paperwork."

Phillip saw a handsome man of slight build with a great shock of dark hair above a thin face.

Dr. Pearlman continued, "Please, join me when you've finished." Each man appraised the other. Phillip would be next in command in an emergency.

Two young officers entered the mess, one a freckled faced redhead flashing a smile like a beacon. "I'm Red MacPherson." His high spirits evident, he shook Phillip's hand and nodded to the other. "This is Pete Beagly, our reigning dentist."

Pete reminded Phillip of a small alert terrier. He shook Phillip's hand and said, "I hear you're from San Francisco. Any chance you're from UC Medical?" Pete asked. "I graduated from University of California Dental School there."

"That's my home base." Phillip sat down at the table. He helped himself to several pieces of fried chicken.

The men joined Phillip at the table and began heaping food onto their plates.

Pete asked, "Has San Francisco changed much?"

"Frankly, Pete, I was so tied up with leaving the hospital leaving I saw little of it. What every coastal city is facing I expect, dim-outs. The place is crawling with service personnel, bringing people in from out of state."

"I don't want that city by the Golden Gate to change. I love it."

"You're lucky to grow up in San Francisco. I grew up in Fresno. My dad grows acres of almonds. Not a big bay in sight." Nickers stuffed a spoonful of potatoes with chicken gravy into his mouth.

Captain Pearlman finished his lunch and left the mess hall.

"I hear we're headed for Pago Pago," Red said. He sipped his coffee in loud slurps.

Phillip rose from the table and smiled. "Your guess is as good as mine. Right now, I haven't a clue where we're going. I do know that after the surrender of Singapore the Japanese will be moving toward New Guinea and on to Australia. We'll be somewhere close to the fighting, picking up patients. Nickers, if you're ready, why you don't conduct me to the captain? On the way, perhaps you could give me a look-see around the ship?" He nodded toward the officers as they left.

A comely nurse met them in the passageway. Nickers introduced them, "Lieutenant Day, this is Lieutenant Commander Barron."

Phillip saw chestnut eyes, bright red hair, and a quick, crooked grin. "Glad to meet you, sir."

Phillip nodded. "Likewise."

She left them and walked toward the mess hall.

Phillip and Nickers continued onto the deck.

"I heard she's top notch." Nickers observed, "and she looks like a sweater girl."

Phillip glanced at him. "Concur."

Walking the quarterdeck with Nickers, Phillip was relieved to see the wide deck. When the landing crafts brought the wounded men aboard on stretchers, they would need a lot of space to maneuver and classify the men for treatment.

Phillip enjoyed the feel of sea air on his face. "I hope I get my sea legs before long."

"It's amazing how few people get seasick once we're underway. If they do, they damn well better get over it fast," Nickers chuckled.

The wards were empty. Nickers explained that the patients on the ship during the bombing at Pearl Harbor had been moved to base hospitals. The two men moved quickly through the modern operating room, bed wards, X-ray department, and dental rooms. Then to the eye, ear, nose, and throat department. Finally, they investigated physiotherapy, the pharmacy, and the laboratory.

Phillip said, "Nickers, I heard the *Solace* is the best. I believe it."

"The *Solace* is the only hospital ship operating in these waters," Nickers said. "I have faith in Captain Pearlman's abilities. After a battle, I just hope we doctors and nurses can keep up the grind."

They found Captain Pearlman in the hold. "This time we're lucky. The *Solace* was hit at Pearl, but no serious damage." He turned to introduce a Corpsman First Class Henry Taylor. Henry was a good-looking young man with a slender build, fresh skin, clear eyes, and dark hair.

Nickers said, "Taylor was on the *Solace* at Pearl. He'll have to tell you about it."

"Be glad to, sir."

Phillip promised himself he would take the time to hear the story. He had wondered exactly what had happened that morning.

Captain Pearlman continued, "This is Bosun First Mate Archie Berg." Archie was slightly overweight and balding early. He gave Phillip a toothy smile.

Before the day was over Phillip learned there were fourteen doctors aboard, including two dentists, eight nurses, and an indefinite number of corpsmen and technicians. While night descended, Phillip expected the *Solace* to turn on her powerful floodlights to illuminate the red crosses across the hull and the stack, but the ship moved in darkness. That evening, alone with Captain Pearlman in his quarters, Phillip asked, "Isn't it mandatory to turn on our lights? Aren't we following the Geneva Convention Rules?"

"Captain, are you asking whether we are immune to enemy attacks if we light up?" Captain Pearlman spoke quietly with authority. "Everyone knows a light from a single match can be seen for miles. Why should I believe the Japanese subs would obey the Geneva Convention after Pearl?"

Phillip listened with respect, but he felt uneasy about the news. He looked at a plaque above Captain Pearlman's desk that read,

First Operation of the *Solace*
To Enter Active Combat Area and Receive Casualties Direct from Combat
Operations

Phillip felt a surge of admiration for the man sitting before him and the job he had to do.

"Good night, sir."

"Good night, Doctor. Sleep well." Pearlman smiled.

Phillip was uneasy, having read recently that their navigation maps had not been updated since 1939. There were many indications America was not prepared for war.

Phillip found Nickers reading alone in his bunk. He repeated his recent conversation with Captain Pearlman. Nickers listened for a minute. "I did some research about ships before I came aboard and found out that we Americans put everything—I mean everything: all accommodations of officers, crew, and navigating bridge—smack in the middle of our ships. We're sitting ducks. The point being, British and Canadian living quarters are fore and aft. Everything on the ship doesn't go at once."

Phillip, already in his bunk, said, "Those are comforting words to go to sleep on." He laughed. "Good night." He rolled over, but he lay in the dark and listened to the deep throb of the ship's engines for a very long time before drifting off into a fitful sleep. Carmel's image slipped in and out in his dreams.

CHAPTER 27

Three days passed before Phillip asked Corpsman Taylor to tell him the story of the *Solace* at Pearl Harbor. Phillip suggested they meet in a wardroom. Word got around and all the corpsmen, technicians, and officers that were off duty came to listen to Taylor.

Someone called the radio room and asked them to turn off Glenn Miller's "One O'clock Jump" being piped in over the loudspeakers.

Phillip sat with two steaming cups of coffee and asked Taylor to join him. Taylor took a sip of coffee. "That Sunday morning I was going to the cathedral for services. The *Solace* was tied up between the repair ship, *Dobbin*, and several destroyers. We had a good view of Battleship Row and Ford Island. Our liberty boats were due at eight o'clock.

"In the mist, some planes came down, and I thought it was another one of those sham battles. I remember there were five planes. They dropped torpedoes on the *Utah*, then flew over us. The pilots were so close we could see their faces. 'My God, those are Japanese. Get the damn hatch shut,' I yelled.

"I saw the *Utah* jump in the air. The deck was covered with piles of lumber—we used it for target practice. The lumber was loose and knocking some men twenty feet in the air. Some were jumping into the water. Three of us closed the iron cargo hatch. It usually has to have an electric winch. I'll never know how we did it. The officer of the deck was in a panic. A chief came on deck in his socks and told the ensign to tell the bridge to get underway as fast as possible. He called the boiler room and told them to fire up. 'We're movin' out.'

"The men from my ward learned from our drills to cover the windows with metal covers. I could hear the planes comin'. I turned around to see one drop a bomb down the stack of the *Arizona*. It blew the bow loose. I saw men flying through the flames and smoke. I can still hear them screamin'."

The room was silent. Taylor took a sip of coffee.

"We finished our windows, as you know," he said, looking around at the group around him. "This is a converted cruise ship—our windows are kinda high up." The men looked behind them and nodded to confirm his words.

Phillip said, "Please continue, Taylor. You're doing a hell of a job. We appreciate it."

"We went to our ward room to get ready for the patients that we knew would be coming. We had been told to make plaster of Paris bandages as fast as we could. We could hear the Japs over Ford Island. I knew we could be a target any minute.

"One guy was naked with only his belt and badge left on his body. He was from the USS *Nevada*. The scalp of one guy was cut so deep I could see inside his head every time he breathed. All our sheets were dark brown from the tannic acid. We made it out of tea and brought it from the galley. The men were like burned hot dogs, ears and noses gone. We did what we could, mostly gave them morphine. We must have gone forty-eight hours without sleep. I couldn't have slept. I was so full of adrenaline, I started staggering around. A nurse insisted I get some sack time. I guess I slept an hour before they needed the bunk.

"The awful part, the next day boats from the *Solace* had to go around the battleships and pick up remains of bodies that floated to the surface. We had to bring the parts back, clean the oil off them, and try to identify by teeth or fingerprints.

"I hear the *Oklahoma* turned over in thirty minutes; the *West Virginia* took seven torpedoes and is on the bottom. The *California* is on the bottom and the *Arizona* lost a thousand men. The *Utah* capsized and the *Nevada* took five bombs and a torpedo. I don't know what happened to the *Tennessee* or the *Pennsylvania*."

Taylor looked into his empty cup. "That's about it, sir."

The group of men filed silently out of the wardroom. Corpsman Taylor stood.

Phillip looked at him, "Thanks, Taylor."

"Yes, sir," he said, and he left the ward.

CHAPTER 28

The *Solace* received orders to proceed to Samoa, Pago Pago, and the Tonga Islands.

Lieutenant Molly Day looked forward to seeing the islands. Though it was hot and humid, she went ashore with Nickers and Ensign Lucille Danner. She wiped perspiration from her forehead with her handkerchief and made a face. "Gosh, I thought we would at least have a breeze."

Ensign Lucille Danner, a petite brunette, said, "You talked me into coming ashore." She looked at Molly. "Somehow you talk me into everything—becoming a nurse, joining the service, and even signing up for a hospital ship."

Molly laughed. "You'll never regret it. You'll have tons of stories to tell your grandchildren." She was thinking about the history of infectious diseases that troubled some of the islands. She asked, "Have you ever seen any cases of elephantiasis and leprosy?"

Nickers, walking behind them listening to their conversation, said, "No, but I read about the woman that carries her breasts and stomach in the wheel barrow."

Lucille shivered. "How awful for her."

Molly said, "She's probably been stared at her whole life and is used to it, if that's any consolation."

Nickers had escorted them off the ship onto the dock. "Let's continue our walk and see the island."

Before them was a thick jungle of dark green. A soft trade wind made rustling noises in the tops of the tall, swaying palm trees as they reached for the clear blue sky. The *Plumeria* trees produced an abundance of pink, red, and yellow flowers. The spicy odor of ginger filled the air. The scene reminded Molly of a Gauguin painting.

They wandered onto a side street. Molly said, "Even with all this island beauty, there's an unexplained feeling of pessimism surrounding it."

Nickers said, "I feel the same sadness. Perhaps it's because these islands sit defenseless against the enemy."

Brown, barefoot children played a game with seashells on the dirt street. Picking the child hiding the shell, they bent over with laughter at the shared discovery. A long wooden fence ran along the dirt walkway. It led to a wooden gate on which hung the word *Leprosy*. Someone had drawn a large skull and crossbones on the gate.

Molly felt like an intruder in her immaculate white uniform staring at the afflicted.

Old people sat on straw piled outside the small wooden buildings. Their faces and arms were covered with sores, some of them bright red. Their skin appeared hard and scaly on limbs large as tree trunks. They had no toes.

Children played inside the area, romping and chasing each other, not upset by the ugliness around them.

"I've had enough; let's go back," Lucille said.

"I've never seen a person with leprosy," Molly said.

Nickers said hopefully, "You're not likely to see it again."

"What causes it? Do you know?" Lucille asked.

"Apparently a microorganism marks those ulcerations and deformities in the beginning. Mosquitoes infect the blood stream. This causes worms to invade and grow until they are five inches long. Leprosy isn't a killer, because circulation is not affected. Someday something will be done about all of this filth and especially the mosquitoes." Nickers kicked at the grime on the dirt walk.

"This heat must add to their misery," Molly said.

Lucille shuddered. "I won't forget this walk very soon."

Silent on their way back to the dock, they saw three gray navy destroyers had arrived and anchored in the harbor.

Once they boarded the *Solace*, Nickers said, "I hear they have commissioned another hospital ship called the *Relief*."

Molly said, "That's a relief. I wonder how many months before it'll be ready?" Her effort at humor failed to ease the stressful afternoon.

A week later, Phillip and Nickers stood on the quarterdeck and watched the Samoa Islands disappear in the distance.

"Difficult to believe such beauty is home to so many suffering people," Nickers mused. He cupped his hands around a cigarette and lit it.

"It sure upset the nurses. The suffering they saw is all they've been talking about."

"I hope the pain they witnessed at the beginning of our tour is not an omen of what's to come. Captain Pearlman said we'd be doing the drills every time we leave port and new personnel come on board," Nickers said. He cocked his head and grinned. "I don't mind the nurses romping about, up and down the ladders."

"Have you forgotten they wear trousers now?" Phillip silently agreed with Nickers. He admired the vigor of the nurses climbing the ladders as they followed mandatory drill orders. He reflected on Molly Day, who had caught his eye. Her uniform fit in all the right places. But Phillip didn't intend to break the rule he made. Don't get involved with any of the nurses, especially in such close quarters.

Pete joined them on deck. "Do you know how we find out if there's a battle and where?"

Phillip crossed his arms and leaned back on the rail. The *Solace* was underway, but with a calm sea, the quarterdeck barely seemed to move under his braced legs. "From what I understand, Admiral Halsey or General MacArthur lets Captain Pearlman or the skipper know there's going to be a battle."

"How much time will that be?" Pete asked.

"They hope to give us at least three days, maybe five." Phillip's face was grim. "We should get patients from the Coral Sea battle any time now. You'll probably be called to do more than dentistry before we're through."

Pete said, "Rumor has it when General MacArthur left the Philippines, he promised to return."

Nickers added, "Being forced to leave must have been hell. The Philippines suffered great losses before they were captured." After a moment, he said, "I believe any promise from a man who smokes a corncob pipe."

Phillip moved past the two doctors. "See you in the morning."

The *Solace* had arrived at the Island of Tongatabu. The medical personnel and ship's crew had left the ship to stand on the dock. In spite of the early morning, the heat of the day couldn't be avoided. Perspiration appeared on foreheads, and uniforms were damp.

Captain Pearlman and the skipper received large bouquets of flowers from the bowing natives. Pearlman and the skipper thanked them. After a moment, they handed the flowers to the nurses.

A small brown man, wearing short pants and a flowered shirt, spoke in his native tongue. When he finished, he stood, smiled, and waited. The interpreter informed the Americans that Queen Solate, Ruler of Tongatabu, wished to offer them a cemetery to bury their honored dead.

Nickers, standing behind Molly and Lucille, said, "That makes sense. I hope the Captain accepts."

Molly observed Nickers always seemed to linger near Lucille. She said, "I think these wonderful people appreciate what we've done for them." She was referring to the natives, who were treated aboard the *Solace* for infections, toothaches, and other body ailments. The natives were as inquisitive and enthusiastic as children about the dental chair, X-ray machine, and medical equipment.

She noted Phillip stood away from the group. She thought about asking him to join the three of them. But his aloofness, almost indifference, stopped her. Nickers seemed to be the only person Phillip spent time with. And that wasn't much, as far as she could see. Molly wondered if he was just as aloof in San Francisco.

She decided to chance it. "Let's ask Phillip to join us."

Lucille stopped her. "Mr. Iceberg? Let's not."

Nickers laughed. "He's not so bad. I guess he is rather unapproachable, but I like him."

"He sure is good lookin'," Lucille added.

CHAPTER 29

Phillip had stood in the rear of the crowd and watched the service. The proud old queen, with her entourage, displayed great dignity. He was touched by the respect and love these island inhabitants had maintained for each other through generations. He hoped the war wouldn't destroy their way of life.

Phillip felt puzzled. Lately, no matter how busy he was, Carmel kept popping into his thoughts. Sometimes he had a prick of contrition that he hadn't called her before he left. He was not quite sure how to approach his feelings for her. In his mind, she remained no more than his sister's best friend, and he wasn't ready to think beyond that.

He hadn't found out what happened in the hall of the Palace Hotel with those marines. He knew she had not encouraged their treatment of her. When he heard her sing Christmas Eve, he had no doubt she was blessed with talent. Now she appeared to be fulfilling her dreams of becoming a popular singer.

The voice of the officer of the deck blurting over the ship's loudspeaker interrupted his thoughts. "Stretcher bearers lay aft to the quarterdeck."

Once on deck, Phillip saw whitecaps on the water and felt a stiff breeze. He knew the choppy sea might cause problems boarding the patients. He called for all hands to join the staff and offer assistance.

Each landing craft held fifteen to twenty casualties. They were lifted, one at a time, in litter baskets onto a four-legged swing. The swing hooked onto a winch, and a small boom brought the baskets on board. On the wide decks the crew and staff moved the men rapidly. Working quickly, the doctors practiced triage. By the severity of their wounds, they determined which patient they would treat first.

Many of the wounded men were in shock, their bandages blood stained and the stench of jungle rot surrounding them. Corpsmen worked swiftly preparing patients for surgery and assisting the doctors and nurses to set fractures and apply splints.

The brisk morning wind that made loading patients aboard so difficult had subsided. Phillip, along with Captain Pearlman and six other doctors, operated in three surgical rooms. The oppressive heat of the South Pacific hung over the ship and added to the somberness. The nurses continually wiped the foreheads of the perspiring doctors.

Phillip fought to remain impartial to the patients. To save their lives, it was necessary to stop the bleeding and keep infection from spreading.

Young men with smooth skin and taunt muscles had their once healthy and muscular legs severed from their bodies. Hands with class rings still on their fingers were chopped off forever.

Phillip and the weary doctors and nurses continued with the arduous work. For twelve hours in the operating room, one heard only the slap of surgical instruments being placed into the doctors' rubber gloved hands and the deep breathing of a patient under the mask, being administered to by the anesthetist. When night fell, the sounds were only of the wounded, moaning and swearing. Nurses spoke in low voices offering encouragement and hope.

Close to dawn, Captain Pearlman said, "Barron, I think we can tidy up. This group took care of 180 men. There's another bunch coming aboard at 0600. I have ordered more plasma. The crew may have to contribute. Get some rest. That's an order." He walked out of surgery.

Phillip saw the fatigue in Captain Pearlman's face. He looked at his watch and realized eighteen hours had passed. He decided to get some air. As he left surgery, the interior battle lights gave off enough eerie blue light to see in the wards and passageways.

He passed through the blackout curtain onto the deck and was surprised to see the black night. There were no stars. The wind had died down, and the ship rolled with the swells. He could hear the *Solace's* motor keeping the auxiliary batteries stable.

Nickers joined him. In the distance, they could see intermittent flashing. "Those lights are from a battle?"

"Yes. They must be miles and miles away, but they look like they're sitting on the rim of the earth. Tell me this," Phillip said. "Do you feel more secure knowing, while we're sitting at anchor, steel nets surround this ship?"

"Hey, old man, do you think those nets dropped twenty feet into the water will really protect the ship if a submarine finds us and fires a torpedo? No. I'm not too sure about their usefulness."

"Maybe the nets slow the torpedoes down a bit so it causes less damage. Thank God we're at anchor with all that surgery. A rough sea would really slow us down." Phillip sighed. "What did I learn in medical school? Stop the bleeding and chop off what can't be saved. Come on, Nickers, let's get some shut eye."

The doctors left the dark deck. The *Solace* rode the swells of the Pacific Ocean alone and anchored through the night.

A month later at 3:00 a.m., it was another night as black as coal. Nickers and Lucille pushed aside the blackout curtains and slipped out onto the silent, unlit deck.

Nickers whispered, "Some of the patients have exchanged sleeping quarters with the crew. They sleep out on the decks at night."

Lucille whispered, "I don't blame them." After a moment she said, "I heard we're receiving patients from carriers, air battles, and ground casualties. Look at the miles of water the *Solace* has covered in the last month. No wonder the Solace is called the 'Workhorse of the Pacific'. We've been shuttling between New Zealand, Australia, New Hebrides, and the Fiji Islands, picking up servicemen and then delivering them to Auckland?"

"One of the corpsmen who puts the bodies in the wicker baskets stacked in the morgue told me many will be buried in the cemetery that Queen Solate offered us."

"Nickers, that ceremony seems so long ago."

Nickers leaned against the rail and toward Lucille, just enough to smell her faint bouquet. "Lucille, everything seems a long time ago to me." He paused and then whispered, "From your conversations, you and Molly have known each other a long time."

"Ever since we were kids, in the third grade. I can't imagine life without her."

They stood thinking their own thoughts and listening to the faint sound of splashing as the *Solace* cut through the water.

"That reminds me," Lucille said, "sometime today I heard one Marine tell another Marine, when asked if he prayed, that he was only interested in metaphysics. The other marine said, "I thought you said you were a Presbyterian." She giggled.

Nickers chuckled quietly. "That remark will carry me through the rest of the night. It's time to go back to work."

CHAPTER 30

When Carmel first began to sing, "casuals" was a word describing bands or small combos that played a single night for private parties and dances. As a result, when she wasn't called for a job, she might have three nights off in a row.

One night, Jerry suggested, since they both had a free evening, that they see the nightlife of San Francisco. Delighted, Carmel accepted, anticipating a night to remember.

She wanted to look especially pleasing and wore her red silk suit. She dressed early for their evening out and went downstairs. As she entered the morning room, the phone rang and she heard her uncle answer.

"Hello, Andrew. Yes, thank you. We're all fine. I hope you are, too. Yes, I heard the confirmation. That General Doolittle must be some kind of officer. Yes, I had heard Roosevelt in April when he first announced they had bombed Tokyo.

"No, Andrew, I've never been aboard a carrier. I suspect the *Hornet* has got to be one of the biggest, with sixteen aviators taking off from her deck." He paused. "We'll never know for sure how many made it. We'll know after the war's over." He listened again. "Some of my friends bounced around the bay in their own boats guarding the entrance to the Golden Gate. They watched for Jap planes the first days after Pearl."

He grunted. "Yes, Andrew, they are *my* friends. And they were physically miserable sitting out there. That Gate is one of the coldest. I understand that steel nets are under the water and stretched across the entrance protecting us against submarines. Just keep that information under wraps at the moment." He laughed. "Listen, we're tough cookies. Oh, my God, yes. Lydia's into everything—Red Cross, Bundles for Britain, and planning a Victory garden. That sister of yours is one of a kind. That's nothing new." He laughed. "Yes, yes, she's fine. We enjoy having her. I'll get her for you. Good to hear from you."

Carmel picked up the phone. "Hello, Dad. How are you?"

"We're all fine. Now that it's spring, we're waiting for the buds to start popping. I thought you might hop on a train and pop down here." He laughed at his own words.

"I can't do that, Dad. I'm working casuals."

"Sounds like a big gamble to me, hardly a secure job." The tone of his voice changed. "I was counting on you coming home for a few days. You can't be making enough money to feed a bird let alone take care of yourself."

Her voice became warm and persuasive. "Now, Dad, I miss you, too. I haven't been here very long and I have to follow their rules. The bandleaders must be able to count on me. I'm really working hard, learning songs, and keeping my clothes in good shape. I'll come home when I can and spend a few days."

"Well, all right." He sounded reluctant. "Good-bye, my dear."

Carmel finished her conversation with her father as Bannister met Jerry at the front door. Jerry whistled when he saw her. "Wow, you look terrific, but then you always do."

"Thank you, Jerry. You're quite handsome yourself in you blue suit."

"I have a cab waiting."

Russell emerged. He wore his glasses on the end of his nose, a newspaper folded under his arm. "I'm Carmel's Uncle Russell." The older and younger men shook hands.

"How do you do, sir."

"Heard you say you had a cab waiting. I won't keep you. Have a good time, Carmel."

"I intend to, Uncle. Jerry's going to show me San Francisco's nightlife."

"Well, good luck. I doubt you'll see it all in one night." He chuckled.

"But we'll try. Won't we, Jerry?" Carmel said as they went out through the blackout drapes and out the front door.

In the back seat of the cab, Carmel asked, "You said you had a surprise for me."

"You'll have to wait."

He said to the driver, "Three sixty-five Market."

In the blackout, streets, buildings, and cars were barely discernible. Carmel said, "These streets are so dark it gives me the creeps. This great city is teeming with life. You can feel it. Whatever is goin' on, it's behind blackout windows and doors."

Jerry laughed. "Probably a good idea we don't know what's happening behind those blackout curtains."

The cab driver drove at breakneck speed as if it were daylight and he could see for miles. Carmel tried to remember something that Elka had told her. "I heard you say 365 Market. Is that where Marlena dances?"

"That's where Marlena performs. I wanted to surprise you. We'll go there first but not stay long. I'd like to take you to North Beach, too."

"This should be fun."

Jerry saw in the dim light of the cab that she was smiling. "Have you seen your family since you've been here?"

"My father and brother Scott are in San Jose. With gas rationing, it's difficult to visit them."

The cab pulled up to the building on Market Street. Jerry assisted Carmel out of the cab and handed the driver cash.

Carmel said, "I think we're lucky to arrive in one piece. He drove like a madman."

They entered the club and went through the blackout curtain. Jerry said, "The bar is upstairs."

They climbed a wide carpeted stairway. Two sailors came down the steps, arms around their giggling girls. At the top of the stairway, Carmel saw a large room crowded with customers. She noticed well-dressed men and women seated at the tables. Showgirls wearing abbreviated red, white, and blue outfits were tap dancing on a stage with a large orchestra. Jerry ignored the room, guiding her into a crowded, noisy bar on the right of the stairway.

He said, "Let's head for the end of the bar. Maybe we'll get a seat. At least we can try."

The room exploded with humanity. No one seemed to mind getting shoved and pushed by strangers. There was laughter as they forgave the friendly jostling of their companions. To Carmel, everyone seemed to be in uniform. She wondered if it bothered Jerry to be one of the few men in civilian clothes.

Moving to the end of the circled bar, Carmel noticed an empty fish tank not quite three feet long sitting high behind the bar.

In a few minutes, a couple got up and left. Jerry and Carmel quickly moved into their empty seats. "What do you want to drink?" Jerry asked.

"Vodka and tonic."

Jerry ordered a scotch and soda for himself and when the bartender brought the drinks, asked, "When does the gal perform?"

"Every half hour."

Jerry checked his watch. "We'll have time."

In a few minutes, the light went on in the fish tank. It began to revolve slowly. A tiny nude woman lying on her back on a table covered with black velvet moved her legs and arms in a swimming fashion. As one leg bent to her chest, her arm crossed her body, covering herself. As the alternate leg and knee bent, she crossed her body with the other arm.

Carmel recognized Marlena. "Why, she looks only seven inches long."

The men around her began to whistle and call out to the woman in the fishbowl to put her legs down. "How does she do that?"

"I'll tell you later." They watched the little mermaid swim and wave until the light in the fishbowl went out at the end of the ten-minute show.

Carmel sat completely fascinated. She could never in her life take everything off, keep her legs and arms moving, and keep the intimate parts of her body hidden with hundreds of people watching her.

Carmel was insistent. "Tell me, do you know how Marlena does that?"

Jerry laughed hard. "You gals amaze me. I bet you would like to be a mermaid. Marlena is naked on that table. It's in the basement of the club. A periscope projects a miniature image of her onto the mirrors. This has been going on since the thirties. A friend of the owner, a magician, invented it."

"She's Caesar's girl, isn't she, Jerry?"

"It would appear so. I guess they're together a lot." Jerry stood up. "We'd better leave. I want to take you to another club. It'll be curfew before long."

Carmel laughed. "If the next event is as exciting as this one, all I can say is 'let's go.'"

They caught a cab and shared it with two Marines. The cabby explained times had changed. Riders had to share—it was the only way to catch a ride.

The El Gomez was an upstairs club. The staircase, narrow and dingy, led to the second floor and a huge room with a pine bar running the length of the long room.

Carmel saw a tall, broad-shouldered man coming toward them. He wore a dark suit, somewhat worse for wear, and a dark fedora.

"Well, old friend, you haven't been here in a long, long time." He grabbed Jerry's hand.

Carmel heard a slight accent she couldn't place.

"I've been working long hours, Izzy. I'd like you to meet a great vocalist, Carmel St. John."

Izzy doffed his hat to Carmel and quickly put it back on his head.

His large eyes prompted Carmel to think of an owl. "Miss St. John, you're very beautiful. She's very beautiful, Jerry." He led them to a table and seated them. "I'll get you a waiter."

Carmel looked about the smoke-filled room. Again, the room overflowed with servicemen and women dressed in a variety of styles. One woman sitting at the bar wore a full-length mink coat, which dragged on the floor. Carmel wondered if she was a socialite.

"You're the prettiest girl in the room. You just received the highest compliment Izzy could pay you. He took his hat off to you. He *never* does that."

"Is he Italian?"

"No, he's Portuguese and greatly loved. He has a heart as large as his hat. This place is the number-one stop on the tourists' list."

Wordless, Carmel gazed about her. The walls were bare. No one wore hats. Small tables and the long bar supplied the decor. A small combo across the room played jazz. Couples glided by. Carmel didn't see a glum face in the crowd. "I love places like this; makes me feel good."

Jerry's fingers beat to the rhythm. "Let's order a drink and then we can dance."

Carmel looked at the crowded floor. "I'm happy just watching."

Jerry gave their drink order to the waiter. "William Saroyan made this bar the background of his play *You Can't Take It with You*. Have you read it?"

Carmel nodded. "I read it in a high school English class."

Their drinks arrived. Carmel sipped hers and watched the crowd. She felt comfortable sitting with Jerry. "Do they gamble here?" she asked.

"Yes, as a matter of fact. How do you know that?"

"I hear the guys in the band talking. I'm not as naive as you might think." She smiled at him.

"There's a back room for gambling."

"How do they get away with it?"

"San Francisco's a wide-open city. Mayor Rossi looks the other way. Even the city council's open-minded. I hear Vanessie's stays open until four."

She looked at the crowd around her. "Where do these people come from?"

"They work in the shipyards around the clock. No one wants to go to bed. They might miss something." He laughed.

The band took a break.

"Now you can hear me better. Izzy is known for some very funny and wise remarks. He told me once, 'When you come to a pool of water, don't make it muddy. Maybe you'll pass there again, and you'll be thirsty.'"

"He sounds like a philosopher. I like him."

Jerry nodded. "Let's drink up and shove off."

"I thought we were going to dance?"

"It's almost one o'clock, Cinderella. I want to show you the International House in the Settlement. It has sawdust on the floors; everyone sits on barrels. You'll like it. I want to take you to the Fillmore. Saunders King is playing at Jacks. I think Bob Barfield is working there. He plays a hot sax. There's plenty to do in this old city, but later we'll have coffee at Coffee Dan's."

"I'm game. I've having a great time." She thought, He has no idea how glad I am to get out of the house and experience the excitement of San Francisco. Without someone who knew his way around, she didn't have a chance. Singing nightly with a band did not allow her to see any nightlife. She felt lucky to be with Jerry. He was fun and very handsome, especially tonight. In addition, she didn't have to worry about any hanky-panky. She had a feeling they would always be good friends.

They said good night to Izzy. This time when he doffed his hat to Carmel, she was flattered. Jerry managed to hail a cab.

"Jerry, this has been a wonderful evening, much more than I anticipated. Why don't we call it a night and save the International House and Coffee Dan's for another time. I promised Aunt Lydia I'd be up early to help her pack at the Bundles for Britain meeting. I don't want to disappoint her. May I go home now?"

Jerry laughed. "Of course. I'll look forward to the next time."

CHAPTER 31

Andrew sat quietly at his desk in his small office. Only the snap of oak logs burning in the fireplace broke the stillness. The phone conversation confirmed Carmel was well, but the rest had been a waste of time. A tiny hope had remained in his heart that she might have had enough of San Francisco and want to come home to her family.

Though music had taken her away from him, Andrew was delighted Carmel loved music. As a small baby, she formed the habit of going to sleep at night in her crib with the phonograph playing. He granted singing with a big band must be a heady experience, but he asked himself, what is this casual stuff? It sounded a little too casual for him.

Scott limped into the room. He wore a brown wool shirt, making his eyes, Andrew thought, look like his mother's, brown as buckeyes.

Andrew saw Scott frown as he moved.

"Was that Carmel?" Scott asked. "Did you get her pinned down on will she come home?"

"No, I didn't. She says she'll show up one of these days."

Scott heard the disappointment in his father's voice. He said, "Dad, let's have a drink. I want to speak to you. Something I'm very serious about." He faced his father across the big desk

"Sit, son. I'll get the drinks." He reached for the brandy and glasses kept handy on a shelf, poured brandy into two snifters, handed one to Scott already seated, and returned to his chair. The men raised their glass in a salute.

Scott said, "Dad, I know, you're not happy over Sis's move to the city. Maybe my timing is lousy, but I have to talk to you." He saw his father lift his hand to interrupt him. "Please, listen, Dad. I'm still determined to master the canning business. I have an opportunity to work with the crew at the San Jose Cannery down on Twentieth Street. They start canning peaches in June. I want to learn processing, how to set up the machinery and put the lines in."

"I thought you wanted to open a plant someday in Watsonville?"

"I sure can't do it and make a dime if I don't understand the business."

"Watsonville doesn't handle a lot of fruit. I believe it's mostly cauliflower and sprouts."

"Exactly. It's necessary I learn everything I can. That's my main idea. Dad, the government's paying these packers to produce. When the war's over, they'll have to turn to something else to pack, or they'll sink. I have an idea there'll be a great future in frozen vegetables. Packaging frozen food is going to be one hell of a marketable product."

"You'll be nothing but a glorified mechanic," Andrew said. "Just how do you plan to do this? Don't you feel you have a responsibility to Costalotta? Right now, we should be building the new storage bins for the walnut crop. I don't plan on paying storage anymore on anything we harvest on this ranch. We'll do it all here."

Scott interrupted, "Todd Brenner—he's the plant manager—says I can come over at night and start working on the equipment. You have enough help. You've said so yourself. I grant you because of the war it'll be mostly women … doing the picking in the orchards. I'll get my work done here. I have the lumber now to start the new bins."

"Tell me this, son: just how do you expect to get the labor you will need?"

"I've thought of that. I think the *bracero* program is as good as we have. I have investigated and Todd says the Mexicans come in on a green card. While they're working here they have to put an amount of their wages in reserve to take home with them. Granted it's mostly students, but it includes anyone that wants to work. When the season's over, their money is sent back to a bank in Mexico."

"I'm no longer—"

"No, Dad, Grandfather James wouldn't be able to do now what he did years ago. The workers will have enough money to get their education, or if they are married take care of their families. I intend to be good to anyone working for me, just as you have."

Scott rose and sat his empty glass on the desk. "I wanted to tell you, Dad, so you would know what I intend to do and what I'm doing about it." He limped to the door, turning to look at his father. "Who knows, Dad? Maybe one day you can send me your crop of strawberries, and I'll freeze them all." He grinned at his father before he left the room.

The cozy room seemed suddenly chilly to Andrew. He felt deserted. Working all his life for this land and ranch, it had never occurred to him that his three children wouldn't want to inherit the ranch and work it.

Apparently, Carmel needed a big city to satisfy her needs. She was going to be twenty-one in a few days and she was no longer his little girl. Grant, according to his letter, was working in vice for the police department in Honolulu. He obviously had no intentions of coming home. Vice, what an ugly word. If only one son had graduated from Stanford. The degree alone, plus the contacts made playing football and joining a fraternity, could last a lifetime. Andrew asked himself why didn't they want the opportunities offered to them. Even if Scott couldn't play football, he could have stayed at Stanford and obtained his degree.

Andrew was beginning to understand he had taken for granted the love he thought his three kids had for the ranch.

Andrew finished his brandy and poured another. He sat deep in thought. Once on a trip to Paris with Elizabeth Rose, he had bought her beautiful, expensive long dresses. Andrew had kept them to give to Carmel someday. She would need the dresses: he'd send them to her. Bruno and Howard pushed their noses against him. He patted their big heads, finished his brandy, banked the fire, and left the room.

In her room, Anna removed her robe and slippers and sat down on the edge of the large double bed. No other light burned in the room, except the flickering light from a fire in the fireplace. She knew it was Andrew before the door opened. She asked, "Scott gone to bed?"

He saw her smile in the dimly lit room. "He left early and then came back."

Andrew slipped out of his wool robe. He stood naked before her. He approached the bed, lifted the bedding, and slid in beside her.

She felt his body heat and strength even before he touched her. Anna moved over for him. "Guess Scott's been over to Laura's. He seems so restless. I hear him pacing up and down at night. Do you know why?"

"Yes, I know why, but I can't let him go, not yet. Let's not talk about Scott." He kissed her neck. "I want my Anna. You took your night gown off; I like that." He pulled her to him and moved his hands over the warmth and smoothness of her skin.

His desire for her grew. He leaned her back against the pillows and began to kiss her mouth. Her breath was sweet. He took his time, tasting her before he left her mouth. He kissed her throat and neck, and then his tongue circled her nipples. They became hard at the gentle nibbling of his mouth.

Anna enjoyed the slow and sensuous lovemaking of Andrew intent on her pleasure. His hand moved across her flat stomach and down to the moistness already starting between her legs. He enjoyed waiting for her heat. When she began to moan, he felt her hips begin to twist and arch for him. He rose above her on his knees, lifted her, and entered her slowly, beginning a rhythm that brought them both to the crest of passion.

Afterwards, neither of them spoke. At these moments, Anna wanted to say she loved him.

Andrew muttered in her ear, "How long have we been doing this?"

Anna, silent for a moment, answered. "Fifteen years."

In the light from the fire she looked beautiful to him. Her hair, released from its braid, spread around her face and shoulders. Her dark eyes, shining and full of love, watched him. He asked himself for the hundredth time. Why can't I say it to her?

Anna understood Andrew would not marry her because she was a Mexican. She held no grudge. After all, for generations, the prejudices had been deeply ingrained not only into his family but also into hers. Andrew, always kind, spoke not a word to hurt or indicate possession of her. However, when they were alone, desire and passion consumed them.

CHAPTER 32

Two months later on a hot June afternoon Laura sat on a bench in the shade on the St. John's back terrace. She watched a fat frog sit blinking on a lily pad in the koi pool. The fish fascinated Laura. Their brilliant colors of gold, bright orange, and red flashed as they swam in the clear green water among the roots of the yellow and white water lilies. Laura wished the screeching jays in the crab apple trees above her head would stop scolding so she could think.

Since Laura grew up on the ranch next door and Carmel was Scott's sister and her best friend, she was in and out of the house nearly every day. It was natural during the many days Scott spent recovering from surgery that Laura befriended him. They often did their homework together. From the beginning of Scott's surgeries, while he lay in bed waiting to heal, Carmel and Laura sat on the floor by his bed singing to him in their children's voices. He read to them out of the books they brought to him. Eventually, Laura came alone for the stories. Gradually they began to take turns reading to each other. People commented on the two blond, brown-eyed children, saying they might pass for brother and sister.

Their relationship changed when Scott left home to attend Stanford. During Christmas week, he had accepted an invitation to spend the holidays at Lake Tahoe with a college friend. Then, after what seemed an eternity for both of them, he came home on Easter break. The long absence had been difficult for each of them. Laura missed his gentleness and strength. Scott missed her compassion and intensity. Their feelings exploded and they confessed their love for each other.

Scott had held her close. "I guess we're alike as two black-eyed peas." He laughed. "You have to stop grabbing me from behind hedges and in doorways.

I want you just as much as you want me. If you want me to stay in control of myself, just take it easy."

Laura said, "I promise, only until our wedding day."

She heard the tractor rumbling from the back of the orchards. Scott would be stopping work for the day.

He limped toward her across the terrace. "Hi, good lookin', what ya' got cookin'?"

Laura looked up into Scott's brown eyes, his hair as blond as hers from the sun. His tan, muscular body always managed to make her heart skip a beat.

"What brings you over so early? Scott asked. "I thought I was to pick you up at your place?" He took off his wide-brimmed straw hat and fanned himself with it, then sat in one of the chairs beside her. "Wow, you found a hot place to sit."

A frog jumped into the water with a loud plop. "Even he thinks it's too hot to sit in the sun." They both laughed.

Laura's shampooed blonde curls gleamed golden in the sun. In her pale blue sleeveless blouse and blue cotton slacks, she looked rosy, tan, and scrubbed.

Scott took her hand, turned it over, and kissed her fingers. "Can't you wait and tell me tonight?"

She felt the coolness of his lips. "I guess so. You amaze me how you always read my thoughts."

"Good, Dad and I have to check some accounts and I have to shower." He pulled her up on her feet. "See you at eight. It's Harry James and his band. Be ready to dance." His lips brushed hers. She watched him limp into the house. He was the sexiest man she knew.

Laura wanted to look irresistible for Scott when she presented her plans to him. She decided on a white printed voile dress with a splash of pink and coral flowers. The neckline was low and revealed the slight swell of her breasts. Because August nights in San Jose were warm, she never wore stockings. Her legs were brown enough. She put on her white high-heeled shoes.

The ceiling of the Civic Auditorium in San Jose arched over the huge dance floor. The seats against the walls rose in tiers from the floor, already filled with spectators and girls waiting to be asked to dance.

Scott escorted her across the floor to join the crowded dancers. Harry James's band played "I Had the Craziest Dream" while Helen Forrest sang.

Scott wore a light tan jacket and trousers. Above his pale yellow sport shirt, his skin appeared very tan. She giggled, "You look like an ice cream cone."

"Thanks a lot. I guess you want to take a bite out of me." He pulled her closer and whispered in her ear, "I've got the prettiest gal here."

In their small space on the floor, Laura nestled in Scott's arms. It did not bother her that he was not able to dance as vigorously as other men. When he held her, they moved their bodies to the rhythm of the romantic song. Two couples they knew danced by. "I think everyone in San Jose's here," Scott said as he swung her in a circle.

The huge auditorium was stifling. Laura looked flushed. "After Dick Haymes sings one more time, let's go get a beer. I'm too warm. You'd think they would have fans to blow this hot air out of here."

The band started to play "One O'clock Jump." Scott led her out of the auditorium into the wide hall and crowded bar, where beer was served. Scott gave the order and then he heard a familiar voice say hi. The voice belonged to Bill Ralston, a neighborhood rancher and an old friend.

"Great band, great crowd," he said, his words slurred. He had his arm around a pretty brunette. "Laura," he bragged, "this is Alice. Alice is taking care of me."

Alice grinned. "I think you're doing a grand job of lying," she said. "Long time no see."

Scott smiled at Alice. "Seems that way, doesn't it? Bill, you told me last week you would be in the army in two days."

"That's right," he hiccuped, "I brought my girl to hear Harry James play the trumpet." He tried to bow to her and stumbled, almost falling.

Alice said, "Bill will be on his way to camp in the morning. I'll see to that."

Laura admired Bill. He had enlisted though he could have gotten a deferment from the service. His family owned acres and acres of crops and farmland south of San Jose.

Bill said, "Hey, I hear Dick Haymes and Helen Forrest singing."

The foursome moved toward the doors of the auditorium. Scott said, "Look at that crowd."

"You look," Laura said. "I can't see anything."

They stood still and listened. Dick Haymes and Helen Forrest were singing "It Had to Be You." The crowd was noisy and they couldn't hear his words.

Scott whispered in her ear, "Honey, let's leave. We have so little time together." She nodded. Scott tapped his friends on the shoulder and waved good-bye.

Scott drove Laura's blue convertible with the top down. He headed for the Circle in the east hills above San Jose. Laura said, "This air feels delicious."

They reached their favorite area to park under the trees, a site that overlooked the San Jose valley. Before the war, the valley sparkled with lights. Now the distant bay, lit only by a quarter moon, stretched in darkness to San Francisco.

Scott pulled Laura over next to him. "I know you have something on your mind. Out with it." His arms around her, he waited.

Laura silently crossed her fingers. "Scott, you know I love you with all my heart, and we agreed to talk over everything."

"Yes, I know, go on."

"Soon, I'll be at county hospital, and the year after that I'll graduate as a nurse. I want to be involved with the war. I've been thinking I might go to San Francisco and be a nurse on a hospital ship, just like the one Phillip is on."

"What made you change your mind?"

"Well, you're working all the time. Like you said, we don't see each other much anymore. Aren't you planning on leaving here and going to Watsonville to start you own business?" She looked at his handsome face in the half-light. She hoped her words would make him realize how negelected she felt.

"That's going to change. I have to stop working every night at the cannery for a while. We're too busy on the ranch. After the product is changed at the cannery, I hope I can go back there to learn all I can. I don't want to miss the opportunity. It's high time we get started on our project for the Watsonville frozen food plant before some jay bob beats us to it.

"You're right about Ron and me. We must find a shed in Watsonville and start building our own equipment. I don't feel good when you talk about leaving, especially with a war going on. You're talking about two years away from now, anyway. We don't know how long this war will last. Laura, I have a busy time ahead. If I'm going to make the business a success. I'll always want you beside me. Let's not talk about it anymore."

Alone on the hill, the dark gave them the privacy they needed. Laura felt his hand move across her breast and gently knead it. His lips, soft and warm, tugged at the corner of her lips. As she yielded to him, he slowly began to push her lips open and thrust his tongue into her mouth. Laura ardently returned his kisses. His hands moved down across her, slowly moving her dress up over her thighs. Caressing her, he unzipped her dress, which fell away from her body. A fragrance of perfume rose from her. He reached his hand up her back, unhooked her brassiere, and released her full breasts. He bowed his head and searched for the crests with his tongue; her nipples were hard. Slowly he sucked them. Laura moaned. He held her with one hand and with the other caressed her parted thighs, the top of her mound, and pushed her panties aside. He found the entrance to her sex. She felt him begin to gently massage her, waiting for her spasm. When the pleasure flooded her and was gradually over, she reached for him.

She whispered, "Hold me. I love you so, darling. I'll always love you."

Each time they made love, he took the time to satisfy her. When they first began to make love, Laura felt guilty about him holding back, but the excitement and passion he brought to the very core of her being made her helpless to stop him.

He held her, their bodies warm against each other. "We've gone this long. A promise is a promise, but it isn't easy."

Scott kissed the tip of her ear lobe. He heard himself whisper, "I guarantee you won't be leaving on any hospital ship."

CHAPTER 33

❀

Carmel felt San Francisco in the summer wasn't much to shout about. She found the days bleak with fog. In case she forgot, the continual bellow from the foghorns was sure to remind her. Having grown up in the Santa Clara Valley with a profusion of flowers and sunshine, she realized she had been taking glorious weather for granted. Carmel had forgotten what every native knew. When the valley temperatures in California rose and crossed the mountains to the ocean, seacoast cities remained overcast and foggy, leaving the nights chilly.

She sat at Aunt Lydia's piano trying to concentrate on a new song, "I Cover the Waterfront." The words wouldn't stay in her mind. No matter how many times she played it, nothing stuck. She tapped her foot and tried to feel the rhythm of the music. It was hopeless. She closed the lid and rose from the piano.

She had stopped thinking it might be Caesar each time the phone rang. He hadn't called, and she hoped he had lost interest in her. Discouraged, she walked to the window and looked out onto the gray day. Her angora sweater and wool dress didn't help. She felt cold. The fog was thick and close to the ground. The pink, red, and white azaleas lining the walkway beside the house were almost hidden.

Making love to Phillip had been what she wanted most, but now she felt she had not handled their evening well. What must he have thought when he saw her at the Palace Hotel with her blouse ripped open, her breasts exposed. She shook her head. She had been heedless to be so willing.

She leaned her chin on the cold windowpane. Fog from her breath obliterated the view. She heard distant horns across the bay and felt the damp seeping around the windows. Her spirits sank even lower. The waiting to hear had become unbearable. She decided to call Laura and find out something, any-thing, about Phillip.

Laura answered the phone.

"Can you come to the city this week and visit?" Carmel asked.

"I would love to come, but school keeps me busy, and Mother needs me. She hasn't been at all well. I'm really sorry; I can't come up. How are you? Scott says you're singing in some glamorous places."

"Yes, I guess you could call them glamorous. It's usually for an officer's dance in one of the hotels. I have to be sure I keep up with current songs."

"Have you met anyone interesting?"

"Jerry, the piano player, has taken me out once." She couldn't wait much longer. "How's Phillip?"

"He seems to be fine."

Carmel felt like strangling her friend. Why didn't she volunteer any infor-mation? "Where is he?"

"Just what he told us before he left. He's on a hospital ship, the *Solace*. I don't know where."

Carmel felt there was nothing more to say. "I hope your mom's better. Come and see me when you can." She hung up.

How could she bear the long days that stretched ahead of her? It would be weeks, maybe months, before she would see Phillip again. She ached to see him, to hear his voice. Why, oh why, had he left and not called when he said he would? She wanted to look into his black eyes, to reach out and feel his arms around her, the softness of his lips.

What do you do when you love someone so? My feelings are like geysers. They keep spouting up like Old Faithful. How do you stop them? If you try to crush them, they spread like molasses and creep into your heart and body. The tears, the helplessness, and the emptiness are still there.

Uncle Russell spoke from the doorway. "It's dark in here," he said, flipping the wall switch.

Carmel forced a smile. She knew her false smile didn't fool Uncle Russell.

"Lydia tells me you're singing in the hotels."

"That's true. It's not a steady job, however." Carmel sat on the couch by the window.

Lydia came into the room wearing a bright green dress. She immediately started to pull the blackout curtains across the large windows.

"Auntie, let me do this room." Carmel went to a window and began to pull the drapes.

"Thank you. I'll finish the other rooms." Lydia left the room.

"Lydia and I are having martinis. Would you like one?"

"Yes, I would, Uncle."

Lydia came back into the room and sat down beside Carmel. Heidi and Hilda followed her yapping and sliding through the doorway.

Russell observed. "I swear this is their favorite time of day, racing Lydia to each room while she closes the heavy curtains."

Seeing that the three adults settled, the dogs stretched out beside Lydia's feet. Russell handed each lady an icy martini. "Well. I hear you practicing. You sound great."

"I love your martini, Uncle. I know it's the best in San Francisco."

"Thank you."

"Actually, Jerry says if I'm to get anywhere, I have to make a recording."

Lydia asked, "How is that done?"

"Sing with a name band in order to make a successful record. But most of the big bands are on the road."

"And?" Russell waited.

"I don't want to leave San Francisco. I want to be able to go home once in a while. My father would have a fit if I went on the road. Uncle, where are they fighting in the Pacific?" That's where the *Solace* would be, or close to it.

Russell crossed the room to a large world globe on a stand. "Ladies, come here and I'll show you." He twirled the globe around and pointed. "To help you understand, most people in these United States don't know where Hawaii is—here." He pointed to the Hawaiian Islands. "That's where your brother Grant is, Carmel, here in Honolulu. This whole area is called the Coral Sea." He ran his hand across a wide expanse of ocean. "A big battle was fought there in May. We lost a carrier, the *Lexington*, but the Japs lost more than we did. The battle was fought off the decks of carriers. The big guns weren't even fired, or so I understand. Across from these waters is Midway on the edge of the Coral Sea." He pointed a finger at the tiny speck. Lydia and Carmel leaned over the globe to look at the speck.

I'll never know, Carmel thought, where Phillip's ship is.

Russell continued, "It was a crucial battle because Midway is so close to Australia. If we had lost, the Japs could have easily moved on to Australia. Actually, the papers don't tell us much. We know we lost the *Yorktown*. The fighting lasted three days. Now we're fighting in the Solomons. Those Japs are tough little buggers; they would rather commit suicide than give up. The marines are fighting somewhere around here." He pointed to Tulagi.

Lydia asked, "Is that near where the ship the Sullivan boys were on sunk?"

"We aren't told that, Lydia. That's not going to happen again. The navy will make it official that only one member of a family is on any ship."

"What are you saying?" Carmel asked.

Lydia answered. "Five brothers from the Sullivan family were on one ship and it sank."

Carmel shook her head. "How awful for their family," she said.

Russell refreshed the drinks.

Lydia said, "I know you're upset about General MacArthur leaving the Philippines and General Wainwright's surrender."

"It'll be a long time before we have official word on how many Americans died in Bataan, The Japanese enforced a sixty-mile death march. With the Russians, the Japanese, and Nazis fighting, the losses in Europe mean a third of the world is at war. I believe we can stop worrying about the Japs coming to these shores. At least, they won't arrive by plane."

"Everyone says the war will be over in a year," Lydia said, hoping to sound cheerful.

"Good, heavens," Russell protested. "That was repeated about the American Civil War and World War I."

The thought occurred to Carmel that Russell might resent being left out of the war. "You're busy, aren't you, Uncle?"

"Busier than a cross-eyed rat watching two rat holes," he laughed.

"Oh, Russell, you say the corniest things. Dinner smells about ready; we're having sweet potatoes and apple pie." Lydia left the room in a flash of green silk, the dogs instantly at her heels."

Russell's eyes twinkled. "Her nose is so good she could be a bloodhound if she could run fast enough."

"Thanks for trying to cheer me up. Please don't try too hard."

Later, that evening in bed, she thought about facing day after day of not knowing and decided maybe her aunt was right. Even though she had heard the rules were stringent, she would volunteer time to the Stage Door Canteen. Carmel had been asked to sing for the patients in the local hospitals—now she would accept. She intended to keep herself as occupied as possible. If Caesar called, she would be unavailable.

Lydia and Carmel were home when the large trunk arrived, addressed to Carmel. Madison helped the driver carry the trunk into the living room. Carmel stared at the battered trunk. "I can't imagine why my father would send me this old thing."

"I agree. My brother does some strange things. Do you have a key?" asked Lydia.

"Yes, Dad mailed a key to me several days ago. I'll get it." She disappeared upstairs. Back in minutes, she said, "I don't think it's anything bad." She knelt down by the trunk to insert the key in the lock, snapped the lock open, and lifted the lid.

Both women peered into the trunk. It was full to the top, and there was a great amount of tissue paper. A faint aroma of perfume rose from the trunk. Somehow, it seemed familiar to Carmel, but she couldn't place it.

She reached into the trunk and lifted off the tissue paper, "Oh, my, Auntie, look at this." She lifted out a red dress of the softest chiffon, a voluminous skirt, and a bodice covered with tiny sparkling beads.

Lydia took the dress from Carmel. "My dear, this name tag is Mainbocher. What about this dress?" With her free hand, she lifted the next garment from the trunk, a black taffeta with tiny jet beads around the neck. "This tag says Dior. Oh, here's your note." She handed Carmel an envelope.

Carmel sank onto her knees, pulling the letter out of its envelope. She recognized her father's clear handwriting. "It's from Dad." She began to read,

> "Daughter, here are dresses and a cape of your Mother's. She went on a shopping spree when we were in Paris. You look about the same size as your mother. I think you can use them now. Love, Dad."

"Oh, Auntie." She let out a hoot. "Can I *ever*."

"Carmel, they are all *haute couture*."

Carmel stood and held a full-length peach georgette against her body, kicking her feet out to make the yards of material swirl about her. "Oh … oh! This is glorious. I checked the label—Givenchy—and cut low in the back, and look at this darling flowered bow at the waist."

The contents of the trunk included a black crepe skirt with a heavily embroidered bolero jacket in bright colors by Dior. Also, a green wool cape lined with duchesse satin to be worn with a dark green bustier and a matching silk evening skirt, created by Schiaparelli.

In particular, a Chanel beige silk chiffon skirt and hand-embroidered sequin top delighted Carmel. "I must call my father. What grand taste my mother had." She rushed from the room, leaving Lydia on the floor.

CHAPTER 34

With the arrival of an early fall, Carmel agreed autumn was the season when San Francisco natives had reason to brag. The crystal-clear air from the sea swept across the bay and the days were full of warm sunshine. Flowerbeds filled the yards with color: borders of pink and white impatiens; cyclamens; blood red and palest pink flowering perennials of pink buckwheat and blue *Ceanothus.* She stared out of her open bedroom window at the view and felt that with a single stretch of the arms her fingertips could reach the sparkling sea and the clear sky. Carmel's resolve to keep busy started on such a September morning.

When Lydia appeared, Carmel had finished breakfast. Wearing her usual worn slacks and sweater to work in the garden, Lydia carried her garden basket of seeds and small gardening tools for her Victory garden.

Lydia said, "My, my, I just spoke to your father on the phone. Since the Japanese have been put into those camps, their gardens are dying. Some of their homes have been vandalized. I don't understand people sometimes. How can civilized people rob each other? But then I've always known I'd make a lousy judge. I could never put anyone behind the awful high fences that enclose those camps."

"I remember how hard Mr. Koto worked, helping Dad make things grow. Now I hear they live on barren ground," Carmel told her.

Russell walked into the room. "I cannot believe this conversation. Have you forgotten how many boys lie at the bottom of the *Arizona* at Pearl Harbor? Did you know a Japanese sub came into San Diego Harbor last week? We don't know how many American Japanese have been spies, relaying plans of munitions and oil fields to Japan. I don't want to ever hear anyone defending the

Japanese in this house—ever!" He took the newspaper on the table and stomped out of the room.

Lydia sputtered. "Well, well, he does carry on." She started out of the room, then stopped. "You're up early. What do you plan today?"

"I've volunteered to sing at Letterman Hospital for the patients this afternoon. Jerry's going with me to play the piano."

"I'm proud of you, my dear."

"Thank you, Auntie. I hope the patients like me. We'll see how it goes." She stood. "I'd better get busy. I need to wash my hair."

"Tell me all about it later. I'm behind in my planting. Guess I'll plant radishes, beets, spinach … let's see." She looked down at her Ferry-Morse seed packages. "Every vegetable I've started is in small flats. Vigoro is the greatest fertilizer and really gives a boost to the plants."

Carmel laughed. "Auntie, if you keep this up you'll be able to feed the entire neighborhood."

The young doctor stood in front of the closed double doors leading to the ward. He faced Jerry and Carmel. "Some of these men have lost their arms or legs. Are you sure you want to go into this ward?"

Carmel looked at him with wide gray eyes, bright with curiosity. "You're sure they'll want me to sing."

"Oh, there's no doubt they'll want to hear you, Miss St. John." He pushed open one of the double doors and held it for her.

Carmel looked up at Jerry beside her for support. "He's right. You'll wow them." Jerry winked.

They walked into the ward. Behind them were two orderlies pushing a small piano on wheels. In the long, narrow room there were at least twenty beds occupied with men, a few with their heads wrapped in bandages. Others had legs in traction attached to pulleys above their beds. Some bodies were wrapped entirely in bandage. Nurses in white uniforms stood beside the beds. The room was very still. The smell of antiseptic was strong.

Jerry put a chair in front of the piano. He sat down and looked at her expectantly. "What will it be, kiddo?"

Carmel felt her breath become shallow. She stood in front of men who had given parts of their bodies for their country so she could sleep safe. Awe and shame swept over her.

Jerry started playing softly, encouraging her. "Are you all right?"

Carmel couldn't think of one song to sing. Every song had words referring to something the men could not do. She thought of "I Don't Want to Walk without You." She prayed, God, help me. I don't know what to sing.

She said, "Hi, I'm Carmel St. John and I'm here to sing for you. What do you want to hear?"

Male voices called out, "I'll Be Seeing You," "Honeysuckle Rose," "Back Home Again in Indiana."

Carmel said, "I'm going to start with a great and popular song, 'These Foolish Things Remind Me of You.'"

Carmel sang the haunting words. Her warm and intimate voice flowed out to the heart of each patient. At the end of the first song, only the nurses applauded. Carmel saw tears streaming down the faces of some of the young men. Forgetting the time, and herself, she wanted desperately to make them smile. When she sang "Dixie," she asked them to sing with her. Her urging helped, and the young voices could be heard singing the words. She sang for an hour.

When it was time to leave, the men and doctors invited her to come back.

Later, in the cab Jerry asked her, "Can you do it? Go back and sing for them?"

"Go back? This has been one of the most important days of my life. I think I grew up a little there singing for those young men. I have to go back." She smiled through the tears in her eyes. Jerry squeezed her hand.

Carmel, keeping her promise to keep as busy as possible, went to the Stage Door Canteen on Mason to volunteer her services. She was surprised to see so many women waiting to be interviewed by a large woman seated at a small table.

When it was her turn, she learned the stiff, unbending woman was Mrs. Fiddler, who spoke in a strident voice and to the point. "Miss St. John, we have the cream of San Francisco serving these men in uniform. Ina Clair, a wonderfully talented actress from New York, traveled across the United States to set the rules. They're rigid, and we expect them to be followed. A hostess must wear simple dresses and very little cosmetics. We prefer you use only first names and not arrange dates with the young men. Please do not expect to see them after the evenings are over. You'll be expected to serve coffee, tea, and Cokes. Sometimes you'll serve sandwiches and doughnuts. Any letter writing for the boys is usually offered at the USO, which is on O'Farrell. We have music here for dancing. You may dance when you're asked. We will let you know if we can use you." Her smile was as frigid as her voice.

While Carmel waited to be registered with the Canteen, she saw across the back of the room a bar for serving drinks and sandwiches. Next to it was a small stage. Placed along the edge of a dance floor were small tables and chairs.

Carmel heard a voice say, "Don't let that old bag scare you away."

Carmel turned to see a girl about her own age in a hideous purple dress. The girl smiled at her. "She's practicing. She wishes she was a sergeant in the BAM s." At the question in Carmel's eyes, she said, "That's Broad Ass Marines. I'm Angie McDonald." She put out her hand.

"I'm Carmel St. John." She shook Angie's hand. "I don't think they'll call me."

"Oh, yes they will. Any gal as pretty as you is called. In spite of Fiddlesticks, we do have a lot of fun. Guys drop in from the big bands in town and play for us to dance. Sophie Tucker was here last week. Boy, can she belt them out. The Canteen opens at six o'clock. I have to go home and change. I'm sure I'll see you around."

In spite of what Carmel thought, they called in two days and said she had been accepted. Wednesday would be her evening.

Carmel made an effort to get there early. She wore her flowered yellow jersey and hoped she was dressed simply enough to suit Mrs. Fiddler. She went to the sandwich center to offer her help but found the sandwiches made. Four musicians played on the small stage. She listened to them for a moment and thought they performed well together.

She heard someone say, "It's time to dance." A tall sailor stood looking down at her. With his pointed chin, he reminded her of the tall, thin dancer in a Toulouse-Lautrec painting. He smiled. "Would you dance?"

They whirled away in time to the song "It Had to Be You."

"My name's Walter Peabody. I'm from Virginia."

"I'm Carmel, and I'm from San Francisco."

"You're a good dancer."

"So are you." They both laughed.

"Those are excellent musicians. I play the clarinet."

"Really? I play the piano."

When the music stopped, Carmel said, "Let's find out who they are." She and Walter walked toward the bandstand. The four musicians were from Dick Jergen's band and would play until eight o'clock, when another group would replace them.

Carmel and Walter stopped at a counter to eat a hot dog. Other service men asked Carmel to dance. All the men seemed to be homesick, but they were enthusiastic to have a place to meet and talk to sympathetic listeners. She hadn't danced so much in months. Happily exhausted, she was relieved to go home at ten o'clock.

Caesar, along with two well-dressed men, entered the door of the towering and impressive Victorian on California Street. They were smiling and a little drunk. A petite woman greeted them. She wore a long red velvet dress that revealed her ample breasts and smooth shoulders. Her hair was beautifully styled in the current pageboy fashion.

"Well, look what the night blew in." Her voice was low and husky.

She looked at Caesar and lifted her head for a kiss. "It's been a long time, Caesar."

"Yes, Ivy, it's been a long time," he said, referring to the nights he had spent in Ivy's arms in her spacious bedroom and luxurious bed.

Caesar eyed the large sumptuously, furnished parlor. Seeing it empty, he turned toward the group. "Ivy, this is Dancer and Jake. They're friends of mine, and I'd like you to treat them to some of your special hospitality."

"Evening, gentlemen. How about a little book learning?"

She pulled a silken cord hanging against the wall.

In a moment, five very pretty young ladies walked into the room. They wore hip-length transparent blouses, revealing pink nipples. Large red bows tied under their chins held white bowler hats on the back of their heads. Carrying school slates and pens, they wore high-heeled shoes and nothing else.

The eyes of the two men grew large.

"There's enough for everyone. Take your pick." Ivy laughed and looked at Caesar.

Caesar knew Ivy was feeling frisky. He smiled and shrugged. "I'll stick around. Just bring me a brandy."

In Ivy's apartment Caesar reclined on one of Ivy's huge settees.

"Caesar, your thoughts are elsewhere. What is it?" She stared anxiously at his face and waited for an answer.

He lifted his glass, indicating he wanted more brandy. "It's not you, Ivy. God knows you know how to relax a man. I just need to talk." She added brandy to his glass. He sat and sipped.

Ivy had changed into a peach silk robe and in the soft lights of the room she presented a voluptuous invitation. She sat down on the chair opposite him. A wise smile slid over her face. "It's a woman. I knew it. Caesar, you're the guy no woman can get. Who is it?"

"No one you know. She's from an old family in San Jose. I'm not sure why she's even in San Francisco."

"What does she do?"

"She sings and works here in the city. God, she's driving me nuts. I want to take her to dinner; I can't figure how to do it. She'll refuse any offer I come up with."

"Does she know about Marlena?"

"I guess she knows I see Marlena once in a while."

"Once in a while. Ha! I think you kid yourself." Ivy studied his handsome face for a minute. She cared for the big guy.

She finally said, "Stop thinking about the fact you can't see her. Act as if you've solved the problem and *are* seeing her."

"What do you mean? I don't get it."

"Where does she sing?"

"Carmel used to sing at the Chez Paree, but she didn't belong there. I ran into her and gave her a ride home. She told me she works for casuals." Caesar sat quietly for a moment and then smiled at Ivy. "Okay, I gotcha."

"Yes, you dummy. Haven't you got a birthday coming up? Use your head. Make her obligated to you. You'll have your dinner date if that's what you really want."

Caesar put down his empty brandy glass on the table and stood. "Guess I needed to clear my head. I don't think straight about this woman."

"Are you leaving? I thought maybe …" She stood. When Caesar first started making love to her, he had been the only man in her bed, but that was a long time ago.

"No, Ivy, you have become my friend, and I have to start planning my birthday party, right?" He gave her a hug and a pat on her backside. He reached inside his coat breast pocket, brought out an envelope, and handed it to her." This should take care of the boys. Thanks for the beautiful shoulder." He doffed his hat and went out into the cold night.

CHAPTER 35

On a gray November day in August 1942, the *Solace*, anchored, rolled on the long swells. The heavy steel net surrounding the ship had been dropped into the sea.

A familiar call came over the loud speaker. "Stretcher bearers lay aft to the quarterdeck."

Phillip had learned of the savage campaign for the Solomons, which began in August 1942 on the islands of Tulagi and Guadalcanal. The marines going ashore were under fire. In the beginning, they were without air cover or naval protection. The Japanese, entrenched in the hills above the valley of jungles, fought with determination to secure Guadalcanal and its airstrip. It was their stepping-stone to Australia.

Phillip climbed on deck to watch the small boats come alongside carrying casualties from Guadalcanal. Nickers joined him at the rail. "The rumor is they're throwing the book at us this time. These casualties are coming from flat tops, air battles, *and* the jungle."

"Thank God the water's calm," Phillip said. "It's rough as hell on the injured when the small boats bang against the sides of the ship."

The first boat was loaded with marines; the bandages covering their heads and bodies were blood soaked.

Phillip said, "Let's shove off." Both men headed for the operating area.

He was proud of the way the medical staff worked. Speed was essential in getting the men aboard and classified. The men were losing blood. Corpsmen knew the wounds from bullets and shrapnel caused fractured jaws, paralysis, and sometimes blindness. This necessitated X-ray immediately. Bullets in the abdomen required instant surgery to stop the bleeding; those patients were sent to Phillip and other surgeons. Orthopedic surgeons received the patients with broken bones. Twelve auxiliary army nurses had come aboard in Auckland to assist in treatments that included removing shrapnel and stitching wounds. Some burned men were barely recognizable; they bit their lips not to cry out from the excruciating pain.

Phillip noted that the two operating rooms had filled in record time. The stench of body dry rot was overwhelming. From constant heat, humidity, and sweating, a fungus grew that left sores on the legs and under armpits. It caused unbearable and continual itching both day and night. The Atabrine, taken daily, yellowed the skin but kept the men from getting malaria.

Phillip knew the men would die if the bleeding couldn't be stopped. Chopping off legs and arms was now routine, but he would never get used to it. He didn't like to dwell on the future of these brave young men, who were now without arms or legs. Phillip felt for a pulse as he ran his hand over a young marine's leg. The toe was black. The leg would have to come off.

The marine, groggy with anesthetic, mumbled, "Don't cut me, Doc. My leg don't hurt."

Phillip dreaded when a young man needed immediate surgery. He wished there was time to wait before the operation. By then, the patient would be in such pain he would demand Phillip remove the leg. Later, many patients blamed the doctor, never convinced the amputation saved their lives.

The oxygen mask was placed on the young man's face. Phillip received the nod from the anesthetist. He cut through the man's flesh. An hour later, with surgery over, the wound was generously sprinkled with sulfa and the patient was moved to recovery.

Phillip turned to the next patient, a man with maggots burrowed into his scalp. He ordered his head shaved and sent him to a surgeon to be inspected for brain damage.

Molly stood beside Phillip through the long hours of surgery. She wiped the moisture from his forehead in the stifling room and put instruments into his gloved hand.

For twelve hours, they continued their backbreaking schedule until they had treated all the patients. When the weary staff met in mess for a late supper, Phillip asked Captain Pearlman, "How many patients came aboard today?"

Captain Pearlman wiped his mouth with his napkin. "I understand the number is close to five hundred. The grand news is we got them aboard and classified in two hours."

"And I feel like it," Nickers said. "Those twelve nurses from Auckland saved our life." He took a bite of potatoes. "How long are we here? Then where to?"

Phillip said, "Plus they're very hard workers. To answer your questions, we can expect to be here two more days. We need to get as many patients as possible on board before we leave."

The captain agreed. "That's correct. When we're through here, we're sailing on to Auckland. The men not able to return to active duty are being evacuated to the base hospitals. We get these burn victims into the hospital."

Molly joined them. She poured herself a cup of coffee and asked, "Captain Pearlman, aren't they sending out more hospital ships this year?"

He shrugged, "We thought the *Relief*, a new hospital ship, would be heading out to sea before now. There're supposed to be several ships. I hope they won't be a reconverted something or other. We need more hospital facilities on our existing ships. New ships should have the facilities we've never had."

Phillip's back and legs ached from standing long hours at the operating table. The workload could be worse the next day. Gangrene, a deadly infection, was a nightmare that sometimes followed surgery. He forced himself to eat a pork chop, some potatoes, and drink some coffee.

A surgeon must remain detached and impersonal. Otherwise, he might lose his control of the situation. On the other hand, nurses were allowed to murmur comforting words to a young man about to lose an arm or leg. They understood how to ease the pain. Sometimes in the night before the anesthetic produced sleep, Phillip would hear a marine cry out, "Look out. They'll get you! Get down, Nurse! Hurry!" Some mumbled for their mothers.

Finally, many hours later, as Phillip settled into his bunk for the night, he asked, "Will, are you asleep?

His voice heavy with fatigue, he said, "It's your nickel. Shoot."

"I looked in on a Marine, one of the men that I amputated. I'd heard he was a dancer and won a lot of jitter bug contests. I didn't tell him his other leg had a bullet hole as big as a tennis ball. He asked me if he'd dance again. I said they wouldn't be able to stop him."

"Did he believe you?"

"He has a lot of guts, said he'd be the first one on the dance floor."

Phillip muttered, "Those kids and their fight to live make this never-ending job bearable. What would this war be like if we didn't have penicillin? Now that we've got sulfa, that boy will have a life, one way or another." Once he saw a guy who danced with artificial legs. That was the truth, wasn't it? Or was he dreaming? He closed his eyes and was instantly asleep.

Three evenings later, the *Solace* steamed toward Auckland and the Marine hospital. Phillip stood by the rail, staring at the moisture-ridden clouds pile one upon another. Sunsets always replenished him when he managed to slip away from the wards. He watched the sun begin to sink behind the clouds—the colors of raspberry, pink, and deep purple were outlined by a golden light.

Molly joined him. She looked as weary as he felt. "Looks like the sky's been touched by an angel's wand dipped in gold. It's a religious experience to watch these sunsets," she said.

"You feel that too?"

She nodded. "Makes me think that life is the way it has always been, normal and safe. God is in his heaven and the sun will shine tomorrow. Do you ever worry about our being unprotected, sailing around by ourselves?"

"To be honest with you, Molly, I try not to think about it. Protection would announce we were a combat ship. What could we do about it, anyway?"

The tropic twilight faded fast. They could see the bright full moon rising over the distant water.

"Try to get some shuteye tonight, if you can," Phillip said. "Do you have a bunk?"

"Oh, yes. The rumor is the crew had to give up their bunks, but not mine. At least, not yet," she laughed. "The guys from Guadalcanal have had enough sleeping in a jungle. They wanted to sleep inside."

"I heard the scuttlebutt that many of the guys slept in the trees to get away from the snakes." She shuddered. "How many patients do we have aboard?"

"I think the count is twelve hundred."

"We sure needed those extra nurses. I guess they leave us when we reach Auckland. Actually, I'm grateful as hell there aren't many bodies stacked in the morgue. At least they'll have a decent burial in Tongan."

"Molly, I'm headed below for coffee. I suspect the night will be a long one." In the evening light, he saw the glints of red hair caught under her cap. He thought, What a good-looking gal. She's much too young to carry so much responsibility. She worked long hours, never complained, and was always cheerful. He hoped there was a great guy waiting for her.

Later, as Phillip closed his eyes, the *Solace* steamed through the dark night. Without lights, alone and unescorted toward Auckland. Its human cargo depended on Captain Pearlman, the crew, and God for safe passage.

CHAPTER 36

❀

Phillip stood with Captain Pearlman on the quarterdeck. As the *Solace* approached the Queens Dock at Auckland, the day was bright and sunny. A large crowd, full of admiration and appreciation for the ship and crew, stood respectfully waiting for the ship to dock. The ship carried the twelve hundred casualties from Guadalcanal and the four US cruisers in the battle of the San Juan Islands.

Captain Pearlman confided to Phillip he had received word the crew and staff of the *Solace* were to receive awards. The awards would make a well-earned surprise. After one more trip around the islands, the ship would get underway for Pearl Harbor. There, Admiral Nimitz would present the awards.

He stood by as Captain Pearlman greeted Captain Aston and his delegation from Auckland. Ambulances lined the dock. Although New Zealand soldiers volunteered to be litter bearers, Captain Pearlman learned they lacked experience in handling the sick and wounded, so he declined their offer. The volunteers were thanked, and the trained, weary personnel aboard ship carried out the long and arduous task.

Phillip joined Lucille and Nickers on the deck. They stood in silence watching corpsmen and crew carry the patients from the ship.

Finally, the evacuation was over. On the way to their separate quarters, Phillip said, "I heard there was a trout farm on the shore. Twenty-four-inch rainbow trout, weighing twelve pounds, swimming about in a tank! I planned on catching enough fresh fish to have the cook prepare our dinner." He chuckled.

Lucille laughed. "At least you're optimistic. Did you forget? We can only disembark in big cities. No liberty or R&R except on the islands."

"I doubt he forgot," Nickers added. "Too bad his fishing will have to wait. I heard from my dad the American public doesn't know where we are. That the kids in school are learning about the battles, where we're fighting, and educating their parents."

"I'm not surprised," Lucille said. "I didn't have any idea where Guadalcanal was before I started this part of my life. Good for the kids."

"We better get some rest; we're to leave tomorrow. The plans are to shuttle for the next few months between Australia, New Caledonia, the New Hebrides, *and* the Fiji Islands."

As darkness came on, the *Solace* steamed toward Esprito Santo. The night air felt humid. Calm water made for a comfortable roll of the ship. Phillip walked into a ward. He joined Molly, checking on a young ensign who had spent six hours in the water fighting off a shark.

Anxiety consumed the young man. "I'll never forget the feel of shark's teeth. I knew he hit me, but I didn't know how many times."

Phillip saw the young man's legs and arms were badly lacerated, covered with bruise marks. "We'll get you all cleaned up. After some rest and sleep, you'll begin to forget."

"You don't understand!" the ensign screamed. "I hung on to an empty oil can in the water for hours—they said six goddamn hours. The shark circled and struck me about every fifteen minutes. I had nothing but my legs and arms to hit back. I aimed for his nose."

Phillip took the prepared needle from Molly and gave the ensign his injection. The medicine worked immediately. The ensign screams stopped. He muttered and then became quiet.

Molly tucked the sheet up around the young man and shut off the lamp. "They have such mental stress, exhaustion, and they're so young." They walked slowly from the ward.

Molly joined Lucille in her quarters. "I thought you'd be in bed by now. It's nearly midnight."

"I'm going. I want to finish a letter before I quit for the night." As Molly stood up, sounds of rupturing steel followed by a popping noise filled the room. Lucille saw Molly put her hand to her forehead, covering her face. Blood filled Molly's fingers as she slumped to the floor.

Lucille leaned over Molly's body. "Dear God." She heard men yelling and running. The lights flickered and went out. She groped for a flashlight in the net hanging over her bunk. The auxiliary battery lights flashed on. She turned to her friend still on the floor. "Molly."

Another loud concussion hit the ship. The *Solace* shuddered. Lucille was knocked off her feet. She struggled to stand as she heard over the loudspeakers, "Break out the life jackets."

She staggered as she pulled open the door, hearing someone say, "Get those damn distinguishing lights on those crosses." Another blast rocked the ship. There was the rat-a-tat sound of machine-gun fire.

Lucille called, "Oh, help me somebody! Molly's bleeding to death!"

In the murky light, a corpsman appeared and yelled, "Where is she?" He found Molly and picked her up her. "Gang way. I'll get her to surgery." He disappeared down the passageway.

Lucille, frantic and desperate, followed the corpsman to operating quarters. Molly's small unconscious body was placed on the table. Lucille wiped the blood from Molly's face.

She asked, "Where is Phillip? We've got to get Phillip. There may be a bullet in her head."

Phillip entered the ward with Captain Pearlman. Captain Pearlman said, "We have turned on our distinguishing lights. They have ceased firing." He paused, seeing Molly. "Phillip, what have we here? My God, it's Molly."

Phillip leaned over her. "She's got a nasty wound." He glanced at Lucille, who was covered with Molly's blood, and asked, "Are you all right?"

Lucille nodded.

Phillip continued to exam Molly. He thought, How could this have happened? He had just left her. Her life was fast slipping away. He shined the light in her eyes. The pupils did not react. Molly, of all the personnel on the ship, was the best. Now she was dying. He realized he couldn't help her.

Captain Pearlman stared at the straight line on the cardiac monitor. He felt for her pulse, "Phillip, she's gone." He stood by the surgical table. "Too, bad, she was tops. We needed her so badly."

Phillip told a corpsman to take her body to the morgue.

Lucille mopped at her tears. "This is more than I can bear. I've known Molly all my life. How can I be in this world without my friend?"

A voice blared, "Keep on your life jackets."

Phillip placed his hand on her shoulder. "Go and get your life jacket. I'll come and give you a shot. You need some rest." Then he and Captain Pearlman made their way to the captain's quarters.

The upper deck lights had been turned on. The *Solace*'s red crosses on the stack were illuminated by powerful floodlights. Captain Pearlman issued orders for Bosun Berg to report the extent of damages. Berg appeared in the

Captain's quarters in his white tee shirt and boxer shorts. Berg's arms hung too long for his short body and his legs were bowed like a small gorilla's. He moved over the ship swiftly. He knew what was going on all the time in every department, including surgery.

"Do we know who fired on us?"

"Yes, Captain. Uh … we do, sir, one of ours."

Captain Pearlman was silent for a moment. "Berg, give me the damage report."

"The damage was on the bow, just above the water line. They fired at least fifty rounds before they stopped. The first round went through the nurses' quarters. Shrapnel penetrated the metal bulkhead and Nurse Molly Day received the brunt of it. The rest of the shrapnel banged around but didn't do enough damage to prevent us from normal procedure. We are seaworthy. Damn good thing our lights came on."

Captain Pearlman dismissed the bosun. Berg saluted and left.

Phillip's thoughts were of Molly. He didn't speak as Captain Pearlman took a cigarette from his pack, lit it with his Zippo lighter, and walked down the passageway. Molly's body had been put into a bag, placed in a basket, and carried to the morgue to await burial. Phillip checked on Lucille; he gave her a sleeping potion and sent her to bed. Then he joined Nickers and the others in the wardroom. No one wanted to go to bed. They talked about Molly and the *Solace*, lit up like Broadway at Christmas.

The experienced, seaworthy crew objected to the ship being lighted up. They were conditioned to believe a U-boat could sight them from miles away. On the other hand, when their own men fired on them because they could not see those red crosses, it was a strong argument for the lights. This subject had been the topic of long discussions by the ship's personnel.

Phillip and Nickers returned to mess for coffee. Nickers filled Phillip's cup, one for himself, and sat down on a bench. He said, "What a senseless war! Losing our best people, and for what? The ones that took the best care of those needing care the most get hit. Molly never complained, no matter how weary she was. She was a super gal. Lucille is brokenhearted."

Phillip stared at his coffee. "We just lost someone incredible; it's difficult to know the reason why. The firing was from one of our ships, and it didn't need to happen if the lights had been on. We're not in convoy and have no escort. We're not in conflict and carry no artillery. Now, I suppose we're a target for any U-boat."

Phillip stood and yawned. "Old chap, I'm hitting the sack. I don't think we can solve anything further tonight. Just sweat it out."

In his bunk, Phillip thought about the risks the ship was taking and the strain on the personnel. He thought about Molly and how her family would feel at the news of her death. He had become accustomed to her standing beside him in surgery. She had been one of the best surgical nurses in his professional life. He would miss seeing her ready smile and red hair under her nurse's cap. If only he had been able to stop the bleeding. He guessed it was a miracle that she was the only casualty.

Then, as sleep drifted closer, he saw Carmel staring at him. He saw her dark hair, eyes sparkling, full of mischief, and he thought he could hear her sing to him. The song was unfamiliar. He wondered if she was seeing anyone. He mumbled, "Too good looking not to."

CHAPTER 37

As time passed, Carmel worked three to four nights a week. Local bandleaders heard about the engaging singer, who was always on time and knew the current songs. She felt it was important to learn as soon as possible the new songs about the war. Some of the most popular were "This Is the Army, Mr. Jones," "You'd Be So Nice to Come Home To," "White Christmas," and "That Old Black Magic."

On a cold and wet December afternoon, Carmel arrived at the hospital, where Jerry waited for her. Doctor Anderson, in charge of the amputees, took her aside.

"Miss St. John, we appreciate you coming every week. I've already spoken to Jerry, and he understands this ward is crucial. These men are trying to face the fact parts of their bodies are missing. Most have lost much blood. They lie here in a state of depression." He saw Carmel's anxious look and hesitated. "Some have heard you sing before and have asked for you again. What I'm sayin' is … please try to sing as many happy songs as you know. It'll mean a lot to us all."

"All right, Doctor. I'll do my best."

Carmel tried, but after she sang "On the Sunny Side of the Street," she felt helpless. It seemed all the songs were overflowing with sad memories. A young, handsome patient called Georgia had been there since Carmel first came to the hospital. He had no arms. He made his usual request. She sang the song "Georgia on My Mind," hoping to make him smile. The expression in his eyes told her he was far away, recalling some memory. She doubted it brought him contentment.

Carmel found it impossible to ignore their requests of sentimental songs about girls they left at home and the promise they would see them again. After singing, "I'll Be Seeing You," she felt tears on her cheeks. Georgia was sobbing and unable to wipe away his tears. Other men wept quietly.

Outside the ward, she leaned on Jerry's shoulder. "I certainly failed everybody today."

Doctor Anderson heard her words. "Maybe I shouldn't have told you about the men, but think about it this way, Carmel. Those tears released a lot of pain. Some of the men will sleep better tonight, I promise you."

Carmel said defensively, "I can't stand to see grown men cry."

In the taxi, she said to Jerry, "I'm going to the Canteen tonight. I want to see some healthy, whole American men."

That evening at the Canteen she was asked to sing with the musicians sitting in from Carl Ravazza's band. This time she enjoyed singing the crowd's requests. Her spirits lifted, although the afternoon remained heavy in her thoughts. She couldn't help comparing the joy of seeing whole men before her to the sadness and pain of the afternoon of broken men.

When she told Jerry how she felt, he said, "Don't torture yourself. You're doing your part for the war effort, giving of yourself the best way you can."

In the middle of December she received a telephone call from John Canepa. "Miss St. John, I would like you to work for me December 21. It's a birthday for someone special. Would you be available?"

Would I? Carmel thought. John Canepa was a very popular bandleader. She tried not to show too much excitement. "I'm checking my calendar, Mr. Canepa." Silently she mouthed, "Wow." Then she said, "Yes, sir, I'm free."

"Good. We're playing at the Palace Hotel in the Gold Ballroom. A very big crowd. Do you know any Italian songs?"

"I can sing '*Vieni Su*' in Italian."

John chuckled, "Okay, we'll give it a try. See you at eight sharp. Be on time."

After Carmel hung up, she was puzzled. Why had he called her? He already had a popular vocalist. However, she was glad he had.

Carmel arrived before eight o'clock at the resplendent Gold Ballroom in the Palace Hotel. She had not sung there since her awful encounter with the Marines. She wondered how she would feel to enter the ballroom. She admonished herself to tend to business and pushed back the heartbreaking memories of Phillip. The band was setting up at the far end of the room. She walked over to the tall, impressive man in a tuxedo standing in front of the musicians.

"Mr. Canepa, I'm Carmel."

"Well, young lady, glad you're on time. Your gown's perfect."

"Thank you." Carmel wore one of the dresses her father had sent her, Dior's black silk taffeta. Her skin glowed against the low neckline trimmed in black jet beads. Her aunt's borrowed ruby earrings sparkled in her ears.

The expression in Mr. Canepa's eyes was warm and his smile friendly. She relaxed. He was very handsome. The women, she thought, must be nuts about him.

John said, "As soon as you grab a minute with Jimmy, the piano player, tell him your selections and we'll get the ball rolling."

She greeted Jimmy and they quickly set her keys. Once seated on her chair by the piano, she took time to look around the room. A huge Christmas tree twinkled with bright lights, and decorations touched the ceiling of the ballroom. At least ten large tables edged the dance floor, covered with red and green tablecloths. Each one could easily seat twenty people. Centerpieces of tinsel, colored balls, and candles looked festive. Waiters in red coats rushed around finishing the place settings. Just who was celebrating a birthday? And before the evening was over, she planned to find out where John's vocalist had disappeared and why. Maybe she would be asked to return for another engagement.

People arrived amidst happy shouting of greetings and laughter at seeing old friends. The men were in tuxedos, and the women wore long, glittering Christmas dresses. Carmel thought the evening promised to be one of the best holiday parties she had sung for. The seventeen-piece band opened with "Oh Johnny, Oh Johnny, Oh!" The musicians were exceptionally good; the band had rhythm and a great beat. Carmel looked forward to singing. Couples had begun to dance and passed before her on the shining floor.

Then she saw him. Caesar, the man with the wicked eyes. She stumbled over her lyrics but recovered her composure and finished the jump tune. She intended to ignore him.

Caesar saw Carmel at the same time. He watched her for a minute. People drew his attention away. "Happy birthday, old boy," they said, shaking his hand.

He laughed, calling loudly, "Thank you, thank you. Hold on. I'm not thirty-nine until mid-night!" More guests surrounded him to shake hands.

Marlena waited beside him, ravishing in red silk, her blonde hair piled on top of her head. Diamond earrings glistened in her ears.

Carmel heard Marlena shout above the commotion, "Let's sit, Caesar, before they knock us down."

They were led to the main table, where four couples joined them. During the break Jimmy, the piano player pointed out Caesar's lawyer, Tom Courtney, with his wife, Vivian, and two county supervisors, Hal Kelly and Ken Bartlett. He told her both men supposedly kept their fingers dipped into the big pie known as the black market in San Francisco. Carmel saw their wives eyeing Marlena's diamonds and the neckline of her red dress, revealing a large amount of bosom. Finally, there was Judge Catlett with his wife, Gloria. An old timer, it was rumored he knew where the skeletons were buried of more than one prominent man.

Jimmy said, "Looks like Caesar Almato has them all here to celebrate his birthday." He glanced around the room. "Even Old San Francisco is here. There's a police captain, politicians, bureaucrats, union officials, and restaurant owners. It doesn't look like he missed anyone."

Carmel knew the war kept food supplies limited and rationed, but not at this party. A single table offered a choice of fresh prawns, lobster, and oysters in their shells piled high on mounds of ice. Three chefs stood behind tables ready to carve selections of prime rib, ham, and venison. Fresh pastas, light as air, were served with red or white sauces. Waiters brought baskets of San Francisco's sourdough bread. French wines and champagne were poured at each table.

Mesmerized by Caesar's presence, Carmel worked hard to keep him from knowing she watched him. He was indeed a handsome man. When he and Marlena got up to dance, Carmel wasn't surprised at how gracefully he moved on the floor. Once he came close to the bandstand and barely nodded in her direction.

Carmel sang several songs. The noise in the room rose as the evening wore on. The next break, she joined John for coffee in the kitchen.

John said, "Carmel, Mr. Almato requested your presence this evening. He would like you to sing a special happy birthday to him."

Carmel struggled to hide her consternation. "I'm really surprised you asked for me. Mr. Canepa. I know you have a vocalist."

"She couldn't be here tonight. You're doing a great job." He didn't wait for an answer and returned to the ballroom.

Carmel felt uneasy. She had to sing to Caesar alone in front of this whole crowd. Now she knew he had ordered her presence. When the time came, John requested the dancers return to their tables. Lights dimmed and a huge candle-lit cake on a table was rolled in. The band started to play "Happy Birthday."

Carmel managed to stand in the spotlight and sing to Caesar. As he watched her, she felt his pure animal magnetism from across the room. His dark, pulsating energy excited and frightened her. She dared not look into his eyes. She purposely looked over the heads of the people in the room.

Carmel sang the words softly and, as the crowd listened, the song became personal for Caesar. She had not planned it that way and was relieved when the second time around John asked the crowd to sing along with her.

When the evening ended, Carmel felt her singing had touched everyone in the room. But Caesar disturbed her. Because of him she was here, and if John used her often, she'd be indebted to Caesar. It could be an overwhelming debt, impossible to pay.

CHAPTER 38

❀

For two hours, maybe more, Grant rode in a Honolulu police car with Sun Lee, a Chinese police officer. Grant had been riding with Sun Lee for the last few months. Grant's nature did not allow him to abide by rules. Off duty for the evening, he felt restless and bored.

The wheels of the police car screeched suddenly, barely missing a dog in the street. Sun Lee asked, "You be in old Honolulu Sin-A-Lot before seven-thirty curfew?"

"You bet." Grant's expression remained passive. He felt the war held him captive and it was useless to resist. Lately, he had a hard time finding a reason for anything he did. There was no special girl at home. He didn't miss his family. When he did think of them, his father came to mind. He knew his father was disappointed the Spartans hadn't played football in Hawaii.

"I take you. Bettah not let chief catch you," Sun Lee said.

Grant laughed. He had discovered a bar he liked with music and gambling. And he liked the whores in the place. They knew him by name. Sun Lee dropped Grant at the curb in front of the Sin-A-Lot and drove away. Grant walked through the blackout curtain of the club. The bar was full.

A Hawaiian woman, large as a sumo wrestler and wearing a saffron-colored *holoku*, greeted Grant. "You come foah good time? Yoah numbah one."

He gave Big Mama a thumb up. The whores in their bright satin robes fluttered around her mammoth size. They reminded him of brilliant colored butterflies. Two giggling girls joined him. He put an arm around the waist of each and led them across the cavernous room to the bar. Overhead fans, barely turning, supplied little relief against the heat. The few lights in the high ceiling spotlighted several tables surrounded by gamblers.

The smallest girl asked, "You like nookie?" Eyes shiny and black as kona beads looked up at him.

Grant laughed. "I feel lucky, Lia. I think I'll gamble for a while." He signaled Knee-Hi for his usual as well as drinks for the girls. The bartender, whose short arms barely reached across the bar, set a boilermaker in front of Grant and served each girl a Coke. Knee-Hi stood on a box behind the bar.

Grant observed that most of the customers were sailors. They'd be drunk soon and he'd clean up.

He asked to join five players at a table. They made room for him and he slid into a chair.

It was his deal. "We play same rules, aces wild."

At ten thirty, he had been winning steadily for an hour. Grant realized his head was getting fuzzy. He had smoked too many cigarettes and drunk too many boilermakers.

A beefy sailor with a New York accent sitting across from him rose from the table. "Lia," he yelled. "Get your sweet little ass over here. It's my time to screw."

Lia walked over and looked up at him. "You mistake. Time was eight thirty. I have customer."

The sailor slapped her hard across the face. The blow resounded in the room. "You miserable scheming whore. I'm horny *now*."

Grant felt the blood in his body explode through the top of his head. "You sonofabitch." He rose so fast, he lifted the table with him. Chips, glasses of booze, ashtrays filled with cigarette stubs, and cards flew across the room. Girls screamed.

The sailor loomed over him. Grant saw something frightening in the other man's eyes. He had seen rage before, but not this madness. Grant dove at the crazy bastard, his head hitting him in the stomach. He was fast enough to surprise the sailor and knock him off balance. He followed the surprise by slamming a fist into his face, and he heard the sickening sound of bone crushing. Blood spurted over the sailor's face.

Sailors, marines, and locals, surprised at the savagery of the attack, welcomed the excuse to get rid of their frustrations. They joined in the melee and began to pound on each other.

The bloodied sailor picked up a broken beer bottle and waved the jagged edges at Grant. Grant made a miscalculation on the sailor's left fist. His neck snapped as the fist landed hard on his chin. Dizzy from the blow, and knowing the guy was off his rocker, his next punch had to count, but he had to stay away from that bottle. Grant lunged for the sailor, pushing him back, trying to pin his arms to his sides. Someone raised a heavy chair and crashed it onto the sailor's head. The sailor fell to his knees. Grant felt delayed pain in his left cheek. As he sank to the floor, he put his hand to his face. He felt sticky blood.

In the hospital, Chief Kana stood at the bottom of Grant's bed, staring at him. "You feel bad?"

Through blurry eyes, Grant saw him. "I'm okay." His head throbbed. His cheek felt as if a baseball had been shoved into his mouth. It was difficult to speak.

"The doctor said you have eighteen stitches in your cheek, will leave scar." If Chief Kana had any sympathy for him, he kept it hidden. The man's black eyes gleamed like a seals when rising out of the water.

"How did I get here?"

"Big Mama."

Grant tried to remember why he had fought. He didn't care about Lia. Then he remembered the slap. He could not tolerate a woman being hit, whore or no whore.

"Fight numbah three. Always military police come; always shore patrol come. You make trouble, bad temper. Now you make big decision—number one, join the marines; number two, join the marines. Or I lock you up. You trouble. I don't want."

To avoid infection, Grant was to be kept in the hospital two weeks. Then he would be released to Chief Kana.

The chief asked a nurse to bring a mirror to Grant. He looked at his scar and saw that it ran from his left eye to his chin. The sonofabitch had just missed his eye. The cut was an angry red, stitches pulling across his swollen cheek. His skin was purple and black from the bruises. The right side of his face looked normal compared to the hideous left side. Something had happened to his mouth, too. The stitches made his lip lift in a perpetual sneer. He looked like shit.

Heavily bandaged, Grant was finally released to face Chief Kana in his office. The stitches and bandages made it difficult for him to speak. He didn't care what happened to him. He stood silent.

The chief sat behind his desk. There were no smiles, and the chief's message was brief. "You fly stateside Air Transport Command plane. Plenty time to see family. Report in San Diego."

Grant shook the chief's hand and promised he would see his family before his induction into the Marines in San Diego.

Inwardly, he knew he'd return stateside, but he had no intentions of letting anyone he knew see him or his face. Maybe later. Maybe not.

CHAPTER 39

❀

As the Christmas of 1942 approached, Carmel felt as if the whole world was fighting the war. In the windows of many homes hung a square blue satin emblem with one star in the middle. This indicated a soldier from the household fought in the war somewhere in the world. A gold star in the center of a white satin emblem meant he had given his life.

Movie stars were marching off to war. Morale was boosted by the news that Jimmy Stewart registered for the Army Air Force. Clark Gable, the King of Hollywood, joined the Army Air Force after his wife, Carole Lombard, selling US War Bonds died in a plane crash. Bob Hope traveled overseas to camps and bases, taking along famous movie stars to entertain the troops. Betty Grable posed for pictures, showing kids how to wear gas masks. Victor Mature joined the navy, and Tyrone Power became a marine.

A week before Christmas, Carmel sat with her aunt and uncle in the morning room. President Roosevelt had just finished his radio address, which he called his fireside chat, beginning with the words, "My friends ..."

Russell put his newspaper down. "Lydia, if the President told us to be careful of saboteurs and spies, that's exactly what he meant."

"Oh, that's so presumptuous, Russell. Who do I know who could be a spy?"

Russell made an effort to be patient. "According to the newsreel we saw in the theater last week, spies are everywhere, sending coded messages with invisible ink. We should pay attention to what we say when speaking to our neighbors and even the butcher, especially if we know someone who's expected to arrive on a ship."

"It's true," Carmel volunteered. Suddenly, she knew Phillip would never send word; he'd just appear. He could be on his way home right now. He had to return sometime. Her heart leaped at the thought. She didn't dare allow herself to think he might be home for Christmas.

Lydia was saying, "I think it's awful the way women are wearing slacks to work. The first thing you know they'll wear them everywhere. It's *so* unlady-like."

Russell said, "Climbing over steel girders, I think it's a splendid idea for *them*." He grinned. "As for me, I'd rather see them climbing girders in skirts."

"Sometimes, Russell, I wonder why I married you."

Russell chuckled. "I heard you were so determined to get me you would have climbed Mount Everest if I was the prize at the top."

Carmel stifled a smile.

"That's hearsay." Lydia went back to her paper. "Oh, my God, the *Normandy* burned while it was docked in New York. Do you remember that beautiful ship? Russell, we went to France on her."

Russell exclaimed. "That could very well be sabotage."

"Oh, Russell, I suppose you think when the Coconut Grove in Boston burned last week and four hundred people were killed, that was sabotage?"

"For Sam's Hill, Lydia! We're at war. Anything that happens should be questioned."

Lydia ignored her husband. "Russell, I'm trying to buy a war bond every two weeks. They cost $13.75. Do you think that's excessive?"

"Not when they'll mature at twenty-five dollars. Indeed, I do not."

Before she left to spend Christmas in San Jose, she sang two more times with John Canepa's orchestra. John did not refer to his apparently former vocalist. Carmel knew Caesar had something to do with her working for John and avoided the subject. Before she left for Christmas in San Jose, John asked her to sing for a New Year's Eve dance and she accepted.

In San Jose, sudden gusts of winter wind shook the house. The rafters creaked under the strain. Windowpanes rattled. Logs piled high in the large fireplace gave off the scent of burning wood, and the tang of Christmas pines filled the rooms. Red satin ribbons tied around large pots of white and red poinsettias decorated the house.

Carmel, seated at the long dinner table with her father and Scott, thought, This is a magical place. But as much as she loved and missed her home and family, she would miss San Francisco more.

Anna had prepared a Christmas dinner of Carmel's favorite foods. Carmel cut a piece of lamb. "This roast is heavenly, but so much work to prepare."

Andrew said, "You're worth it. Getting you home for Christmas is something to celebrate." His blue eyes twinkled. "Your tangerine silk dress is very becoming. Are you taking care of yourself?"

"Oh, Dad, don't worry about me. I'm fine."

After dinner, they lingered at the table over Anna's famous chocolate cake and coffee. "Have you heard from your brother?" Andrew asked.

"I never hear from him," Carmel answered. "What have you heard?"

Scott pushed a large piece of cake into his mouth. "Nothing. He's not writing."

Carmel said, "There's one thing about our brother: he always lands on his feet, completely innocent and untouched."

Scott laughed. "That's true."

The doorbell rang. Scott rose. "I'll answer it." He limped from the room.

Carmel and her father heard young voices from the front hall.

Scott reappeared, "Dad, did you promise these kids some scrap metal or rubber?"

Two young boys with serious expressions stood beside him inside the doorway.

Andrew got up from his chair said, "I sure did. It's piled out by the terrace." He looked at the boys. "Its pitch dark out here. I thought you were never coming. Here, follow me." He left the room with the young men.

"Dad's constantly gathering all this junk for the war effort," Scott added.

In a few minutes, Andrew returned. "Those kids are making a penny a pound; they're real businessmen." He laughed and sat down at the table. "Have you seen those full-sized cardboard cartoon images of Hitler, Mussolini, and Tojo at the scrap metal depots with gaping holes for mouths? Ugly as sin. Metal is pushed through their mouths, where it's dropped onto piles of scrap." He poured a fresh cup of coffee for himself and asked, "Carmel, how many nights a week are you working?"

"I've been lucky. One of the best bandleaders has begun to call me. Plus other calls probably adds up to five nights a week, always four."

Scott said, "I guess a singer would have to be pretty good to keep getting jobs."

Carmel smiled at her brother. "You have to know your songs and the key you sing in."

"Who does that?" Her father held a cigarette paper in one hand and poured tobacco into it from a small white bag of Bull Durham he kept in his shirt pocket. She had watched this old familiar habit since she was a very little girl.

"Well, Jerry, a piano player and good friend of mine, sets the keys." She thought, Thank goodness, they never found out she sang at the Chez Paree. A strip joint! It would make no difference how famous a celebrity Tempest Storm was. Carmel could well imagine what her father would say.

Her father asked, "Where will this band singing lead you, Carmel?"

"For one thing, the navy thinks I'm special. They asked me to break a bottle of champagne on the bow of a cruiser." She laughed at the prospect.

Scott said, "I like that idea. Hate to see them waste the good bubbly."

"Dad," Carmel said, "something has happened recently in the music world. A man named Petrillo is head of the American Federation of Musicians. They call him Little Caesar."

"Jerry told me this. Petrillo asked a man named Selvin to see if musicians were losing jobs because records were being played on radio and jukeboxes. Selvin investigated and found the opposite to be true. Musicians were getting more jobs than ever. Petrillo ignored the information and instructed radio and jukeboxes not to play their records. Can you imagine? They stopped recording all these great bands in the whole USA." She shook her head.

"What happens to you?" Scott asked.

"Oh, I'll keep working as long as there are dance bands. We're not recording."

"You actually mean there are no more recordings?" Her father's tone indicated his disbelief.

"That's right. I don't know when they'll allow recording again. Singers can record in groups, I guess. As a result, more people are showing up to listen firsthand to their favorite bands. Right now, Sweets, a ballroom in Oakland, is the place the name bands play. It's packed. People come from all over the bay area to listen and dance."

"Well, sis, sounds risky to me, but then you've always loved music. Enjoy it while you can." Scott stood. "I'm going next door to see Laura. Great to have you home. See you in the morning." Scott limped out of the room.

"Tell Laura I'll see her tomorrow." Carmel called. She and Andrew followed him out of the room and started up the stairs. When they reached her door, they stopped.

Andrew hugged his daughter. "My little girl, learning about the big bad world."

"Sometimes I believe you want me to remain at home and not find out what it's all about. I love to see San Francisco's finest turn out for a dinner dance. The women dress in their expensive dresses and jewelry, and the men in their tuxedoes. After all, didn't you take Mother to Paris to buy all those gorgeous clothes, to dress up, and dance all night?"

"Yes, I suppose that's what we did." He looked at her. "You be sure you act like a lady with all that folderol going on."

Carmel crawled into bed. She had brought two new books with her just in case she wasn't sleepy, John Steinbeck's *The Moon Is Down* and *The Company She Keeps*, by Mary McCarthy. She had started to read again, especially on the nights she couldn't sleep, but tonight she was disturbed to think her father called her life *folderol*, as if she was wasting her time.

The day after Christmas was full of warm sunshine. Carmel and Laura wore sweaters and sat outside on the St. John's terrace. They watched a greedy jay strut across the terrace. Carmel laughed. "He's so full of *Pyracantha* berries he'll never get off the ground, let alone fly."

Laura said, "You sure aren't staying here very long."

"I hate to mention it, but Christmas isn't the same without Grant. Besides, I do have a job to return to. Traveling from here to San Francisco isn't what it used to be. The trains are so crowded. There's never a place to sit." Since she had learned nothing new here about Phillip, she might as well return to San Francisco. Compared to San Francisco, San Jose was a sleepy village. "I thought you were coming to the city to see me."

"My nurse's course takes a lot of studying. When you came to the house yesterday, you saw how Mom is. In spite of Christmas Eve, Dad and I stayed home, just so she would remain in bed. Mom gets so tired."

"Is her arthritis worse? Have you written Phillip about your mother?"

"Yes, I think she's worse. Dad says Phillip should get a leave soon. He'll find out about Mom soon enough when he comes home. It's awful when he isn't here for Christmas."

The expression on Carmel's face didn't change. "Do you think he'll be home soon?"

"According to what I can gather from the men in our family, the ship'll have to go into dry dock sometime."

"Carmel. Scott and I spend our evenings at home. We just sit and listen to *One Man's Family* or *Fibber Magee and Molly*. There's really a lot to hear on radio these days." She paused. "What are some of the interesting things that happen in the city?"

"I met a famous man named Izzy Gomez. He never takes his hat off. He has a bar and a place to dance and gambling in the back room. The club is not very attractive, but glamorous people come to his place, even Bohemians." She laughed. "Jerry took me."

"You must like Jerry. You talk about him a lot."

"He helped me get my first job. He's a great friend." Carmel hadn't realized she talked about Jerry so much. "I just thought of something. Jerry took me to see the girl in a fishbowl."

"Doesn't sound too interesting."

"She has no clothes on. Marlena—that's her name—moves around in a fishbowl that sits on top of a bar on Market Street."

"Just a minute—"

"It's all done by mirrors, and Marlena is in the basement, on a table. When it's projected in the bar, she's about seven inches long. Anyway, I met her when I worked at the Chez Paree with her sister, Elka, who's a dancer."

"Carmel, you'll have a lot more to tell your grandchildren than I will." She laughed. "Do you ever hear from Grant?"

"No, and I think not hearing worries Dad. Grant has never realized how much he hurts other people by his downright thoughtlessness."

"Maybe the new V-mail will encourage the men overseas to write more."

"I haven't seen any, but I just heard it's like tissue paper, weighs nothing, and makes for lighter mail. I doubt if that would have any effect on my brother."

Howard and Bruno had been stretched out beside them on the broad-back terrace, dozing. Suddenly, they raised their heads and started barking. They rose and dashed to the front of the house. Both girls got up and followed the barking dogs. They saw a car traveling down the long drive toward the house. A man got out of the car and paid the driver. He was speaking to the dogs. Carrying two suitcases, he started toward the house.

Laura said, "Speak of the devil! It's Grant!" She called to him, "We were just talking about you."

Carmel walked toward him. "Put those suitcases down and give me a hug." She was shocked to see her usually meticulous brother unshaven and wearing wrinkled clothes. Something terrible had happened to the left side of his cheek.

He reached for his sister and hugged her hard till she let out a little yelp. "Gosh, beautiful, it's good to be here." He grinned at Laura and gave her a hug.

Andrew appeared at the door. "I heard the dogs barking, but I thought this guy was a thief." He reached for Grant's hand, but Grant brushed it away and gave his father a bear hug.

"No, Dad, it's just old me. I'm the thief. Settle down, boys." The dogs were milling around him and trying to lick his hands.

Andrew tried to pick up Grant's suitcases, but Grant pushed him aside. Andrew asked, "When did you leave Hawaii? How did you get here? Why didn't you tell us?"

They walked into the house. "Well, let me get my bearings, and I'll tell you. I hoped to be here Christmas Day. Oh, the house looks great. Did you do all this, Carmel?" He set the cases down.

"No, Grant. Anna and Lupe decorated this year." She was glad to see her brother, but she couldn't stop feeling that something was not right.

Anna walked into the room. "Oh, Grant, it's really Christmas now. How brown you are." Smiling broadly, she reached out her arms for a hug and kiss.

Grant was pleased to see the woman who raised him. "You look as young as ever, Anna." She beamed at the words. "My brother, is he around?"

Scott walked into the room. "He's around, but when I heard the commotion I thought somebody important had arrived. Who's this guy?"

He gave his brother a hug; the two big men appraised each other.

Andrew looked at his watch. "Hey, it's after five o'clock. Let's celebrate with a drink."

The group followed Andrew to the room and the wheeled bar. "Come on, Anna, you too. Let's everyone sit and I'll mix. My son has come home."

Scott asked, "How did you get here."

"I flew over on an Air Transport Command plane. Then I hitched a ride from the base." He skipped mentioning the two weeks he spent in Oakland with an old friend to give his stitches more healing time.

"Aren't there priorities for flying and being able to secure a seat?" Carmel asked.

"You have to know someone. My chief at the Honolulu Police Department got me a seat on the plane." There was no use telling them anymore. Grant planned on being long gone before one of the old team returned and brought gossip from Honolulu about his fight. "Thanks, Dad," he said, taking a sip from his martini. "Nothing like your martinis."

Andrew asked, "How's it over there, son?"

"Curfew's at seven thirty. And I mean curfew. No one does anything without authorization. The people are still very jumpy and excitable. I'm glad to get out of there. What's the scuttlebutt here?"

Carmel suspected her brother was leaving things out of his conversation. "We have a midnight curfew in San Francisco and follow blackout rules," she said. "The cars still run into each other at the corners."

Scott said, "We're not worried about the Japanese bombing us anymore from airplanes, but we still worry about Japanese submarines. I would guess our ships zigzag between here and the islands in case a sub is sighted."

Anna spoke up. "We have Victory gardens. Butter is rationed, but we have our own meat ..."

Everyone laughed. It was so unlike Anna to draw attention to herself.

Scott said, "We never know if we do without because Anna manages so well. You should have had a bite of the lamb roast we had last night."

"Anna always took good care of us," Grant added. "Do you have a big garden?"

Anna blushed at the compliments and nodded her head.

Andrew finally asked. "Grant, how did you get that scar on your face?"

"Oh, a small altercation. I'm healing fine now."

Scott asked, "What happened to the other guy?"

Grant laughed and lifted his glass for a refill.

Andrew got up to make a second round of drinks. "What will you do now, Grant? Return to college?"

Grant looked down for moment at his long legs stretched out before him. "No, Dad. I've enlisted in the Marines. I report to San Diego, then on to El Centro."

The room remained silent. "That's a hell of a decision, Grant. I hope it's what you want." Secretly Andrew didn't like it, but he didn't say more.

CHAPTER 40

Carmel would agree, if anyone bothered to ask, that Caesar had maneuvered her into a corner. John Canepa's band was the trap. She felt clever knowing she understood Caesar's maneuver. Big scary Caesar. He had arranged all these jobs with John's band; now he thought she owed him. But he hadn't caught her. She laughed aloud at the joke.

Carmel felt in the long run she had indeed lucked out. She loved singing with John's band. He gave her many songs to sing, and the musicians in the band liked her. He had introduced her to extraordinary San Francisco people. Carmel decided she wouldn't run away from Caesar when he called. Determined not to reveal her true feelings, she would see him just once and get it over with.

As she expected, Caesar was courteous when he called. He asked if he might pick her up at the house, but Carmel decided the lobby of the Fairmont Hotel was more appropriate. She didn't plan to see him again, so there was no need for her aunt and uncle to meet him.

Carmel waited in the sumptuous lobby of the Fairmont Hotel with its grand staircase and European Baroque furniture. She sat on a satin covered couch behind tall green palms next to one of the marble columns. She saw him first and watched him move with charismatic intensity across the lobby. He looked as big as Phillip in his black suit and topcoat. He carried his hat. She rose to meet him and realized she was trembling. And was instantly furious with herself.

She saw admiration in his eyes.

"How lovely you are, Carmel."

If he had meowed like a tomcat, it wouldn't have surprise her. She was glad she wore her red silk suit.

Caesar picked up her Persian lamb coat from the couch. "May I?" He held her coat as she slipped into it. "I have my car waiting."

People stared at the good-looking couple as they left the hotel lobby.

Jake was at the wheel and easily drove Caesar's big Cadillac through traffic. Caesar asked, "Are you familiar with Chinatown?" He looked directly into her eyes and waited for an answer.

Chinatown frightened her. She remembered stories her aunt and uncle had told her about what happened to girls there. In her mind, Chinatown resembled a black panther crouching in the dark, watching and waiting to take what it wanted. You had to be careful—if you got too close, the shadows, crooked streets, and expressionless faces would hide the clues to escape. It was possible to be swallowed, to disappear, and to be lost in the maze. "I don't know much about Chinatown."

"I'm not taking you there. We're going near there to Forbidden City, a club called the first and only Chinese nightclub in America. I think you'll enjoy it."

Carmel felt the name itself hinted of the prohibited royal city in Peking.

It was only minutes before they arrived at Forbidden City. She saw on the front of the building an enormous poster of a pretty Chinese woman holding a large fan in front of her nude body. The letters read Noel Toy, the Chinese Sally Rand

They entered through the heavy blackout curtain and climbed a wide stairway to the club on the second floor. A huge green dragon carved on the wall greeted them. The club was noisy and crowded. Caesar checked their coats and his hat. The Chinese captain came immediately to Caesar and bowed. "Good evening, Mr. Almato. We have your table ready."

Carmel followed the captain across the dark carpet to a table next to the dance floor. As they passed the bar, she saw it was three deep with customers. People looked at Caesar and commented. Carmel thought she recognized guests who had celebrated his birthday party. She wondered if everyone in San Francisco knew him.

After they were seated, Caesar said, "Wearing red tonight showed great foresight on your part. The Chinese believe red brings good fortune. See for yourself."

Carmel looked about the room. Dark red walls glistened like silk. Elegant Chinese tapestries covered the walls. Massive ornate red and black lanterns hung from the ceiling. Rising around the dance floor were three tiers of tables and red lacquered chairs. Carved black teakwood handrails lined the aisles and the dance floor. The room was full of merry customers eating and laughing. Chinese musicians played swing music for dancers on the crowded floor.

A short, smiling round-faced Chinese man, impeccably dressed in a tuxedo, stood before them. "Good evening, Mr. Almato." He bowed, smiled, and giggled.

Caesar said, "Hello, Charlie. Charlie Low, please meet Carmel St. John."

Charlie bowed. "Very pleased to meetcha, Miss St. John. New show tonight, start in few minuets. Bing Crosby here last night. He enjoy the show very much. I'll send your waiter. Enjoy the show." He giggled and left the table.

Carmel smiled. "Is he always that happy?"

"I've never seen him any other way. He used to be a stockbroker and dress designer. He's making a killing on this place. In his mind, every one's a friend. Do you have a preference in Chinese dishes?"

Carmel thought Caesar had the blackest eyes she had ever seen. "I'm at a loss. I'm not familiar with their food." She looked away from his gaze and the expression in them. What would he think if he knew he reminded her of another man?

"Would you like an appetizer? May I order for you?"

Carmel nodded and Caesar called for a waiter. He ordered a Mia Tia for Carmel and a scotch and soda for himself.

A waiter holding a large menu, bent over Caesar as they discussed dinner. Caesar was courteous and patient to the waiter. Carmel heard the words braised duck, *moo shu* pork, sweet and sour prawns. Their drinks arrived as the show started.

A young Chinese man, Larry Ching, billed as the Chinese Frank Sinatra, sang "I'm Stepping Out with a Memory Tonight." Carmel enjoyed listening to him, but she thought he didn't sound much like Sinatra. There was wild applause when he finished.

The waiter brought their appetizers before the next act.

Eight pretty Chinese girls introduced as Chinese Dolls followed Larry Ching. They danced an energetic tap routine, and the audience loved them.

Carmel looked around the room. She noticed there were no Chinese patrons sitting at the tables. "Why aren't there Chinese customers?" Carmel asked.

"All these performers are from out of town. San Francisco's Chinese natives are shocked at this club. They would never permit their daughters to perform. They discriminate against their own. It's unfortunate."

Carmel tasted the soup. "This soup is marvelous."

"It's seaweed soup with shrimp," Caesar said.

Customers, many of them servicemen and their dates, filled the tables. Several of the patrons came to Caesar's table as if to pay homage to him. His good looks attracted women and they openly flirted with Caesar. He didn't seem to notice.

Carmel watched him and wondered what made him so important. He lived a life she knew nothing about. She wondered why she felt he surrounded himself in darkness. Perhaps she felt uneasy with him because he controlled that very darkness. She guessed it might be due to the fact the words black market suggested crime. At the same time, she felt protected sitting beside him.

The meal he ordered was exotic and fascinating: dishes included braised duck in soy sauce, shrimp in bean curd sauce, chicken with shitake mushrooms, and chestnuts. Quickly, Caesar spooned small amounts of food onto a plate and presented it to her. She refused the chopsticks he offered, but he chose to use them.

The waiter brought to the table a small bottle in a bowl of water and two tiny cups. Caesar said, "The water is hot. This is sake." He poured liquid from the bottle into each cup and offered her one. "It's very pleasant."

Carmel thought it tasted sweet.

The floorshow continued and the music was too loud for conversation. Dottie Sun, a slim Chinese girl's act, brought laughter and applause. She crossed her eyes and mimed hypnotizing a snake trying to bite her. Noel Toy, the exotic dancer, appeared with a large white fan. She waved it across her body to hide her nudity. Twice she bumped into tables and people thought she might fall. Customers sat perplexed, not knowing if her clumsiness was part of the act.

Afterwards Caesar whispered, "Her awkward act was no doubt because she's new and shy. I hope she improves or Charlie won't keep her."

Then a short, plump, expensively dressed singer called the Chinese Sophie Tucker electrified the room, just as her namesake would have. Carmel enjoyed listening to her.

When the floor show ended, Carmel was relieved Caesar hadn't suggested they dance. She asked, "Do they still drop people down trapdoors and leave them in holes under Chinatown?"

"Are you referring to what they call *shanghai*? I'll tell you a story about old Chinatown. Would you like more sake?"

At her nod, he poured sake into their cups, then reached inside a coat pocket for his gold case, opened it, and took out a slim cigar. "Do you mind?"

Carmel shook her head and took a sip of sake. Caesar lit his cigar. "In the 1800s before the gold rush, San Francisco was already a thriving port. The worst thing that could happen to a man was to be told he would sail to Shanghai. It was the longest sea duty. When the gold rush came in forty-nine, the sailors didn't want to return to the ships. They wanted to seek their fortunes. At one time, seven hundred ships sat in this bay. The embarcadero was overrun with pickpockets, thieves, and murderers. Men, called runners, made a great deal of money in those days by supplying a crew for a captain. They approached the huge schooners in small boats, got themselves aboard, and managed to get a liquid soap into the soup. When the men became ill, the runners offered to take them ashore and supply them with booze and women. The main point was to get them drunk at Shanghai Kelly's."

Carmel was fascinated with the story. Caesar continued. "He ran a club with two trap doors in front of the bar. When his customer drank enough from the drugged liquor, the trapdoors opened. The men fell on mattresses so there were no broken bones to keep them from working. The poor souls were shipped aboard another schooner. When they sobered up, they were far out to sea, bound for another long voyage. Sometime the men wrapped clothes into bundles shaped like bodies and dumped them into the hold. They were paid by the body, and the captain was none the wiser until they were at sea." His black eyes bored into hers.

Caesar had just told her a story about a terrible life of misdeeds. She felt too innocent and naive to even begin to ask the right questions.

"Elka tells me you're from San Jose." He sipped his warm sake.

"That's right, until a short time ago. Now I live with my aunt and uncle." Not wanting to reveal anymore about herself, she asked, "You love San Francisco, don't you?"

"Yes, I grew up here. There's no place like it." He puffed on his cigar. "Don't you want to know your fortune?" He passed her a plate holding two fortune cookies, one for each of them.

"Yes. I'm as superstitious as the next Irishman." She laughed, looked at the paper from the broken cookie shell, and read out loud, "*Unseen circumstances change path you travel.*" She handed it to Caesar. "I think the war is the unseen circumstances for everyone. What's yours?"

Caesar's expression was blank while he read. Then he laughed, handing the slip to her. *Highway of life sometime slippery—wear boots.*

Caesar asked for the check. She started to thank him for the evening, but he interrupted her.

"The night's still young. You love music—I thought I'd introduce you to some great jazz in the Fillmore, a place called Jack's."

She would appear ungrateful not to go with him. Charlie Low, still smiling, was at the door to thank them for coming. On the wall, Carmel saw pictures of him standing beside Alfred Hitchcock, John Wayne, and Bob Hope. Charlie grinned.

It was a short ride from Chinatown to the Fillmore.

"Carmel, I have a feeling you enjoyed the shows tonight."

"I thought they were smashing. I heard Chinese girls were bow legged and had no rhythm. Those girls were adorable."

Caesar laughed at her remark. "Maybe we'll go again. They change the show every two weeks."

The arrival at Jack's relieved Carmel from answering.

They heard a piano and a saxophone playing as they walked through the blackout curtains into a dimly lit room full of cigarette smoke. The place was jammed. Well-dressed white and black customers sat at the tables. They were listening to four black musicians play the music of familiar standards and blues. There was no bar. A waiter appeared carrying two cups of coffee. He sat a cup in front of each one. Caesar took a silver whiskey flask out of his pocket and poured some into each cup.

Caesar looked around and laughed. "This place is strictly after hours. There's a lot of coffee drinking all over the city at this time of night."

A piano player, a bass player, and a saxophone player swayed to "Honeysuckle Rose." The drummer made strange grimaces and rolled his eyes. The good-looking piano player spotted Caesar and nodded in recognition.

"That guy on the piano is John Horton Cooper, an old friend of mine. I'll introduce you."

At the first break, John joined them. Carmel liked his voice. It sounded rough, like water running over a creek bed. "I'm glad to meet you, Miss St. John. I've heard musicians say you sing very well."

Carmel noted his eyes were blue and his skin was the color of butterscotch. "Thank you, Mr. Cooper, I like your playing. Reminds me of one of my favorite piano players, Art Tatum."

"Please, call me John. Would you sing a number for us?"

Carmel looked at Caesar. "I'd like to, but some other night."

John said, "I'll look forward to it. Caesar, excuse me. I have to say hello to some other cats. It's a pleasure to meet you, Miss St. John."

They stayed for one more set before Caesar indicated it was time to leave.

When Caesar escorted Carmel to her front door, he took her keys and unlocked the door. He returned the keys to her, taking her right hand. She felt his lips brush it lightly. "I enjoyed tonight. I would like to see you again. I leave for Nevada in the morning. I'll call you when I return."

It was three o'clock when Carmel climbed into bed. *I saw him once, as I planned, and now he expects to see me again.* Too tired to think what to do, she turned her thoughts to the Chinese people who wouldn't support their own, especially the Chinese who needed to make a living. How could any parents believe a talented daughter or son was an insult to their family and ancestors?

When Caesar left her side, she missed his energy, so like Phillip's. Oh, what she wouldn't give to have an evening with Phillip like the one she just had with Caesar.

Sleep was fitful—she dreamed of sleek black panthers roaming around Chinatown and of a pretty Chinese girl who played a saxophone and charmed a snake.

CHAPTER 41

Carmel sat at the piano and struggled to learn a song, but the words wouldn't stick in her head. Some songs were difficult; this song was one of them. That evening the band was playing for a private party, and she had been asked to sing the members "Anniversary Waltz." She patted her foot to feel the rhythm of the music.

The phone rang and Carmel went into the hall answer it. The caller was a man with a pleasant voice and a slight English accent.

"Miss St. John, my name is Lancing Tevis. I was at the Palace Hotel last week. I passed the ballroom and heard you singing. I was very impressed."

"Thank you."

"I obtained you name from publicity at the hotel, and discovered I knew your father and mother. I met you when you were very small. Are your parents still on the ranch in San Jose?"

Even though Carmel didn't know him, she felt comfortable speaking to him. "My father is. My mother passed away some years ago."

After a moment of silence, Mr. Tevis said, "I'm so sorry. She was a beautiful woman."

"Thank you for your kindness." She wondered where this conversation was going. "How did you get my phone number?"

"Well," he laughed. "I hope you won't mind, but I called the Musicians' Union. I also know your father's sister, Lydia."

Carmel thought, He certainly has gone to a lot of trouble.

"I was hoping you would allow me to take you and your Aunt Lydia to lunch. I'll send my car."

"Why don't I mention it to her?" Carmel couldn't imagine either of them going to lunch with this caller.

"Fine, Miss St. John. If I remember correctly, your Aunt Lydia has a delightful sense of humor, and I would enjoy seeing her again."

"Thank you, Mr. Tevis. I'll tell her. Perhaps we can join you some day." There, she thought, that should finish it.

However, when Carmel told her aunt about the call, she saw the color rise on her cheeks. Lydia said, "Why, that old rake. I haven't heard from him in years. He did, indeed, know your father and mother. He's from one of the oldest families in San Francisco. I think his aunt or some of the family started Well's Fargo Bank. His brother, Willie, is wonderful with horses; he plays polo." She preened a bit. "I think it would be fun to see him again."

Lansing Tevis called the following week and Lydia accepted his invitation. He said he would send a car for them and meet in the Garden Court.

The appointed day arrived. After a week of fog, the bay sparkled under the blue sky. Mr. Tevis's chauffeur arrived with the car. As Lydia and Carmel prepared to leave the house, Carmel noticed the front yard swarmed with hundreds of brown and yellow butterflies.

Lydia commented, "You can be sure it's October when the yard fills with Monarch butterflies. They love the flowering eucalyptus trees." The butterflies hovered in masses over the large red blossoms.

Lydia wore a dusky pink wool dress with a matching coat. Carmel wore her yellow gabardine suit with a tiny yellow hat perched on the back of her head. Carmel thought Lydia's eyes would dance out of her head as they were escorted by Mr. Tevis's chauffeur into the car.

Each time Carmel walked into the Garden Court, she tingled with anticipation. The chatter of the patrons over the violin music sounded happy.

Lancing Tevis, already seated, rose to greet them. He used a cane and was a tall, imposing figure in his navy suit. His navy-and-white checked silk tie and matching handkerchief gave him the assurance of a *boulevardier*. The handshake he offered Carmel was firm, his blue eyes bright and friendly. He indicated to the captain where to seat his guests.

Lancing Tevis was from a San Francisco family often referred to as "old money." Carmel learned from her aunt that he was a bachelor and content to remain so. He enjoyed a position of control on many San Francisco boards, and he scanned the backgrounds of applicants who wished to be members of the distinguished and prominent private clubs in San Francisco. Nothing made him happier than entertaining attractive women.

"Well, well, two of the most beautiful women in the room. This is my lucky day," he said, sitting down.

"You always were a flatterer." Lydia rolled her eyes and shook out her napkin.

"It's wonderful to see you again, Lydia, and to meet you, Carmel. May I call you Carmel?"

"Yes, certainly. It's nice to meet you." Carmel liked this man, with his broad face and penetrating eyes. His short-cropped white hair added to his distinctive appearance.

"Would you join me in a before-lunch drink? I'm having a martini."

"I'd enjoy a glass of wine," Lydia said.

"I'll join my Aunt Lydia and have wine."

"If I may—as we're celebrating—I'll order a bottle of champagne." He motioned for a waiter and gave the order. "You ladies look like part of the rainbow and do this old heart good. How's my competition, Lydia?"

"Russell is very well, thank you. He's right in the middle of everything."

"You're referring to the war, no doubt? Russell's a good man." Directing his gaze on Carmel, he asked, "What about you, Carmel?"

"Oh, Lancing," Lydia interjected, "she has the most beautiful voice."

"You do have a beautiful singing voice. Have you ever thought about singing on the radio? A marvelous friend of mine, one of the best voice coaches in California, lives here in the city. She's busy with the networks and might take you on as a student. Her name's Edna Fischer."

"I have heard she's very difficult to see."

"Let me see about that." He smiled and said, "Remember, my dear Lydia, the wonderful salad we used to eat here?"

"You mean The Green Goddess? I certainly do. I also see Adolph." She winked at Lancing.

"You may be wondering what we are referring to, Carmel. George Arliss was a marvelous actor in the twenties and appeared here in San Francisco in a play called *The Green Goddess*. A local chef by the name of Roemer here at the old Palace Hotel created a special salad for him called The Green Goddess. Adolph served Arliss his first Green Goddess salad, and Adolph is still here."

Carmel laughed. "I love stories like that."

The tall, slim Adolph Steinhoff was called to the table. Carmel recognized the maitre d' as the one who had pinched her as she walked through the kitchen in order to reach the Gold Room.

Lydia asked, "How long has it been, Adolph?"

"Can you believe it's seven years? If you'll permit me, madam, you're as lovely as ever."

"Thank you, Adolph. We're looking forward to you preparing us the perfect Green Goddess Salad."

"Thank you, madam. I'll do my best."

Quickly, a small table covered in white linen was rolled beside their table. On it sat a large clear bowl the size of a punchbowl. Beside it were several smaller bowls filled with various ingredients.

Adolph explained, "It's necessary to first rub the inside of the bowl with garlic. Next, mince eight to ten fillets of anchovies with mixed green onions. Then add parsley and tarragon, and scoop all these ingredients into the mayonnaise. Lastly, add a small amount of vinegar and chopped chives."

Each time Adolph said a "small amount," he smiled. Carmel watched closely. What a performance! He heaped salad onto three plates and dribbled one tablespoon of dressing on each portion. He then served their salad, and, waving his napkin to signal the waiter to pour the wine, he rolled his table away.

Lancing asked, "Carmel, what do you think of that as an accomplishment?" He passed her a silver basket with sourdough rolls.

Lydia said. "He didn't wait for us to taste it. How sure can you be?"

Carmel took a bite. The salad lived up to its reputation. After today, she hoped Adolph would treat her with more respect.

Lancing asked, "Carmel, could you stand some more history?" Carmel nodded. "In 1919, President Wilson, who had received the Nobel Peace Prize, came to San Francisco to deliver a speech here in the hotel. When he finished his speech, the hotel, to show their appreciation for his peace efforts, released a flock of white doves. They flew to the top of the ceiling here in the Palace Court and nothing could get them down. So they had to hire someone to shoot them. I doubt if you can see the bullet holes in the ceiling."

Lydia and Carmel looked up at the ceiling and could see nothing. "So much for peace, eh?" Lancing chuckled.

Lydia said, "Lancing, I think that's rather a grim story."

"I believe it also displays the lack of foresight one puts into a plan. They made fools of themselves."

During lunch, Lancing asked about the family. He was distressed to hear about Elizabeth Rose and interested in Scott's determination to have his own frozen food plant. He indicated his concern for Grant's future in the marines.

When lunch was over Lydia said, "Lancing, I've found this luncheon enjoyable and educational, to say the least."

"I hope you ladies will honor me again. Carmel, I'll put in a word for you with Edna." He rose slowly, leaning on his cane. "Martin's waiting to take you home."

On the way home, Carmel asked Lydia, "He's lonely, isn't he?"

"He didn't say much about himself. He has his older brother, Willie. I don't know who else."

Carmel thought about Edna Fischer. She hoped Lancing would keep his promise.

CHAPTER 42

How about another night on the town?" Jerry stood in front of the raised bandstand and stared up at Carmel, who was seated on a chair by the piano.

"You mean tonight? We're playing for a wedding. I should finish by ten."

"Yes, tonight. I'll wait for you at the bar."

The resplendent Gold Ballroom in the Fairmont Hotel, with its mirrored walls and frescoed murals, was full of wedding guests drinking champagne. However, the bride and groom were not in sight. Jerry walked over to the open bar and ordered a scotch and soda. Carmel got up to sing. Her gown of lime green satin was cut low over her full breasts and fell in folds about her slim hips. The men stared as they danced by. The lights dimmed and the dancers moved to the rhythm of the romantic ballad "Dream," the last song of the night.

When the band finished, Carmel hurried toward the bar and Jerry. She hadn't seen him for a month. He looked handsome in a dark suit. His brown hair swept back from a high forehead and his deep-set blue eyes always twinkling, he seemed as if he were enjoying a private joke.

Jerry greeted her. "You're singing better each time I hear you—if that's possible."

"Thank you. What have you planned for our night—as you put it—out on the town?"

He helped her put on her coat. "Don't ask any questions."

"That's what you said the last time."

"Wasn't it worth it? Let's hurry so we can get a cab."

They shared their cab with two sailors. Jerry told the driver to take them to the Mark. The sailors, in high spirits, said they wanted the Tonga Room. The driver dropped them off at the Fairmont Hotel's side door on California Street. More than once, they wished everyone a "grand night." Carmel thought they were fun. The cab climbed California Street to the top of Nob Hill. The driver stopped under the portico in front of the Mark Hopkins Hotel.

After the sailors left the cab, Carmel studied Jerry. "Do you have something special to tell me?"

Jerry smiled at Carmel in the darkened ca, "I'll share it with you when we get to the hotel."

The cab climbed California Street to the top of Nob Hill. The driver stopped under the portico in front of the Mark Hopkins Hotel.

Jerry guided Carmel through the lobby. "We're going to the Peacock Court."

They entered the Peacock Court. The majordomo knew Jerry and greeted him warmly.

"Fritz Bergdorf, I want you to meet Carmel St. John. She's a vocalist and maybe the star of this room someday." Another time, Carmel thought, Jerry's words would have embarrassed her but tonight she felt they might be true.

"How do you do, Miss St. John." Fritz's brown eyes appraised Carmel. "It's my pleasure."

Carmel sensed this tall and slim, rigidly formal man was important to know. Fritz led them to a small table on the edge of the dance floor.

"Miss St. John may I take your coat?"

"Yes, thank you."

Jerry gestured at the room. "What do you think?"

Carmel gazed around. A massive gold peacock tail fanned out against the wall behind the band's platform. Walls of pale beige silk held crystal lamps cast a soft glow on red and gold tablecloths. Brilliant red and blue upholstery adorned the chairs. A high gold ceiling embellished the room's beauty. "It's breathtaking."

The band started to play. "Come on, let's dance." He led her onto the dance floor.

After a few minutes of smooth dancing, Carmel said, "Most musicians are terrible dancers. You are a definite exception."

"Thank you." He whirled her over to the band stand. "Dick Foy, meet Carmel St. John. She's a vocalist."

Dick Foy, jet black hair and ebony eyes, slender and elegant in his black tuxedo, leaned down and shook her hand. "Pleased to meet you, Miss St. John. You must sing for me sometime."

"Oh, no you don't. I met her first." Jerry laughed and danced them away.

"The music stopped and they went back to the table. "Let's have some champagne." He placed the order with the waiter.

"How much longer do I have to wait for this surprise?"

"I've been offered a job at NBC."

"Oh, Jerry, that's wonderful news. You deserve it."

"I don't know about that."

"Tell me what happened."

"One of my best buddies, Harlan Roach, has been called into the service, and I'm to replace him. I may get a chance to conduct the orchestra."

"You look so happy. I'm thrilled for you."

The waiter brought the champagne, filled each glass, and placed the bottle in the ice bucket.

Carmel announced, "Let's toast to your job and its success." They touched glasses and drank.

"Let's have something with our Champagne. Would you like some oysters?"

"I would love it."

He ordered the oysters. The band had struck up a rumba. "Let's dance." He was a remarkable dancer and Carmel was enjoying herself.

Returning to the table they found oysters in their shells served on a mound of ice.

Carmel served herself. Swallowed a oyster and took a sip of champagne. "This is fun," she said.

They ate and drank in silence, enjoying the food. When the band took a break the room became quiet.

Jerry took each of her palms in his. He turned them over and brushed the backs with his lips. He stared at her for a moment and his voice was soft. "Carmel I've loved you for a long time. I want you to be my wife. My new job gives me the security to ask you and provide you with the life you deserve. I believe I can make you happy." At her surprised look he quickly said, "Don't make up your mind now." He released her hands.

She had sensed Jerry cared for her, but to announce his love did surprise her. "Oh, Jerry, I do care about you but only as a valued friend."

"I want you to think about it, I can wait. I hope this hasn't destroyed our relationship."

Carmel reassured him, "Nothing will destroy our friendship." She patted his hand.

Dick Foy announced the last number and they agreed it was time to call it a night.

.Leaving the hotel lobby, Carmel saw a huge crowd at the far end of the hall. "What are they doing, Jerry?"

"They're waiting for the elevators to take them to the Top of the Mark. It's one of the most popular rooms in the city. The guys go up there to tell their gals good-bye and have their last drink. It's tradition. The bottle is bought for a squadron, signed, and kept under the bar. Every drink is free. The last drinker buys a new bottle. I'll take you up there sometime."

Headed home in a cab, Carmel asked, "Jerry, do you know Edna Fischer?"

"No, but I've heard of her. She's a voice coach. I don't think she teaches just everyone though. Why?"

"I met Lancing Tevis, a friend of my aunt's, who says he will introduce me to her."

When they said goodnight, Carmel wasn't exaggerating when she told Jerry she had enjoyed the evening.

CHAPTER 43

San Jose's summer days in 1943 were long and hot. Residents swore they could see heat waves simmering above the dry earth. The green foothills rising around the valley turned the color of straw.

Andrew's top priority in the month of August was watering. It was time to divide the bearded irises and fertilize the roses for a heavy fall bloom. The war had taken Jesus from the ranch. He volunteered for the Merchant Marine early. Only Jose and Pedro remained to help Andrew.

Mr. Penbroke arrived from the fish hatchery, driving his small truck onto the gravel driveway. Mr. Penbroke had replaced Mr. Kato, who now lived in a concentration camp surrounded by barbed wire.

"Let's get those fish into the pools." Andrew assumed all the huge milk cans full of fish in the back of the truck were his.

"You tell me all those cans are not for me?" Andrew's voice rose.

"Oh, no, Mr. St. John, I have only one can for you," Mr. Penbroke said, sliding out of the truck.

Mr. Penbroke opened the back of the truck. Andrew stood beside him and reached for a large metal can. "I'll help." He grasped at the heavy can but failed to hold on. The can full of goldfish fell on the toes of his left foot.

"Damn," he yelled, pushing it off.

"Mr. St. John, if you move I'll lift the can." The wiry little Englishman easily lifted the can and started for the first pool. "You only get one," he muttered under his breath. Andrew limped behind him, wondering how much the damn can full of fish weighed.

"Let's put the fish in the first pool." Andrew stood by and watched Mr. Penbroke put the can on its side and slowly slip the rim of the can into the water.

He watched the koi, a myriad of deep oranges, whites, and blacks, dart among the new goldfish around the small pool. At the sight of the beautiful fish waving their fins in the water, Andrew began to relax. Caring for his three backyard fishponds was his joy.

Mr. Penbroke said, "I can't get you more fish for two weeks. It's the war." He took the empty can back to his truck.

"Yes, yes, I know. I can only get goldfish now. The Japanese had all the koi. Everything is because of the war." The pain in his foot was becoming unbearable.

"Good-bye," Mr. Penbroke called as he quickly backed out of the driveway.

Andrew ignored him. He limped across the brick terrace to the front door. The house, with its high ceilings and thick walls, shut out the summer heat.

"Anna," he called. He sank onto a soft chair and leaned over to remove his boot and sock.

Anna came into the room and saw the foot. "Good heavens, what have you done?"

"It's not what I've done. It's what the damn can did." The big toe was an angry red and already swelling.

Anna pushed a stool toward him. "Let's put your foot up. I'll get some ice."

Scott limped into the room and brushed dust from his pants.

Andrew saw him. "You'd better not let Anna see you do that. You know how she hates dust."

Scott stared at his father's foot. "What happened to you?"

"Mr. Penbroke brought a can of goldfish from the hatchery, and I managed to drop it on my foot. It's nothing to fuss about."

Anna came into the room carrying towels and a round, shallow basin of water with large piece of ice floating in it. She knelt down and lowered his foot into the cold.

He jerked his foot away. "Yipes! What are you doing?"

Anna waited a moment and again put his foot into the basin. "Is that better? The ice water will help take the swelling down." Andrew gritted his teeth and waited for the throbbing to stop.

Scott watched them for a moment. "You are always in good hands when Anna is in command. I have a heavy date. Better I get cleaned up." He left the room.

"Will you soak for ten more minutes if I go to the kitchen?"

"Yes, *conchita*."

She left the room.

As soon as she was gone, Andrew lifted his foot, dried it with the towel, and pulled on a sock. He limped to the door. He had to see the fish.

Scott had arranged for his meeting to be in downtown San Jose at Marty's on Park Avenue, a popular gathering place for beer drinkers, many of them college students. Marty was a jolly, short man. His rotund shape gave evidence he enjoyed the food he served as much as his customers. A stein of beer came with beans and bologna sandwiches. By the time Scott arrived, the old building on the corner of Park Avenue was full of young students, most of them from San Jose State. He heard the Andrew Sisters singing "Rum and Coca-Cola" on the jukebox in the corner. Fifty cents paid for sixteen songs. The jukebox played steadily.

Two men at the table nodded at Scott when he came into the huge room. One called above the noise. "Come on over, Scott! I'll get you a beer. Want some beans?" Al Dressler rose from his chair. His mass of shaggy blond hair, needing a cut, framed alert and friendly brown eyes. A work shirt and jeans hung on his thin body like an afterthought. Al's flat feet registered him 4F.

"A beer is fine." Scott eased his lanky frame into the chair opposite the man at the table. "Hi, Ron."

Ron Whipple, as lean as Al, was a dapper contrast to Al's disregard for fashion. Brown hair was brushed back from an aquiline face, featuring a long nose and thin lips. His green eyes dismissed Scott after a quick appraisal. He wore an immaculate navy blue weather jacket and navy trousers. He nodded at Scott's greeting. Ron was 4F due to the loss of two fingers on his left hand.

Al came back to the table with a beer for Scott and one for himself. He waved away Scott's offer to pay. "You can get the next one."

The three men lit cigarettes, stared at the ceiling, looked at each other, and began to speak at the same time.

Ron asked Scott, "What is so damn important we had to meet tonight?"

Scott inhaled deeply and blew smoke through his nostrils. The three men were about the same age. However, sometimes Scott felt Ron was a hundred years old. "Al will tell you."

Al blurted, "Aren't I supposed to be finding a place for us to start a cannery?"

"That's the idea." Scott answered.

"Well, I've found a building in Aptos, back of the Bay View Hotel. Old man Schiller's doctor says Schiller has to quit working because of his health, so he's retiring. It's been a drying shed for cots. The place needs a lot of work, but there's room enough to build our product line."

Scott was interested. "What makes you think he'll deal with us?"

"There's no machinery. We'll be buying just the building." Al answered.

Ron said, "It'll be an investment for our future." His voice was sharp.

"That's one way of looking at it," Scott said. "Our agreement is, Al and I build our machinery and push out the product. Your job is to find buyers and sell it."

Ron was worried. "You are talking about building the line for one product, then tearing it down to start another? Brother!"

Scott, exasperated, said, "That's the only way we can start. You know the brokerage business. Al and I will get the product going and you sell it. Damn it! This war will be over one of these days and those big government contracts will stop. We have got to learn the business and be waiting to supply and sell our produce on demand." He grinned at Al. "I know we can do it. Let's look at the shed Saturday."

Ron remained skeptical. "If you're going to dream, might as well dream big. We're so far from getting a plant, I can't believe it."

"We're not pushing, Ron," Scott continued. "If we can get that shed by sharing our down payment, then we can apply for the loan to build our equipment. If you want out of this, it's all right with me." Scott found relief at his words. It would be no skin off his nose if he never saw Ron again.

Ron's voice was low. "I'm staying. See you Saturday. Good night." He didn't wait for their good nights.

Scott waited until Ron walked out the door and then limped to the bar and ordered two beers. He brought them back to the table and slid one in front of Al. "That guy is a pain in the ass, but we haven't got enough know-how to kick him out."

"An empty wagon makes a lot of noise. He'll calm down."

"It's lucky you know how to tear that machinery apart and put it back together."

"Funny, that's all I've ever wanted to do. Dad sure wanted me to go on to college."

"My two years at Stanford were enough for what I wanted. I feel lucky, my friend. Let's see if anyone is playing the slot machine. I have a few nickels." The slot machine was in a closet near the phone. The room was so small only one man could play at a time.

Scotts's friendship with Al was no gamble. Pale and thin, Al never went in the sun. Black grease under his fingernails was part of his life. Scott, on the other hand, was robust and tan from the California sun. He could fall into a barrel of sawdust and emerge looking shiny clean.

As summer waned, Scott continued to work on his project and follow the war. Newspapers and radio carried reports of the Japanese. They had withdrawn from the Aleutians. In Europe, the Sicilian campaign was over. Italy had declared war on Germany. Mussolini, forced to resign from his government, was rescued by the Germans to become a puppet without authority. In the Pacific, General Douglas MacArthur advanced with Americans and Australians in New Guinea to stop the Japanese at the Owen Stanley Mountains. After his success in Africa and the Mediterranean, General Dwight D. Eisenhower was promoted to supreme commander-in-chief of the Allied Forces. He was preparing for the invasion of the continent in 1944. Hitler attacked the Russians, but after five days of fierce fighting his army was stopped. The Allies bombed Germany. Fifty thousand fell on Hamburg alone.

Following these events in the fall of 1943, Scott read the words of Winston Churchill: "There is no halting place at this point. We have now reached a point in the journey where there can be no pause. We must go on."

CHAPTER 44

Carmel began to feel Saturday night was the most difficult night of the week. She wished she could wave a wand and push her loneliness away. Sitting on the bandstand waiting to sing, she watched the dancers.

Couples glided by under the whirling mirror-covered ball. She envied their closeness, how they hugged and clung to each other. Perfume drifted up to her from women dancers, their bare shoulders moist and pale in the dim light. The men wore crisp uniforms. Pinned on their chests were colored ribbons of battles fought. The room spun under the spell. The evening dragged on her soul. It was the war; she wished it were over.

The unlined faces of the young men were faintly alabaster in the dim lights—her heart ached for them. Their expressions had changed since the start of the war. At the beginning, she had seen hope and anticipation there. Now they wore looks of acceptance and resignation. It was as if everyone was always saying good-bye.

She thought about how she felt when entering the bars. An atmosphere of "drink up, be merry, for tomorrow you die" filled the rooms. Boisterous sailors hung onto their women and drinks. Bearded pirate-faced Merchant Marines wore rings in their ears. Grim expressions shadowed the faces of paratroopers, and the young—always young—Army airmen wore their caps with the bills worn backwards. As the evenings wore on, they let you know they were the ones winning the war.

Watching the dancers, she wondered what it would be like to dance with Phillip, to have him hold her close as they moved to the music. She wanted to smell his cologne, crisp and tangy. She wanted to feel the warmth of his body as he held her in his strong arms. Carmel sighed. She prayed to herself, Please, God when the war is over, let him come home to me.

It was time for her to sing. Time to sing a song that would carry memories. Time to watch the men as they leaned down to the uplifted faces in front of them. She had to pinch herself to stop thinking about it all.

Carmel received the phone call from Anna saying her father had injured his foot. Anna insisted he was taking care of himself and not to think of coming home. Carmel headed for the garden to find Lydia and tell her about her brother.

The sun remained glazed behind a heavy fog bank, turning the late afternoon chilly. Carmel pushed her hands into her sweater pockets for warmth. In the distance, she heard sounds of bellowing whistles from the ships in the bay. None of them sounded alike. She had heard that long ago, they fired a cannon when the fog became thick. In the foggy summers, the bay must have sounded like the Fourth of July.

An essence of purple and white alyssum filled the air. She found Lydia in her heavy wool jacket and thick gloves, shears in hand, attacking the thick shrubbery of English Ivy crawling over the red brick wall.

When Carmel told her about Andrew, Lydia said, "My brother's a grouch when he's hurt."

"Dad has never been one to stay down."

"Why does he insist on having those fish?"

"They've been a project he's very, very proud of. I wouldn't dare try to convince him to stop doing anything once he's set on it." As Carmel watched Lydia whack at the vines, she noted that stubbornness ran in the family. Her aunt could have left the vines; they didn't grow that fast. She said, "Auntie, you're working too hard. Shall I help you?"

"No, this thick fog is keeping things cool enough for me to get some clipping done. I'm glad there's no wind. My favorite gardener called last week. He's joined some reserve and won't be around for the next few months. Oh!" She jerked her hand away from the thick leaves and pulled her glove off to inspect her hand. "Well, it's just a pinch. Carmel, do you have time to go inside for a cup of tea?"

"That's a lovely idea, Auntie."

The warm country kitchen felt good after the chilling fog. From the wooden beams in the kitchen, Helen had hung baskets of dried flowers. Spaghetti sauce simmering in a pot on the huge gas stove smelled wonderful. The picture of a large cow with soulful eyes looked down from the wall. Lydia had found the picture in Holland on one of her trips and sent it home. Growing up, Carmel visited her aunt often. The cow was part of her childhood.

Carmel brought cups and saucers to the table. "Where are the dogs, Auntie? It's unusually quiet."

"Oh, Helen took them for a walk. I can't handle the garden shears and the darlings too." She laughed. "They'll be back soon enough."

Lydia lit the fire under the kettle. "I've got really tasty brown bread for toast. I managed to get some marmalade to top it off. With sugar and butter so hard to get, marmalade will have to do."

"I don't mind. Sounds delightful."

Toast made and tea poured, they sat down at the kitchen table. Carmel bit into the thick bread "Uhm … I didn't know I was hungry."

After a moment Lydia said, "Forgive me, Carmel, but Russell and I are worried about you. We think you're getting too thin, not eating enough. You are very seldom home, day or night. Do you think you might be burning the candle at both ends?"

Carmel knew her aunt meant well. I can't tell her, she thought, that *everything* reminds me of Phillip, *every* single day. I think about him constantly. It's impossible to get away from the reminders.

Servicemen and women in uniform were everywhere. Being a volunteer at the hospital was difficult, especially when she saw doctors in their officers' uniforms. She was tired, but she wanted to be tired enough to sleep. She didn't dare risk coming home to sleepless nights. If she didn't keep busy, she might go mad wondering where his ship was, when and if she would see him again.

Carmel's gray eyes darkened. "I feel whatever I do, I'm doing what I can for the war effort. To sing at the hospital and volunteer for the Canteen does take time above my singing."

"I was hoping you would call Edna Fischer and arrange to sing for her," Lydia continued. "I'm not trying to tell you how to live your life, my darling, but your hours are so late. I thought there was a curfew at midnight?"

Carmel studied her aunt's expression of concern and felt a sudden urge to hug her. "Auntie, the band quits at midnight. They have to pack up. After that, time is spent getting home."

Lydia sipped her tea slowly. "I heard the clock strike three o'clock last night when you came up the stairs."

"That's true. I did stay out late. I went to Jack's tavern, an after-hours place in the Fillmore. I heard some really great jazz musicians. I don't know if I can say it right, but late at night in the middle of the city, the musicians pour out their birthright. Saxophonists wail their version of the composer's music, and drummers beat a rhythm from the beginnings of time. A vocalist sings the words that sometimes slip like honey over the top of the rhythm. The crowd eats it up."

Lydia's mouth popped open. "I've never heard it said exactly like that."

Carmel had left out the dusty smell of the small club, the odor of bodies packed close together. For some, it might be the last time to feel. The music released the rage against the war, helping the men and women remember happiness and loneliness mixed together. It was a time to be free, to escape, and to forget the obligations to do their part. They let the music and the noise of the crowd roll over them.

"The fellows from the band asked me to go, and I went with them. Afterwards, we stopped for breakfast at Coffee Dan's Restaurant. The customers beat on the tables with little wooden hammers. I guess that sounds ridiculous, but it's perfectly harmless."

She stood. "I do plan on calling Edna Fischer. I know you feel responsible for me, and I don't intend to be a bother. The guys in the band treat me wonderfully and are very protective. I have to change. I'm doing my bit for the Canteen tonight. Thanks for the tea." She kissed her aunt and left the room.

Lydia sat in the quiet room. The ticking of the clock was the only sound. She muttered, "Do I really understand what is happening in this crazy world of 1943?"

CHAPTER 45

The last days of October brought glorious sunshine. Carmel woke on such a morning, dressed, and went downstairs to eat breakfast. She found no one at the table and was surprised Hilda and Heidi were not jumping at her feet. Not being hungry, she drank her orange juice and took her coffee into the morning room to sit by the window.

She watched the city around her glisten in the marigold sunshine. From the windows of the house on Russian Hill, she saw the bay sparkle, spanked by the sun.

She opened the window and leaned out for a better view. Coit Tower dominated the azure sky. The tower, shaped like a fire nozzle, had been donated by Lily Coit, in honor of the San Francisco firemen. Carmel planned to see the murals inside the building someday. The bay was full of ships. They steamed back and forth under the Golden Gate Bridge, their whistles and horns shattering the air.

San Francisco had crept steadily into her blood. She became accustomed to the best parts of the weather. Brisk winds from the bay cleansed the air, filling her with energy. In spite of the time it took to learn songs and take care of her clothes, Carmel made an effort to walk often. On those days, she thought less about herself and slept much better.

Carmel knew her uncle was delighted with her interest in San Francisco. He enjoyed telling her how he believed part of San Francisco's charm lay in its "sevens." The city was seven miles long and seven miles wide. It sat on seven hills facing a bay formed by a rupture in the earth that eventually allowed the Pacific Ocean to pour through the Golden Gate and cover the sinking marshes.

He told her in the beginning the city streets were laid out to cross sand dunes, as if the dunes were flat. Owners with homes perched on top of the dunes had to use ladders to climb to their front doors. In those days, lumber was plentiful. The roofs and porches were trimmed with carved scrolls the natives called gingerbread. The houses, built in rows, reminded Carmel of attentive soldiers waiting for orders.

Russell said San Francisco's leaders were concerned about the empty hundred thousand acres of sand dunes stretching from Stanyan Street to the Pacific. They asked McLaren, a Scotsman, to make a park out of the land. He requested three provisions: horse droppings for fertilizer, all the water he wanted, and thirty thousand dollars a year. His demands were granted. He immediately built two windmills for pumping the needed water, and in due time the land became Golden Gate Park.

In 1915, the Panama-Pacific International Exposition was celebrated in the park. Now, in 1943, thousands visited eleven lakes, an aquarium, the Hall of Sciences, and Fleishhacker Zoo. They toured the De Young Museum and the spectacular glass Conservatory modeled after the Kew Gardens, London.

Carmel's curiosity led her to wooden stairs bordering private properties hidden by overhanging trees, clumps of blood red azaleas, and flowering bushes of pink and white oleander. They led her up and down hills to breathtaking vistas of the bay. Watching a sudden sweep of white gulls riding the breezes over the city never ceased to thrill her.

She loved to climb Nob Hill and walk by the great mansions of the wealthy families on Nob Hill, men like Huntington, Crocker, Tevis, and Hopkins. The city encouraged a closeness that bred familiarities steeped in tradition. Memories of the past became romantic if not exaggerated. The columnists for the *San Francisco Chronicle* and the *Call-Bulletin* kept readers aware as to where they ate and drank, and in which clubs they held memberships.

On bright, sunshiny days she walked as far as Chinatown. Its history of underground tunnels, opium dens, and the gambling fascinated her. In her mind, she entered a foreign city where colorful balconies of red, green, and yellow decorated the second-floor exteriors. She passed Chinese children, who reminded her of tiny blackbirds, playing on the sidewalks. Old Chinese men, wearing traditional black pants and their boxy jackets, sat outside their shops smoking, enjoying the sun.

The sights in the storefront windows captivated her: live turtles swam in a tank; flat, plucked chickens and ducks hung above them; barrels of eels and octopuses sat beside varieties of fish, packed in ice.

Streets during the day teemed with servicemen. Occasionally, she passed a building with sand bags still stacked against it. No one ever bothered her. If she listened, she heard the hum of life and energy that fed the city. Three times a day, the Ferry Building blasted its siren. Cathedral bells rang in Chinatown, followed by the Grace Cathedral chimes on Nob Hill. Clocks on the street corners chimed the hour. Bells clanged on streetcars rattling up and down Market Street.

Sitting by the window, she thought about the people she had met since her arrival. Jerry with his constant encouragement was one of the best things that happened to her. She treasured her friendship with Elka.

Caesar was another story. She wished she didn't feel indebted to him for the introduction to John Canepa. Every time the phone rang, she wondered if it was Caesar. Thank goodness he seemed to spend a lot of time in Nevada.

At the Canteen, she didn't mind listening to a lonesome man talk about home and his girl. Many were good dancers and the music was exceptional, especially when popular musicians sat in with the band. But her trips to the hospital, even with Jerry's moral support and accompaniment on the piano, were becoming difficult. The pain she saw in their eyes stayed with her for hours afterward.

Engrossed in her thoughts, she was startled when the ringing phone pierced the quiet house.

She reached for the phone.

"Phillip Barron here. Is that you Carmel?

"Yes," she replied after a moment of stunned silence.

He laughed, "I hope you're well."

"Yes, I'm well."

"Guess I'm surprising you. I'm surprised myself. The *Solace* is here in San Francisco. I have a few hours. I've borrowed a car and want to take a run home and see the folks. Later, I hoped you could join me for an early dinner." Carmel's mind raced. He was nonchalant as if he called every day. "Carmel, I have to be back on the ship tonight."

This was her regular night for the Canteen, but nothing, absolutely nothing, would stop her from seeing him. Her voice was strong and clear. "Yes, I would like that."

"Good, I should be able to pick you up around five thirty. Is that too early for you?"

Oh, his dear, wonderful voice—just to hear him was a thrill. Now she would actually see him. "That would be fine."

"Good-bye, Carmel. See you then."

"Good-bye, Phillip."

She let out a yell. Energy roared back into her shaky knees. She thought she might dance an Irish jig. She froze. Oh, what to wear? She looked at her watch. It was just ten o'clock. In seven hours, he would arrive.

Upstairs in her room, she began to pull clothes out of the closet. Black wool dress, yellow plaid suit, red suit? No, no. She wore it on her dinner date with Caesar. Oh, she hadn't called the Canteen. It would be all right. It would have to be. There were always plenty of girls to talk and dance with the guys.

At five o'clock, Carmel was ready and downstairs waiting.

When the bell rang, Helen opened the front door. Carmel heard Phillip's voice and went to greet him in the hallway, her heart thumping. He looked absolutely perfect in his officer's uniform. He removed his hat, and a smile flashed across his tanned face. Brown eyes held hers for a moment.

"Hello, Phillip."

"You look great, Carmel."

Her skin glowed against a pink silk dress with matching jacket. She wore black velvet heels and a small black velvet hat. Gold earrings sparkled in her ears. "Thank you, Phillip."

She had thought about him every hour of every day, and now he was actually here. Lydia and Russell entered the room and she introduced them.

The men shook hands. Russell said, "I hear you've been all over the Pacific?"

"It certainly feels like it, sir."

"I don't suppose you've seen MacArthur?"

Phillip's eyes twinkled. "No, but I've seen Nimitz. Will he do?"

Lydia gushed. "Carmel said you took a quick run to San Jose. I've known your folks for years. How are they?"

"They're fine, Mrs. Bannister. Thank you for asking. Mom's a little under the weather. My sis is fine; so is Dad. Everyone seems busy, busy." He turned to help Carmel put on her black wool coat.

Phillip shook Russell's hand. "It's nice to have met you folks."

Lydia and Russell echoed their good nights. Once outside, Carmel saw a taxi at the curb.

"I only borrowed the car to drive to San Jose." Phillip said. "I had to return it." In the cab, he told the driver to take them to Alfred's restaurant. "I'm so hungry for a steak. I hope you are too, Carmel."

At this moment, hunger was not on her mind, but she wanted anything he wanted. "A steak? I'd love it."

She was aware of Phillip's body next to her and his long legs stretched out beside her. She could touch him, feel energy flowing from him, and smell his cologne.

Carmel hesitated to speak about his ship, the war, his work. His arrival was so unexpected, and she had so many questions.

They both said at once, "How are you?" their laughter afterward breaking the ice.

Phillip said, "I'm surprised to see so many people on the streets."

"You *do* love this city, don't you?"

"Yes, indeed I do. This is the city the boys so far away promise themselves they'll see again. Don't you love it?"

"Good heavens, yes. It's in my blood."

"You must know it fairly well by now. You can probably tell me a few interesting stories."

"My uncle has told me a lot about it. Montgomery Street was once the very edge of the waterfront. At one time seven hundred ships sat here, abandoned. Sailors jumped ship to mine the gold fields and left the enormous schooners to rot. Buried beneath us are farm tools, mirrors, mahogany bars, and furniture. Many predicted that the tall brick buildings would sink into the mud and the landfill." Carmel stopped. She realized she sounded like a tour guide. "I'm sorry, Phillip, I didn't mean to say all that."

He laughed. "Let's see if I can top you." He began to speak in an even tone, as if giving a lecture. "Now, ladies, San Francisco has endured five fires and the 1906 earthquake. During the quake, they formed lines and emptied their wine kegs to douse the fires. The aroma that rose above the city was never to be forgotten. The city has survived the Gold Rush, Vigilantes, the earthquake, and now the war." He paused. "Well, how did I do?"

"You're much better than I am. That was interesting, though, about the wine."

The cab stopped at a stop sign. "How do these people keep from running into each other at the corners?"

The cab driver heard him. "Sometimes we don't. I've been smacked twice."

It was a short ride down Russian Hill, to the top of Broadway and to Alfred's. They entered through the blackout curtains. Phillip left his cap and their coats with the hatcheck girl. The captain at the door greeted him warmly. A handsome officer with a beautiful woman was always welcome.

Carmel saw a long Victorian bar running the length of one wall, and though it was early, the seats were already occupied. The red walls in the large dining room were lit by a huge crystal chandelier. Center tables were filling with customers.

"We have your table, Commander Barron." They were led across the room to a commodious red leather booth.

They sat opposite each other. She noticed the booths were separated by walls of dark wood. Curtains could be pulled across the entrance to ensure privacy. A small lamp on the table added to the intimacy.

A waiter appeared, wearing a knee-length white apron over his tuxedo uniform. Phillip asked, "Would you like a martini, Carmel?"

She nodded. He ordered and said, "I think before a steak the absolute best drink is a martini." He grinned. "You're looking great. Whatever you're doing is very becoming."

"Thank you, Phillip. I was thinking the same about you." God, she thought, he couldn't be more handsome. The same brilliant dark eyes. Fatigue showed in the lines on his face. He looked older. A slight shadow of a beard crossed his upper lip and jaw. This man she loved could turn her heart upside down. She said, "This booth's something else. You could lie down here if you wanted." She felt herself blush at her implication.

"With these curtains here, some might do exactly that." He laughed as the waiter brought the drinks and left them large menus.

Phillip raised his martini. "Here's to my good luck that you were able to join me."

"Thank you. Cheers." They each sipped their drinks.

"Do you mind if we order? We haven't a lot of time. If you feel like it, I wanted to take you to another place after dinner." He looked at the menu. "What steak would you prefer?"

She was thrilled to realize he had planned to take her someplace else.

"Would you like to share a chateaubriand? Do you like medium or rare?"

She nodded. "Rare would be fine."

The waiter reappeared and Phillip ordered a bottle of Cabernet to be served with dinner. "I'm having another martini while we wait. Would you like another?"

"I'm fine."

"Are you still singing?"

"Yes."

"Are you singing in the same place? What was it? The Chez Paree?"

"No, I'm now on call for local band leaders who need a vocalist."

"Here in San Francisco?"

"Yes, and sometimes down the Peninsula."

"Tell me about your glamorous life. Seems one could get used to all that attention."

He smiled, but the look in his eyes bothered her. Did he resent her singing?

"Phillip, I'm very sincere about my music. I do sing in the big hotels with a big band, but I work hard to learn the current songs."

"Yes, I don't doubt you do. Laura says you're singing in the hospitals. That's very brave of you, Carmel."

"Well, thank you. I don't know anything about being brave. The men I sing to in the wards are the brave ones. For many, it must seem like the end of their lives." She was silent for a moment, twirling the stem of the martini glass in her hand. "Jerry plays the piano for me when we go into the wards."

"That's the man you met on the train?"

Carmel was surprised he remembered. "Yes, he's helped me a lot. He's working at NBC now."

"Good for him."

Carmel took a sip of her martini. "Tell me about meeting Admiral Nimitz."

"We were in Pearl. He was there and came aboard. He's a forceful leader and a quiet man—perhaps not as colorful as Admiral Halsey—and he demands a great deal of respect. He awarded 270 Purple Hearts and 1 Gold Star. Everyone aboard deserves a medal as far as I'm concerned. We have an amazing staff and crew. No one ever gripes when there's work to be done."

"Are you still the only hospital ship?"

"No, I understand they've sent out a ship called the *Relief*. We need several more, however."

"Do you think the war will be over soon, Phillip?"

"No, I don't. They have to finish off those Germans before they'll get the much needed men and equipment to the Pacific."

The waiter set a platter of antipasto on the table.

Phillip offered the plate to Carmel. At her refusal, he served himself. "There's nothing like San Francisco food."

Their conversation was interrupted by their waiter rolling a small table next to theirs. He carved the chateaubriand, added vegetables to the plates, and served each of them. He opened the wine and poured some for Phillip to taste. Phillip found it acceptable. The waiter poured wine into Carmel's glass and left.

"Cheers." Phillip lifted his glass. His brown eyes looked into hers.

"Cheers."

The light from the small lamp on the table flickered and she felt her world tip. Something clicked in her mind. Phillip was there with her because he chose to be. She fought to keep from reaching for his hand.

Phillip took a bite of his meat and said, "This is heaven."

"Do you ever get off the ship?"

"Actually, large cities are for disembarking, to move patients on or off the ship. Our orders are no R&R except on an island." After a sip of wine, he continued, "One time we were in Auckland and the city fathers treated the staff to a tour of a trout farm. I saw a twenty-four-inch rainbow trout weighing twelve pounds, swimming in a tank. I knew without a doubt with my fishing gear, I could catch enough fish for dinner." He laughed, then shrugged. "It doesn't work that way, however. I didn't get a chance to fish until much, much later."

"Are there many doctors and nurses?"

"About fourteen doctors, but that includes dentists and specialists. We have many nurses and we need every one."

"What do you do about getting the supply of blood you need?"

"We give our share."

"You, too?"

"Have to. I've given five times."

Carmel watched Phillip cut his meat. His hands were clean and strong. He wore no jewelry. The skin across the back of his hands long fingers was smooth, the nails clipped straight across. Surgeon's hands. A wave of love for him swept over her. For a moment she imagined him coming home every day, needing her. She forced herself to stop yearning and searched for something to ask him. "Do you have movies on board?"

"Oh, yes. The men watch movies and get all the ice cream they can eat." He smiled.

"Just like a city on the water."

"Exactly. The USO came aboard once and entertained us. Sunday mornings, religious services are conducted for all. Our chaplain plays a great harmonica and the men like him. Now, enough about me. Are you going to stay in San Francisco?"

"That's my plan." She stopped. Why didn't she tell him she wanted to be a doctor's wife and live where he lived. Give up her singing and be with him. She wanted to tell him she'd stay in San Francisco waiting for him. She wanted to ask him when would he return, but she remained silent.

"Will you continue your singing?"

"I'm planning on auditioning for a great coach, Edna Fischer. I'd like to sing on the local radio station."

"You sound as if you have it all planned. Guess you won't return to San Jose?"

She didn't have a chance to ask him what he meant. The waiter asked, "Would you like an after dinner drink or coffee?"

They settled for coffee.

"Laura told me your father wants you to come back to his clinic in San Jose."

"I suspect I'll go back to the university hospital to practice when the war is over. That's my present program."

She wondered what might make him change his mind. Did that beautiful blonde she saw him with have anything to do with his decisions?

"What do you hear from Grant?"

"He left Hawaii, came back to San Diego, and joined the Marines. We don't hear much from him."

"I suppose he's not too interested in the ranch?"

"I really don't know what my brother's interested in, beside girls."

Phillip laughed. "Your brother, in fact both your brothers, are fine men." He checked his watch. "I really would like to take in the Top of the Mark. Have you been there?"

"No." She was suddenly glad she hadn't been to the top of the famous hotel.

They left the restaurant and found a cab. When they reached the hotel, they waited in the lobby for the next elevator with the happy crowd of high-ranking officers and noncoms.

They shared a booth with another couple so engrossed in each other that Carmel didn't think they knew anyone else was there.

"I'm having a cognac. What would you like?"

Carmel ordered the same, and they sat looking out at the scene before them. A full moon hung high in the sky as round and blank as a head of cheese, outlining the two bridges over the black bay and silhouetting tall buildings against the faint sky, their windows dark.

"The last time I was here the buildings were ablaze with light."

Phillip became quiet. Suddenly, she felt his distance. She wanted to reach for his hand. It should have been a beautiful night, but it wasn't. The silver moon looked cold and left an empty feeling. The couple beside them sat close together, and couples around them embraced and kissed unashamedly. He must feel a loneliness she would never understand. She was glad she hadn't mentioned it was customary for a service man to bring his girl to Weeper's Corner at the Top of the Mark for their last evening together.

Carmel and Phillip left shortly after their drink. Once in the cab, Phillip spent the short ride telling her how streptomycin was saving lives on the ship. At her front door, he stood looking down at her. Carmel felt he wanted to say something. He put his arms around her and drew her so close she could feel his warmth and the slow beat of his heart. He pressed a cool cheek against her. Then lifted her chin and she felt his warm lips for only a moment.

"Thank you for a wonderful evening, Carmel."

"Thank you, Phillip. I had a wonderful time, too."

All so damn formal, she could have shrieked.

She watched him walk down the porch steps, his body outlined in the moonlight. Before he climbed into the waiting cab, he turned and waved to her.

In bed, she pounded the pillow with her fist. She knew so little about him, yet she had committed her life to him. She felt so close to him all evening. She was positive he was glad to be with her, but at the Top of the Mark, the place that should have been romantic, he had changed. Phillip was attentive, but he might as well have been across the Pacific. What had happened? Tears rolled down her cheeks. She didn't know if he would write, if he would see her again. She felt the same old frustrations. She wanted to die. How could she go through the awful loneliness that stretched ahead of her?

CHAPTER 46

Carmel felt her spirits rising as she climbed the stairs to Edna Fischer's flat on Clay Street. Edna greeted Carmel at the door. She was shorter than Carmel, with auburn and gold curls piled on top of her head. Soft brown eyebrows arched above her hazel eyes, giving her in an inquisitive, friendly expression. She appeared very glamorous.

Carmel heard the charming lilt in Edna Fischer's voice. "Lancing Tevis, my old friend, called. He told me I should hear you sing."

"That was kind of him."

"Give me your coat and I'll just leave it here on this chair." She placed Carmel's light gray coat on a small chair. Edna Fischer's silk dress was the color of peaches. A wide peach colored belt encircled her small waist.

"Thank you." Carmel, curious about this famous lady, couldn't help herself but stare around the large room. The decor of the flat captured the essence of San Francisco. Sunlight flooded through the windows facing Clay Street. There was a huge, comfortable couch, with plump pillows scattered on it. An Oriental rug covered the floor. Gold framed a mirror reflecting the fire burning brightly in the hearth. A radio and record player, along with a record collection, stood next to a wall. A bookcase was filled with books and interesting looking carvings in wood and ivory.

Edna Fischer's jade earrings swung from her ears as she moved gracefully to the baby grand piano. Framed pictures sat on top of the piano: George Burns and Gracie Allen, Ginny Sims, the Andrew Sisters, and pictures of famous people in the theater. All dedicated to Edna Fischer.

"What would you like to sing?"

"Please, *tell* me. I can sing 'Sunny Side of The Street' or 'Stormy Weather.'"

"Let's do 'Stormy Weather' in E flat."

Edna Fischer vamped some chords and began the melody. Carmel's soprano, her voice full of warmth and melody, filled the room.

After Carmel finished, Edna Fischer stared at her for a moment. "Lancing is right—you do have a lovely voice. I believe with your looks and hard work … What is it you want to accomplish?"

"Thank you, Mrs. Fischer."

"Please, call me Edna."

"Edna, I'm interested in learning to sing on the radio."

"Well, Carmel, you have the voice you'll have all your life—if you don't abuse it with whisky or smoking. Your voice is certainly one that could become popular on the radio, but singing on the radio is not like singing in front of a band. The musicians can't hear you. On the radio, *you* have to *hear* your conductor. Totally different, because you apparently have a good ear and know pitch. Like anything else, to be good takes hours of practicing to find your special voice and phrasing. It's not just the words and music; you need the dedication to succeed."

"I don't smoke, but I do drink once in a while." She wanted Edna's approval more than anything in the world. "Will you take me as a pupil? I promise to work hard."

"That's exactly what it takes, hard work." Edna folded her arms.

"I had decided to cut back my time teaching, but Lancing was so enthusiastic about you I promised I would see you. Yes, I will take you as a student."

"How long are your lessons and what do you charge?"

"I teach for an hour and its five dollars. I'm thinking about raising the fee, but I won't for you at this time."

"Thank you. Lancing told me you were a headliner with George Burns and Gracie Allen."

"That's right. They are true professionals."

"Don't you play at the Stage Door Canteen here in San Francisco?"

"I certainly do. I play for Ginny Simms. Carmel, the voice must have character. We are wind instruments, and ample breath is indispensable. Pant like a dog …" Edna began to take short breaths to show her. "The breath comes from deep in the body, like a succession of sighs. The solar plexus moves in an out when you pant from the body and indicates correct breathing. Do you understand?"

"I believe I do."

"That's enough, for now. All comes with practice."

Carmel asked, "So now you do *Stars in the Making*?"

"I have wonderful guests: Carl Ravazza, Anson Weeks, and Del Courtney, very popular band-leaders. When they're in town, they come and listen to the singers' auditions. They select a winner, who then has the opportunity to sing on the show. It's the way the young people get started."

"How lucky for the winners." Carmel listened, mesmerized. "When may I come back?"

Edna laughed and searched through a brown book on the piano. "Call me after Christmas and we'll work out something."

Carmel left the flat, Edna called out, "Stay wonderful," two words Carmel was to hear often from Edna. Carmel knew a new door had opened in her life. How wonderful it would be if she did become a success on radio. She intended to do just that.

CHAPTER 47

Carmel went home for Christmas in 1943 and found her father walking with a cane, his foot still bandaged.

She put her arm around him. "Why haven't you told me you're still having trouble with your foot?" She noticed his usual ruddy complexion appeared pale in the room's light.

"Because it wasn't necessary." Andrew, dressed in a tailored navy jacket and trousers with a red and black checkered ascot tucked into his collar, stood erect as he greeted her with a kiss.

"A blood clot formed after the incident with the fish can," Anna said. "He has to stay off his foot and keep it up. Doctor's orders. You can see how well he minds." She maneuvered him into his chair and pushed a stool under the bandaged foot.

"That's enough, woman. She continually fusses over me." He stared gloomily at Carmel.

"It's a good thing I came home. It seems no one was going to tell me anything. Where's Scott?"

Andrew answered, "Watsonville—he'll be home soon. Carmel, it's close to five o'clock. Will you join me in a cocktail?"

"He's not supposed to be drinking, either," Anna said.

"You'd better mind her." Carmel admonished. "Not yet, Dad. I want to get rid of my trappings. I have presents to unpack. Anna, the house looks beautiful." In the corner, the tall Christmas tree glistened in the firelight, and garlands trimmed the windows. The banister was wrapped in garlands of greenery and red ribbons.

"Thank you, Carmel. We try, but this house needs your enthusiasm." Anna began picking up Carmel's suitcases and boxes.

"Anna, send for Lupe to help Carmel."

"Dad, I'll call Lupe." Anna looked tired. Carmel suspected her father was worse than he and Anna admitted.

Lupe came immediately. Her black eyes danced when she saw Carmel and the packages she was carrying.

"There are more packages sitting on the bench on the patio."

Lupe returned with them and the girls struggled up the stairs. Lupe said, "I don't know how you managed this on the train."

"None of them are heavy, just cumbersome." She set her suitcase down on the floor. Carmel looked directly into Lupe's eyes. "I expect an honest answer. Dad doesn't do much does he, Lupe?"

"No, Anna makes him sit with his leg up most of the time. I'm glad you're home for Christmas."

"So am I. You're wearing your Christmas skirt, I see." Embroidered blue birds and angels with gold wings decorated her skirt and blouse. Lupe and Anna along with Rosita made it a custom to dress in long red skirts and white blouses at Christmas.

Carmel was especially fond of Lupe. She was Jose and Rosita's daughter, twelve years older than Carmel, and had grown up on the ranch. A hard worker, she helped Anna with the cleaning and cooking. Andrew refused to treat her as a servant and paid her well. After finishing high school, she stayed and had her own bedroom in the little house she shared with her parents. Carmel knew Lupe loved hearing about San Francisco, the hotels and dance bands, and about the big house on the hill where Andrew's sister lived.

Carmel also knew how attractive Lupe was to the men. She was like a small doe, curious and cautious. Carmel asked, "Are you engaged yet?" Lupe shook her head and giggled. "Please tell my father I'll be down in a few minutes."

Carmel quickly put her things away and sorted her packages. Something was different. The house seemed chilly. Before leaving the room she pulled on a white cashmere cardigan over her coral wool dress, adding a gold necklace and a spray of perfume behind her ears.

She carried some of her packages downstairs to the huge room, where her father waited. She heard Bing Crosby on the radio singing "White Christmas."

Scott appeared at the door wearing slacks and a green shirt. "Hi, sis. Whoa! How many presents have you brought? Glad you decided to embrace your family." He gave her a kiss on the cheek before he took some of the gifts and put them under the Christmas tree.

Carmel frowned at him. "That doesn't sound very hospitable, my pet."

Her father said, "Come on, you two. It's so good to have you home. Let's have our first Christmas drink. I've opened the champagne. There's plenty of food. I thought we'd enjoy a buffet tonight."

A red damask tablecloth covered the long library table. Anna had attached red and gold satin ribbons to the corners. In the center were large silver chafing dishes keeping baked salmon, Anna's ravioli and meatballs, and garden-fresh vegetables appetizingly warm. A cranberry mold sat next to them. Red and white tapers in silver holders stood beside the crystal and silverware.

"Anna, you and Lupe have prepared a feast. It's lovely," Carmel said.

"They've worked all day," Andrew added.

"Anna's very good to you, Dad."

Scott lifted a bottle of Dom Perignon from a silver bucket on the movable bar. He served Andrew and Carmel.

Andrew took a sip of his champagne and said, "Here's to us."

Carmel raised her glass to the salute. She saw dark shadows under his eyes and wondered if he was getting enough sleep. She sat on a chair by the fireplace, where a bright fire burned.

Andrew stared at the fire. "I wish your brother was here."

"Have you heard from him?" Carmel asked.

"Yes, we have a letter. He's somewhere in the South Pacific with the Marines. I cannot imagine my brother taking orders from anyone, much less a Marine officer," Scott said.

He stretched out on the end of the couch. "Well, sis, when are you going to quit singing, leave the bright lights, and come back home to the really good life?"

"As long as I earn a living I'll stay where I am."

"I didn't realize you *knew* that much about music. I didn't *know* you knew that many songs well enough to sing?" The sarcasm in his voice was new to her.

"I didn't *know* you cared. You haven't been to San Francisco to hear me sing with a big band." She wondered why her brother was being so nasty. "And what about you? Are you still planning on going to Watsonville?"

"Those are my plans—haven't changed a damn thing."

She understood perfectly. Scott wanted to leave the ranch and he expected her to come home and take his place. She knew very little about raising walnuts, fruit, and crops. That's what she did not want to do.

Andrew listened. "It's true, Scott, I think we've let your sister down. Let's plan a trip to the city." He smiled at his daughter.

Carmel was sorry they were upsetting her father, but why was Scott being so irritable? He had been her knight in shining armor. She remembered her big brother comforting her when she hurt, holding her to wipe away the tears. She loved her brother, but she tonight he was being difficult and she didn't like him. The realization stabbed at her.

"Scott has promised me he'll stay here until the war is over. Let's have another, son."

"Comin' right up." Scott rose to do his dad's bidding. "How about you, sis?" Carmel nodded her head. "Did you see *Life* magazine? What the hell will be left of Berlin and London?"

"I wonder how the people will feed themselves, much less grow anything. We'll be feeding the world, no doubt," Andrew said.

"Well, that's exactly what I mean. The world will be wide open for my frozen food."

Neither Carmel or Andrew responded.

Carmel watched Andrew reach for the small package of cigarette paper on the table beside him. He opened it, held the paper between the fingers of his right hand, and reached into his shirt pocket with his left hand. He managed to remove the white sack of Bull Durham, pull the string with his teeth and fingers of his left hand, and shake the tobacco into the narrow slip of paper. He pulled the string with his teeth and fingers, shutting the bag, and put it in his shirt pocket. Holding the paper between his fingers, sealing the edge with his wet tongue stuck the cigarette in his mouth, lit the end, and inhaled. Gray smoke rose from his mouth. He smiled. "*Real* cowboys do it with one hand."

"You're real enough to me."

The room was silent except for wood snapping in the fire. Carmel asked, "Dad, what time are the Barrons coming over?"

"Only Harold and Laura are coming. Cynthia won't be joining us. They're due any minute."

When Laura arrives, Carmel thought, my brother will snap out of his surly mood. Maybe I'll find out something about Phillip.

The doorbell rang. Lupe opened it to let Harold and Laura arrive full of good cheer. The dogs raced into the room from the outside ahead of the Barrons. Bruno went under the tablecloth. Howard went straight to Carmel to be petted. Carmel obliged him. "Hello, Howard, missed me?" She bent down to look into his brown eyes and Howard licked her face. Then, with his tail wagging, he joined Bruno under the table.

Harold said, "Merry Christmas, all." He smiled at Carmel. "Glad you're home." He shook Andrew's hand. "How's that foot doing?"

"I'm doing better. It feels better, anyway."

"Ignoring a blood clot won't make it go away, you know."

Andrew muttered, "I'm not ignoring it."

Harold placed the packages he carried under the tree. Scott took their coats and gave Laura a kiss.

"Thank you, Scott." Harold wore a red cardigan over his white shirt and red bowtie.

"Laura, you look wonderful in lavender." With a pang, Carmel thought, Laura's facial expressions were like Phillip's.

"Thank you."

"Would you folks have champagne with us?" Andrew asked. "When you are ready, help yourselves to the buffet. For dessert there's apple-filled puff pastry with whipped cream."

Harold laughed and sat down. "A drink will be fine. No thanks to any food. I don't plan on staying long."

"Scott, would you do us the honors?" Andrew looked at Harold. "How is Cynthia?"

"You never know about arthritis. Some days are better than others. Today is one of the good ones. She's holding her own. Thanks for asking. I understand from Laura, you've heard from Grant?" Scott served Harold and Laura champagne.

"A short letter. At least we heard something from him," Andrew said.

Harold surprised. "Grant in the marines? My, my."

Scott sat on the couch beside Laura and put his arm around her shoulder. Laura nestled into him. "That's right. Never, never thought my brother would volunteer for the marines," Scott said.

Carmel watched them. She knew Scott would walk Laura home early. Goodness radiated from Laura. Her dear friend was without an ounce of guile in her whole body. Laura's requests of life, Carmel thought, were too simple. Became a nurse, marry Scott, have babies, live in Willow Glen on Minnesota Avenue the rest of her life. To be honest, her plans were similar to her friend's. They hadn't gone much beyond marrying Phillip, but lately a new thought began to lurk in her mind. If she were married to Phillip, would he ask her to give up her music?

Laura asked, "Carmel, have you seen any good movies?"

"Yes. *The Outlaw* with Jane Russell."

Scott slapped his knee with enthusiasm. "Hey! I haven't seen it yet. Any good?"

"I think you'd like it. Jane Russell fills up the screen." Carmel laughed. "I liked *For Whom the Bells Tolls* better. Ingrid Bergman and Gary Cooper are wonderful together."

Laura said, "Oh, Scott, let's see *The Outlaw* soon."

Andrew interrupted, "Scott, get the letter from your brother. It's on the chest by the door.

Scott brought the envelope and handed it to his father. Andrew opened the envelope. "It's not very long, but considering it's from Grant, I'm grateful for anything." He began to read.

December, 1943

Dear Dad, Scott and Carmel,

I can't tell you much. My main objective is to let you know I'm alive and healthy. As you know, I left with the intent to hook up with the marines. Any rumor you heard that the marines are tough is true. Somehow, I survived boot camp. I'm so tough, I could bite a nail in half. I understand now why a Mean Marine is a Fighting Machine. Ha!

The grub is tops. My biggest event occurred when the USO came to camp and Betty Grable picked me to dance with her on stage. I have a picture to prove it, but can't send it to you. Need it for solid reference. This is a doubting bunch. I can't tell you when or where we are headed. Just hope you get to see Aunt Francis for Christmas. Tell Anna to start those cookies coming.

Love to all,

Grant.

Andrew asked, "Harold, do you know where Phillip is?"

"When he was here the last time, he said wherever there's a battle the *Solace* is close by. She waits to take on patients. If there's fighting in the South Pacific, that's where Grant and Phillip are. But who knows where."

Andrew signaled Scott to refill the glasses. "We do know that for the past twenty months the Japanese have fortified the islands in the South Pacific, planning their attack on Australia. We need to establish bases for B-29 bombers for raids on Japan. We read the assaults between the Americans and Japanese on the Gilbert Islands were brutal."

"The November battle on Tarawa must have been fierce. It was reported the largest force of navy vessels ever assembled in the Pacific, including battleships and aircraft carriers, was joined by the Second and Twenty-seventh Marine Divisions against four thousand Japanese. At the end of the four-day battle, out of three thousand American men only a few hundred escaped wounds or death."

Scott listened to his dad. "Well, they have destroyed forever Japanese hopes of landing in Australia."

Laura asked, "Carmel, will you be around tomorrow?"

"No, I have to be back early tomorrow afternoon. I'm doing a Christmas benefit for the Stage Door Canteen. We'll have some great entertainment. The place is always jammed."

"Carmel, I don't have anything special to tell you. Mary Alice Watson and Emily Fish have joined the navy. They are in New York at the US Naval Reserve Training school. Before they left we gave them a farewell get-together. The only thing different around here for me—nothing ever changes." She sounded wistful. "After I finish this drink, I'm going back to the house. Don't want to leave Mother alone very long. Dad can stay here and visit."

Scott filled his plate. "I like that! Nothing ever happens. You have me to watch out for. You want to go running off like my sister?" He grinned at her. "When you're ready to go, I'll walk you home."

"I'm ready now." She turned to Carmel. "I really came to say *hello* and wish you Merry Christmas!" Laura got up to leave. "Patti had a new litter of pups. Wish you could see them."

"I will next time. Tell your mom Merry Christmas from us all."

"I will. Goodnight, Mr. St. John."

Both dogs crawled out from under the table and followed Scott and Laura out the door.

Carmel observed Dr. Barron. Well over six feet and every bit as handsome as Phillip, he had a perfect profile. His dark hair, as black as Phillip's, was cut short and high over his ears in the current style. His dark eyes, though not as black as Phillips, were alert and attentive. Even though he was older than her father, his skin was unlined and his bearing was of a younger man. Harold always appeared well groomed. His movements were brisk and full of authority. He was a modest man, devoted to his family, and treated his patients well. Laura told her of his many anonymous good deeds, such as arranging the adoption of several underprivileged children—not cute babies easily adopted but already school age and needing a family. She wondered, Is Phillip that tender hearted? Does he even like children?

Tonight she learned absolutely nothing about Phillip—where he was or when he was coming to San Jose. No one seemed to know.

She heard her father say, "Those Japs have dug deep into the islands. It'll be hell to get them out. The Marines will have to do it."

"Grant will do it," Carmel said.

There were chuckles all around. Andrew rolled another cigarette. Harold watched him. "You're a stubborn man, Andrew, he said. "You know I don't approve of your smoking, especially when you are trying to recover from a blood clot."

Andrew exhaled slowly. "You worry too much, Harold. What do you think about the Russians?"

Harold took a swig of his drink. "Granted, we don't know what happened in Cairo in November with Chiang Kai-shek, Roosevelt, and Churchill met to plan the futures of Germany and Japan when the war was over. We don't know what happened when Roosevelt and Churchill met with Stalin, but I'm relieved the Russians are coming over on our side."

Andrew wondered. "How do you account for that?"

"Don't you believe Roosevelt realizes he needs Stalin on our side? Andrew, the Russians have been fighting a bloody battle. I think Roosevelt believes if and when Eisenhower is ready for the invasion of Europe, we'll need a signed pact with Russia."

Andrew shook his head. "I'll never trust those Russians. Too many have been killed by their own regimens. They sure are scrappers though. Those women are as tough as the men. They dug ditches in frozen ground to hide and fight. After months of German attacks on Russia, the Red Army and women succeeded in pushing the German army 775 miles away from Stalingrad."

"What do you think about the government ordering us to start income tax withholding?" Harold asked.

"By taxing, the government will know how much money there will be to spend. With the war continuing, the government needs to know." Andrew laughed. "No one will escape."

"I hoped by Christmas we would read that the Allies had captured Cassinio. Even with advanced heavy bombing and artillery, little ground has been gained and the losses continue." Harold shook his head.

During this conversation, Carmel carried dishes of food out to the kitchen to be put away. Lupe was with her family on Christmas Eve. Anna had quietly joined her. In a short time, the two women had the table cleared. "Thank you, Anna, for a lovely Christmas Eve." Carmel hugged Anna.

Anna hugged her back. "You warm my heart, Carmel. I'll always want you home."

Carmel gave her father a kiss. "I'm going to bed. You guys can solve the world's problems. Good night, Dad. See you in the morning. No, don't go, Dr. Barron. Stay and visit. I've had a long day and tomorrow is another. Merry Christmas and to all a good night."

Carmel entered her darkened room. She walked to the window and opened the drapes. The night was clear and bright with a full moon.

Troubled she leaned her forehead against the cold window. "I'm a singer," she said to the pepper trees swaying in the moonlight like gray dancing ghosts. Before this evening, Carmel thought Scott and her father were proud of her singing accomplishments. Now she realized they felt she had accomplished nothing.

If the talk with her brother discouraged her in the beginning, now it simply put fire and determination into her veins. One thing was certain. She was going to stay in San Francisco, begin her lessons with Edna, and continue to get better and better in hopes of singing on the radio. She lifted her shoulders and promised herself it would not take long. And she would remain patient, knowing Phillip would arrive again just as unexpected.

CHAPTER 48

Jerry waited, seated at a table in Jack's Restaurant on Sacramento Street. When Carmel arrived, he stood and brushed her cheek with a kiss. "You're fresh as a spring day."

Carmel wore a becoming pale green wool dress that fit her slim curves. Her dark hair was pulled back from her face under a tiny green hat.

Her smile was radiant. "Thank you. You're looking wonderful yourself," she said, referring to his black and gray checked jacket and yellow bowtie. "I'm glad you could meet me." A waiter took her coat, hung it on one of the brass hooks lining the wall, and waited for their order.

Carmel said, "I'd like Chardonnay."

Jerry ordered a bottle of wine.

They sat for a moment and enjoyed the noonday crowd. The waiter brought the wine, received Jerry's approval, and poured it into each glass. He gave them menus and disappeared. Jerry raised his glass to her.

Carmel looked around the restaurant. "This is quite a place; I've never been here before."

In the long, narrow room, moldings of dark wood with garlands and strands of laurel in gilded plaster decorating the walls. Ornate brass coat hooks held coats and hats. The table linens were blinding white, and the chairs dark bentwood.

"It's been here since 1864. It survived the 1906 earthquake and the fire. It was dynamited and later rebuilt on the same spot. There are six private dining rooms upstairs which can be locked from the inside for hanky-panky." He laughed.

A tall, thin waiter appeared. "Okay. What'll it be?"

"How are the sand dabs today?" Jerry asked.

"Same as yesterday."

Jerry asked, "Carmel, would you like sand dabs?"

Carmel studied the menu. "No, I'd like the Rex Sole."

"Good choice. I'd suggest their green bean salad with vinaigrette dressing and small roasted red potatoes." Carmel nodded. Jerry turned to the waiter and ordered.

"Do you think he likes his job?" Carmel asked.

"These birds are like New York waiters. Just on the edge of being surly. As you can see, they are all past draft age."

The room was noisy with conversation and bursts of laughter. "The place is sure crowded, so the food must be excellent."

"Actually, it is."

Jerry said, "Jack's is popular at lunch time for lawyers, judges, and newspapermen. This is a gathering place for the politicians of the city." Jerry looked across the room. "Mayor Rossi is there with his gang from city hall. Harry Bridges is across from him."

Six men sat at a table across the room, laughing at something someone said. One of the men, looking well fed and prosperous, seemed to be the center of the group. Carmel supposed he was the mayor. The man Jerry called Harry Bridges was slightly built and wore a gray suit. His thin face and high forehead belied the force of the man. She heard he controlled the powerful Longshoreman's Union in San Francisco. He was in an intent conversation with one of the men."

Jerry narrowed his eyes at her. "You sounded mysterious on the phone when you called."

"I've decided. You're the only one to help me. I'm feeling lost in the music world. There are so many bands and musicians, and I don't think I know anything about them."

The waiter served lunch. He refilled their glasses of wine.

Carmel savored her fish, smothered in butter and herbs. "I understand what you mean. This fish is perfection." After a moment she asked, "Jerry, tell me about some of the leading bands."

"Sure, we can start with Mickey bands. They play sweet sounding ballads for dancing. For example, there's Guy Lombardo, Lawrence Welk, and Freddie Martin. The swing bands, like Goodman, Glen Miller, Artie Shaw, and Dorsey, play music that is crisp, clean, and exciting. For example, 'Stomping at the

Savoy' or 'Take the A Train."" He poured himself a cup of coffee and took a gulp.

"Let's see. There are the jump bands—Count Basie, Kenton, Herman, and Lunceford—they are more brisk and decisive sounding. Then there are jazz bands like Jack Teagarden and Ellington, who play everything. Del Courtney, Carl Ravazza, and Ray Noble are usually in the hotels. Here in town, Lu Waters, his Yerba Buena Jazz band, and Turk Murphy are very popular, as you know. Take the southern parts of the country. There's music with fiddles and guitars, called hillbilly. In addition, there's the Grand Old Opera. If you picked up a copy of *Down Beat* magazine, you'd know the scene, as they say."

Carmel was impressed. "I bet you know some wild stories about your compatriots?"

"Some. A lot is hearsay." He took a cigarette from a pack of Chesterfields, lit it, and exhaled before he continued. "Charlie Barnett, a good-looking cat, was the first to bring black musicians into a white band. I guess he was the first white band to play in the Cotton Club in New York, an all-black club. People thought they were listening to black musicians. Barnett has the rich sound of Ellington and Basie, even some Lunceford. When he's on the road and hears there's some good fishing, he stops his bus, and all the guys go fishing. He's some kind of cat."

"I love his theme song, 'Cherokee.' Didn't Billy May write it?"

"Ray Noble wrote it, but Billy May arranged it. Yes, he did. See, you know more than you think you do."

Carmel grinned. "Where did you start, Jerry?"

"My father died when I was sixteen. I lied about my age and went to work playing piano in backrooms and bars. My first real job was playing piano on the ferries crossing the bay to Sausalito."

"You know so many musicians. How come you didn't go on the road with a band?"

"I don't dare go too far from my mother, who has chronic heart problems. I'm her only child. She still lives in our old house in Redwood City. I'm lucky to have the job at the station."

"Do you know Glen Miller?"

"Just to say hello. He looks more serious than his bouncing music. He's a dedicated arranger. Right now, he's got a great band in the army. I used to listen to his band on the radio at night, coming from the East. The broadcasts here, heard three hours earlier, were done to give them publicity. When they arrived in California, the musicians were surprised to find how popular they were."

Carmel said, "I went to sleep at night listening to them broadcast from Hotel Pennsylvania and the Meadowbrook. Tell me more."

"Well, a lot of these birds are in the service. Woody Herman's band enlisted right away, so did Artie Shaw's. Musicians love to play with Woody. He's a great, warm guy. I hear Artie is an intellectual and perfectionist. He's hard on his men."

Jerry stubbed out his cigarette. The waiter brought the check and Jerry paid the bill.

He continued, "Goodman is tough. He's meticulous and demanding. In 1937, when he played at the Paramount Theater in New York, his fans built bonfires in Times Square." Jerry laughed. "I have an idea that upset Benny. He's a quiet and serious man. The musicians with his band are outstanding, especially Lionel Hampton on vibes and Gene Krupa on drums. Benny's an old friend of mine. When he comes to Sweets Ballroom in Oakland, let's try and see him."

"I'd love that."

"Benny recently recorded with the Budapest String Quartet. Carmel, anyone that is any good is demanding. Musicians have the highest respect for Miller and Goodman." Jerry frowned. "Dorsey fires someone in his band just about every night and hires him back the same night. He does put the booze away."

"I don't notice narcotics in the bands I sing with."

"They're not in every band. Some musicians get high regularly, popping bennies. Where there are musicians, booze, babes, and gambling are all part of the scene. Cocaine has killed many top artists. Traveling, sleeping, and living on buses gets old. Now, obtaining the gasoline they need has become almost impossible. Leaders try to control marijuana, but you can't baby-sit your men. Gene Krupa, while here in San Francisco, was arrested on a marijuana charge—did ninety days in the county jail."

The waiter brought Carmel's coat. "I was so fascinated. Our lunch sure went fast. Thanks, Jerry. I felt absolutely ignorant."

"How're you doing with Edna Fischer?"

"She's coaching me. I'm working on some songs now. She's adorable."

"San Francisco loves her. She knows everyone in broadcasting, and they *all* know her."

They stood outside the restaurant to say good-bye, Jerry put his black snap-brim hat on and said, "Keep working hard. I have a good feeling about you. If Edna took you as a pupil, that says volumes. See you at the hospital Thursday."

"You bet. Thanks Jerry." She thought, It will take me forever to learn what he knows.

CHAPTER 49

Carmel, suddenly awake in her own bed in San Jose, for a moment wasn't sure what woke her. Under the warm blankets, she listened to her father yell at the dogs. Bruno and Howard had treed a cat. They weren't going to stop barking until someone did something. Her father giving orders to barking dogs were sounds both familiar and comforting.

The decision to come home was not prompted by anything special. She had worked steadily since Christmas and decided to take a few days off. After informing Lydia, she packed a small bag, rode the Hyde cable car downtown, caught a bus to the railroad station, and boarded a late-afternoon commuter train to San Jose.

Now wide awake, she got up and opened the blue velvet drapes. Sunlight flooded the room. The bright, sunny February day reminded her spring was not far away. She hurried through her shower. Afterwards, dressed in navy slacks and a pink cotton shirt, she gave her hair a quick brush and put color on her lips. The barking had stopped. She guessed the cat had been rescued.

When Carmel entered the kitchen, she saw that the tops of the trestle tables were covered with cardboard boxes and wax paper. A large bowl full of popcorn sat on the table. "The house smells delicious. This looks like a bakery. What's going on?"

Lupe giggled. "You wouldn't believe what we're doing!"

Anna said, "Since Grant wrote and ordered cookies, I see this recipe in Sunday's church calendar. It shows me how to ship cookies overseas so they not so many pieces. I'll stop and fix you breakfast."

"No, you won't. I'll fix my eggs and toast. I see there's coffee."

It didn't take long to scramble eggs and pop bread into the toaster. She placed the eggs on a plate with toast and honey and sat with a cup of coffee to watch the women work.

Anna explained, "First you wipe the inside of this sturdy box with a damp sponge that Lupe sprinkled with vanilla. Next, line the bottom of box with a layer of unsalted popcorn." Anna scooped popcorn from the bowl and spread it over the bottom of the box. She tore off a sheet of wax paper from the roll beside her and laid it over the popcorn.

Lupe spread cookies over the paper. Then she tore off a sheet of wax paper and spread more popcorn.

Anna continued, "Next time a layer of cookies with nuts and dates. You keep doing with wax paper until box is full."

Carmel rinsed her dishes and set them on the sink. "I want to help."

"You get a box and pack if you like. I'm going to bake cookies. I want to fill six boxes. Each box holds forty cookies. Grant and his buddies will have cookies." Anna went to the end of the large table. There were bags of flour, sugar, and mixing bowls. She began to measure and mix.

Carmel rolled up the long sleeves of her shirt. "How did you manage to get sugar?"

Anna laughed. "Many people on ranch gave up ration of sugar when I say I make cookies for solider boys. Drink coffee without sugar. Carmel, use this rubber band, tie your hair back."

Andrew limped into the kitchen and watched the activities. He put his arm around Carmel and gave her a squeeze. "It looks to me, Carmel, like you've taken up wearing slacks."

"Why not, Dad? They're comfortable. Many women in San Francisco wear them, especially women who work in the defense plants."

"I'll never get used to it. I like a woman to look feminine, wear skirts." He reached for an oatmeal cookie and munched on it as he left the room. "Boy, will Grant and his buddies cheer when they taste these."

The three women worked through the morning into the early afternoon, baking and packing. They made peanut butter, date cookies with nuts, and oatmeal cookies. Carmel broke eggs, sprinkled powered sugar, and chopped nuts, anything Anna asked her to do.

In the early afternoon, her father stood in the kitchen doorway. "Look what I found on the terrace."

Phillip stood behind her father, a look of amusement on his face. Carmel gasped. She felt as if someone had punched her very hard in the stomach. Staring at him, she responded by accepting his handshake.

For him to appear suddenly was embarrassing. She knew she had flour on her face, powdered sugar across her apron, and here she faced this immaculate officer in navy blue. "What a surprise," she sputtered.

Her father said, "Phillip's here for a few days. Come on, Carmel. You've done enough in the kitchen. Come away and visit with Phillip."

"Phillip, I'll be with you in a minute. Would you like some coffee?" She was untying the apron Anna had tied around her.

"No. Your father already offered me a drink. Don't let me interrupt the cookie factory."

Anna said, "Carmel, go entertain your guest. We'll finish."

Carmel walked slowly into the living room and found Phillip alone. "Where's my father?"

Phillip had taken off his heavy navy top coat and stood looking out the window. "One of his men needed him. Your father seems to be limping even more."

"He's being very stubborn. The doctor said he might have to use a wheelchair. I don't think he listens to his doctor. He smokes constantly."

"Maybe I'll have a talk with him. Carmel, you look very domestic in the kitchen, decked out with flour on your nose." He laughed.

"Oh, sit down. I'll get you something. What would you like?"

Phillip pulled her down beside him on the couch. "Nothing. I called you when the ship docked in San Francisco. Your aunt told me you were here."

She was at eye level looking directly into his black eyes. Carmel wondered what would happen if she fainted. "You're not as tan this time." What an insane thing to say.

"I don't spend much time on deck sunbathing." He grinned.

Carmel scoffed, "All right, smarty."

She moved off the couch, away from his closeness. "I know your family is anxious to see you. Will you be here very long?" Her breathing was uneven. She wanted to ask him why he'd shown up with no warning.

"I've seen my mom and dad. I think Laura is off somewhere with your brother. I intend to spend a day with my folks. Then I wondered if you would go to Santa Cruz with me. I have two days. There's a beautiful place I'd like to show you. I've borrowed a car from a friend who owes me a favor. I'll be able to drive you back to San Francisco. Please don't say no."

She looked at this man she loved. She knew she should say no. This wasn't proper, she thought, going away with him. But what if she would never see him again? She instantly forgave him.

"I'll pick you up at four o'clock tomorrow, here."

Carmel nodded her head.

Phillip stood. "See you tomorrow." He put his coat over his arm. "Wear something warm. We'll walk on the beach." His lips lightly kissed the top of her nose. "Don't forget to talk Anna out of some cookies." He left the room.

Carmel heard the front door close. Oh, damn, she thought, her beautiful clothes were in San Francisco. She had nothing spectacular to wear, nothing to knock him off his feet. She had waited so long to spend time with him. What a joy this was, happening to her. The gods were kind. Now she knew why she had come home.

CHAPTER 50

Carmel was waiting, pretending to leave for San Francisco when Phillip arrived. Andrew limped to the door and told them to drive safely. Carmel would face the guilt later. She would not spoil it now.

In the small Chevrolet coupe, Phillip's hand brushed her thigh when he moved the gearshift. She wanted to stare at him. Watch everything he did. Sitting next to him, she could feel his body heat. She liked his cologne and wondered what it was.

Carmel watched the landscape go by. "These mountains are spectacular. They remind me of pictures I've seen of Germany."

"And Switzerland. These trees go right down to the edge of the sea. I'm looking forward to walking on the beach. Did you bring the cookies?" Phillip asked.

"Yes. Will a dozen be enough?" She grinned.

The day was clear with a blue sky full of white clouds buffeted by the wind. They passed few automobiles on the highway. Carmel felt the drop in temperature as they drove closer to Santa Cruz and the ocean.

"We're going to a famous Victorian hotel called the Beach Hill Inn. It's a block from the beach and boardwalk, which I imagine will be closed for the winter. Carl, the caretaker, told me Mrs. Lyon, the owner, is in Mexico City. The inn is closed during January and February. Carl, whom I've known since I was a kid, arranged a room for us. Maybe you remember our family spent part of the summer at the inn."

"I do remember, but I always met Laura on Cowell's Beach, which was more fun than the beach in front of the boardwalk. Cowell's was closer to the mile-long wharf and the bigger waves. If you caught the top of one, it gave you a longer ride.

"I had no idea you were a surfer."

"I kept away from Steamer Lane by the lighthouse. It was hard for me to stand on the board. The boards were hollow and filled with water and I had to have help dragging it up on the beach so the cork could be pulled out to let the water out. I was a nuisance." She laughed. "Santa Cruz is so clean. Did you ever notice Santa Cruz has a different sun than San Jose?"

"Why is that?"

"The sun is blinding here. I think it's because the air's so clean."

Santa Cruz, a thirty-minute drive away, was a picture postcard town nestled on the edge of the sea. They drove down Pacific Avenue toward the beach past two-story frame and brick buildings. Phillip drove up the hill and parked in front of a large Victoria mansion. A sign hung on the entrance, Beach Hill Inn. "I'll just be a minute." He got out of the car, ignored the front door, and followed a pathway leading to the back of the building. Carmel watched him disappear and wondered if she was about to make a mistake.

She pushed the worry away, looking with interest at the three-story white wooden building. There were many green shuttered windows of different sizes. Vines covered the pillars of a large verandah encircling the first floor. It was empty of the chairs and couches. Two tulip trees about to burst with pink and lavender blossoms stood inside the low rock wall rimming the property. Thick wisteria vines, now dormant, covered an arbor extending into the garden. Purple and white alyssum edged the walkway.

Phillip came back to the car and opened the door. "Carmel, this is Carl Kruge, my old friend."

"Good afternoon, Miss Carmel, velcome." His accent made her think of Elka. A slightly built man, he had bright, unblinking eyes and tanned, wrinkled skin. His bushy hair was streaked with gray. She was fascinated by his gray mustache, which curled under his nose and touched his chin in a graceful swirl. He wore dark green corduroys and a heavy jacket.

Carl picked up the two bags and led Carmel and Phillip into the front lobby furnished with ornate Victorian couches and chairs. A massive floor-to-ceiling mirror, framed in gold, hung on a wall and reflected the luxury of the room. They followed him across a plush Aubusson rug to the wide stairway.

On the second floor, Carl took them down a long cool hall, passing closed doors. He stopped in front of one and opened it. Carmel almost gasped when she saw the large, high four-poster bed with ornate owls carved in the middle of the headboard. There was a stool for climbing into the bed. Carl set their bags in front of a tall mahogany armoire. A table and two chairs upholstered in green velvet sat in front of French doors. A small couch beside the fireplace was covered in the same color velvet.

"You have room with a view. You can go out on balcony. You can see Monterey Bay." He pushed open the French doors onto a small deck facing the gardens and the sea. He opened a door to the bathroom.

Phillip said, "Carl, this is great."

Carmel looked past Phillip and saw a stack of thick white towels on a chair, beside a massive claw-footed bathtub. A large, round mirror hung over the sink. Green and gold paper covered the walls.

Carl said, "Sammy is Chinese cook. He will cook meals served here or dining room. Let him know vhat you vant."

"Thank you, Carl. Is it all right with you, Carmel? We'll eat dinner here." He looked at Carmel. At her nod, he said, "Let's have dinner at eight. I'd like to show Carmel the place before it gets any darker."

"You're velcome. Show secret passages; don't forget dungeon." Carl laughed.

Carmel's eyes grew large at his words.

Phillip said, "If she's naughty, we may lock her up."

Carmel took off her warm coat and hung it in the armoire. She said, "What a beautiful room." The floor-to-ceiling brocaded draperies, in gold and green, were trimmed with gold fringe and tassels. The same brocade covered the bed. An emerald green rug matched the stripe of the green and cherry in the wallpaper. Dark moldings near the high ceiling added to the elegance of the room.

Phillip said, "Before we start, I'm going to change." He took clothes out of his suitcase and went into the bathroom, closing the door. In a few minutes, he returned in brown slacks, a red and brown plaid shirt, and brogues. He hung his uniform in the armoire.

Carmel hesitated, unsure in this new situation. Phillip put his arms around her and looked into her gray eyes. "I'm glad you're here. We'll have a great time. Come on and grab a sweater. I think it'll be cold in the halls."

Carmel, in her gold silk blouse and navy skirt, wasn't dressed for warmth. She pulled her navy sweater from her case and put it on. She was looking forward to exploring the old inn.

"Mrs. Lyon bought two Victoria mansions in the early 1900s and had them placed side by side. This gave her forty-five guest rooms. Carl built fireplaces in twenty-five of them. Now it's a three-story building. And Carl says there are seventy Seth Thomas clocks throughout the inn."

Carmel enjoyed listening to Phillip tell the history of the Beach Hill Inn. They started on the first floor; the labyrinth of rooms was impressive. Both a piano and a harpsichord stood in the music room. A small library contained shelves of books, comfortable leather chairs, and lamps set on small tables. Carmel thought the large dining room, with its parquet floors and many tables and chairs, would be friendly on a summer day, especially with flowers on the tables and bright lights, but in the winter afternoon the room was uninviting, cold, and full of shadows. French doors opened onto a large deck with an arbor beyond.

In the front parlor, Carl had carved words above the hearth. Carmel stopped to read the words.

Behold, how good and how pleasant it is for brethren to dwell together in unity.

Carmel stayed close behind Phillip, peeking into the warren of rooms. They opened doors and went up and down endless steps. All the rooms were tastefully decorated with antiques. Pictures painted by early California artists hung on the walls.

As the early winter dusk began to settle, the dimly lit halls and rooms had become eerie. Carmel began to feel increasingly uneasy as she walked along the long dark corridors. On the third floor, the halls grew quite narrow. A shutter banged in the wind, making her jump.

Coming out of one of the rooms into the gloomy, narrow hall, she suddenly realized Phillip had disappeared. She called his name. No answer. Then the wall beside her began to move away, making a horrible scraping sound. It stopped moving and there was silence. Her breath became shallow and she began to tremble. She had a feeling something terrible was going to happen. Where was Phillip?

She stood at the threshold of an open doorway leading into a room that had not been there before and stared into total darkness. There were no windows, and it smelled of old newspapers. The wind had increased, and in the cold silence Carmel waited. Her heart pounded.

Phillip emerged from the room, grinning impishly.

"Doctor, you nearly had me as a patient."

"You do look pale. I'm sorry. I meant to scare you a little for the fun of it, not to frighten you." He put his arms around her and held her close for a moment. "There are three hidden passages in the inn. We used to hide in them."

"I'll not go a step further, unless you promise not to do that again."

"I promise. Had enough of this spooky place?" He took her hand. "Let's go back to the room."

They returned to find Carl had set a fire and drawn the blackout curtains across the windows. The room felt warm and cozy. He had also brought a bottle of champagne in a silver ice bucket, glasses, a tray with crackers, and a small dish of caviar.

"How like my old friend."

Carmel pulled back the heavy silk spread, folded it, and laid it on a bench at the end of the bed. Kicking off her shoes, she climbed onto the bed and watched Phillip open the champagne. Her emotions were on hold. He was before her, talking to her, planning the next day. She felt with a clap of her hands he would be gone.

Phillip filled two glasses and handed her one. He sat on the stool by the bed near her feet. Carmel didn't dare look at him. She felt the pleasant odor of his closeness. They were quiet as they watched the fire and drank. Phillip got up to refill their glasses. This time he raised his glass and looked into her eyes. "Carmel, I want to make love to you."

She heard herself gasp. The wood in the fire snapped. Somewhere at sea a foghorn blasted. She was speechless.

"Don't feel shy." He placed their champagne glasses on the table and sat down on the stool. Taking hold of her silk-covered foot, he began to gently massage it.

Carmel felt pleasure from his hands. A slow flow of excitement spread up her leg. His hand moved toward her thigh and released her garter. Taking his time, he removed the stocking, leaving her foot bare. Carmel watched him remove her other shoe and stocking. He lifted her foot to his mouth and kissed a toe, continuing to massage her foot, first one and then the other. Carmel wanted to reach for him.

He moved easily onto the bed beside her. He began kissed her eyelids, her brow, and the tip of her nose. He found her willing lips and began gently sucking her tongue. Carmel moaned softly. His kisses covered the creamy skin on her throat, down to the deep crevice between her breasts. He unbuttoned her blouse, and as it fell away from her body he reached behind her back and unhooked her bra, releasing her breasts. Their rosy color revealed, his mouth sucked on a pink nipple. Carmel gasped at the pleasure his lips brought to her.

Carmel was greedy for his kisses. She helped him slip off her skirt and out of her panties. She lay nude before him. Revealing her naked firm breasts, tiny waist, and long tapering legs in the firelight

His voice was husky. "You are beautiful, Carmel." He removed his clothes and stood before her. She reached for his chest and rubbed her fingers in the hair. She trailed her fingers over his stomach and down between his legs, feeling him, until he lowered himself and kissed her lips with passion.

She saw the desire in his eyes. Overwhelmed to make love to the man she so desired, Carmel gave herself to him, matching the fires of his passion. Now strong arms encouraged her, teaching her what to do. His ardor carried her to a release of unfamiliar ecstasy.

Afterwards she remained beneath him, holding him until the trembling stopped. Carmel could feel the beating of his heart.

A knock at the door brought back reality. Phillip called, "Just a minute." He left the bed and pulled on his trousers. "This is a hell of a time for company."

Carmel yanked the covers up to her chin.

Phillip turned up the light and opened the door. A Chinese man held a tray. "I bring dinnah."

"Are you Sammy? Thank you." Sammy nodded. He placed the tray of dishes covered with silver salvers on the table by the windows and backed out of the room.

Phillip inspected the dinner. "He's brought our dinner early and it looks appetizing. It's fresh salmon. Do you want to eat, Carmel?"

Carmel, already off the bed, found her blue wool robe. "Yes, I'm hungry. I'll be back in a few minutes." She stepped into the bathroom.

She returned in her robe. Phillip had put on his shirt and replenished the fire with the wood Carl had left. He looked into her eyes for a moment then held her close before he led her to the table. He lit the candle on the table, refilled their champagne glasses, and sat down.

It began to rain tapping against the windows. Phillip teased her when she finished every bite of her food.

Carmel felt time had stopped and she would wake up finding it all was a dream. With only the candle and the fire, she saw their silhouettes were long dark shadows against the walls.

After dinner, Phillip took a blanket off the bed, spread it on the floor in front of the fire, and added two pillows. He invited Carmel to join him. His strong arms enfolded her. They were silent listening to the rain and the cracking fire. Carmel sighed. She was where she always wanted to be.

"Please take off your robe and stand in front of the fire," Phillip asked. "I want to remember how you look." Carmel removed her robe and stood before him, naked in the firelight. Her skin glowed the color of honey. Dusky hair covered naked shoulders. The pink nipples of her full breasts waited for his kisses. Her curving hips and the hollow between her thighs invited him. She looked at him with tender and yielding eyes.

"You could drive a man crazy desiring you. Are you a witch?" He rose and removed his shirt and trousers and returned to the blanket.

She joined him. With a sparkle in her eyes, she pushed him back on the pillow. "If I'm a witch, then I can make you do what I want." Crouching over him, her nipples barely touched his chest. Carmel's hair fell like a curtain over their faces.

"What would you have me do?"

"Love me again, just love me." She nipped his ear.

Her request renewed fires of passion. Phillip lifted her to the bed. He took his time teasing Carmel with his lips. He traced her brows and the very edge of her ears, nibbling the soft skin around her lips. His breath was warm and excited her. She was hungry for his kisses and searched his body with her mouth and hands. He resisted her attempts and made her wait as he moved, barely touching her shoulder, moving to her breasts with his mouth. His tongue was warm and wet as he drew her nipple into his mouth. His lips followed the curve of her waist, across the smooth satin of her belly. Her skin was becoming moist with the pleasure his caresses aroused. Only then did he cover her with his body and gently and slowly enter her. Carmel opened herself to him, matching his rhythm and returning his passion. To Carmel, there was only this moment.

Later, she curled in his arms and slept peacefully.

Carmel was the first to wake the next morning. Enough light escaped from the half-open drape and she watched him while he slept. She could hear the soft flutter of his breath. His beard was darker this morning and his lashes formed crescents on his cheeks. She looked at his full lips and remembered he had explored every inch of her with those lips. She could feel her body warm for him.

Suddenly, black eyes opened and caught her staring at him. He smiled. Her eyes were soft and full of love. Her face flushed at being caught staring. "How's my tormentor this morning? Did you sleep well?" He pulled her to him.

She felt the heat from his body and started to reach for him.

Their love making was interrupted. Sammy knocked on the door with their breakfast. Phillip slipped on his trousers. He took the tray, closed the door, and sat the tray on the table. He threw back the bedclothes, uncovering Carmel's nude body, and left her.

Carmel laughed, and by the time she reached down to pull up the covers he stood with a cup of coffee for her. "There is juice and a roll if you like. Come on, lazy bones. I'll run your bath water." He went into the bathroom, carrying a cup of coffee. She heard him turn on the faucet.

In a few minutes, Carmel finished her juice and coffee. She sat in the warm-scented water, watching him shave, soaping herself, when Phillip said, "Let some of the water out. I'm joining you."

Carmel did so. Phillip flipped off the towel he wore around his waist and slid in beside her.

He said, "Here let me soap you." Facing her, he reached around her and began to rub her back with the bar of soap bringing her closer to him. The creamy skin on her shoulders glistened with water, her breasts swelled against his chest.

Phillip took the soap away from her and began to sing in a clear baritone, "Rub a dub dub, a man and woman in a tub."

Carmel listened for a minute. "It's too much. I'm here with you. We're alone in a huge, empty inn. There's a terrible war everywhere, and you're singing nursery rhymes." She began to cry, tears running down her cheeks.

When Phillip saw her tears, he put his arms around her and pulled her close. "This is my fault. I've moved too fast for you. You're feeling vulnerable and perhaps a little frightened."

She nodded her head and kept her face buried in his chest. "Oh, Phillip, I love you so. I never know when I will see you or if you care for me." Tears continued down her cheeks.

"Part of what you say is true. I don't know when I will see you again, but I do care, Carmel. I care."

"Do you think about me on the ship, sometimes?" She looked up at him.

He smiled, kissed her wet lips, and held her close. "Yes, sometimes I do." He was silent, holding her. "Let's get dressed and go for our walk."

She nodded and Phillip got out of the tub, dried his body, and wrapped a towel around his waist before he lifted her from the tub.

Carmel stood still as he dried her and wrapped her in a huge bath towel. Sitting down, he lifted her onto his lap.

She said, "I'm sorry."

"You're acting like a woman who cares—there's nothing to be sorry for."

She felt relief at his words and nestled into his arms.

They dressed, put on their coats, and headed for the beach. The wind was strong but the air warm and the day sunny after the rain. They walked close to the waves, Carmel snuggled under Phillip's arm.

The bay was empty of the usual small crafts. Only two boats bobbed next to the mile-long wharf. They walked alone on the beach, high swells pounding the shore. Seagulls flying above the waves had given up riding their crests.

Phillip said, "This area is a haven for the migratory birds that fly every year between Alaska and Mexico. Even mountain quail fly down to this level in the winter."

"I always thought our heavy winter storms came from the Gulf of Alaska."

"No, the Gulf of Mexico gets the blame, but our most damaging storms are from tropical and subtropical Pacific winds."

A small dog with a fuzzy black coat covering his eyes barked at them until Phillip found a small stick. He tossed it in the air, and the dog was fast after it on his short legs. They laughed watching him. They went to the mile-long wharf and discovered guards in uniform. Visitors were forbidden.

Then they climbed the steps from the beach to stroll along the famous boardwalk. Windows and doors of buildings were closed and covered with boards. The shooting gallery, Little Pigs game, and the entrance to the merry-go-round were boarded over. Looking through the cracks in the boards, they saw the Plunge, the enormous indoor pool, devoid of water. The trapezes hung from the ceiling, empty and silent above the pool.

They continued their walk, listening to the wind blowing across the top of the Giant Dipper roller coaster, the machinery rattling and creaking.

"Phillip, let's go find somewhere more cheerful. This place is creepy with no people around."

"I agree. We'll go back to our room and bribe Carl to bring us hot chocolate."

Carl, glad to fill their request, arrived in a short time with hot chocolate and a piece of fruitcake.

Phillip took a sip of his hot chocolate. "I could go for any one of those cookies you baked."

She brought the cookies from their bag and placed them on the plate.

"Would you tell me what life is like for the men on the islands?"

"Carmel, if you're thinking about your brother, I can't vouch for him. I have to go by what the men tell me. Those battlefields are not laid out in sunshine and dry land. Our men are fighting in swamps, walking in water up and over their hips, battling mosquitoes; some even try to sleep in trees."

"I remember you said snakes are everywhere."

"That's what I hear. The field hospitals experience a dreadful time with mosquitoes. They bring malaria. A system has been worked out to use long pipes that spray oil through the trees tops. On the ship, the sea breezes keep mosquitoes away unless we are anchored. Then oil is sprayed on top of the water."

"What does that do?"

"The mosquitoes can't breathe.

"What happens when you lay at anchor? Is the ship protected?"

"A steel net is dropped around the ship to protect it from torpedoes. We're too busy taking care of our patients to notice much."

"When you're at sea, what do you remember back home that makes you feel good?"

Phillip thought for a moment. "Listening to cable car bells clang as they travel on Powell Street. How Coit Tower looks through the fog and the sun setting behind Golden Gate Bridge. A drink at the Top of the Mark, dinner at Fior d' Italia, Tadich's, when a little guy I've operated on smiles at me for the first time after surgery. Oh, Carmel, there's so much to remember about the good life in San Francisco. What about you? What do you miss?"

"I miss all the flowers on the ranch, listening to Dad's Chopin recordings. Picking a ripe apricot off the tree and eating it right then. Walking with the dogs always barking and chasing shadows, having breakfast on the back terrace in the early morning. Hearing a fish jump in one of the pools. Funny, you miss San Francisco and I miss home. What about people, your mom and ..." She waited.

He grinned. "Yes, and I miss you." He stopped. "That's enough of this talk. Let's go down to the restaurant for dinner."

She suspected he wanted to forget the ship and the continuous pain that accompanied it and this seemingly endless war.

The Ideal Restaurant was next to the wharf, a short distance from the inn. Their table was by a window, but with the blackout curtains drawn they couldn't see the waves sweeping against the pilings. They felt the shudder of the building when the waves hit. The low ceilings and the fire in the pale rock fireplace added a cozy atmosphere to the restaurant. Red and white checkered tablecloths and napkins added cheer. A jukebox played softly in the background. Other customers in the restaurant were as oblivious to Phillip and Carmel as they were to them. Phillip held her hands, gazed into her eyes, and kissed her fingertips.

The steaming bouillabaisse, served in colorful country bowls with crusty sourdough bread, was mouth watering. To their mutual delight, they discovered that fried sand dabs were their favorite fish. They shared a bottle of wine.

Carmel said, "I heard a German managed to get into the top of this restaurant and tried to signal submarines in Monterey Bay."

"I heard that, too, but the rumor was never confirmed."

They spoke of acquaintances they both knew and Carmel told him of local San Jose gossip. They found they shared the same taste in music from Mozart to Ellington, enjoyed good food, and both loved dogs. Phillip told her about Captain Pearlman and how much he was respected.

"Phillip, the Germans are sending a secret weapon to bomb the English. The weapon doesn't need a pilot. Uncle Russell told me about it. It makes a horrible noise, like a screaming teakettle. Oh, I wish the invasion of Europe would start."

"I'm sure General Eisenhower feels the same way."

Carmel took Phillip's hand. She looked very serious. "Do you know what I would like you to do?"

Phillip had finished his dinner. "What would you like?"

Carmel continued to hold his hand said, "You have a wonderful speaking voice. When we get back to the room I want you to read to me."

"Read to you? I suppose I could, if we can find anything to read."

"I'll find something. I promise you."

The rain was light when they left the restaurant. They hurried the short block to the Beach Hill Inn without getting too wet. Phillip built a fire while Carmel looked for something for him to read. She didn't want to go downstairs to search in those dark and spooky rooms. In a drawer she found a copy of *Tale of Two Cities.* "Please read to me," she said, nestling on the couch.

Phillip sat on the floor with his back to the couch. "Charles Dickens. I'll read only for a short while." He turned to look at her. "I have other things on my mind."

Carmel looked into his eyes. His promise of lovemaking made shivers run down her back. Phillip began to read. His voice was vibrant and clear.

"'It was the best of times, it was the worst of times, it was the season of Light, it was the season of Darkness, we had everything before us, we had nothing before us ... in short it was a period very like the present.'"

Her father had read *Tale of Two Cities* to her and Scott when Scott was recovering from surgery. She found the words comforting. Carmel made up her mind to memorize everything in the room. The green velvet drapes, the pictures on the wall, the four-poster bed with its brocaded bed cover. She listened and tried to learn by heart his voice, the rain on the windows, and the sound of firewood burning.

He finished the first chapter and closed the book. "Let's go to bed. I want to hold you."

Phillip was gentle and took his time bringing Carmel to heights of passion. They made love for a long time, knowing it was their last night.

Carmel was grateful Phillip understood her tears when they were in the tub. She hadn't planned to tell him she loved him, but now that she had, she was glad.

When dawn came, they packed and found Carl to thank him. He refused money and told Phillip to come back when the war was over. On the drive back to the city, Phillip told her stories about the inn's famous guests: Charlie Chaplin, Al Jolson, the Hearsts, and Greta Garbo. Carmel was certain they had slept in the same four-poster as Garbo.

She didn't ask when he would return or if he would write.

The night fog in San Francisco dripped like rain. Phillip placed Carmel's bag on her uncle's front porch and held her close. She buried her face in his heavy top coat. Moments passed. She raised her face to look at him. "Thank you, Phillip."

He kissed her. His lips were gentle and warm. "Thank *you*, Carmel."

And then he was gone.

CHAPTER 51

In the days following Carmel's return to the city, everything and everyone brought memories of Phillip. Navy uniforms, a whiff of cologne, tobacco smoke, singing at the hospital, but most of all doctors and nurses in white uniforms.

She spent many sleepless nights listening to ships horns blast and whistle in the bay, wondering where the *Solace* might be. Was the ship near a battle in the middle of the Pacific? Any of the prospects frightened her. Every day she searched the newspaper for news of fighting in the Pacific.

She went over and over the trip to Santa Cruz with Phillip. She tried to recall those words between them. When he had made love to her, he touched her with gentleness and sometimes with bold savagery, as if he couldn't get enough of her. She became warm remembering his kisses over her body. Hadn't he held her on his lap and wiped away her tears? But when he said goodbye, he hadn't said he would write or see her when he returned. She had to fight back the tears.

How important was it for her to stay in San Francisco? Her father wasn't obeying his doctor. Was she responsible for him if her brother left? If Scott left, could she manage the ranch?

She knew Scott was furious with her. He wanted her home so that he could leave, but was Scott wasting his time on some half-baked scheme? She told herself she was too young to feel guilty about the future of her brother.

Carmel realized if she was to remain sane she would have to put her thoughts on hold. There were no easy answers to the decisions facing her. Her mind swung back and forth like a pendulum, leaving her with a sense of hopelessness and rendering her helpless to form a plan of action. She did the only thing she could do. She waited and prayed for Phillip. After all, the whole world was waiting and praying for someone to come home.

A winter storm had blown in from the Pacific and heavy rain and strong winds raged all night. The following day the winds had quieted, leaving overcast skies and intermittent rain. Carmel canceled her afternoon walk.

Carmel sat in the morning room sewing. Lydia entered, followed by Hilda and Heidi, their nails clicking on the hardwood floor. "Carmel, do you know what I just found out about the Grahams next door? They have a blue star hanging in their window. I knew they had no children, so I had to ask them what it all meant. Their dog, Buster—you know, the big German shepherd—has gone to war."

"That sounds very patriotic. What will he be trained to do?"

"The Grahams said dogs are used to sniff out bombs, bodies, and I guess snipers." She turned to Hilda and Heidi. "Do you sillies want to go to war?" The alert dogs knew their mistress had asked an important question. They stared into her face and barked in unison, tails wagging.

Carmel and Lydia laughed at the idea of Hilda and Heidi at war. The Fourth of July they were always under the bed at the first burst of a firecracker.

"Dear, you appear thinner. Are you losing weight?" Lydia sat on the chair opposite Carmel.

"Maybe a little, but I feel fine."

Heidi trotted up to Lydia and stared up at her. "Oh, come on." Lydia reached down, cupped one hand under Heidi's bottom, and lifted the dog onto her lap. Scratching Heidi's head, Lydia watched Carmel for a minute. "I'm glad you're able to use the skirt. I so seldom need a long dress these days."

For the past two years, Carmel had worn the dresses she inherited from her mother. They remained as beautiful as the day they were created by the European designers. In addition, Lydia's seamstress had made her three lovely dresses.

"I do feel guilty using yards of fabric when fabric is needed for uniforms. This skirt just needs shortening and will work with my white silk blouse and a red cummerbund. Also my polka dot blouse."

Lydia asked, "Someone mentioned wearing an Eisenhower jacket. Do you know what they're talking about?"

"Oh, that's a battle jacket like General Eisenhower wears. It's cut off at the waist to save material. I saw Jo Stafford wearing one with a short skirt. I may get one. With material so difficult to find, only zoot suiters have the nerve to wear voluminous clothes."

"I saw a zoot suiter the other day in a purple outfit. Carmel, there were yards of material in his baggy trousers. He had on a long jacket, a hat with a huge brim, and on his belt loop was a gold chain that he was swinging around. He was walking funny."

"That's called hep or hip." Carmel laughed at Lydia's expression.

"Dear, I see you walking around with a short chopstick clenched in your teeth. What does it do for you?"

"Oh!" she giggled. "Edna has me doing singing exercises with the chopstick in my mouth to give my muscles the right start and to set my jaw. Another exercise, I have to wobble my jaw and speak at the same time without the wobble affecting my words." Carmel wobbled her jaw while she spoke to show her aunt, and both were laughing before she quit talking.

"What happened to the plan of singing on the radio?"

"Auntie, in the first place, San Francisco doesn't have many spots for singers. The big shows come out of New York and Hollywood."

"What about Mrs. Fischer's 'Monday Night Jamboree'?"

"That's an audition for a singer to be heard by some popular band leaders like Del Courtney and Anson Weeks. It's an audition only for her show 'Stars in the Making.'"

"And ... go on."

"Aunt Lydia, I intend to audition. If I'm lucky and get selected, I would only sing once in a while. I should stay available for calls from band leaders, or they might stop calling me." Carmel realized she sounded impatient, but she felt her aunt pushing for an answer.

Lydia mulled over Carmel's words. "Well, it seems there're many opportunities on the radio. I would hate to see you give up trying. This house would be silent as a tomb if we didn't have at least five radios. Do you think anyone in this household would miss hearing Gabriel Heater or Edward R. Murrow's broadcasts from Great Britain? He begins: 'This is ... London.'"

Carmel couldn't hold back her laughter. "Auntie, you sound just like him." She continued sewing her skirt.

"Have you heard Mayor LaGuardia of New York City read the Sunday morning comics to the children over the radio? I guess he'll continue as long as the newspaper deliverers stay on strike. It's worth getting up to hear him."

Hilda decided she wanted to be in Lydia's lap and started barking. Lydia looked at Hilda. "I can't hold you both, and Carmel hasn't got room on her lap. I'll hold you later. I heard someone say radio provides stability by repeating the same programs every week. If that's true, your uncle should be steady as a rock. Our Sunday night ritual begins with Jack Benny and Fred Allen's famous feud. We never miss Charlie McCarthy." She looked sheepishly at Carmel. "I would never, never give up my favorite, *One Man's Family*."

Carmel was well aware of her aunt's attachment to the radio story of the Barbours, a San Francisco family living in Seacliff. Lydia wouldn't answer the phone when the program was on.

"Yes, I hate to miss the *Hit Parade*."

"I hear you singing. Your voice is truly lovely. I know you'll be ready to sing on *Stars in the Making*, and who knows what it will lead to?"

"I know only one thing—I want to sing and become a success. Who knows what changes big bands will be facing after the war? I seriously wonder if I'd be able to find enough steady work on the radio."

They were interrupted by her uncle carrying his helmet and wearing his Civil Defense uniform. "I can't believe I found my two girls at home at the same time."

"What good does that do? You're leaving, and where are you going?" Lydia asked.

"To my usual defense meeting," he said.

"Are you busy, Uncle Russell?" Carmel asked.

"Busy? I'm busier than a one-eyed cat watching two rat holes."

Carmel and Lydia laughed.

Lydia said, "Do you know it's still raining?"

"Yes. It's raining so hard it's stacked up two inches high waiting to get to the ground." He roared at his own humor."

"Carmel, are you still breaking the hearts of the ninety-day wonders?"

She knew Russell was irked that men were being promoted so fast in this war. "I hope not." She flashed him a smile. Her skirt finished she stood up. "I'd better truck on up stairs. I have to work tonight."

"Russell, I've hired a senior high school student to wash windows and help with the heavy housework. The market has stopped their deliveries. We need someone to carry the groceries up Chestnut for Helen. He's coming in the morning."

"Aunt Lydia, I'll be glad to help you."

"Well, Carmel, I was wondering if you would take over vacuuming the upstairs. Helen will do downstairs rooms and the young man can help. I must say, if Helen decided to go to work in one of the defense plants, I don't know what I would do. Her friends are pushing her to leave me."

"I'll help any way I can, Auntie. With the Canteen one night a week and two afternoons at the hospitals, I can manage easily. I don't want you to give up your Red Cross or volunteer work."

Russell kissed Lydia on the forehead. "I want you to find someone who can help Helen in the kitchen. Bannister is reaching an age where he'll appreciate it. Find someone who has worked in a hotel. Helen would never leave you—you can count on that."

Carmel reassured her aunt she would be up in the morning to start on her chores. In fact, she looked forward to it.

CHAPTER 52

Tuesday evening, Caesar telephoned as Carmel and Lydia were leaving the house. They intended to see the movie *Meet Me in St. Louis,* a brand new musical with Judy Garland.

Caesar's words were to the point. "Wear something red. I like you in red." He said he'd pick her up at seven o'clock Thursday evening at her home. Carmel hadn't realized until she heard his low voice that she was glad to hear from him. After all, she told herself, because of Caesar, John Canepa called her often to sing with his band.

Thursday morning, Carmel opened her blackout curtains to beautiful May weather. From her windows, she saw the bougainvillea climbing the high brick wall, spilling red blossoms in every direction. She watched the imperious jays chase tiny brown and beige-breasted sparrows away from the bird feeder. Last night from the bandstand she watched a group of officers celebrate their graduation from flying school. Their exuberance was catching. The band really bounced and the crowd complimented her singing several times. The men appeared more handsome and the women prettier than usual. She admitted her spirits had definitely risen.

Thinking about Caesar, she allowed herself to feel excitement. If there ever was the question of forbidden fruit, he was it. Carmel was ready for an evening out, and ready to stop thinking of Phillip.

She wondered what her aunt and uncle would think of Caesar. Earlier she told Aunt Lydia and Uncle Russell, who were leaving the house early, that she was going out with a friend. Carmel hurried to be ready to open the door when he arrived.

Dressed in her red suit, she added a small pearl in each ear and decided to hang a slim gold chain with a pearl pendant around her throat.

Caesar arrived on time, as she knew he would. All in black—black hair and eyes. Oh, my God, she thought, just like Phillip. Caesar smiled at her aunt when she introduced them. "It's my pleasure," he said, helping Carmel slip into her black coat.

Carmel knew his incredible good looks and tailored clothes overwhelmed her aunt. Jerry and Phillip were the only two men she had brought to the house. Lydia managed to mention the weather and wished them an enjoyable evening.

Jake opened the door of the long black Cadillac parked at the curb. The evening was chilly and Caesar made a point of making her comfortable. He tucked a lap robe across her knees.

"Would you like a drink? Anything you prefer?" He pointed to the small bar in front of them. "Perhaps some champagne?"

"Yes, thank you." Carmel watched every move Caesar made. His energy and magnetism did fascinate her.

He easily maneuvered the bottle of champagne and glasses, poured the wine, and handed her a glass. He raised his. "Here's to a pleasant evening." After a sip, he said, "We're going to the Music Box. Have you been there?" Carmel shook her head. "Good, I like taking you places you haven't been. You look beautiful tonight."

"Thank you." Carmel was content to remain silent as they drove through the dark streets in the dim out. She enjoyed the luxury of the big car.

The instant they entered the Music Box through the blackout curtains, Carmel sensed the crowd was full of infectious good-time seekers. Music from the band was deafening. The dance floor burgeoned with servicemen and women.

The captain bowed. "Good evening, Mr. Almato. Your table is ready." He led them to a table on the first tier. Champagne sat in a silver bucket.

Once they were seated and the wine was poured, Carmel looked around the large room. Caesar had said the Music Box was designed for entertainment, that it once had been an opera house. The band played from the stage in front of red velvet curtains. Gold and white columns, intricately carved, supported a second-floor balcony, on which patrons sat at tables eating and watching the crowd below them.

Again, men and women came to Caesar, wanting to be recognized. The women were good looking, wearing expensive jewelry and fashionable in low-cut gowns. The men wore well-tailored clothes and smoked long cigars. Caesar was treated with the same respect he received when they had dinner at Forbidden City. Sometimes he introduced her and sometimes not. Nevertheless, his attention remained with Carmel.

"How do you feel about rack of lamb for dinner?"

Carmel nodded.

"May I order for us?"

"Please do." She began to relax. To have so much attention and not care about what Caesar thought was heavenly.

Caesar ordered escargot and asked Carmel if she'd like some. Carmel refused.

"I raise my own. Snails, that is."

Carmel curious, asked, "Where?"

"I have a few in my house, just enough to eat. Chen, my houseman, takes care of them for me. I raise exotic birds too." He laughed. "We don't eat *them.* Perhaps, sometime I could show you my birds."

Carmel was saved from answering. The waiter set the asparagus vichyssoise Caesar ordered in front of them. The soup was excellent. After a moment, she wiped her lips. "Caesar, you have so many friends, no matter where we go. Have you thought about running for mayor of San Francisco?"

He threw back his head and howled. "Carmel, do you know where I go when I'm out of town?"

He didn't look nearly as forbidding when he laughed. "I have no idea."

"I used to go to Reno. Now I travel to Las Vegas. Have you been there?"

"No, I haven't. I hear there is nothing there except desert and gambling."

"Well, maybe for now, but that's going to change. I have a small club big enough for a lounge show and a main show room."

"What exactly is a lounge show?"

"A lounge show is always next to the black-jack area, slot machines, and crap tables. The entertainment in the lounge keeps customers happy and spending money. Most lounge entertainers want to perform in the big room. They receive more pay. Who knows, maybe you'll come someday and sing in my club."

His words astonished Carmel, but, more surprising, he did not give her a meaningful look or squeeze her hand. Instead he said, "The floor show is starting."

Carmel heard about Sally Rand and her half-nude cowgirls during the 1939 Exposition. She remembered Grant had seen the show and said it was not for ladies. The lights dimmed and the music began. There were a few whistles from the audience. Sally Rand appeared. She was nude, placing two mammoth pink and white fans alternately across and behind her body as she danced. A blonde angel, Carmel thought, with alabaster skin. Carmel didn't find anything offensive about her act. Sally Rand kept her body hidden completely while she waved the fans. When it was over, the audience responded with enthusiasm.

Caesar asked Carmel to dance. An accomplished dancer, he guided her lightly, not holding her too closely. When he suggested they leave and have a nightcap at another club, she willingly accepted.

Caesar said the club called Roberts-at-the-Beach was on the Great Highway that followed the seashore along the Pacific. When they reached the nightclub, a strong wind was blowing in from the sea. A dark night, Carmel barely could see the building amidst the grove of eucalyptus trees. The wind in the tops of the trees made a terrible racket. Carmel pulled her coat tightly around her against the cold as they walked through the full parking lot.

Once inside, the rambling building with its low ceiling reminded her of an old horse barn. Caesar introduced her to Shorty Roberts, who greeted them with a big smile. His nose seemed to disappear somewhere in a face topped with abundant gray-streaked hair; his muscular body was no taller than her shoulder. He wore a white shirt with the sleeves rolled up.

Shorty led to their table past suits of armor standing against the walls. There was something insidious and secret about its darkness. The small band was deafening.

When they were seated, she asked Caesar, "Do they ever turn the lights up?"

Caesar seemed amused. "Customers aren't asked any questions in Shorty's place. Perhaps they don't want to be seen. I'm having a cognac. Would you like something?"

"Yes, I would like a brandy and soda, please."

Caesar signaled the waiter and gave their order.

"My uncle says it's difficult to get scotch, because alcohol is used to make gunpowder. Didn't the government order us not to make anymore scotch?"

"True. In '42, distillers were ordered not to make any drinking alcohol, but if there is *anything* you desire, let me know. I did pick up some cases of scotch from England when I suspected there was going to be a war. It's called exchange." He chuckled. He looked at the crowd. "What do you think of this place?"

"If George Raft or Edward G. appeared, I wouldn't think a thing about it. Is there a floor show?"

"We have time for a dance before show time." Dancing with him the second time, Carmel relaxed.

The atmosphere in Shorty's place was distinctly different than in the other clubs she had been in with Caesar. People knew Caesar was in the room, but they didn't come to the table as the had in the Music Box and Forbidden City. They remained unconcerned, well dressed, and, she suspected, drunk.

The band played a four-bar introduction and the leader stepped up to the microphone.

"Ladies and gents, let's get lined up for the race. If you are entering the race, please come to the bandstand. We have twelve horses."

Chairs scraped, followed by laughter. Men and women lined up in the front of the band. Waiters brought children's hobbyhorses and set them in a row. The horses were blue, yellow, red, and green, many with white dots. A woman in a black dress screamed, "I'll get on this little blue one." Much to the crowd's delight, she sat down on the little blue horse. Both horse and rider toppled to the floor.

"Caesar, they won't let her ride, will they?"

"That's the point of this charade—to make a fool of yourself and win a bottle of champagne."

The riders lined up in front of the band. At a blast from the trumpet player that began a bad version of the "William Tell Overture," eleven people got on the colorful spotted hobby horses.

Six female riders wore dresses showing silken clad knees. The men took off their jackets and in shirtsleeves straddled their horses, trying to walk them to the finish line. The women shrieked, the men cursed, and falling from the horses added to the hilarity in the room.

Carmel was having a great time watching the nonsense.

A man with the buttons popping off his shirt won the race. He was accused of cheating by lifting his horse and trying to carry it, but Shorty gave him a bottle of champagne anyway. Carmel thought the bottle of champagne was the last thing he needed. The customer's antics brought tears to her eyes, but when Caesar suggested leaving for home, she accepted. It was late. The quiet of the car was a welcome relief after the noisy horse race.

"I hope this stimulating evening won't keep you from sharing another one with me."

"It was different."

He escorted her to the door, took her keys, unlocked the door, and put the keys back in her hand. "Carmel, I'm leaving town. I'll call you when I return, if I may? Thank you for a great evening."

She had expected him to kiss her and felt bewildered that he didn't. "Yes, you may. I had a very exhilarating evening. Thank you."

Later, she thought the evening had been delicious, wonderful, and wicked.

She did not choose to think about another night. She felt confident her debt had been paid.

CHAPTER 53

For the past nine weeks the *Solace* had navigated back and forth between New Guinea and the Admiralty Islands picking up wounded.

Nickers found Phillip in his cabin. "There's a young marine in surgery asking for you. Says he knows you."

Phillip wondered who had slipped by him. He made an effort to be alert to every patient who came aboard. He finished his shave and put on a fresh uniform.

The day had been a bitch. Bringing the patients aboard was extremely hazardous. The ship dived into troughs, then rose and dived again. The dense fog and a light drizzle fell for days, increasing the risks of boarding. To cross on LST's in the choppy water from the beachheads to the ship often meant seasickness.

From the distant shore they heard the rumble of big guns. Before the day was over, 325 patients filled all the hospital beds and overflowed into some of the crews' quarters. Phillip checked the manifest and found Grant St. John recovering from an emergency appendectomy. On the chart, he noted Grant had a sore on his left foot. Phillip returned to a quiet ward that only a short time before had been a whirlwind of energy. The stench of sweat, poisoned feet, blood-soaked bandages, and filthy clothes was replaced by the familiar scent of antiseptic, antibiotics, and clean linen.

Phillip stood at the foot of Grant's bed checking his chart. "Neighbor," he said, "you've come a long way to lose your appendix. How do you feel?"

Grant's face was pale. He mumbled, "I'm ready to get out of this bed. Those 'gyrines' need me." A white bedside stand held a glass jug of glucose being injected by tubes into his arm.

"I don't doubt that." Phillip removed the sheet covering Grant. He checked the bandage and incision on Grant's abdomen. "You're lucky we got you before that appendix burst." Phillip inspected Grant's swollen foot. The deep laceration just missed cutting off Grant's toes. Phillip suspected the angry, red wound was already infected. "Some bed rest will do you good. Your foot doesn't look like you should be on it. It needs to heal. Catch some rest, Grant, while you can." He moved on to the next bed. Phillip wondered how in the hell Grant had acquired the long scar on half of his face.

Three days later, Grant limped around the ship in a regulation maroon robe and duck slippers. Phillip heard him beg a nurse to promise to write. "Listen, when this war's over, come to San Francisco. I'll show you the city."

Phillip laughed, "Yvonne, don't let these Marines get away with anything."

"Get away with anything? Yvonne poured a bottle of awful red stuff all over my foot. Look at it." His foot was three times its normal size.

Phillip said, "That awful stuff, Grant, is going to prevent any bug from getting into your blood. I want you off that foot. Hop back into bed. I'll visit you when I can."

That evening, a balmy South Pacific wind brought most able-bodied men outside to enjoy the sunset. Phillip found Grant in one of the deck chairs. He leaned on the rail and studied Carmel's brother. The handsome young man, once healthy and solid looking, was now lean and compact. His red-gold hair and cinnamon eyes were so different from his sister's dark hair and slate-gray eyes. Yellow skin indicated he was taking Atabrine for malaria. "How're you feeling?"

"Hello Joe just got back from Kokomo. I'm ready to join the human race," Grant said with his usual cockiness.

"You've been out here for a while?"

"Yeah, I left Pearl, the police department, and joined up. I shipped out to hit Guadalcanal my first fight."

"What happened?"

"I guess I'm one of the lucky ones I'm still here. Things got bad. The Japs would rather die than surrender. We were so short of supplies we were wearing rags. We chased the Japs out of a spot and found brand-new, never-worn Japanese uniforms. We put the sonabitches on. We ate the food the captured Japs left. I wouldn't give the navy the sweat off a grape to count on them getting us supplies. And the mosquitoes! They have their own history." Grant laughed. "We were so infested, the guys used to say, 'Shall we take 'em with us or eat 'em here?'"

Grant rambled on, "I was transferred to the Second Division on Tarawa. The Japs really dug in. With heavy defenses of forty-foot concrete blockhouses, seventeen feet across on one side, and constant rough surf, we had to go in from the lagoon. I heard the tides screwed us up. The Higgins boats carried tanks to shore but couldn't beach them. I left my best buddy there. We lost a thousand men. Six months taking that damn island. At this rate, this mess is just going to keep going. Scuttlebutt is once the invasion in Europe happens we'll start getting our supplies. I was never so glad in my life when, in our third wave on Tarawa, the navy got the tanks onto shore. 'Kilroy was here' was stamped on the boxes. Can you believe it?" He pulled a pack of Camel cigarettes out of his robe pocket and offered the pack to Phillip.

At Phillip's refusal, Grant lit a cigarette, took a long drag, and blew out smoke rings. "Did you see my dad at Christmas?" At Phillip's nod, he asked, "How is he?"

"He's limping a little. If he takes care of himself and stays off his foot, he'll be fine."

"Just like me, huh? Guess my sister loves San Francisco. She sure won't go home."

Phillip noticed he didn't mention Scott, who, Carmel said, was pushing on his father to leave the ranch.

"I hear you're the only hospital ship out here?"

"For a while we were, but the *Relief* is serving. Soon the *Comfort* and *Mercy* will follow."

Grant laughed. "Those names are something. What do you do with the guys who go berserk?"

"The men refer to it as battle fatigue. Generally, they are the Seabees, older men at the top of their profession. They're always in the combat zone building the runways and bulldozing. They call it 'pushing dirt.' It's usually the constant firing of big guns that gets to them. We keep them for three weeks or so, and then they go back."

"Do you get off the ship?"

"Yes, we went into dry dock in Milne Bay in New Guinea for ten days. I enjoyed some real fishing for rock cod. Do you like to fish?"

"No, Doc. I couldn't sit still waiting for a fish to bite. How do I get a drink around here?"

Grant's smile and a dimple on his left cheek reminded Phillip of Carmel. "You don't. You shouldn't drink with malaria. What do you want, an egg in your beer?"

Grant nodded. "When do I get off this tug—I mean boat?"

"We're headed for the New Hebrides. You'll be dispatched to a Marine hospital there. Good to talk with you, Grant." Phillip put out his hand to shake. "I have rounds."

Phillip admitted Grant had shaken him up. Thoughts and questions about Carmel leaped into his mind. Did he really know her? She wanted a career—that meant being famous, didn't it? Would she be happy as a doctor's wife? Was she actually waiting for him? Trusting him? Carmel's passions had fired his own. No other woman had stirred his emotions to such heights of excitement and pleasure. Her perfume, smooth skin, dimples, gray eyes turning dark with passion, soft lips. He purposely kept Carmel a blur. Past observations taught him a budding relationship blossomed on hope. He had given her none. What could he offer her? It would be a miracle if he came back in one piece. He wouldn't try to guess how many submarines were hunting them through the waters beneath the *Solace*.

He was overwhelmed with work—all the ships' members were. His mind labored with questions. He couldn't afford to think about his safety or Carmel. Stick to the ship's routine and motto, he told himself: "Treat and heal, treat and heal."

CHAPTER 54

Tuesday, June 6, Carmel joined her aunt and uncle at breakfast. Their faces were grim as they listened to the radio. The invasion had started. It was D-Day. German soldiers, artillery, and Panzer tanks waited to stop the Allies somewhere on the French coast. She wanted to cheer, but instead her eyes filled with tears. "Uncle, does this mean the war will be over soon?"

Russell dripped honey onto his toast. "No. Some may think so, but they're wrong. We have a long way to go. Our troops must control the beaches first. Hundreds of thousands of men have to get from those ships onto the beaches.

"I only know the weather is stormy and the seas are very choppy. Rough water will affect the landing craft. Can you believe we're getting our news from the German radio?" He got up from the table. "I'll listen in the morning room; maybe I'll receive better reception."

The pictures Carmel saw in *Life* magazine flashed through her mind: landing craft, ships, and men in uniform crouching, holding guns, running across beaches loaded down with packs on their backs.

Lydia said, "They're closing some of the schools because of the invasion. Oh, those poor boys. I can't just sit here. I think I'll work in the vegetable garden. Russell can tell me what's happening." She looked down at the dogs, their faces upturned, eyes alert. "You may come outside, but no dog business in the garden; you know exactly what I mean." She leaned over to see if they were listening. She left the room with them following quietly behind her.

Carmel tried to remember the faces of men who would confront death today. She had sung for so many. They were no longer fresh recruits but young faces with war-weary eyes who knew they were going back to fight. She called

Edna and canceled her lesson. Edna had already canceled all her lessons, intending to listen to the news.

Carmel joined Lydia in the vegetable patch. Weeds needed to be pulled, and there was planting of vegetables for the next crop. "I read in the *San Jose Mercury*, the canneries are begging for any girl sixteen or older to work this summer to help meet the emergency in California. I didn't realize we produced one billion cans of fruit and vegetables for the armed forces. Maybe Scott is right wanting to build a large plant and freeze food."

"People in California are lucky, dear. We can grow our own vegetables and fruit. Besides being patriotic, any dummy can have a Victory garden."

They worked silently. Perspiration dripped from Carmel's forehead.

Suddenly Lydia said, "I don't know if you know, but the Office of Price Administration has issued the guidelines for War Ration Books. Red Stamps total sixteen points a week, allowing two pounds a week for meats, cheese, butter, and canned milk. Thank goodness Helen's good at all this figuring."

She moved her small wheelbarrow away from the rose beds. "I know your father doesn't have a problem with meat, since he has some butchered every year. Even when I wait in line, I may not receive the food I'm allowed. Butter is the highest priority because the dairies sell it to the army for well more than the prices I want to pay."

Carmel thought, Aunt Lydia is sure wound up.

"Getting gasoline stamps and sugar is the worst," Lydia said. "Blue stamps are used for canned food and dry packaged food. Helen went to the store. She doesn't know how the stamps got loose in the book, but the clerk wouldn't accept them. Stores will not accept loose stamps. She came home in tears. Wages are so high the people of San Francisco are willing to pay the black market prices. Everyone seems to find a source to buy liquor, or they hear about a chef in a hotel or a butcher in a shop who'll sell an extra chop or two—for a price, though."

At lunchtime, Carmel and her aunt ate a sardine sandwich Helen prepared for them. Kate Smith came on the radio and sang "God Bless America." They listened to her big voice as she sang the patriotic words. Carmel ate without tasting. They decided not to return to the garden.

"Carmel, Russell wants to hear the President speak tonight, and then we're going to church. I hope you join us."

"Of course, I'll go with you.

All that afternoon, Carmel stayed with her aunt and uncle and listened to the radio. The news announcer reported young students were sent home and asked to pray. High school teachers left the radio on all day in the classrooms. Neighbors gathered on the street, discussing what family or a friend was fighting on the beach that day. Shop windows displayed signs that read, "Gone to church."

News about Normandy came across the wires slowly, garbled and uncertain. How long would it be before they knew the results? Suspense continued to rise. Carmel heard that evening that Kay Kyser's and Lowell Thomas's programs had been set aside. The local movie houses stopped the movie in order to broadcast the President's speech for the audience.

President Roosevelt asked the American public to pray for the hundreds and thousands of men facing the enemy, for every family in the United States with a relative on the beach. The country came together, praying for the men.

When the long day finally ended, Carmel was caught between guilt and relief. She felt guilt that so many men had to die and watch helplessly as their buddies and friends died, relief that the invasion of France was the beginning of the end for Germany's Europe.

Gradually, as news was released, Carmel learned what happened on D-Day. Eisenhower's speech to his men the previous day had been kept secret, because it revealed where the five divisions would land on the Normandy coast. The men knew the big day they had waited for so long had finally arrived. They stood in line, making out their wills.

The worst storm in twenty years pounded the coast of England. However, the tides were right and failure to strike meant a two-week delay. Seasick men waited to board landing craft. Young men fell into 43-degree water from boats that never reached the shore. The landing crafts banged against the mother ship in the choppy waves. Some were disabled, sinking with all hands aboard.

Between midnight and dawn of June 6, thousands of paratroopers were dropped from planes that flew too low thirty-five miles from their target into enemy territory. Eighty percent were annihilated. American-British infantrymen landed on a mistaken Omaha beach. Mines blew up their landing craft. Bombers overhead, flying through clouds, missed targets of German forces on the cliffs. Unable to see through the gun smoke, Utah's first wave, confused by ocean currents, landed on a lightly defended beach. As a result, most of the Germans surrendered without a shot.

Three waves of Allies faced the best German infantry, who increased their gunfire four times as Allied infantrymen struggled to reach the beach. Allies were told, "Keep running. Don't stop to help the wounded—you'll die." Men tried to protect themselves behind a seawall and the wrecked, stalled equipment.

Germans used wooden bullets. As a result, many an Allied solider died from blood poisoning. Unable to receive aide, the wounded drowned in the water. Colonel George Taylor delivered words of inspiration and courage that saved many lives. "Two kinds of people are staying on this beach. The dead and those who are going to die! Now let's get the hell outta here."

It was three hours before seven navy destroyers provided relief with their constant gunfire. Later, pilots flying over said the stench of twenty-five hundred dead bodies reached them at one thousand feet.

It was another week of fierce encounter before they were linked as a solid front. Many months later, the world learned the coded message that began the invasion, as it came to the Resistance in occupied countries: "Long violent sobs rock my heart in monotonous languish."

Five thousand ships, eleven thousand Allied aircraft sorties and one hundred and fifty-four thousand soldiers, seventy-one thousand of which were Americans. There were two hundred and thirty-seven thousand Allied casualties, all part of D-Day.

D-Day also meant Phillip and Grant would return home earlier. She was only human to believe the war was almost over.

As the days passed, Carmel kept herself busy. Cleaning the upstairs took awhile before she worked out a routine. Hilda and Heidi thought she was playing a new game. They barked at the vacuum and got in her way, until she chased them out of each room laughing.

She sang only four nights a week, which left time for her night at the Canteen. There, new faces arrived every night. Men were eager to forget where they had been or where they were going. Spirits were lifted when they had an evening with lights, music, and girls. Others talked and talked and talked of girls and home. Often a young man wanted to sit quietly, eat a sandwich, and watch the others.

She asked her aunt, "Would it help if I met ships and gave coffee and doughnuts to servicemen?"

"No. That's the Red Cross's job. You contribute much more by singing."

CHAPTER 55

Forty-eight commuter trains traveled every day from San Francisco to San Jose. Signs in the coaches said not to travel unless it was necessary. As usual, the train was overcrowded with servicemen and their bags. Unable to find a seat, Carmel stood part of the way to San Jose.

The June day was hot and she was glad to get off the train into the cool ranch house. Carmel called to Andrew and Anna but received no answer. She had come home unannounced, so wasn't surprised when no one greeted her. She carried her bag upstairs to her room. Then she heard hammering. The sound came from back of the barns. She decided to see if she could find Andrew or Anna. She crossed a thick carpet of freshly mowed lawn. Bruno and Howard appeared, tails wagging, and followed at her heels.

In the slight breeze, the willow tree branches swayed over the fishponds. She could see brightly colored koi flash through the water. In the late afternoon, she smelled the rich essence of her father's rose bushes. It was home.

She walked past the old barn her grandfather had built to find a large new building attached to the back wall of the barn. Her brother and two men were on the roof pounding nails. She watched Scott for a moment. He moved smoothly and swiftly as his hammer hit the nails.

"Hi, up there. What're you doing? This is some building you're putting up."

"Hi, sis. I'm enlarging the barn. We're having a bumper crop of walnuts this year and I'm going to store them here instead of in the old barn. I'll be down in a minute. How long are ya staying?"

"Just for the night."

Scott climbed down the ladder and walked over to her. He took off his weathered straw hat and kissed her.

"My gosh, Scott. Your hair looks bleached white from the sun. You're as brown as one of your walnuts."

He pulled a handkerchief from his pocket and wiped his perspiring face. "Let's have a Coke. I need a break." They walked slowly back to the house. "It's cooling off. Let's sit outside and get some breezes. I'll get the Cokes. Okay?"

"Okay."

Scott went into the house and in a moment returned with two bottles, handing her one. "Colder in the bottle."

They found chairs on the shaded terrace and sat. "You look mighty spiffy."

"Thank you." Carmel's green and yellow jersey dress was one of her favorites. "Why're you adding such a huge addition to the barn?"

"It's not only our crop. I'm adding two crops from Barron's leased crop. I can store them all at the same time. I want to get started early this year."

"Where's Dad?"

"Anna drove him to the doctor."

"How's he doing?"

"I can't tell. If he complains, Anna will have him put in a wheelchair and he'll fight that. She's trying to get him to stop working the ranch."

Bruno and Howard came running, panting. Their pink tongues hung out of their mouths. They stretched out at Carmel's feet in the shade of the terrace.

Scott took a sip from the bottle. "Grant wrote and said he was on the *Solace*, the hospital ship; he had his appendix out. He's looking forward to some R&R before he returns to duty. He saw Phillip."

"What did he say about him?" Carmel struggled to keep the expression on her face indifferent as her heart thumped harder.

"Just that he doesn't see how they can take care of so many men on the ship. Guess the *Solace* was a cruise ship before the war. It's not that big. Didn't say when or where he's going."

"I'm not surprised."

"Are you ready to come home?"

"I resent you asking me that every time I come home. You're a needle stuck in its tracks. No, I'm *not* ready. If I wanted to, I could sing every night. I try to sing twice a week at the hospital, and now it's expected of me. What is it I could do here that you can't?"

"That's not the point. I can't be here and start the work I have to do in Aptos and Watsonville, namely getting the cannery going."

"No, you can't, and I don't know why you would leave Dad now. I can *not* do the things you do here."

"What's so dang great about singing?"

"Well, I never! It's as *dang* important to me as you going to Watsonville."

"Your singing doesn't come close to me starting a business."

"Maybe my singing is *my business*. I am not giving up something I've worked so hard for just so you can start a business. You can do it *after* the war is over. I *cannot* do the things you can do." She felt tears coming and wanted to give him a good smack.

"You'd be surprised what you can do if you took a notion." Scott stood up. "I've got to get back on the roof. I'll see you at dinner."

If my brother, she thought, doesn't stop fussing at me, I'll never come home. Why does he try to make me feel as if I'm doing nothing? What about *his* selfishness? It would be awful to come home now, when I'm working so hard to make a name for myself.

She was getting fed up with Scott. Scott and Laura. Ha! Did her best friend know what a pill Scott could be? She heard Anna and her father returning home and went to meet them. Andrew, on crutches, limped across the terrace, his foot heavily wrapped in bandages. Carmel kissed her father and turned to kiss and hug Anna. "What did the doctor say?" Carmel took Anna's hand. "You tell me. I don't trust my father."

"Same instructions. No smoking, no liquor, and keep off the foot."

Her father growled. "I'll do just that the day you put me in the box, not before. Listen to that hammering. What's the matter with that brother of yours? Acts like he's going to a fire. That barn's not going anywhere."

Scott didn't have dinner with them. He came into the house, showered, and left to take Laura to the movies. Carmel was relieved he wouldn't be dropping snide remarks during dinner. The evening felt like old times. She sat beside her father at the head of the long dining room table. Dinner was simple, with fresh brook trout a friend had brought Andrew. They didn't mention the war or her singing.

"Dad, why do we grow so many walnuts in this valley?"

Andrew was surprised at Carmel's curiosity. "It's kinda interesting. Father Sierra came through here in 1777. This area was called the Valley of the Oaks. There were thousands of oak trees. The farmers would come in, buy land, and cut the oak trees down with a two-man saw. The Indians who lived here cut the wood and sold it for firewood. The farmers would put ten to twelve sticks of dynamite under the trees and blow them up, but the roots were left. They decomposed in the ground and became infected with a fungus and contaminated much of the valley. We can't plant a deciduous tree in the same spot—it'll die—but not a walnut tree. As a result, we have walnuts, prunes, and cherries all mixed together on this ranch."

That evening she delighted in seeing he father's eyes spark like diamonds when she said something to please him, hearing his low rumble of laughter at her stories of his sister and her yoga, and her flirting with Lancing Tevis. Her father remembered meeting Lancing at a dinner party.

Andrew told her about his plans for the new septic tank and how many fish he could add to the pools. He had heard about strange-feathered chickens from Africa and wanted to purchase a few. Anna talked him out of buying noisy Guinea hens. They insisted Anna sit with them and share fresh-baked cherry pie and coffee. After dinner, they went to sit outside on the terrace. He asked if she wanted to join him with cognac in her coffee.

"No, thanks, Dad, just coffee." He drinks too much, she thought, and smokes too much, but I'm not going to say anything to him, not tonight. They sat in the dark. The perfume of the roses in the night air was bliss. Anna put on a recording of the London Symphony playing Handel's "Water Music." The melody drifted out to them.

Carmel tucked the evening into her memories. "Tired as I was, Dad, I'm glad I came home."

"It's a special treat for me when you're here." He sighed. "So saying, I'll finish my smoke. I heard the clock strike ten a while ago. I'm going to insist we retire. As pleasant as this evening is, it's been a long day."

The next morning Carmel went to see Laura. The day was bright with sunshine, and they decided to have their coffee outside on the terrace.

Laura poured coffee into a mug and handed it to Carmel. "Mom sent apologies for not coming downstairs. She stays in her room much of the time, seems to need me more and more. I'm home for the summer session at State."

"What's happening to your mom?"

"Dad says she has rheumatoid arthritis. I guess there's no cure. Her hands hurt terribly. Dad said they might go to the hot springs in Calistoga. The hot baths might help."

Carmel sipped her coffee. "How're you and Scott getting along?"

"I hardly see him anymore. He's planning to get his canning business going real good before we get married."

Carmel thought, What was the big rush? He could wait until the war was over before he left. She smiled at Laura. "You're going to make a great sister."

"I've always thought you were my sister."

"I guess we are at that."

"Look what came in the mail yesterday, for Mom." Laura took a small picture out of her apron pocket and showed Carmel a picture of Phillip. Carmel's heart jumped. Phillip wore a white uniform, his hair was tousled, and he wore a small grin. A man in white was beside him. Phillip wrote on the back of the picture, Phillip B. and Dr. Will Nickers, 1943.

"How's he?"

"Oh, he's okay. You know Phillip doesn't tell you what's really going on."

Carmel thought, You can sure say that again.

"Are you happy in San Francisco?"

"Happy enough that I want to stay there. I'm not planning to return to the ranch."

"Yeah, that's what Scott said."

"Laura, don't you know by this time how important my music is to me? I've worked hard to find band leaders to hire me, and that's where I'm going to stay."

"Well, gee whiskers, don't get mad at me."

"I'm not. It's just that I don't think my brother understands me or even tries to." She looked at her watch. "I must get started back."

"I wish I could take you to the train, but we use the gas to take Mom for her treatments."

"I understand. Give her my love." They hugged and Carmel left through the oleander hedge.

On the train returning to San Francisco, Carmel overheard people talking about a terrifying fire that broke out in the Ringling Brothers Barnum and Bailey Circus in Connecticut and claimed 167 lives. She knew about the excitement of a circus—rings full of clowns, animal trainers, and trapeze artists above them. To think a fire had swept across a tent and crushed people trying to get out. They were also talking about an explosion closer to home, in Port Chicago, near the city of Concord, east of Oakland.

When she entered the house she heard her uncle's loud voice on the phone.

"Yes, the whole town of Port Chicago is about gone. No, I don't intend to go over. The navy asked us not to come. It's horrible. Yes, I'll let you know. Good-bye."

Carmel walked into the morning room. "What happened, Uncle Russell? Coming back on the train, I heard everyone talking about Port Chicago."

"Oh my, Carmel," Russell answered. "Come and sit down. Let me tell you."

Carmel sat by her aunt, so stunned that she hadn't taken off her jacket. She had never seen her uncle so agitated. He was almost wringing his hands. His voice was heavy with agony. "Never, never has there been anything like this explosion. There was an explosion in Halifax in 1917 and one in Bombay this past April. Those cities were forewarned by fire. Port Chicago had no warning."

He paced across the room. "Port Chicago is on the deep channel part of the Sacramento River. Two liberty ships, one the *E. A. Bryan,* were being loaded with five thousand tons of ammunition by three hundred and fifty Negro Navy personnel. The SS *Quinalt Victory* stood empty beside her, waiting to be loaded the next morning. Near where the ships lay at dock, railroad engines were bringing in sixteen trains loaded with four hundred and sixty tons of ammunition to the docks and were busy switching boxcars." He dropped his head, his words muffled. "It happened at 10:19 last night. Three hundred twenty-five are dead. Five ships were obliterated, plus one diesel engine and sixteen boxcars. The blast made a hole a hundred and sixteen feet deep in the river bottom. It's a miracle more weren't killed.

"We heard the detonation here in San Francisco, thirty-one miles away. There were two explosions. The first blast brought people to the windows, and the second blast ... the glass splintered in their eyes. Hundreds were trapped in their homes."

"What about the town?" Carmel asked, her heart racing.

"The explosion destroyed three hundred fifty homes and twenty-seven stores in Port Chicago. The streets are full of glass, wires and poles, and shells that didn't explode. It's frightening. Twelve other towns are damaged. Camp Stoneman, eight miles away, is a demarcation center for the South Pacific. Fortunately, Stoneman's army units got medical aide, field kitchens, and tents down to Port Chicago by two in the morning."

Lydia had been listening. "Now the men won't return to work."

"What do you mean?" Carmel asked.

Lydia folded her arms. "I would be petrified too. They work seven-hour shifts around the clock. They form a human chain of men getting the ammunition aboard. They might as well be working in a mine."

The explosion brought the war close to home for Carmel. Though San Francisco was a point of embarkation and thousands of servicemen and workers in the shipyards surged through the city constantly, they didn't have to watch for snipers hiding on roofs and behind doorways. Or wait anxiously for a screaming bomb landing on top of them. Carmel imagined those men working in the hold of that ship, working in the heat, handling dangerous bombs. Some of them were barely eighteen years old. She shuddered.

Russell paced up and down, too agitated to sit. "After making all the headlines in the world newspapers, now it's all hush, hush. Our men in the South Pacific needed that ammunition, and it's bad for morale to talk about not having it shipped to them. The negroes refuse to go back to work loading ammunition on another ship. If they continue to refuse, Rear Admiral Wright of the Twelfth Naval District says the men will be accused of mutiny. They will go to Mare Island into the Ryder Street Barracks."

Carmel tried to accept the horror. "What caused it? The explosion I mean."

"The Twelfth Naval District is investigating now. Some hinted at sabotage, but that property was surrounded by a cyclone fence, topped by barbed wire. Marine sentries, who have suffered an injury in the South Pacific and recovered, patrol the area with guard dogs."

He started to leave the room and then hesitated. "I do have some *good* news. Premier Tojo is no longer a leader in Japan. He has been kicked out. And the Americans are in St. Lo in France. The bad news is German generals tried to assassinate Hitler and failed."

Carmel went to bed that night thinking about the horror of Port Chicago. She had nightmares of a battlefield, surrounded by men screaming, covered with blood, begging for help. The news frightened her—so many men being blown apart, so young, suffering in a hot hellhole, scared of every jar or bump. They must have been in terror of fire and destruction or death, hour after hour, day after day. What a horrible day it had been between Port Chicago and the circus fire, where families with children had been anticipating a wonderful time.

In order to sleep, she concentrated on remembering the picture of Phillip, his hair tousled, a small grin on his face.

CHAPTER 56

Marlena finished her last appearance for the evening and hurried home. Tonight she wanted to be home before Caesar. He had sublet a one-bedroom apartment for her and told her to decorate it any way she wanted.

Her home in Germany, with its massive furniture, dark velvet hangings, and large gold-framed pictures, depressed her. She bought Louis XIV chairs, a couch with silk fringe around the bottom, and ordered it all upholstered in satin the color of Alaskan salmon. Large nude figurines, painted gold, held lamps with massive pink shades. The lamps sat on small gold tables and appeared top heavy in the crowded room. Caesar said the chairs were uncomfortable.

In her favorite room, the bedroom, Marlena hung frothy lace curtains with pink satin draperies held back by pink and gold tassels. The view from the two large windows was limited to San Francisco rooftops. She didn't mind—she had no reason to look out of her Bower of Love, her name for the room. Two chairs and a chaise upholstered in pink velvet sat in a corner. A mirrored headboard on the mammoth bed reflected a bedspread of pink satin, while pink silk and lace draped the dressing table. Prints of cavorting nude cupids hung on pale pink walls.

Caesar covered his eyes when he saw the room and said it was better than a French bordello.

There wasn't much she could change in the large bathroom, with its marble floors and walls. Mirrors covered one wall. She stacked thick pink towels on a settee upholstered in pink brocade, added a pink shower curtain with silver fish swimming across it, and placed white angora rugs on the floor.

Before she met Caesar, she had heard he was rich. It was a challenge, scheming how to pluck some of his wealth. Granted, he bought her everything she needed. She took each necklace, bracelet, or ring he gave her to the appraiser for assurance the pieces were genuine. Then she put the jewelry into a safety deposit box at the bank. She didn't mind going to the bank each time she decided to wear a piece. Knowing her jewelry was safe was worth the inconvenience.

She remembered the days in Germany when her family took their way of life for granted, thinking it would never change. Then they lost everything. Marlena promised herself as long as she was breathing, she would keep every item given to her. She knew as long as she performed in the fishbowl, men would provide her with the gifts to safeguard her future. Preserving her figure was part of the insurance.

She liked Caesar well enough. He was an exciting man, but she didn't love him, and he didn't demand love from her. But when she went to his apartment for the first time and saw his attachment to the birds, she got the idea. Since then the thought had been growing in her mind. Caesar needed a kid. That would tie him up like a fish net.

In the past, the sisters thought Elka would have the first baby. Now, however, Marlena had a plan. If she had Caesar's baby, he would be so crazy about his kid she would be able to claim anything she wanted. Her mind went only as far as the obstacle before her. She believed when a problem arose, a solution was easily found.

Marlena went into the bathroom. She turned on the faucets for her bath and poured fragrant oils into the water. She removed her clothes and dropped them on a stool. Standing before the floor-length mirrors, she stared at her naked body; the men who saw her perform in the fishbowl said she was perfect. Her breasts were firm and full, her stomach flat, her long legs tapered to her small manicured feet. She took pride in her luxuriant golden hair, although she wanted to cut it so she and Elka would look different. Their hair was the only remaining feature to remind them of their shared past. Elka became very vocal. "Do not to cut hair short." Marlena knew Elka resented her desire to eliminate anything that reminded her of their life in Germany.

Because she took care of herself, Marlena always scrubbed her body with sea salt before she left her bath; the salt left her skin like velvet. One night a week, when she knew Caesar wasn't dropping by, she rubbed her body with Vaseline, leaving it on while she slept; this kept her skin smooth as a baby's.

Marlena slipped into the tub and waited for the warm water to relax her. She allowed herself to plan the conversation with Caesar. Thinking of the baby, she smiled. After the birth of her baby, she would follow a rigid regimen to regain her former figure. Caesar told her many times he was not planning on marriage or kids, but she watched how he was with those damn birds, gentle and concerned. Marlena knew once he got used to the idea of having his own child, he would love it and want to give the child a home, even if they didn't get married for a while.

After her bath, she rubbed her favorite lotion on her body and splashed on cologne. Tonight was important and she intended to be her most alluring. She heard Caesar arrive and knew he was in the bedroom waiting for her. Wearing a negligee, Marlena returned to her bedroom. Caesar lay naked on the bed. In the softly illuminated bedroom, he watched Marlena slowly remove her negligee. She stood in front of the mirror with her back to him watching his eyes glide hungrily over her body. It thrilled her to tantalize him.

"You're waiting for me, *ja?*"

"Bitch, you can see what is waiting for you."

Turning to face him, she stared at his swollen organ. "I'll cool you off." She ran her tongue across her lips. Her silk nightgown slid off creamy shoulders, revealing naked breasts and pink nipples. She began to massage her rosy tips until they grew harder. Marlena glided slowly over to the bed. She crouched on her knees over his naked body. Moving lower on his body, she placed a breast on each side of his penis, teasing him, intent on his enjoyment. She flicked her warm and moist tongue across the tip and slowly up and down the shaft. He groaned with pleasure. Caesar reached down, lifted her up, and holding her above him slid into her moistness.

Caesar found his satisfaction immediately. Pushing her away, he rolled over and sighed, "Jesus." He was asleep.

Tonight Marlena didn't care if he went to sleep without satisfying her. The diaphragm remained in the bathroom.

CHAPTER 57

The headlights of Scott's old Ford truck picked up Laura, waiting for him at the entrance of her driveway. It would be another hour before dawn. She climbed into the truck. He asked, "Are you freezing?"

"If I'd waited much longer, I would be. I'm all right. I wore my heavy coat." She placed two paper bags on the floor by her feet. Laura turned to him and their lips met in a quick kiss.

"Are you sure you want to go with me?" He shifted the gears and pulled onto Minnesota Avenue.

"How else am I going to see you? You're in Watsonville or Aptos as much as you're in San Jose."

"You're right. I don't see anything changing for now."

"Couldn't Ron or Al do more?"

"Laura, we've been over this before."

When they reached Highway 17, a ground fog covered the highway, making it difficult to see. Laura wondered if she had made a poor decision coming with him.

Scott slowed down. "Damn fog. It'll just take us a little longer. One good thing—there's never any cars at this hour.

"The simple truth is Al and Ron don't care as much as I do. This is the chance for all of us to get started, to make our names in the canning business. When the war's over, I see myself making big money. Ron doesn't know beans about machinery. He can't fix anything. The only thing he can make is reservations—and he doesn't even do that very well—but he'll be good as a food broker talking up contracts for us. I know he thinks I'm an eager beaver, but somebody has to push."

"You have chores to do on your own ranch and your dad's health is failing."

"Yep."

Laura knew he was thinking about Carmel. "In all honesty, Scott, could your sister learn to take charge of a big ranch? She's never displayed five minutes of interest."

"Yes, but she could learn. If I can get going now, I'll get a head start. I want a big, big business, and that's what I intend to do. I want to go beyond dried fruit. If we can figure out how to freeze food, keep it frozen while being shipped, we'll have it made in the shade. Do you realize we have no place to store food and keep it frozen except in freezers in the back of the meat counter? Thank God business is so damn good. Hitler stopped all imports and exports from his country when the war started. They grow their own produce. As a result, the Lend-lease agreement our country made with Russia, France, and Belgium has created a market for our dried foods prunes, apricots, and dried apples all over the world."

He loved talking about his plans, and his voice grew louder. "Laura, the *whole* world needs food. If we can get this fruit cocktail canned and fill a contract on time, it'll be our first big job. I've got to do it right. We can't afford all the machinery we need. We have to break down this equipment and set up for the next job. Al knows about machinery and, between us, I hope we can put it together. You know that's what I've been doing at night. Our equipment is so old. After the war, all those damaged countries will need food. It's for you too, for us. Just stick through it with me for now." He held her hand. In the tiny light on the dashboard she saw him grin.

They passed the Summit and started down the mountain toward Santa Cruz and the sea. As the fog lifted, they saw the majestic redwoods, green in the morning mist. Laura felt his impatience. She didn't question her love and commitment to him. She looked forward to their marriage, intended for the fall of 1945. When she became a nurse, she would probably work in her father's clinic, stopping only to have babies. Her desire to leave San Jose seemed a long time ago.

Once she felt envy for Carmel and the glamorous life she led. Everything Laura heard about her friend in San Francisco was exciting. How she wore gorgeous clothes, sang in the best hotels, and met famous people. However, Laura was beginning to recognize the change in her best friend. Once they were close friends and shared all their secrets. Now, when Carmel came to San Jose, she was preoccupied and indifferent. Laura missed their old friendship and the sharing.

"I don't know what would make your sister leave her way of living and come back to San Jose."

"My grandfather and his father worked hard to accumulate this land we call home. These acres are going to remain in our family, and someone has to run it. Eventually, I will earn much more money than Carmel does with her lollygagging around in San Francisco."

Although Scott had told no one, he ran ads in the local newspaper the *San Jose Mercury* for a foreman. He received one response. The man was over draft age and bent with arthritis. Scott found out that anyone suitable had been drafted, enlisted, or had their own ranch to manage.

"And Grant?"

"He shows little interest in the ranch, or its future. I have no doubt the devil has stuck his tail in Grant's ear. I wouldn't trust him to cultivate a window box."

Laura laughed. "I've got a surprise in the lunch I packed for us. I made you apple turnovers. The other sack holds *The Fountainhead*, by Rand. I finally bought it." Their habit of reading together had continued.

"You're my sweetheart. I don't think I can take much time for reading today. You'll have to read alone. The sun will be out by noon and we'll go down by the Aptos Creek and have our lunch. That packing shed gets hot as fired steel for those gals running the lines. We've got to figure out how to improve the place. Ron is supposed to be taking care of the women here. The plan is to get air moving across the shed. I haven't figured it out yet."

The truck jolted as they turned off the road and drove onto the property. Laura took hold of the door handle to steady herself against the bouncing. She saw the one-story empty, packing shed. The long wooden building was badly weather stained. Crooked stairs and a slanting ramp led to a bowed porch. Steam rose out of the vents on a swaybacked roof that sagged in the middle. She didn't doubt that a strong wind could rip the whole building off its foundation. She said nothing.

Scott was explaining, still occupied with his future. "Right now I've got Jose running the pickers at the ranch. We can store walnuts in the new barn this year.

CHAPTER 58

Late October in San Francisco was the golden time, when the natives looked forward to days of burnished sunshine. Russell sat on a garden bench puffing on a large cigar, enjoying the sunshine. He would take a San Francisco fall with sparkling sunny days and brisk evenings any time. It was a day to savor and made one feel glad to be alive.

Someone had stepped on the thyme growing between the rocks on the pathway and its odor was pungent and pleasant. Lydia's rock garden spilled with Irish moss. Baby tears and alyssum tucked themselves among the rocks.

A light breeze ruffled the tops of the copper beeches and the cut leaf maples. Crab apples lined the drive behind the bird feeder. Russell found himself wondering why Lydia kept the messy trees. He guessed it was because the birds loved the crab apples. An aggressive dove pushed tiny gray-capped sparrows from the feeder; they fought back. Six small bundles of feathers fighting for their rights amused him.

Hilda and Heidi sat motionless at his feet, following orders. He watched Lydia and Carmel on their knees digging in the Victory garden. Both women wore large-brimmed straw hats. The day was warm enough to wear sweaters with colorful smocks over them.

Lydia was the president of the neighborhood Victory Garden Association. Members came regularly to ask for advice. The two women knelt to transplant rows of cool season vegetables—cauliflower, cabbage, and broccoli—for early spring growth.

"My favorite girls are as fair as the flowers in the garden," Russell said.

Lydia stood and rubbed her lower back. She sighed. "I hope the war is over soon. This garden is killing me." She knelt back down in the dirt and continued to separate small heads of garlic into cloves and plant them.

"Do I see you planting garlic?" Russell asked.

"Yes, you do. I won't live in San Francisco with all this good Italian cooking around me and not cook with garlic. My yogi says it is good for your heart and fights infections." She glared at him. "If I'd known your intentions were to imitate Winston—sitting there in that huge hat, wearing a parachutist's jumpsuit, and smoking that big cigar—I'd have ordered a suit made for you, if I could find the material." She smiled at him. "You're such a darling old fool."

Winston Churchill had started the fashion of wearing a one-piece romper with buttons closing the front. Russell thought the suit looked exceedingly comfortable. "Thank you, Lydia. Your remark is noted and appreciated." He blew a great cloud of smoke.

Lydia asked, "Where ever did you find such a huge cigar? I've never seen one so large. Please don't blow so much smoke on us."

"Mayor Rossi gave me this cigar last night. It's called a Winston Churchill. Rossi appeared at the Defense Council meeting. We're celebrating the news of Leyte."

"What is Leyte?" Carmel stood to reach for plants in a wheelbarrow sitting on the garden pathway.

"Leyte is one of the Philippines Islands MacArthur said he would return to. Goddamn it, he did. If the Japs captured the Philippines and Luzon, the door would have opened for them to have the oil and rubber needed to continue the war. We just fought a four-day battle and won. There're a thousand miles of islands in the area."

He put his cigar in his mouth and puffed clouds of smoke before he said, "I read the three top admirals, Halsey, Spruance, and Vice Admiral Kincaid, assembled our entire fleet and faced Kurita, the Japanese admiral. The Japs sent out false news that we were destroyed. I don't know exactly what did happen. I do know it was the largest sea battle ever fought.

"Admiral Kurita's cruisers could have sat safely at a distance and pounded us with their big guns. We didn't have the kind of force to reach them. I guess it was a game of hide-and-seek. That battle means the Japs are done. They are whipped, done for, kaput." He slapped his leg. "We lost ten ships and the Japs lost three battleships, six heavy cruisers, and four aircraft carriers." He took another great drag on his cigar. "The Japs will never manage to come back with enough sea power to attack again. The Japanese admiral finished with his flagship destroyed under him and had to hit the water. Our subs did a lot of damage; so did our air attacks."

Carmel listened to Russell ramble on about the battle. She heard only that it could be the last one. When she listened to any news about the war, her mind went immediately to the *Solace*. Where was it?

Restless and grumpy for the last three days, she thought she might be getting a cold. She was not in a happy mood. She would be glad when her aunt wanted to quit for the day.

The dogs were on their feet, barking at the approaching mail carrier who ignored them.

"Hi. I heard you out here. Wanted to see Lydia's Victory garden." His bright blue eyes were alert, his face flushed. He carried a huge leather bag over one shoulder on his short body. He found Lydia concealed behind the tall beanpoles and trellises of vines. He stood looking at the rows and rows of vegetables. "My, my. You have some garden here."

Lydia stood up. "Thank you, Herman. My niece deserves some credit, too." Lydia, sputtered, "Oh, Russell, keep those darlings quiet."

Russell tried to quiet the dogs and take the mail. "You're early today, Herman. Anything interesting?" He was thumbing through the letters. "Uh … look at this, Carmel, one for you. Overseas … has an APO number. Here you are. Must be Grant." He handed the thin letter to her.

Carmel stared at the letter. She held her breath. "Excuse me, I want to read this."

Lydia sorted her mail. "Go ahead. The garden can wait. Let us know what Grant says."

Wanting privacy, she walked slowly away from them. Maybe the long-awaited letter had finally arrived. She didn't recognize the handwriting.

Once in her room, settled in the chair by the window, she looked at the envelope for a moment. A sense of dread filled her thoughts. This letter could change her life forever. She opened it and quickly glanced at the signature at the bottom of the single sheet. She saw one word—Phillip. Her heart raced.

October 20, 1944

Somewhere at sea,
My dear, wonderful Carmel:

I feel I must express my feelings for you at this time. Too much has happened between us for me to be with you and not touch you.

Being close to you has given me much joy, but I know it must stop.

The end of the war could be a long way off. My life is a precarious one, to
say the least. If I come home, I'm not sure what I'll do about going back to
the hospital or the clinic.

It's not fair to ask you to stand by for my unexpected arrivals. I doubt I'll
be coming to San Francisco for a long time. You are a good and beautiful
woman and you deserve to live a fulfilling life.

My wishes are for your happiness.

Fondly,
Phillip

Carmel looked out the window at the bright sunny day. No tears fell. Her
mouth was dryer than it had ever been in her life. She doubted she could swallow. She tried to rub the sudden headache from her head. She was empty, the
whole inside of her. What was next? How could she stop caring because he said
to? She suddenly understood the stories of women throwing themselves on the
burning bier where the body of their loved one was placed.

Her pulse throbbed like a freight train. She struggled for air. She swore she
could feel her nostrils dilate; her breathing was shallow. She got up.

She had been right. The letter had changed her life. She was released; she
could go home. Staying in San Francisco gave her hope. Going home was
admitting defeat, knowing it was over. Many people would be happy if she
went home. She stared out the window and mouthed, I'll never stop loving
you, Phillip.

CHAPTER 59

When Phillip took Carmel to Alfred's and after dinner, he became so distant with no mention of letters or when he would see her again. Carmel had gone to visit Elka at her apartment searching for comfort. Elka had listened and consoled Carmel, telling her that Phillip would probably just show up unexpectedly again.

Today Carmel had asked Elka to meet her at Coffee Dan's on O'Farrell. The crowded restaurant overflowed with noisy customers escaping the pelting rain and gusty winds of an early November afternoon. Elka found her already seated.

"*Himmel!* Glad we're not out in the rain." Elka draped her raincoat on the back of the chair. "What's this?" On the table before her was a dish of apple pie with a scoop of ice cream and a cup of coffee. The same order sat in front of Carmel.

Carmel laughed. "When was the last time you had pie and ice cream?" She took a bite of pie. "Yummy." She stared at her friend. Elka wore a navy wool dress and a becoming navy rain hat. "Elka, you look exactly like your sister today. Sometimes, I'm not sure which sister you are. Only when I see the birthmark by your neck do I know for sure."

"We get older and find easier to fool people. One thing for sure, my sister would not eat pie and ice cream, not with *her* job."

"How are things with her?"

"Oh, Marlena's got her hooks in Caesar, think he marry her. Caesar finished fixing two houses he bought. They're next door to each other; I hear he built bridge between them. He's spending time here and in Nevada. While he's gone, I think he doesn't know the gifts men give Marlena. She's greedy little bitch."

Carmel winced at the anger in Elka's voice. She finished her pie and ice cream and sipped her coffee. "Have you seen his houses?"

"*Nien*. Marlena said Caesar keep birds in one house."

Carmel had a hunch Caesar knew what was happening. She was astonished to hear her sweet friend complaining. "What's new with you, Elka? Have you found somebody?"

"*Nien*. You know Chez Paree packed with men every night? I don't see anyone I want. You said you want to tell me something."

Carmel opened her purse, took out the letter from Phillip, and handed it to Elka. "My 'Dear John' letter, only in reverse," she said.

Elka read the letter, "Maybe better to know now, to not keep hoping?"

"You're looking at me, and I appear sane and in control. Elka, inside I feel empty and abandoned. We went away and spent two days together."

"Has nothing to do with it. Oh, maybe he's little bit guilty. Maybe Phillip feels he ask too much of you. His life is uncertain. Carmel, last night a Merchant Mariner said hospital ship *Comfort* fired on. Oh, I'm sorry I said that."

Tears filled Carmel's eyes. "If he would just ask me to wait, I could stand anything."

"*Liebchen*, I'm truly sorry. I don't say right thing. You're still at Canteen and sing at hospital?"

"Yes, but my family wants me back in San Jose. My brother wants me to move back home. He thinks I can run things at the ranch so he can leave. Dad just wants me home."

"You stay in San Francisco to see Phillip. When he comes?"

"No one but you knows why I stay here. Elka, I can't think straight anymore."

"Then stay. Not do anything."

"I'm such a nut, Elka." Carmel wiped tears from her eyes with her handkerchief. "I'm lucky to have you for a friend. It means so much to be able to talk to you. I realize many people have problems worse than mine, but I don't do well waiting. Every day I imagine the ship has blown up. It's hard not knowing where he is." She gazed outside at the rain.

"You can always talk to me. Let's go see movie *Laura*. They say Gene Tierney with Dana Andrews is great. Movie is at Fox Theater. If we don't like second feature, we can leave."

Carmel nodded. They put on their raincoats and Elka looked out. "It's pouring. I forgot umbrella. Did you bring one?"

"Yes. The Fox Theater is only a short walk. We can make it."

Huddled under the one umbrella, they walked to Market Street. A gust of cold wind and rain whipped at their coats. Elka said, "My grandmother say, 'Walk between the raindrops, sugar will melt.'"

Carmel gripped Elka's arm and laughed with her friend at the nonsense words.

Phillip's rejection consumed Carmel, filling every breath and every cell of her body. The hurt loomed above her and around her like a violent storm.

The first days and nights following the arrival of Phillip's letter, Carmel traced over in her mind the shared words, kisses, and lovemaking. In the secret part of her mind, she couldn't bear to think she might never see him again.

She ate little. Her skin lost its gentle radiance. To appear attractive while working and to cover her pale skin, she began wearing more makeup. The words to love songs and romantic ballads became irritating with the dancers mooning around her.

Her aunt commented on her niece's silence and lack of interest in daily matters. Then, as suddenly as they started, Carmel's silences broke. Phones began to ring and strange men's voices asked for Carmel. Good-looking men in uniform came to the house.

Now a quiet fury possessed her. She stopped questioning herself. Anytime she felt like doing something, she did it. The first change came while sitting on the bandstand. She started accepting gifts the men sent to her. At first, she accepted only flowers. Recently, a marine officer named Humphrey H. Packard brought an ivory bracelet from Hawaii inlaid with gold, especially for her. He was so sincere, she couldn't refuse his gift.

Lydia and Russell expressed delight she was feeling better. Carmel told herself she was happy and deserved to have fun. Her loyalty to Phillip had brought long, lonely evenings while she watched others enjoying themselves. She now dated some good-looking men who felt lucky to find a beautiful, lighthearted, and carefree companion.

She danced to Harry Owen's orchestra in the Mural Room at the St. Francis Hotel, laughed with the crowd at Hilo Hattie in her silly hat and muumuu. Carmel thought she might go to Hawaii someday if the natives were this happy-go-lucky. She enjoyed drinks in the famous Patent Leather Room next to the St. Francis lobby, nicknamed the "Black Coffin." Sprays of white calla lilies in large vases at the back of the bar supplied the only relief from the black walls, tufted banquettes, and bar stools covered with black patent leather. The long, popular bar, where many a flaming romance started, remained three deep with men in uniform.

She struggled to eliminate Phillip's shadow of rejection. Humphrey made her feel he was thrilled to be with her. Besides being handsome, slim, and a great dancer, he had boyish charm. Raised in Southern Tennessee, he treated her in a courtly manner.

One night they went to the Sinaloa, a nightclub on Powell Street. The place was awash with customers, mostly service personnel. A navy commander stared at Carmel too long and Humphrey punched him, turning over the table. The punch started a fight among the other customers. Carmel heard someone call for the MPs. She managed to lead Humphrey out of the club through a side door.

There was always someone to escort her wherever she wanted to go. She loved dancing at the Starlite Room at the top of the Sir Francis Drake Hotel. The bandleader, Charlie Lyons, knew her and asked her if she wanted to sing a number. Twice she sang and relished every minute of it.

She also welcomed Caesar's invitation to have dinner at Alfred's restaurant. They sat in a booth next to the one where she and Phillip had eaten. Remembering, she welcomed the chance to feel anger. Carmel wore an electric blue satin dress with a wide collar, open to expose the swell of her breasts. Three crystal buttons, sparkling like diamonds, fastened the front. Small diamond earrings hung on her ears.

Caesar ordered their martinis and watched her with an amused smile. "What's going on in that beautiful head of yours?"

"What does it look like?"

"Would you be plotting?"

"The only thing I would be plotting is having a good time," she said, feeling reckless.

"I'm glad to hear that. Have you been to the show at the Sinaloa?"

"I was there. I didn't see the show."

"I heard you've been kicking up your heels lately."

"Who would care enough to gossip about what I do?" Carmel broke off a piece of sourdough bread and took a bite. A shriek of laughter came from the booth next to them. Carmel noticed the curtains were closed. She smiled. "I think everyone in the room is having fun." Women and men, expensively dressed or in uniform, packed the large room. Beneath the chatter of voices, the pleasing sound of music played in the background.

As Carmel listened to Caesar, she thought how handsome he was. She wondered how he managed to wear fashionably new and costly clothes with the shortage of materials. Before meeting him tonight, she felt she might be skirting danger.

Sitting this close to him, she allowed his magnetic energy to push all thoughts of Phillip into a forgotten abyss. Once she believed in a little girl's idea of love. If one person loved, the partner would love back. She had learned that didn't happen. She stopped her thoughts and listened to Caesar telling her something about Las Vegas.

"The town wasn't much in '41, but Highway 91 runs right through the middle of Las Vegas. So anyone driving east or west can't escape Highway 91."

"I heard there're dude ranches to visit while waiting to get a divorce."

Caesar laughed. "I wouldn't know about that, but there're plenty of hotel rooms to stay in. Let me tell you what's happening and where I think Vegas is going."

Carmel didn't interrupt him, but she wondered why it was so important that she know anything about Las Vegas.

"During the time Hoover Dam was being built, the town was full of construction workers. When the dam was finished, the town dwindled to a gasoline stop. Now, Tommy Hull has opened his El Rancho Vegas outside the city limits, and Jackie Gaughan's El Cortez has opened downtown. They're two good-sized clubs and very popular."

Their waiter appeared with another martini. Caesar asked, "Carmel, would you like a serving of escargot?"

"Yes, I would like a small order."

Caesar gave the order and then raised his glass. "Here's to you, Carmel, a beautiful woman. May you sing for me again." He gazed into her eyes for a moment as they touched glasses.

Carmel met his look over the top of her glass. "Who knows?" She felt almost brazen staring into his eyes, black as ink. Flirting with Caesar was a new experience and she took pleasure in it. She felt alive.

"Yes, who knows what this life holds for us." The moment passed. "You might be interested to know I raise my own snails. I mean, my houseman, Chen, does."

"I remember you told me once before. I hear you built a bridge between your houses, and it's all glass."

"That's right. You'll have to see it sometime, and my snails." His black eyes challenged her. The escargot arrived and Caesar scooped her snails onto her plate. She enjoyed having Caesar serve her. She ate one and dipped sourdough bread into the hot butter and garlic.

"These are incredibly good." She finished the snails, tapping her mouth with her white linen napkin. "Caesar, why are you telling me about Las Vegas?"

"Big things are happening in the town. Six thousand soldiers are enrolled to train in the Army Air Corps Gunnery School. A basic magnesium plant near the little town of Henderson employs hundreds of workers. The town is popping, and I intend to build a club."

"You would leave San Francisco?"

"Are you saying you would miss me?" He flashed a smile at her.

She sputtered, "I thought you had a club."

"Not large enough. I have an idea to entertain the gamblers with top-notch performers in the lounge. The big star will be in the main dinner showroom. If the customers hear the show going on in the lounge and it costs nothing, the wife'll stay and listen while waiting for her erstwhile to gamble."

"It all sounds great, Caesar, but I know nothing about gambling or lounges."

"That's what I'm getting to. I want you to sing in the lounge. I have a hunch about you. You're headed for stardom in the main showroom."

Carmel thought he was exaggerating but was saved from saying anything by the waiter arriving with the steaks. "Carmel, this steak calls for a bottle of Cabernet." He told the waiter.

The owner, Alfred, approached. "Mr. Almato, how is your dinner?" He was short, with dark hair, and wore a tuxedo.

"Thanks to you, Alfred, your chefs are still cooking steaks over Mexican mesquite charcoal. They are perfection, as usual. Alfred, this is Miss St. John. She sings locally."

"How do you do? I have heard you on the radio. You sing beautifully."

"Thank you." Carmel was surprised and delighted to be flattered in front of Caesar.

"Come in more often, Mr. Almato. We miss you." Alfred smiled and left.

"I *heard* you were singing on the radio." Caesar's tone was teasing.

"I've been on only twice, and as a guest, nothing steady. Edna Fischer introduced me on her *Blue Monday Jamboree on KFRC.* I felt lucky Edna let me sing. She's a tough coach." Carmel had been so nervous being on the air, she wasn't sure she wanted to sing on the radio again.

"I know how well you sing. I've heard you. Remember?"

Yes, she did remember. She felt his black magic, the wild, out-of-control feeling she had the first time she saw him at the Palace Hotel. Exciting and forbidding. Under his stare, she looked away.

As happened before, people came to greet and pay Caesar their respects. Like the previous time, sometimes he introduced them. At the end of dinner, he asked, "Would you like to go to the Sinaloa? Garcia, the owner, is a friend of mine."

"To tell you the truth, I would like to see your birds and snails." She giggled.

Caesar looked astonished. "It'll bring me great pleasure to show you my menagerie. We'll have a cognac at the house."

They had arrived at Alfred's in a dim-out. When they left, it was over. Riding beside Caesar, she said, "It's a relief to see where we're going, especially at the corners. San Francisco drivers have to be the biggest bluffers in the world."

At the top of Bay Street he stopped in front of a two-story framed house. Caesar helped her out of the car. Chen greeted at the front door. "Chen, this is Miss St. John." Chen bowed and smiled at Carmel. He took their coats.

"We'll have cognac later, Chen, in the upstairs bar. Miss St. John wants to see the birds and your snails."

Chen bowed. "Yes, boss."

Caesar reached for Carmel's hand and guided her up the carpeted stairs to the second floor. On the way, Carmel caught a glimpse of large rooms, high ceilings, and comfortable furnishings. Enormous paintings full of color hung on the walls. Caesar led her onto a passage-gallery with windows facing north. Through them, Carmel could see the lights of the Golden Gate Bridge.

"I made the back half of this house into an aviary." He crossed in front of her, opened the door, and snapped on the lights. They walked into a conservatory with tall palms, banana plants, and vines trailing a trellis. Purple and white orchids grew in pots. Large tubs held water plants, and small gold fish wiggled under lily pads. The lights woke the birds, and the cackling started.

"Oh, Caesar, this is wonderful, but you woke up your friends." A cockatiel turned a slow somersault on its perch. Carmel laughed.

"They're pretty sleepy at this time, but they get lively in the daylight."

"How many do you have?" She saw a large aviary behind a glass wall. Birds, large and small, fluttered across the view.

"There are about thirty in this room. We'll let them sleep; I'll show you the snails." He walked to a large wooden box on a corner table, lifted the screen, and pointed inside. Carmel looked in and saw snails in their shells and pieces of greenery on the floor of the box.

Caesar said, "That's cornmeal on the bottom of the box. It cleans out the snails so we can eat them. The green bits of lettuce and celery keep them alive."

Carmel stared into the box at the little shells moving and knew she would never eat snails again.

"Come; let me show you my view." He took her arm and led her out of the room, across the bridge, and back into the house. Candlelight lit the room. They walked through open doors onto a balcony facing the ocean. The lights of the bay spread before them. The glow disappeared into the marine headlands across the bay. Carmel could barely distinguish the ships under the Golden Gate Bridge, silent, dark monsters headed for uncertainty.

She stood next to him, staring out at the darkness, smelling the night and sensing his closeness. She could feel her nipples growing hard. Taking a deep breath, she hoped he wouldn't see. His sexuality was overpowering. Phillip, help! Phillip, she pleaded. In the candlelight, Caesar reached for her. His warmth spread like syrup, overpowering her. He took only her arm. "It's chilly. Let's go inside and have our cognac."

They sat on a voluminous couch by windows facing the bay. Chen had lit a fire. The snapping wood reminded her of home. She remembered Christmas was coming. The memory brought her to her senses. "Caesar, one cognac and I must go home. I'm singing at the hospital in the morning."

Caesar didn't try to persuade her to stay. He took her home. At the door, he held her hands in his, and his mouth, warm and sensual, kissed the back of her hands.

She was aware Caesar knew he was tempting her. He would be an exciting lover. She felt goose bumps rise on her arms and legs.

He said, "Thank you, again, Carmel, for a lovely evening. I'll call you before Christmas."

CHAPTER 60

Caesar didn't call and Carmel went home for Christmas. It was almost nine o'clock Christmas Eve before she entered the silent house. She stood a moment, staring at the scene before her. At the far end of the room a fire burned in the stone fireplace. Andrew sat unobserved in his wheelchair. His handsome profile and high cheekbones were outlined by the light of the fire, his hair worn longer than usual. His chin rested on his chest and on his face was an expression of total dejection. Carmel, seeing it, felt a pang of guilt. She placed her bags by the door, removed her heavy coat, and dropped it onto a chair by the doorway.

Bruno and Howard raised their heads when she entered the room. They got up from Andrew's feet and walked to her, their tails wagging. She laughed and petted them. "Is this the welcome committee?"

Andrew, hearing her voice, straightened. A smile lit his face. "Daughter, I thought you might not come home this Christmas."

She chose not to tell him she had been thinking exactly that. She went to him, bent to kiss his cheek. He wore his red cardigan over a white shirt and a red bowtie. She said, "Uh-m-m-m … you smell good. I had to wait for my ride. A brother of one of the gals at the Canteen brought us down." She looked at the tree heavy with glistening adornments and the Christmas presents on the floor around it. "Where's everyone?"

"Your brother's off with Laura. Some pal of Laura's is leaving for the service and plans to be married on Christmas Day. Tonight is a pre-wedding shindig. Dr. Barron's at the hospital waiting to deliver a late baby. I have my Anna."

Anna came into the room and stood beside Andrew. She wore her favorite long red Christmas skirt with a white blouse and a blue velvet vest. Anna patted his shoulder before she turned to hug Carmel. "We're glad to see you, Carmel. Christmas started off lonesome."

"Anna, you look beautiful." Carmel thought her father and Anna were becoming more open with their affection. Well, why not?

"Thank you, Carmel. You look quite sophisticated." Carmel wore a black silk dress with gray satin collar and cuffs.

"Thank you, Anna. What I need right now is some brandy. How about it, Dad? Want to join me?" He nodded. She went to the wheeled bar, found glasses, and poured brandy for the two of them. "Anna, have some?"

Anna hesitated only a moment, "Later I'll have a nightcap with your father. Now I have to check the dough for the breakfast rolls. You two visit. You haven't been here for a while." She headed for the kitchen.

"That's right, Dad. I've been busy." She handed him a snifter of brandy. Carmel sat down beside him with her drink. "How're you feeling? Show me your leg."

Andrew grunted and stuck his left leg out from the wheelchair. He wore a wool sock. "I'm getting better. No one else thinks I am, so I have to stay in this damned chair."

She stared at his foot. "Dad, it's still swollen."

"Yes, I guess it is." He put his drink down on the small table beside him. "Give me my humidor. I'm going to have one cigar."

Carmel put down her drink, opened the carved wooden box on the table, and placed it before him. "I think this is why you're always in trouble, Dad. You're stubborn, just like Aunt Lydia."

Andrew put down his glass, selected a cigar, reached in his sweater pocket for his silver cigar clipper, and snipped the end off. He lit it and blew out a great cloud of smoke.

"Ah … stubborn. Well, it's Christmas Eve. Stubborn, eh?" He laughed. "How're Lydia and Russell?"

"They never change—they're great. Dad, do you think maybe the war is coming to an end? The people in San Francisco think so. I heard there won't be as many dim-outs. We're already bombing Okinawa and Tokyo. In Europe we're finally in Belgium taking a stand."

"That's tommyrot. Carmel, our First Army is surrounded by Germans somewhere near Bastogne. The ground's thick with snow and fog. That means our planes can't cover for them. Both sides are immobilized. They're calling it the 'Battle of the Bulge.'" His voice dropped and Carmel barely heard him.

"Germany's fighting with its best troops, including tanks and planes. A lot of our men are dying over there, and it's Christmas." He stopped talking and stared at the fire.

Carmel stoked the fire then added another log. She hated asking her father about war news. "The boys at the Canteen say with the success of Lyete and the brouhaha over the bombing of Tokyo by giant super fortresses, the war has to be coming to an end. Aren't the Japs about ready to quit?"

"If the boys at the Canteen, as you put it, have all that information, then they also hear what I hear. The Japanese do *not* surrender. In fact, they have pilots calling themselves *kamikaze* who dive into a ship and die with the plane as it explodes. They die for their emperor. And as far as Europe goes, you've heard me say this before: Napoleon said the Germans were born in the mouth of a cannon. They'll always be fighting. Now they're bombing cities in England with their damned buzz bombs. Their range is two hundred miles. I understand there's nothing left after they explode. No, Carmel, you can count on this world war lasting for a while longer. It sounds to me like you're not reading the newspapers."

Carmel hoped to hear the end of the war was near. Instead, he made it sound even further away. Many people in San Francisco thought differently. Some said the black market was over; people could get anything you wanted. She believed her father. He always told her the truth no matter how grim. The thought of the war going on and on depressed her.

Andrew looked at her. "Tell me about you. What're you doing now? Lydia told me you sang on the radio, but I didn't hear you."

The question irritated her. "Dad, I've sung on the air only twice. Right now jobs for singers on the radio in San Francisco are few." She got up. "Honestly, Dad, my job singing with bands keeps me very busy. Do you want another brandy? I'm having one."

"Yes. This is a special time. I have my special gal at home." He raised his glass for more. "I want you to sing for me before you leave."

Carmel didn't want to tell him she was having one of the best times of her life. Her popularity had increased, and she was more in demand by the bandleaders than ever. When she finished singing at night, escorts wanted to take her wherever she wished. Sometimes she went to the California Club or downtown to Izzy's or to the Old Poodle Dog. If her father was in San Francisco, he would recognize the citizens felt the war was coming to an end. There was a sense of recklessness in the air.

He interrupted her thoughts. "I'm sleeping downstairs. It's easier for me to get around and easier for Anna."

She finished her drink and put down the glass. "Guess I'll go on up to bed." She leaned over her father and rubbed her cheek against his. "I love you, Dad."

Her father patted her shoulder. "I love you, too. Goodnight. It's good to have you under the old canopy called home."

"Did you see the full moon tonight? You can read a Christmas card outside it's so bright."

"No, I didn't see it."

The house had been quiet for some time. Andrew, unable to sleep, rose from bed, pulled on his heavy winter jacket, and got into his wheelchair. He threw a blanket over his legs, wheeled himself to the bedroom door, and opened it. Wheeling himself out to the terrace, he sat there, staring at the dark forms. Trees, bushes, and plants were black silhouettes under a sterling silver moon. The moonlight was bright enough for him to read his watch. Its hands pointed to 3:00 a.m. Carmel was on his mind. Something was keeping her in the city besides her singing. How long would it be before she stopped searching for whatever it was and come home?

The night air was chilly, but he liked sitting in the moonlight. He didn't tell Carmel more tough battles were coming in the Pacific, especially for the Marines. As for Grant, there was a good chance he would never see his cocky son again. Andrew wanted to see him, listen to his bragging—especially about the women who spoiled him. Andrew chuckled.

In the distance, he could see the roofs of the barns under the eucalyptus grove. Three trucks were parked in the old barn. Scott wasn't around when the men worked long hours storing the walnuts. In fact, Scott was home less and less these days.

If Elizabeth Rose was here, she would understand the problems of the children. She would find Carmel's reason staying in San Francisco. She would grasp Scott's ambitions and have the patience to understand Grant's refusal to accept responsibilities. He remembered their trip to Paris. Elizabeth Rose had wanted to sleep in a chateau and purchase clothes in the great haute couture houses. She didn't sleep in the chateau, but he bought her the clothes. He enjoyed seeing her face full of happiness, listening to her laughter, and watching her twirl around in the salons.

Could he believe his eyes? Elizabeth Rose stood before him, arms outstretched. Her hair shining like spun gold, bright as the sun, blinding him. She was telling him something he didn't understand. He woke with a start. No, it wasn't her hair; the bright light was coming from the barn. My God, he thought, the barn's on fire. He started to roll his wheelchair forward. It was too slow. The flames were curling around the roof on the back of the buildings. Andrew threw off his blanket and pushed out of the chair. He hobbled toward the barn.

The first explosion woke Carmel. She saw the flames from her window and men running. She grabbed a robe to cover her thin nightgown. Running down the stairs barefoot, she yelled, "Call the firemen."

She rushed into the yard. Flames shot across the barn roof and reached for the eucalyptus trees. She saw the overturned wheelchair. "Dad, where are you?" She tripped on the edge of the rock garden and fell on her face. Despite the pain from a cut on her cheek, she threw off her robe and ran. Her sheer nightgown clung to her body.

She heard someone behind her. It was Anna. Searching together, they found Andrew on the ground. He muttered. "Get the trucks out of the barn."

Anna bent over him. "My *muchacho*, what are you doing? Are you hurt?" She tried to lift him, but he was too heavy.

Jose appeared. "I'll help you. Pedro called the fire department." They managed to lift Andrew to his feet. All the color had drained from his face.

Anna yelled, "Let's get him to the wheelchair."

Carmel, relieved her father was alive, ran for the barn. Over her shoulder, she called, "We have to get the trucks out of the barn. Where's Scott?" She heard a horrendous sound. The barn wall and roof had collapsed at the same time. She tasted blood in her mouth from the cut on her face.

Flames reached the trees. Another explosion was followed by a great sheet of brilliant orange-gold fire and black smoke. The blaze had a sound of its own. It roared as it climbed and sucked at the eucalyptus. Ashes filled the air and covered the ground. The smell of burned rags, walnuts, and a heavy resin made it hard to breathe. Sparks flew. She heard another tree explode. If the fire crossed the grove, it would reach the huge butane tank by the old barn.

The new barn was an inferno. She struggled to get clean air into her lungs. She ran to the old barn and prayed the keys were in the trucks. She felt she would never get all three trucks out. Where in the hell was Scott?

She climbed up into the old Chevy. The keys were there. Pedro was suddenly by her side thrusting his heavy shirt at her. He jumped down, hurried to the next big truck, and climbed into the front seat. Carmel hadn't thought about her body. Looking down, she saw her nightgown torn away, one breast uncovered. She heard sirens as she backed the truck out of the barn. It was the last thing she remembered.

Carmel opened her eyes to see Scott standing in front of her. She was under a heavy blanket on the living room couch. She tried to get up and fell back with a groan.

"Take it easy, sis. You've got a hell of a bump on your head."

"Where's Dad?"

"He's in his room. Dr. Barron and Anna are with him. I've been waiting for Dr. Barron to talk to you. Here is the robe from Anna."

Realizing she was still in a torn nightgown and Pedro's shirt, she reached for the blue wool robe he held. Scott turned away while she slipped her arms into it.

"What about the fire?"

"It's been out for an hour. I'm sorry, Carmel, I wasn't here."

She ignored his apology. "What about the barns?"

"The truck they said you backed out and the one Pedro got out are what's left."

Again, Carmel started to get up. A sharp pain pounded in her head, holding her motionless for a moment. She managed to stand and wrapped the robe around her. Scott reached to stop her. She pushed by him. "I want to see. Oh, my God."

In the first streaks of daylight, she saw debris covering the large area where the barns had been. It reminded her of war zone pictures in *Life* magazine. Burned timbers stuck up grotesquely. In their midst was the charred remains of the truck. Piles of ashes covered unrecognizable forms. Only a few gaunt eucalyptus trees, vacant of leaves, remained in the once large grove. "The trees are gone?" Carmel sat down, her eyes blinded with tears.

"They blew up. Their shallow roots couldn't support them."

Harold Barron came into the room, "Well, young lady, you're awake. Stay perfectly still so I can get a look at you." He felt her head and checked her eyes. "Carmel, you have a small concussion. You must remain completely quiet." He looked at Scott. "Your father has had a stroke. It's too soon to tell how much damage he suffered. We'll keep him in bed for a while. I'll check him and your sister every day. If your father gets stubborn with me, I'll leave orders to move him to the hospital. Understood?" Scott nodded.

"Carmel, you're very brave. Now it's bed rest. I want you flat on your back with your head between two pillows. Anna will take care of those cuts on your face." He turned to Scott. "You're in command. See that my orders are carried out."

Scott said, "Carmel, I'll send Lupe to help you. Anna won't leave Dad."

Lupe came immediately after the men left. "I'm going in to see my father before I get into my bed. Help me."

The two women walked slowly to the end of the house to find Andrew asleep in his four-poster bed. Anna napped in the chair beside him. The light from the small lamp by his bed and the fire in the fireplace added a faint light to the darkened room. She saw her usually resolute father with his eyes closed. A white bandage covered one side of his face. When Anna heard them she rose, holding a finger over her mouth. "He's asleep."

Carmel walked over to the bed. She stared down at her father and whispered. "How is he?"

"He banged himself up. This fall keeps him in bed."

Carmel motioned for Anna to follow her to the door. Anna looked as if she had aged ten years. "Oh, Anna, I think I'll never forgive my brother. Where was he? How did the fire start?"

"Now, don't get temper up. Your brother did nothing on purpose. He got home, finally. We do not know how the fire started. Carmel, you mind Dr. Barron. He said you have a concussion. You must not climb the stairs. Lupe, get Pedro to carry Carmel up to bed."

Carmel didn't resist. Her head was pounding, and for the moment she was grateful to be carried. She wondered what could have caused such an explosion.

CHAPTER 61

Carmel woke the next morning to an ominous and frightening silence. There were no familiar morning sounds. No kitchen clatters, no voices in the yard, and no barking dogs. Something dreadful had happened, but for the moment she couldn't recall what it was.

Then she remembered. It was the fire. How the eucalyptus grove was ablaze with flames, the awful sounds of the trees exploding. She recalled falling on the rocks trying to find her father. Tears filled her eyes; her head throbbed. She had to get out of bed and see him.

Still in her torn nightgown, she crossed the room to look at herself in the mirror. Her body ached all over. The jagged cut on her cheek and across her swollen nose had bled; she needed a new bandage. Her nose was becoming black. She must have fallen flat on her face. Then she remembered. Pedro had carried her upstairs and Lupe helped her into bed. Although bruised, she managed to wash her face, tape on a smaller bandage, and dress herself. Wearing slacks and a shirt, she went downstairs to find her father.

She found Lupe staring out the dining room windows at the devastation and went to stand beside her. At the far end of the lawn, where the tall majestic eucalyptus grove had stood when her great-grandfather bought the land, the trees had exploded and fallen across the ruined barn. Some of the crumbled rock foundation remained, exposing the huge, empty space where the old and new barns had stood. In the midst of it all was the skeleton of the burned truck.

Carmel felt as if an old friend had died. She thought of the fun she shared with her brothers. They had played hide-and-seek in the barn behind stacks of hay, climbing into the trucks and pretending to drive. She remembered the musty odor of bins of walnuts in gunnysacks filling the barn. All of it gone.

She saw Scott standing with Jose and Pedro where once the barns had been. Scott waved his arms. Anger surged through her. She'd make him wave his arms soon enough.

"Will the ranch be the same again?" Lupe sighed.

"Certainly. Thanks for helping me to bed."

"You're welcome." Lupe looked at Carmel's bruised and swollen face. "You okay?"

"I have to be." She smiled at Lupe to make up for the sharp tone in her voice. Lupe had nothing to do with the decisions facing her. "I'd better find Dad."

In the dimly lit bedroom, Andrew was asleep and Anna sat near him. Carmel saw the outline of his large frame under the bedclothes. His gnarled hands with palms open looked helpless.

Anna, her finger to her lips, led Carmel out of the room. "He had bad night. He asked for you before he sleep. The firefighters had coffee and ate the Christmas rolls I baked. You supposed to be in bed. Dr. Barron is coming soon. You are staying here?"

Carmel knew she must face Anna's question. To see Anna so rattled frightened her. When Anna spoke of the rolls, she remembered it was Christmas.

Carmel put her arms around Anna. "Thank the Lord no one else was hurt. Just take care of Dad. I don't know what to say about Christmas or dinner. I'll see what Lupe can do, or maybe we'll wait and have a New Year's dinner. I have to see Scott before I do anything."

She found him with Pedro, sifting and poking the ashes with sticks.

Scott looked up. "We're searching for anything of use. How do you feel?"

Pedro lowered his eyes and moved away.

"Outside of a head as big as a squash, I'm fine." Intense anger swept over her. "What caused this fire?"

"The firemen think the explosion might have been caused by gas accumulating from the walnuts."

"Why on *Earth*? Can they be sure?"

"They said an explosion just like this happened at a walnut grove up north."

"Yes, but I don't understand. Why would they explode?"

"I guess the way they were stored."

"That makes no sense. We've been storing walnuts for years."

Scott walked away from her toward the house.

"Where're you going, Scott?"

"I'm going to Aptos."

"Now?"

Scott whirled around, a savage expression on his face. "Yes, now. *I* have a business to run. People are counting on me."

"And just what do you think is happening here?"

"Carmel, this is the day you grow up and take on the responsibilities of the ranch. Dad told me you said if he ever needed you, you would come home."

Carmel, stunned at his anger, felt she should be the angry one. It took a minute, but she remembered saying those very words. Tears moistened her eyes. She promised herself to find out exactly how the fire started, no matter how long it took.

Scott left without saying good-bye. No one mentioned Christmas.

Dr. Barron arrived and stopped to see Andrew before he found Carmel. "Come with me and sit down." He led her to the large couch in the living room. He examined her head and asked some questions about headaches and dizziness. "I recommend you take it easy, but I know you won't. Your father will need bed rest for some time. We have to face the fact his left arm and side may be paralyzed. It's too soon to tell. Looks to me like you'll be making the decisions. You *are* staying?" Dr. Barron studied Carmel's face for a moment, then gave her a kiss on the cheek. "Good girl. If you like, we can have Christmas at our house."

"No, thank you. I don't feel very festive. I think I'll have a quiet dinner here with Anna. I don't know what Scott's doing."

"Laura told me Scott said last night their machinery quit again and he'll be there until it's fixed."

Dr. Barron was right. She had to make some decisions. She was tired, sore, and hurt all over. Scott had turned the ranch over to her. She gritted her teeth. She felt she was struggling for breath after some terrible injury. As far as she was concerned, he had dumped it on her.

Later that morning she met with Jose and Pedro in the kitchen. She asked them to sit down with her at one of the long kitchen tables. The cut on her foot throbbed. She wondered if it was infected but said nothing. She knew if Dr. Barron looked at her foot, he would insist she get off her feet. She put her foot up on a chair.

"Since my brother is working away from the ranch and not here to guide me, I find I am totally dependent on your advice and help." She forced a smile.

Jose, who worked with Andrew's father before Carmel was born, said, "*Conchita*, we'll help you."

Pedro, who was younger and lacked Jose's patience, said, "Tell us what you want to know."

Jose rolled his eyes.

Carmel wasn't sure how to begin. "First of all, we are never to bother my father with questions. I don't care what they are. When the walnut crop was lost in the fire, the income went with it. The firemen are searching for the cause. But I haven't forgotten today is Christmas. We'll have Christmas dinner here in the kitchen. Lupe and I will join you." She paused and looked at Jose's face for encouragement.

"Carmel."

Carmel saw Laura standing in the kitchen doorway. "We can talk in the other room," she said.

Laura followed Carmel as she hobbled into the living room. They sat on the couch.

The morning sun streamed through the tall windows and glanced off the tinsel on the Christmas tree. The Christmas lights were not turned on. Carmel saw the still unopened packages. Her feelings of despair and sorrow intensified.

"Are you all right?" Laura asked.

"I'm fine."

"You don't look fine. You look awful."

Laura asked, "How's your father?"

"Your father said he's still in shock and may be paralyzed on his left side."

"Oh, Carmel, I'm so sorry."

A lump rose in Carmel's throat. She stared in silence at her sore foot.

"Do you want to have Christmas dinner with us?"

"Your father asked me and I said no. Frankly, Laura, I'm furious with my brother and do not want to have dinner with him."

"Yes, I know you're angry. I think he thinks you've done what you want to do, and now he wants to do what he wants."

"I don't look at my singing as doing *just* what I wanted to do. I brought joy and pleasure to people. Besides, to find and keep a job singing took work."

"Well, he believes he'll give people jobs, and if he can perfect his idea for freezing large amounts of food, he'll make it possible for food to be fresh when it reaches the table."

"Laura, I'm not going to sit here and listen to you tell me how wonderful my brother is."

"He won't be here today for dinner because his machinery broke down … again. I'll let you rest. If you want to come for dinner, just come. I'm sorry about your Dad and the fire."

Carmel did not reply. She was far too dispirited. Their friendship was being threatened. It was another reason to be upset with Scott.

When Laura left, Carmel found Lupe and instructed her to plan a simple dinner in the kitchen with Jose, Pedro, Rosita, and her. Anna might join them, although she suspected Anna would stay with Andrew. Late in the afternoon, Bruno and Howard crawled under the long trestle table in the kitchen. Carmel, Rosita, Lupe, Jose, and Pedro gathered at the table to eat the Christmas dinner. The meal was tempting, but the craving for food was small. Conversation was limited to the weather, with January promising to be a month of blustery winds and rain.

Jose asked, "Did you know your father made plans to take out one hundred acres of walnut trees and renew the orchard.

One hundred acres! Afraid to let Jose see how this news shocked her, she bent down to pet Howard's warm head and hide her face. They must not see how bewildered and frightened she was. After a moment, she raised her head and made an effort to smile. "Golly, Jose. One hundred acres and I was afraid there wouldn't be enough to do."

They joined in her laughter.

That night in bed, she struggled to reach some decision. The wind rose and she listened to the old beams snap and pop, adjusting to the cold and the change of temperature. She felt alone, worried about her father, and still angry with her brother. Carmel was also apprehensive about how to manage the ranch by herself. At the top of her worries, she wondered if she could say good-bye to the music for which she worked so hard.

It was time to leave San Francisco. She felt something dying inside her and there was no way to stop its death. She thought about all the wonderful people who helped her. There was Jerry, her aunt and uncle, and Elka. Bitter tears filled her eyes. The tears she held back all day broke loose. She sobbed her heart out. Finally, exhausted, she slept.

The next morning her headache was gone, but her body and muscles remained sore. Each movement caused pain, but this was no time for self-pity. She was determined her father would have no worries, except to get well.

She made a list of immediate necessary tasks. Call Uncle Russell and Aunt Lydia and tell them she wasn't returning to the city. Lydia cried. She was so concerned about her brother it took time before she realized Carmel wasn't coming back. Uncle Russell said he would see her trunk was shipped to the ranch and how lonely the house would be without her.

Inform Edna Fischer. There would be no more voice lessons. Edna accepted Carmel's decision as part of show business. "Carmel, we both know this music business is changing. Even I don't know how long my job will last at the station. You keep practicing. Don't neglect your voice. Come and see me when you're in the city."

Finally, call Jerry and Elka. Jerry was incredulous. "You mean you actually will not be singing at all? Not even in the hospital?" He was quiet for a moment, then in a soft voice he said, "I'm proud of you and I'll be down to see you." Carmel knew the news shook him.

Elka was her sweet self. "*Liebchen*, I miss you. You are true friend." They promised to see each other if Carmel came to San Francisco.

When Carmel visited Andrew, he did not know she was there. Howard and Bruno slept outside his door and then waited each morning for her appearance in the warm kitchen.

Her sleep was constantly interrupted by worries. There was no money to rebuild the barn. Scott kept his small truck to drive to Watsonville. They needed to buy a truck for the chores, one large enough to bring the pickers to the ranch at harvest time.

Somewhere there had to be money, notes, something. She wouldn't allow herself to panic.

She had tried to obey Dr. Barron's orders to remain quiet and off her feet, but every day she saw the horror in the back of the property and knew decisions had to be made. Too much was at risk. She decided to go to the bank and see her father's friend, Mr. Castor. He said he was very busy, but under the circumstances he would set aside time to see her.

The next day she sat at Mr. Castor's desk. Mr. Castor was short and losing his hair. He wore a black suit and a shirt with a too-tight collar, and he sat very straight. She had the feeling if the man relaxed he might deflate. His expression was dour, as if he smelled something bad; his words suited his solemn manner.

He told her he knew she'd moved to San Francisco and sang in the famous hotels. His voice sounded impertinent to her when he asked, "Carmel, how old are you?"

She knew immediately he did not expect her to know much. "I'll be twenty-three in November."

"After your telephone call, I checked your father's account and found what money is available is in savings. If you're careful, the money might carry you until the harvest this year. Andrew was counting on this crop of walnuts."

"Did my father have fire insurance?"

"I'm sure he did, but I have no idea how much. Where is Scott?"

"Well, how do I find out?" She ignored his question about Scott.

"Under these emergency circumstances I'll bring your father's safety box for you to investigate. Excuse me." He got up, walked to the back of the bank, and disappeared. After a few moments, he returned with the long metal box and set it before her.

She found her father's will in an envelope and left it sealed. There were copies of her, Scott's, and Grant's birth certificates. Under them were the insurance papers. She would call the agent and find out how much they could expect. Distressed to find Andrew had lent almost thirty thousand dollars to friends, she wondered if they would pay them when the notes were due. She sighed. Another problem.

Finished with the papers, she thanked Mr. Castor for his time and left. Driving home in the station wagon, she wished desperately this wasn't happening to her father. His pride demanded the ranch must survive. Too many decisions, and she could easily make a wrong one. Too much depended on her. Mr. Castro said there was only enough money to carry them until harvest. She rubbed her forehead and wondered if she should press her father's friends to meet their obligations.

After her visit to the bank, Carmel forced herself to believe life on the ranch was slowly returning to normal. She soon formed the habit of meeting Jose and Pedro at first light in the big family kitchen to discuss the chores for the day.

On the bitter cold January mornings, she enjoyed the fire crackling in the brick and adobe fireplace, the morning chatter, and the smell of breakfast cooking, with fresh coffee brewing on the back of the stove.

The two skinny, hardworking men sat at the table listening. "We'll meet here each morning. At the start of each month, you must tell me what is to be done on the ranch. What to plant. When we use smudge pots. When to hire pickers. Jose, won't we need some men to clear the trees out of the orchard? Let's begin with cleaning up the mess left from the fire. Then we can get started measuring for the new barn." The small fire insurance policy would at least help to get started.

Carmel, worried, had asked Anna, "Can we manage with our ration stamps?"

"Carmel, you forget we have all the meat we need. Your father buys butchered beef, lamb, and pork from neighbors. We always exchange produce. We have plenty chickens and good laying hens. We'll make do with this awful lard. Our problem is sugar, clothes, and no new shoes. You said yourself, gasoline and tires."

"Pedro, Anna said the plans Scott had for the barns are in his room. After I find them, I'll go to the lumberyard and someone can help me figure how much lumber we need. I heard it's very," she took a deep breath, "because of the war, difficult to get lumber."

In the beginning, Carmel knew that Anna, Lupe, Jose, Pedro, and Rosita weren't sure how to accept her. She earned their admiration because she didn't ask them to do anything until she understood what was to be done. Explanations took time, but she listened, and both men were patient.

Finally, two weeks after her father's stroke, she held his right hand and felt a tiny squeeze. She saw in his once incredible blue eyes, now faded, that he knew she was there.

Jose and Pedro's predictions for the month of January came true. Heavy sheets of gray rain followed the cold days, filling gutters and overflowing curbs. Sluice boxes became flooded with leaves and dirt and had to be kept open. Jose and Pedro were outside most of the day digging and pushing dirt to control the overflow.

Following the men, Carmel splashed through the rain in her rubber boots. She felt utterly useless and was instantly relieved when Jose said firmly, "*Conchita*, you're warmer inside. We'll keep the sluice boxes open—it's our job. Later, we prune fruit trees before new growth."

Because of the heavy rains and saturated soil, Anna waited until late January to plant her winter garden. It would be ready for an April harvest.

Gradually Andrew became coherent, but his left arm and leg remained useless. When he was awake, Carmel would join him to eat dinner by his side. She avoided talking about the ranch chores or Scott. If the war news was good, she told him. Many evenings, Anna sat with them and they listened to radio programs. A particular one made her father laugh: *The Happy Island*, with Ed Wynn, playing King Bubbles. Sometimes she returned to tasks on the ranch and worked past midnight. Bookkeeping had to be done, seeds ordered, equipment repaired, and food purchased.

When they had first started to figure how to build the barn, Carmel was lost. Finally, she began to understand board feet and her knowledge of numbers surprised even herself. The new barn, with increased square footage and skylights instead of windows, would be more efficient than the one Scott built.

Carmel enjoyed the dark and moist soil in winter. Bruno and Howard followed her into the fields, chasing intruders in the tall weeds. The tip of Howard's yellow tail waved above the grass. Jose had said, "Let grassy weeds grow. Later we till the land in orchard with tractor. Birds love seeds that fall from wild flowers and weeds."

In February Carmel hired two laborers to help Jose, and they began to cut down the walnut trees.

Jose explained, "We can clear twenty-five acres. These trees have been in ground fifty years. We plant new trees then plenty room to plant rows of strawberries."

Carmel listened and thought how simple he made the work sound. "I think the wood from the large branches and trunks should be cut into logs. We'll sell the firewood. Stack the wood near the front gates, Pedro. I will make a sign, 'Wood for Sale.'"

From then on the days were filled with the sounds of a two-man saw cutting through trees, followed by pick axes striking the roots. Smoke spiraled into crisp winter skies from the small branches of walnut trees.

One day, Fire Inspector Hammermill came to see Carmel. He sounded sympathetic. "There's no doubt the walnuts were stored green and the hulls remained moist. A methane gas formed and caused the explosion. With gunnysacks and old wood, you couldn't help but have a disastrous fire."

"It'll never happen again." Carmel chose not to mention her brother, who in his rush to get the walnuts stored, packed them still green. She was ashamed of him. The fire and Andrew's stroke had been unnecessary.

Carmel knew Scott managed to see Andrew and Jose when she wasn't around. He offered her no help. She had hoped Laura would come to the house and they could share their thoughts and feelings again. There was a rift between them, and Scott had caused it. Carmel felt Laura didn't want to openly side with her and admit Scott might have been wrong to insist she come home. Besides, Laura was busy attending San Jose State, studying and continuing to help her mother. The biggest disappointment remained that Laura *never* knew anything about Phillip, except that he was alive somewhere on the Pacific Ocean.

In bed at night, Carmel heard the locomotive whistles of trains that roared past in the distance. She wondered how many other women listened to the forlorn sound carrying sons, brothers, husbands, and lovers to strange places.

CHAPTER 62

Carmel decided in February to use one of the small rooms off the kitchen for an office. There was room for her father's sturdy old desk and a comfortable chair. She bought two file cabinets. Anna found a large, dark green rug to cover the tile floor. Carmel hung a small mirror by the door. On another wall, she placed a picture of Andrew with his father digging his second well.

She drew a monthly calendar and listed all the tasks to perform and materials they would need. Jose and Pedro were eager to teach her. When she tried to outdo herself, she often caught one of the men rolling his brown eyes at the other. She wanted more than anything in the world to earn the respect of those who had lived and worked so many years with her father and grandfather.

Other times she asked herself, What am I doing here? She didn't have the mind to study dirt and learn how to spray and kill bugs. Aphids, red spiders, and other insects laid eggs on tree bark that might eat up their orchard. She was lonely, but too tired at night to think of going anyplace. Neighbors came by to see her father. They greeted her and said she was a godsend. At night she studied about soil, how to grow strawberries, when to harvest the fruit from the cherry trees, and especially how much area was needed to store walnuts.

Occasionally, she felt the desire to play the piano and sing. I'm dormant like the walnut trees, she told herself. Maybe in the spring she would feel like singing.

March brought bursts of rain and winds that bent the trees in the orchard. Her spirits lifted as the earth moved closer to the sun, the days grew longer, and the soil softened, yet the nights remained chilly. Feelings of bitterness and resentment were occupying her mind less and less. Her love for her father encouraged her to prove to herself she could manage the ranch the way he would want it. She began to take pride in the neighbor's compliments.

Jose and Pedro feared frost would destroy young buds on the trees. They decided smudge pots must be started. The men told her to stay in bed, but she insisted Anna wake her before 3:00 a.m. to join them. She watched them put the pot of kerosene on the ground in the center of four trees. A three-foot stick wrapped with a sack and fastened with bailing wire was dipped into the kerosene and lit with a match. The crude oil in a pot spewed forth black smoke, stinging her eyes and making her cough. The smelly black fog spread through the trees and burned for three hours. The whole Valley of Delight was filled with the rank smoke.

Three months elapsed before the building of the barn could begin. The fire insurance had been settled, little as it was. With the plans drawn, the estimates also had to be submitted and accepted by the county. To Carmel, the wait for the lumber to arrive took forever. Then one day she returned from shopping for Anna and found Jose and Pedro pouring the foundation for the new barn. The lumber had arrived.

Relieved and excited, she rolled her father in his wheelchair to see the great piles of stacked lumber. Andrew's once robust body was scrawny and his voice shook. "We shall open a bottle of champagne to toast the arrival. Everyone must salute with a drink." Carmel filled glasses with champagne and joined Anna, Rosita, Jose, Pedro, Lupe, and Andrew in a toasting the new barn. Life felt good. Excited, everyone talked at once.

Just when Carmel thought the insect spraying was over, Jose said, "We place coddling moth traps on walnut trees. The traps catch moths before they mate." At the crestfallen look on Carmel's face, he said, "That's our job. You learn how to run tractor?"

Carmel found an old wide-brimmed straw hat to wear. The hat was too large and sat far down on her ears, but it kept the early morning sun out of her eyes. She wore her customary outfit of brown corduroys, plaid wool shirt, and jacket to keep her warm. Pedro showed her how to move the gears. At first, she couldn't manage the tractor or the disk. Repeatedly, she ran into trees. But as she worked in the dry earth, she learned to keep the tracks made by the tiller in even circles around them. She was determined to excel as a tractor driver. Following the circles and grooves relaxed her. She thought only of missing trees.

One late afternoon, she climbed off the tractor. Thick clouds of dust had followed her. Dust was in her eyes and mouth, and she tasted the grit between her teeth. She went to the office, took her hat off, hung it on a peg, and caught her reflection in the mirror. She looked brown, maybe too brown. She looked at her hands, with their tan, rough skin and broken nails. I work just like a peasant, she thought, and I look like one.

She found she barely remembered the girl in the haute couture dress singing in a famous hotel. Romantic music, dancers, and listening to melodies in smoke-filled afterhour rooms were distant memories. Her life had changed. She wasn't sure Phillip liked callused hands and sun-browned women.

At night, when Carmel crept into bed exhausted, sometimes too tired to sleep, she tried to visualize Phillip. If she tried too hard to bring him closer, he faded from view. One night she dreamed she was riding in Phillip's small car. She saw the outline of his profile in the dark, could feel his warmth and smell his cologne. When she tried to hold him, he evaporated. She woke crying.

CHAPTER 63

In February, two corpsmen stood on the deck of the *Solace*. They leaned against the rail and peered into the murky air.

"Can you see anything? Is that the coastline of Iwo Jima?"

"I can see the call to arms, the forming of battle lines. Are you crazy? I can't see anything but smoke." The corpsman answered.

"Admiral Nimitz sent word that the bombardment of Iwo Jima was to start. We're to prepare for battle casualties."

"Dummy. Bombardment happens before every battle."

Not giving in, the other corpsman said, "Sometimes MacArthur gives the orders. I heard there's eight hundred ships around us."

"I don't know how those guys on the battleships stand this noise. Seventy-two hours. Yipes! Someone said it's the largest bombardment yet."

The *Solace* rode the rough waters, churned by an armada of ships, including heavy battleships, destroyers, and cruisers. Bombers flew overhead. Phillip stood behind the corpsmen with a wry expression on his face. He heard their exchange before he moved away.

Bosn Berg came to stand by Phillip. Phillip asked, "Are we underway? What's going on?"

"We're too goddamn close. Sorry, sir. We've been ordered to move back another hundred yards."

"I wonder when this softening up will stop."

"Scuttlebutt is we'll have the island secured in five days."

"So much for scuttlebutt." Phillip had witnessed Guadalcanal and Tarawa. Somehow, this attack was different. His sense of foreboding about the island did not leave him. He knew there would be many casualties. Phillip had seen the map of Iwo Jima, a small treeless island formed by a volcano, less than seven hundred miles from Tokyo. On one end of the island a gradual slope led to Mt. Suribachi.

The *Solace* shuddered as she maneuvered in the churning sea, moving away from the island. Phillip went to scrub and met Nickers in the operating ward. "We'll need more plasma today. I'm going to issue orders every other staff member give blood before they hit the sack tonight."

Nickers asked, "Did you know the twenty-six corpsmen ordered to ship with us didn't show? Methinks they'll be sorely needed."

"Or you could look at it this way. Since we just finished a drill on damage control, we won't have to do another at the moment with brand new recruits." He continued, "I heard this Japanese Lieutenant General Kuribayashi is a brilliant strategist. Japanese want to secure the island for a landing strip for planes to bomb American ships. The Americans need it for B-29s to land and refuel on their return from Tokyo. Both sides are seasoned fighters. I'm certain the battle will be bloody. If the Japs continue their usual habit of refusing to surrender, we're in for some heavy casualties."

"It's such a small piece of earth. We should mop it up quick. On the map it looks like a kidney." Nickers made a shape with his fingers.

Phillip dried his hands. "In my book, it looks more like a pork chop."

Later Phillip learned, at the end of the bombardment, both the Fourth Division and the Fifth Division pushed ashore fighting beside each other. Both were caught in crossfire. The Japanese general waited until the third wave of marines were ashore before he ordered the counterattack. Phillips words proved to be true, there were many casualties.

For fourteen hours, patients sat or lay on the beaches waiting to get aboard the *Solace*. That night the *Solace* sat fifteen miles off shore and remained lighted. Phillip worked through the night with other personnel.

He stood by a young patient on the operating table. The marine's head had been shaved and prepped for surgery. Phillip saw the brain pulsating in the man's fractured skull. He began to remove pieces of the fracture where he saw a blood clot had formed. To expose the clot, he would have to cut a flap. With a power drill, he cut across the scalp from the patient's ear to his forehead. He waited for Nickers to start sucking out the clot. Without warning, the brain began to swell. Phillip hadn't time to find out why. He reached across Will and put his hands against the young man's brain to keep it in his head. "Get his blood pressure down."

"His pressure won't come down," the anesthetist answered. During surgery, he used a foot-pumped bellows to provide oxygen.

"We have no time," Phillip said. "Something is wrong. He's not getting any oxygen. I'm not losing this patient."

"My God, his oxygen tube has slipped out of his windpipe." The anesthetist reached for the tube.

Phillip's voice remained calm. "Place it back in his throat." He continued to hold the swelling brain inside the patient's head.

With oxygen restored, the swelling began to recede. The brain slowly shrank to a normal size. Phillip pushed it back into the skull while Nickers began to suck out the clot.

Phillip shoved Nickers aside. "Never mind." He took over and finished removing the tumor, closed the head, and turned the patient over to a corpsman.

Phillip's mind had become a machine. Routine, routine, and more routine. Cut, control the field, repair, sew it back up, leave.

On the second day, the *Solace*, with 667 patients, headed toward Guam and the USA General Hospital. The personnel learned six hundred marines died on Iwo Jima the first day.

Phillip was in the ward when he heard a nineteen-year-old marine explain to the corpsman what was happening on the island. Everyone heard him.

"The sand's black as pitch and movin' in it is like walkin' in a rice bin. Bodies disappear like unseen hands reach for them. The sand slides back as fast as you push it away. I tried to lie down and it was too goddamn hot. Some of the fellows dug down three inches, put their can of rations in it, and within minutes the heat blew the lid off.

"The island is a damn, fucking four-story apartment buildin'. There are five thousand caves, with kitchens and a hospital. They reinforced five-foot concrete pillboxes. Under Mt. Suribachi, they dug in and filled a thousand caves full of ammunition. We were so tired that when we discovered two Japs beside us in our foxhole deader than bees in a blizzard, we just sat beside 'em and ate our rations."

His buddy said, "Stop bellyachin'. I'm only alive because the goddamn slippery and slidin' volcanic ash plugged my bullet holes and stopped the bleedin'. I have more than forty," he bragged. Quiet for a moment, he then asked, "What'd you be doin' if you weren't here?"

"Hell, I'd be settin' out smudge pots in an apricot grove with my old man."

They lit cigarettes and were silent.

When Nickers thought about it, the change in Phillip began in January, after they picked up the survivors off the submarine USS *Mazala*. It was then that he rudely pushed Nickers aside. Though he and Nickers lived and worked in close quarters, there was never time to talk. Phillip spent less and less time in his bunk. His excuse was that he needed to recheck charts after the nurses finished.

At Ulithi the ship received extra blood and supplies. Admiral Halsey came aboard to give congratulations and encouragement to the weary crew. Phillip paid little attention; he stayed with a patient who had lost both his arms.

He walked around with the "bulkhead stare." Some Marines had it, seeing but not having anything register. Saving lives was exhausting and sleep and rest were essential to remain lucid. Phillip wasn't sleeping. At this point he had simply quit feeling. He kept his mind locked where nothing filtered through.

When he finally slept, he had grisly nightmares. There was blood, blood everywhere. Blood-filled holes where eyes and where noses should be were replaced with pools of blood. Brains fell out of craniums full of blood. He watched a heart beat in a pool of blood. He began to go to bed later and later.

Surgery aboard the ship became grim and ironic. On the island, the men were being killed. Phillip and the doctors were trying to save men's lives only to have them go back for a second try at being killed.

On the third day of fighting, Phillip examined a young Marine on the next gurney who had a gunshot wound in his neck. Phillip looked at the wound and felt relief. The bleeding was heavy, but the bullet had gone through his throat and out the other side without hitting any critical arteries. A corpsman would take care of him. He signaled for the next patient.

A corpsman, brought aboard with the wounded, was bleeding internally. He was dying and he knew it, but he struggled to tell what happened on Iwo Jima. He was frantic to tell his story to the nurses who were trying to clean him up. His voice sounded raspy.

"By the third day, all the officers were dead. The noncommissioned men were makin' decisions. The fellows from Guadalcanal and Tarawa that fought in the beginning were killed and replaced by inexperienced recruits. Those Japanese are masters at snipin', hidin' in bunkers and spider traps. They pop out of a hole and shoot you in the back.

"The Japs come out of their caves at night and shoot at us. They carry ammunition under each arm and blow themselves up as well as us. Someone told me their orders were to kill ten of us before one of them died."

The nurses tried to stop him talking. "No, let me finish. On the fifth day, the leathernecks got the American flag onto the summit of Mt. Suribachi, but the fightin' didn't stop. I cried when I saw Old Glory up there. I heard the colonel order a larger flag raised, so we could see it. I knew two of the guys who helped raise a bigger flag."

He stopped talking. The nurse felt his pulse. "He's gone."

Phillip wiped his forehead and nodded.

The *Solace* returned from Guam three times to evacuate two thousand casualties off the island of Iwo Jima. Phillip sometimes wondered if he would ever sleep again.

Finally, on March 26, Japanese resistance ceased and the landing strip could be built. Admiral Nimitz sent words of tribute to all aboard. "Among the Americans who served on Iwo Jima Island, uncommon valor was a common virtue."

The *Solace* proceeded on to Ulithi to pick up corpsman, blood, and supplies.

Before one hundred and eighty thousand fighting troops were to attack Okinawa, Admiral Spruance's armada of fourteen hundred ships, the Twentieth Air Force, and the Marine Tactical Air Force pounded the sixty-mile-long island. This was the largest amphibious operation in the Pacific. The Japanese general repeated the similar assault as to Iwo Jima. He allowed the forces to beach easily on Okinawa while he watched from an old castle high on the hill. Once the whole operation was on shore, he attacked. Phillip again knew the casualties would be high.

There were many more burn victims on Okinawa. Their bodies were black—skin hung in pieces, blistered and covered with blood. Sometimes patients were treated on the shore by medical corpsmen before they reached the ship. The corpsmen carried Burma Shave in their first aid supplies to treat white phosphorous burns. It was cooling and soothing and put out the phosphorous that might still be burning.

For Phillip and Nickers, it was agonizing to treat and heal soldiers who had been on Guadalcanal or Tarawa only to have them return to the ship from Okinawa with more severe injuries. This included the staff of doctors, nurses, and corpsmen.

On shore, the fighting remained fierce. Survivors who came aboard said the dead men were stacked four high. Some had been cut in half, badly mutilated, later only to be identified by fingerprints. The stench of the dead, gunpowder, and sulfur filled the air. Volcanic ash covered everything. The Japs had set sixty miles of tunnels and fortifications.

At last, the *Solace* was able to move under a smokescreen to Guam with 600 patients aboard, 228 of them burn cases. Kamikazes were attacking the American fleet, and every effort was made to move hospital ships under a smokescreen. Once they sailed into bright afternoon sun, Phillip joined Nickers and some of the crew on deck. They saw two kamikaze planes appear in the sky. They were aimed at a United States destroyer a short distance from them.

Feeling helpless, the staff and crew watched as one of the planes peeled into a dive, straight at the ship, did a pylon turn, and zoomed into the starboard side, crashing into the bridge. The plane ripped through the ship and exploded. An orange ball of fire followed by black smoke surrounded the ship. Bodies flew through the air. Another kamikaze roared into view to finish off the disabled ship. American planes attacked and the Japanese plane, billowing black smoke, exploded as it hit the water, just missing the destroyer.

Phillip muttered, "Dead in the water." To the Bosun standing beside him he asked, "What kind of a nation destroys its young men with fanatical devotion to their emperor?"

"Don't want a dedicated kamikaze comin' down our stack," Nickers answered.

The Bosun standing beside them said, "The men in the water'll be picked up by another ship closer to the destroyer. We have no more room. We're overloaded with critical burn cases."

On May 8, the crew heard about V-E Day, the day the Germans surrendered. Some of the tired doctors met in the wardroom for a toast. They raised their coffee cups. The captain said, "Here's to our victory in the Pacific, and may it be soon."

"Hear, hear," the group chorused.

The doctors returned to their duties. On the way, Nickers said to Phillip, "The civilians on Okinawa were told Americans would rape and kill them. Many civilians didn't wait for our men to come ashore; they killed each other and themselves."

"April has been an exceptionally tough month with both President Roosevelt and Ernie Pyle dying. To lose two men so admired left many of the soldiers depressed."

Nickers agreed, "For these kids he was their only President. They feel he was cheated of knowing victory. They've lost a father, part of their family, gone forever."

"And everyone loved Ernie Pyle and his column. I would say, for everyone aboard ship, the morale is lower than a snake's belly. It's those damn kamikazes pilots." Phillip squinted up at the sky.

"Concur, Phillip. To us they're fanatics; to the Japanese they're dedicated war heroes."

Phillip sounded grim, "The fact is, they're so *unpredictable* it makes you nervous. How many hospital ships do we have now?"

Nickers paused. "Let me think. There's the *Bountiful, Mercy, Samaritan, Relief,* and *Comfort.* Did I get them all?"

"At least the *Relief* and *Mercy* have been armed. And we're still running dark at night."

"I've a feelin' when we get these burns cases back to Guam we won't be comin' back this way."

Phillip agreed. "I'm afraid this old lady needs dry dock."

"Let's turn in early, old buddy."

"Can't. I saw Grant St. John's name listed among the burn patients. Come with me."

When they entered the ward, they felt the oppression, the air heavy with pain. Nurses and corpsmen worked silently beside the bandaged figures on the beds. Men whimpered, the only sound that pushed against the quiet.

Phillip found Grant awake, staring. His eyes were round holes in the white bandages covering his face, head, and upper body. The bindings were already turning brown from medicine and blood. Phillip didn't know the extent of the burns covering Grant. He knew the scalp was severely burned and his hair was probably gone. There would be scars on the outside. Phillip wondered how deep inside the scars would be.

Grant, heavily sedated, never knew when they reached Guam. Phillip stayed with him until he left the ship. Phillip wondered if it was too soon to write Grant's family.

CHAPTER 64

Marlena was in an exceptional mood. She was about to get what she wanted. She had planned this night long ago. Caesar usually spent Wednesday night at her apartment.

She entered her enormous clothes closet. At the mere sight of her possessions, she felt intoxicated. The closet was crowded with expensive dresses, suits, shoes, and hats Caesar bought for her. She felt when she appeared in expensive apparel and jewels she added style to his persona.

Her three fur coats hung in the closet. She loved her floor-length dark brown mink from Caesar, her pearl-gray Chinchilla, and her tawny black-spotted leopard from two other men who ogled her in the fishbowl. Men loved giving her gifts. Because it was easy to flirt and lead them on, she promised them nothing. Only Elka knew the jewelry she accepted was genuine and in a deposit box in the bank. Marlena felt her sister wasted her good looks. Elka could have as much as she had. Marlena remembered how fast possessions could disappear.

Caesar would be surprised if he knew how much she managed to squirrel away. She never intended to tell him. When he was out of town, she dated other men, careful not to be seen in the places he took her.

She hurried to undress. Naked, Marlena entered her marble bathroom. She turned on the faucets for a bath and poured in Essence of Rose bath salts. She stared at her nude body in the full-length mirror. She was near the end of her fifth month and wondered how much longer she could hide the slight swell to her tummy. Her body was still trim and her breasts were larger but firm. She had no morning sickness and felt great. Only occasionally she felt like taking a nap. She remained the slender mermaid the public came to watch.

When the tub was full, she slipped into the warm, foamy fragrance of roses and rested her head against the back of the tub. Telling Caesar she was pregnant was going to shock him. However, she didn't doubt once he faced it, he would love the idea of becoming a father.

After her bath, the body oil she applied left her skin smooth as a baby's. Thinking of the baby, she smiled. No one knew about the baby, not even Elka.

By the time Caesar arrived, she had sprayed on cologne and sat in her frothy pale pink nightgown at her dressing table brushing her hair. He dropped his coat on a chair and crossed the room to the bathroom. He pulled off his tie and was unbuttoning his shirt when he said, "Hi, doll. It's been a bitch. Jake was late getting back from Vegas. I'm headed for a shower. Get me a drink, would you?" He shut the door.

No hug, no kiss. She hated it when he was grumpy, impatient, and bossy. She went to the kitchen and fixed his drink of scotch on the rocks, brought it back to the bedroom, and set it on the night table beside the bed. She removed the bedspread, pulled back the top sheet, and sat again at her vanity bench. She returned to brushing her long blonde hair.

Caesar came into the room after his shower. Nude, he took a large swallow of his drink, set it on the nightstand, and lay down. Marlena knew what to do next. She stood at the bottom of the bed, waiting for him to look at her. Her nipples and the curves of her thighs were revealed through the sheer silk. Slowly she moved the straps of the gown from her shoulders. Her nightgown slid to the floor. She stood nude before him. With her fingers she began to massage the rosy tips of her nipples until they were like tiny bullets. She crawled in bed beside him.

She began to kiss him, taking her time, tantalizing him. She searched every hollow of his body with her tongue and fingertips. She knew when he was sated with desire, anticipation, and fully aroused. He pulled her willing body to him. Reaching for her ample breasts, he lifted her body and slid into her heated sex.

Satisfied, he turned away from her. She moved closer to him.

"Caesar, honey, will you talk to me a minute?"

"What is it? I'm sleepy." He lay on his right side, his back to her.

"Caesar, I'm going to have our child."

"Like hell you are."

"I'm already pregnant."

He rolled over to look at her. "I'll find someone to get rid of it."

"I can't. I'm past five months."

"What're you saying?" He was wide awake and sitting up in bed.

"I'm six months pregnant, and I want this child."

"We'll see about that. I'm not bringing any kid into this world." He jumped out of bed and started to get into his clothes.

"No, no, Caesar, talk to me. Don't leave. We could have such a beautiful baby." Tears filled her eyes.

"I'll not come near you again," he said. She had never heard such rage in his voice. "You tricked me. How could you have done this to me? I don't want to be tied down for anything, anything!"

He finished dressing and without a word left the apartment.

Marlena's sobs stopped. She vowed to herself, I'll make him pay for this.

CHAPTER 65

In July 1945, the *Solace* took on fuel in Guam and set a course for Pearl. The day was brilliant with sunshine, the blue sky cloudless, and the sea calm. A clear wake of white water broke behind her stern. The *Solace* carried 280 ambulatory patients, and an additional 240 were on stretchers, 75 in traction. Morale on the ship was high. Men were headed home, and the end of the war was imminent.

After Phillip made the evening rounds, he stopped in the wardroom for coffee. Captain Richards joined him.

Phillip said, "My gut tells me this is our last run. This old lady should head for dry dock. She'll not return to the Pacific, at least not as a hospital ship."

Richards blew on his hot coffee. Took a sip and said, "Bosun told me it's damn good we're going in. Our rudder is responding too slowly, and we aren't maneuvering with the speed we should." He grinned. "But if this weather holds, we should be in Pearl in five days."

Captain Richards replaced Captain Pearlman when the latter completed his tour and was sent stateside. Richards was a handsome, blue-eyed six-footer. Curly blond hair and a slender build made him appear younger than his fifty-some years. He took his position as a naval officer seriously and impressed Phillip with his competence.

In the early dawn of the fifth day, a sudden pitch of the ship threw Phillip out of his bunk. Thick medical books were thrown from the shelves, hitting him in the head.

Knickers held on to his bunk and swore. "What the hell was that?"

Slowly the ship righted itself. Both men threw on their clothes.

Phillip said, "Whatever it is, I bet patients are on the deck. Let's go."

To reach the hospital ward was difficult with the sudden storm pitching and rolling the ship. In the ward, Phillip saw men dangling from their bunks. The corpsmen and nurses were working to get them righted. The patients groaned and yelled questions.

"What in the hell happened? Are we under attack?"

"Jesus … Nurse Button, my crutches fell out of my bunk."

"My leg, everything is loose."

The patients with legs in casts were out of traction. Phillip and Nickers joined the struggle to get them stabilized. The tossing of the ship made it a difficult job. Doctors and nurses tied some of the men into their bunks. Broken glass and bottles holding saline solutions were removed. The ship continued to pitch and roll.

Nurse Lombard asked, "Did anyone check the men on the deck?" The crew now slept on the deck as a matter of routine, leaving the inside bunks to the patients.

The new executive officer, Lieutenant Dean, spoke up, "The men check out, but we lost a few cots over the side."

The wind became a steady roar. Phillip braced his back against the bulkhead. He stood at the end of a bunk checking a young man's feet. Fungus and maggots had eaten part of the flesh. Phillip told the nurse to continue treatment and re-bandage him.

The Bosun appeared. "Commander Barron, Captain Richards wants to see you, sir!"

"I'll come now."

Phillip lurched and bumped against the bulkheads on his way to mess. He joined Richards at the table. "It's the middle of the day and the sky is black. What's the verdict?"

"We could be headed toward a typhoon."

"Don't we know for sure?"

The Bosun, standing behind Richards, shook his head.

Captain Richards explained, "The Third Fleet weather planes report every four hours, but this ocean is too big to be accurate."

Lieutenant Dean joined them and heard the Captain's words. He had boarded the *Solace* in Guam and been in a typhoon. "Can't we get the hell out of here?"

Bosun said, "With respect, sir, we know there is a tropical storm 120 miles away. To avoid it, we must backtrack south. It means we could run short of fuel to make it to Pearl."

Lieutenant Dean appeared pale. "Can't we find out by radar? How about other ships? Can't they tell us what the weather is?"

Captain Richards's voice was calm. "The reports from Kwajalein, Pearl Harbor, and Midway estimate it's a light tropical storm. We'll watch the barometer. For every hour the barometer drops, this'll tell us the number of miles away the storm is. If in four hours the barometer remains normal, this storm will pass."

His conversation was interrupted when the *Solace* was slammed violently, followed by a shudder. The lights went out and the battery-operated auxiliary lights kicked on.

Captain Richards rose and left the wardroom. They heard his voice over the speakers: "Now hear this. This is the captain speaking. It's mandatory for all aboard to wear life jackets at all times. Tie yourself to your bunks. No one is to be on deck except warranted personnel."

Bosun listened to the words. "We have to judge the weather only by what we see ourselves."

Phillip skipped breakfast. He gulped down his coffee and returned to the hospital ward, finding a group of frightened men and women. It was impossible to follow procedure. Wounds needed to be kept clean and freshly bandaged, and men had to be fed intravenously. Phillip was concerned the storm would delay administering plasma to the patients who were near death.

The crew aboard the *Solace* prepared for the typhoon. Lifeboats were battened down. Any gear on the deck that might move was lashed down and secured. Hatches were covered and locked in case water broke through.

Phillip knew the weather had deteriorated. Wind had increased. The seas were mountainous, spraying forty feet over the bow. The ship plunged into black holes large enough to hold a skyscraper. Walls of water fell against the hull as the ship disappeared in the half-light. Water seeped past the bulkheads and the hatches. The sound of pumps added to the cacophony of noise.

Phillip sympathized with the patients. All asked the same question. Could the *Solace* withstand the beating it was receiving? The crew remained somber faced.

The constant pitching made sleep impossible. Men in great pain were kept sedated. Even in their unconscious state, they tore at their bandages. Nurses and corpsmen tied themselves to the bunks beside their patients, watching helplessly as the men rocked back and forth. Each time the ship rolled starboard and hung there a moment, Phillip prayed a silent prayer and held their breath, willing the *Solace* to right itself. The ship fought to stay on course. It was hard to believe how quickly the storm had increased. Winds reached hurricane force at sixty-five knots. Heavy rain fell. The weather worsened.

Only men discharging necessary tasks remained on deck. To keep from going overboard they lashed themselves to the superstructure. Saving any man who fell into the raging sea would be impossible. Crewmembers managed to reach the hospital ward with broken ribs, ankles, and arms, their skin red and pitted from the wind.

Phillip met Bosun in the wardroom with two other doctors. "Could we capsize?" he asked.

"We could, but the *Solace is* charmed. She's a tough lady at eighty-nine thousand tons. She can take rolls of sixty-five degrees." He grinned. On the way out, he confided to Phillip they were taking seventy-two degree rolls.

Phillip returned to the hospital ward and found the chaplain leading the men and women in prayer. It was difficult to hear him above the howling and screeching wind. Those that could prayed on their knees. Then, over the noise, Phillip heard a single voice singing the Navy Hymn.

Eternal Father, strong to save
Whose arm doth bind the restless wave
Who biddist the mighty ocean deep
Its own appointed limits keep;
O hear us when we cry to thee
For those in peril on the sea.

The men, Marines and Army, joined him and sang the hymn again.

Phillip admired these men. They had faced death on a battlefield and were now facing it on the sea. Listening to the men sing, he realized he was as close to death as they were.

Unexpectedly, goose bumps traveled over his body. For a moment, he swore Carmel stood next to him. Her love for him filled his heart and comforted him. Only because he felt he would not return he wrote that letter. Now he knew he wanted to spend what was left of his life with her. Renewed energy began to flow through him.

After five hours of pounding, Phillip felt responsible for telling these men they would make it to Pearl. He turned to the chaplain. "I'm going to the bridge and speak to Captain Richards." He intended to learn the truth no matter how unfavorable the news.

Bosun heard him. "Commander Barron, it's too damn dangerous for you to climb to the bridge."

Phillip ignored him.

Bosun shrugged. "We'll both go. I'm tying you to lifelines."

They climbing to the bridge, the wind and spray were alive, trying to drag them into the sea. Captain Richards shouted above the screaming wind, "Bosun, you're putting the doctor's life in jeopardy."

Phillip shouted back. "I insisted."

Visibility was less than one hundred feet. He heard radios crackling in the background. From the messages, they gathered that other ships were floundering.

He asked, "How much longer?"

"Electricity has just returned to the bridge." The captain answered. "The steering went when the helmsman turned a knob sending signals to turn the rudder—nothing happened. The water short-circuited our wires." Phillip could not hide his concern. "Don't worry, regulations told us what to do in case this happened."

At that moment, Phillip saw the bulk of a ship bearing down on them. It looked twenty-five stories high. Phillip held his breath.

He heard Captain Richard order, "Hard left rudder." The *Solace* rose on the crest of a wave. The huge black shadow plunged into the trough and passed them.

Phillip, shaken at the size of the dark image, knew if the hulk had hit them it would have been certain death. "My God, what was that?"

Captain Richards answered, "Maybe a transport, oiler, or freighter. I don't know. It was a big son of a bitch. His radar wasn't working, probably never knew we were here." He scowled at the instruments. "Believe it or not, I don't think we'll be swimming tonight. The wind is dying down and the barometer is rising. We're finally moving out of the main storm. You may tell them below."

Richards returned to his wheel. "Watch your step."

Phillip thought with the pitching and rolling of the ship, the wind screeching through the rigging, the storm was far from at an end.

He didn't get to tell anyone anything.

He woke up strapped to his bunk. Nickers stood beside the bunk watching him. "Old man, you coming back to the land of the living?"

Phillip felt groggy. "What happened?"

"You slipped on the ladder leaving the bridge and damn near took a header into the sea. Bosun grabbed you. How do you feel?"

"I'm okay … how long have I been out?"

"An hour will do it. Better take it easy."

Phillip was trying to unfasten the straps holding him in the bunk. "No, I want to see what's happening. Help me out of this."

"I'll let you up—just take it slowly. You've got a big bump on your head."

"What's going on out there?"

"We're moving out of the storm; word is we'll be in Pearl in three or four days."

"The ship doesn't seem to be taking such a beating."

"You're right. We're riding the swells better. Visibility has increased. Stay in your bunk awhile. There'll be plenty to do later."

Phillip said, "No. I'll join you. Give me a minute." He attempted to rise and felt a slight dizziness, but he managed to stand.

"I'll stay until you're dressed." He helped him with his shirt and shoes.

Phillip was grateful Nickers supported him through the companionway. The *Solace* wasn't plunging as deeply, and the following shudders seemed less severe. The high pitch of the wind told him they were still in the storm.

He entered the ward and the patients greeted him.

"Hey, Commander Barron, we're coming out of the storm and headed for Pearl."

"Captain Richards ordered us to change our headin' to ride easier," a young patient added.

"Bullshit. I'd like to see what he calls easier." The fear had left their voices. Some had smiles on their faces. Phillip found his staff had maintained an amazing sense of order and calm.

Nurse Lombard said quietly, "You're as pale as one of our patients. Why not return to your quarters?"

Phillip held onto a bunk and ignored her. He spoke to one of the lieutenants. "Let's check out our patients."

His staff, relieved to see their commander on his feet, obeyed as fast as the rolling ship would allow.

Phillip insisted on checking each bedridden patient himself, giving special attention to patients in comas. Fighting the ship to maintain balance, their progress was slow.

Finally, Phillip was satisfied he could leave the wards. He stopped in the wardroom and found Captain Richards smoking a cigarette.

He noted the captain's pale face and the dark circles under his eyes. Phillip realized he must look just as fatigued.

Captain Richards asked, "How're you?"

"Tip top." Phillip smiled to prove he was. "How's the *Solace*?"

"Our rigging is getting the hell torn out of it, and we lost two lifeboats. At the moment everything's working. It could happen again, though. The anchor chain may be burned out. We'll find out when we get to Pearl." He sighed. "We're still taking in weather, but the storm continues to lessen with every knot. Yes, we'll make it to Pearl. The *Solace* is old but sturdy." Richards's eyes lit up. "Aren't you glad you asked?"

Phillip chuckled. "It sounds complicated, but you say you have it all under control. Have any other ships foundered in the storm?"

"Don't know. I suspect many avoided the typhoon. In '44 we lost 790 officers and men in one during a Philippine invasion. Now our communications are greatly improved." He reached in his pocket for a cigarette. "Smoke?" When Phillip shook his head, he said, "I forgot you don't. This is the time I enjoy one. I'd enjoy a good cigar more." He lit his cigarette and puffed.

"Could it have been much worse?"

"Yes, we could have gone in a trough made by the wind and sea and been unable to get out. Its called being 'in irons.' Then we would have capsized. Thank God it didn't happen." He continued to puff on his cigarette. "How're the patients doing?"

"Holding on." Phillip thought, But only due to the remarkable staff of doctors, corpsmen, and nurses. He wanted to say communications on this ocean were inadequate and needed a lot of improvement. Surely the ship could have been informed earlier that it was headed for a typhoon and escaped. He kept his thoughts to himself and said nothing to the tired man facing him. He rose to leave. "Good night, Captain."

"Good night, Commander."

CHAPTER 66

The storm finally blew itself out. The *Solace* at last was underway through calm water under a bright blue sky. Ship routines returned to normal. The crew got the *Solace* shipshape, stood their watches, and slept soundly off duty. The music of Benny Goodman's and Tommy Dorsey's dance bands played from radios. And orders for ice cream were enormous. Phillip was heartened by the enthusiasm. Home was on the wing.

In Pearl Harbor, a huge crowd greeted the arrival of the *Solace*. The air filled with the shriek of sirens, ships' whistles, and foghorns. Well-wishers cheered and waved American flags while a navy band played. Ambulances lined up on the dock and waited for patients. It was a bedlam of joy.

As the *Solace* eased into her slip, she exhibited the ravages of the storm. Her rigging flapped and drooped. The red crosses on the stack and side appeared dull and weather beaten.

Patients, many with tears coursing down their cheeks, waited in line to be transferred to dock side. The staff and crew worked rapidly and efficiently to get them off the ship.

Phillip stood beside Nickers on the top deck and watched the last patients leave. They stared at the scene of people hugging and screaming welcomes. It was over. After all the months and all the miles covered, it was finally over. In all that time, there was never a moment they weren't involved in life and death decisions for someone other than themselves.

Nickers stared hard at Phillip. "How do you feel? Honest answer."

Phillip's felt exhausted. "I've been ordered to have a checkup."

"Glad to hear it."

"Just a waste of time."

"Maybe those doctors can keep you quiet for a while," Nickers chuckled. "We can't leave yet. Admiral Nimitz is on his way here to meet the staff and crew."

"I believe his coming aboard will help make leaving the old lady easier. And it's time to do just that." Phillip said.

Seventeen doctors stood with twenty-seven corpsmen, nine nurses, and a full crew on the deck of the *Solace* to greet Admiral Nimitz. Their faces laid bare the weariness of their last tour. In officer's whites, Admiral Nimitz looked tan and healthy. He shook hands with Captain Richards and said he wanted to shake the hand of each person aboard.

A slight breeze carried his words across the deck toward the standing men and women. "Of all the men and women working to preserve lives, to keep them safe and comfortable, each one of you was cognizant of the peril to the patients, and the *Solace*. Through it all, your integrity and responsibility was constantly maintained.

"Some of you are returning home to loved ones and friends. Others will remain here in the Pacific. Before you leave, we want you to take our eternal thanks for your contribution to end this conflict.

"Four-hundred purple hearts are to be awarded to the men and women on this tour. The *Solace* will receive her seventh battle star."

A loud cheer came from his audience.

"I now have the honor of shaking the hand of each and every one of you."

After the admiral's short speech, Phillip concluded that of all the personnel to come aboard the *Solace*, Admiral Nimitz most of all grasped, with wisdom and compassion, what the *Solace* and its personnel had been through.

Later that afternoon someone brought a copy of the *Honolulu Star Bulletin* paper aboard. A picture of the *Solace* on the front page with the assembled group and Admiral Nimitz filled the front page.

The time for their departure arrived. Phillip made the rounds, telling the doctors, corpsmen, and nurses good-bye. His usual detached manner was gone. He welcomed the chance to express his sincerity. Admiration and love for his fellowman overwhelmed him. His voice raspy, thick with emotion, he shook their hands.

The men, trying not to show their feelings, rushed their handshakes and slaps on the backs, giving him a hurried "Good luck, old man." The nurses cried and hugged each other, promising to remain devoted forever.

Phillip went below to pack his gear. His orders were to check into the hospital for a physical before being released. But first he intended to find Grant.

Nickers joined him. "You've been a true friend these last four years," Philip said, and the two shook hands.

"Well, I guess we'll see you next as the head of a big hospital in San Francisco.

"Not sure about a hospital in San Francisco."

"That's all you spoke of when you first came aboard. Where *are you* headed?"

Phillip chuckled. "That does seem eons ago. Large hospitals seem too impersonal for me now. I realize I like the contact with the patient." He looked sheepishly at Nickers. "How does that strike you?"

"As a matter of fact, if you said you wanted the big hospital, I would be ready to bet you would soon change your mind. Headed back to San Jose and your father's clinic?"

Phillip closed his duffel bag. "Something like that. Maybe I'll start my own clinic. How about you? Want to practice in San Jose? In many ways San Jose is like a Midwestern town." He chuckled. "Ranches, prune pickers, *and* pretty girls. Come and see me after you go home. Are you calling Ensign Danner?"

"I may come and see you. And yes, I intend to see Lucille. She's aboard the *Relief* and a lieutenant now. I just may bring her around," he said, his eyes brightening.

"Good. We'll roll out the red carpet."

Phillip lifted the heavy bag, stood at the door, and saluted Nickers—then disappeared along the bulkhead.

Later that day, before Phillip was assigned to his quarters in the Honolulu Navy Hospital, he was handed several letters. Once in his quarters, he dropped his bag on the floor and sat on his bed by the open window. A slight breeze brought the delicate perfume of ginger into the room. Looking through his envelopes, he recognized his sister's writing. Laura wrote so seldom, he opened it first.

August 1, 1944
San Jose
Dear Phillip:

Guess you are surprised to hear from your sister, especially since I'm not a letter writer, but I promised Mom I would write to you. The poor darling, in the morning her hands are so stiff from arthritis. She's an angel and never complains. You know Mom.

Dad is very, very busy. We still have a shortage of doctors in the area. He doesn't say much, but when you come home, I know he hopes you will join him.

I'm finishing my pre-nursing major this summer. San Jose State has an excellent course. I hate chemistry. I want to get it all over with. Then I'm on to County Hospital. I've heard their training is the best. Guess you thought I would never amount to anything. Ha! You would be surprised how large the County Hospital has become.

Scott and I spend time together when he is here, which is seldom. He works in Watsonville, sometimes all night. I think his partners should do more work. Each time he wants to process another line of fruit or vegetables, he takes the equipment completely apart and resets the machinery to process the next line. Sometimes this takes all night. Someday, when I'm a nurse and his cannery starts showing a profit, we'll be married.

As for the St. John's, Carmel's father sits in his wheelchair most of the day and doesn't talk much. Part of his face and his right arm are partially paralyzed. When he first hurt his foot and was in the wheelchair, he could play poker, but not anymore. Anna takes care of Andrew. She seems tireless.

When Dad wrote you about the fire at the St. John's ranch Christmas Eve, about the barns and the whole walnut crop being destroyed, and Carmel's father having his stroke, no one knew if Carmel would come home or not. Well, Scott was in a state of emergency and wanted Carmel home now, and she did. She doesn't talk about leaving San Francisco and her glamorous life singing. She has only Pedro and Jose to help her. Jose is older than Atlas. Two days ago, I found her driving the tractor through the orchard, tilling the soil, clearing weeds. She can really whip that tractor around. Carmel told me they receive no news about Grant except he is in a hospital in Hawaii. No one knows how serious his injuries are. Carmel thinks that bothers her father a lot. Do you have any way to check on Grant?

Last month Carmel and I spent two days with her Aunt Lydia and Uncle Russell. We shopped the first day, even though there is a shortage of so many things. We met Caesar Almato. I think he is an old beau of Carmel's. She says not. He invited us to have lunch with him at the Palace Hotel.

We had a delicious lunch with lobster and champagne. Musicians played violins and a cello. It was a treat for me. Caesar is very handsome and big like you and has dark hair and eyes. But his eyes are black as olives, and you can't tell what he is thinking. I thought he would take a bite out of Carmel. He never took his eyes off her. He owes a hotel in Las Vegas and said he wants Carmel to sing in his hotel. Carmel said he deals in the black market. I think he has lots and lots of money. People across the room kept nodding to him. Have you met him?

We hoped by this time, since the war is over in Europe, the Japanese might surrender.

It'll be strange with the war over. Being able to eat real butter and meat without ration stamps. At least the blackout is over. We took down those awful black curtains.

You must think I'm spoiled after what you've been through. I admit we are lucky. Nothing bad ever happens here, I mean really bad.

We'll be glad to hear you are coming home. We miss you.

Love and BIG hugs,

Sis

Phillip put Laura's letter back in its envelope. Carmel didn't sound too upset about *his* letter. No doubt, he did her a favor writing to her, but somehow he wasn't convinced. Who is Caesar Almato?

CHAPTER 67

A young ensign approached his bed. Standing at attention, he said, "Commander Barron, sir."

"Yes?"

"As you requested, sir, I found Private Grant St. John. He's in the burn unit. I'll take you there, sir."

"Thank you."

They left the building. Phillip had been at sea so long, he had forgotten how pleasing and luxurious it was to cross the soft green lawn that surrounded the hospital. Coconut and royal palms stood among silk trees. *Plumeria* petals drifted down the fronds. Mynahs or parrots squawked in the tops of the trees.

Suddenly he longed to hear the cooing of California turtledoves and the caw of crows. To smell the fragrance of the blossoming cherry and apricot trees on spring nights. To drive through a forest of walnut trees, feeling their shelter and refuge. He realized how much he had avoided thoughts of home. Carmel was home.

Phillip arrived at the hospital burn area. He was met by a slim, blonde nurse who wore captain's bars on her collar.

"How do you do, Commander Barron. I'm Captain Gilman. Please follow me. Are you a friend of Corporal St. John?" Phillip heard the concern in her question.

"He's my neighbor in California. How's he doing?"

"His burns are healing slowly. He was in critical condition when he arrived a month ago. However, I must warn you his attitude is deteriorating."

They stopped in the hall before closed doors marked Treatment Area—Authorized Personnel Only.

The captain said, "You'll find him in the last bed on your left."

Phillip thanked her, pushed the door open, and entered the silent ward. He walked past hospital beds with bandaged patients. He found Grant sitting up, his back supported by pillows. The corner was dark. The shade pulled down. The bed next to Grant was empty.

"Hello, Grant." Phillip leaned over to shake Grant's hand if he offered it. He didn't. Grant didn't move. The top of his head was swathed in bandages. Phillip saw his right ear was missing.

Grant turned his head, eyes were two dead coals. He said through clenched teeth, "Don't ask me how I am."

Phillip stayed at the foot of the bed. "I can see you are alive and perhaps thinner."

"So what! You call this alive? The top of my goddamn head is burned away." He jerked at his bandages. "Do you want to see?"

Phillip started to tell him that was unnecessary but thought better of it.

"I want you to see. Isn't that what you came for? Go ahead."

Phillip knew Grant wanted him to look. "I'll get a nurse. I'm not sterile." Phillip left the room and returned with Captain Gilman.

She said to Grant, "We don't like to remove your bandages, once they've been dressed."

"Phillip's a doctor. I want him to see."

She looked at Grant's ferocious expression and gently removed the bandage on his head.

Phillip saw Grant's scalp was void of hair. The skin was a bright red, intermixed with zigzagging patches of black skin. Phillip thought Grant's forehead must have been burned black. It was the same tomato red. Where his ear should have been the skin was bright red and raw. Grant glared at Phillip.

"No, they haven't scraped me. What difference does it make what they do?"

Phillip knew sometimes therapy for third-degree burns was to put the burned area of the victim in hot water and scrape the burned skin away with a wire brush. The pain was excruciating. Phillip thought, This once handsome man looks like a freak. He took a breath and hoped he could say something to help the furious man before him.

"You'll heal. It's amazing what can be accomplished to put you aright."

"Put me aright? No hair, no ear, put me aright? I look like something from another planet."

"The doctors can make you another ear, Grant. They can use the soft part of your ribs and form cartilage. You can wear a wig. No one will know unless you tell them."

Grant was silent.

"Have you told your family where you are?"

"They know I'm here."

"Do you want me to write to your father?"

"It's up to you. I don't care."

"Did you know your father had a stroke?"

"I know he's in a wheelchair. If they can't tell me the truth, I don't have to tell them anything."

"Maybe they think like you. They want to spare you worry."

"They'll never see me in San Jose."

"Never is a long, long time, Grant. I'm stationed here at the hospital. I'll be back to see you. Is there anything I can bring you?"

"Yeah, a new head."

Before he left the ward, he said, "Grant, you would be impressed with what these doctors can accomplish."

He realized Grant was facing pain in his mind and his body for a long time to come. Thinking about Grant's future reminded him of home and the letter. Just who was Caesar Almato?

CHAPTER 68

Jake Refugo, though small in stature, called himself Mighty Jake. Behind his back, he was called the Rat. With his large nose, chopped off chin, and furtive, beady eyes, he looked like a rodent. He annoyed Caesar, but Caesar needed him for messy jobs and he kept his mouth shut.

Jake watched the Chinese men crowded around the long table, rapidly clicking the dominoes. They were playing the ancient game of *pai gow*. The room was small and poorly lit. The foul air reeked of sweat and cigarette smoke. The men wore hats, jackets, and trousers, always black to protect them against the white ghosts. Every Chinese knew white was worn only during mourning. To do otherwise brought bad luck.

Jake understood the superstitions of the Chinese. Many of the men visited their Joss temple to burn sticks of incense before coming to gamble. It was safe to gamble only if the smoke drifted toward their favorite deity.

The betting and yelling was deafening. *Ayeeyah!* Jake ignored it and tried to concentrate. He would do anything to get money. Inside the breast pocket of his suit was thirty thousand dollars that Caesar had given him. After the job, he was promised there would be more. He had called Marlena and said Caesar wanted to see her. He would pick her up around midnight. She didn't question the time, since Caesar often arranged to meet her late.

Caesar's orders were to get rid of Marlena, tonight. To Jake, in his simple mind, get rid of meant murder. Caesar had never asked him to commit murder before. He was glad it wasn't Elka. He loved Elka, but he knew nothing could ever come of it. She seldom bothered to speak to him. It wasn't that Jake minded getting rid of Marlena, but he didn't understand why it was necessary. Marlena was a good kid, and that body could drive a man crazy. Thinking of her nude fishbowl act reminded him there was a show of fornication tonight somewhere in the labyrinth of rooms.

The overcrowding of Chinatown and the impossibility of extending its boundaries forced the Chinese to dig rooms and passages below their streets and buildings. In this subterranean world, vice, opium dens, gambling, and prostitution were rampant. Jake had witnessed the sex shows before, and tonight wasn't the night. In the past, he had joined the crowd of men as they moved through the gloomy corridors, built crooked to ward off evil spirits, since bad luck moved in straight lines. They would wander deep into the cellar, through a warren of rooms, and finally up three flights opening to a large, faintly lit room. Then they stood on the wide stairway that circled the wall of the chamber to watch and bet. A nude young Chinese girl, probably the daughter of a prostitute, drugged so she never knew what happened, sat in a net dangling from the ceiling. She was dropped down over a nude man on a pallet who bet he could penetrate her on the first try.

Jake had other things on his mind. It was time to pick up Marlena.

Elka just sat down to her dinner when Marlena called. "Hi, sis. I know it's your night off. I've been in Reno for two days. I'll be home before morning."

Elka learned a long time ago Marlena had her own code of conduct. Anyone could get anything they wanted, as long as there weren't too many rules to mess things up. A phone call meant she wanted something. Marlena asked her to feed her cat. Elka knew Marlena wasn't with Caesar because her sister cautioned her not to tell him.

Elka said she would but took her time getting to Marlena's apartment, arriving after ten o'clock. Marlena's white Persian cat stayed hidden most of the time. Elka knew it would take forever to find him. She was searching when the phone rang. She recognized Jake's voice. "Hi, Marlena."

Elka, without thinking, lowered her voice to imitate Marlena's. "Hi, Jake." She spoke in Marlena's sultry voice

"Night off ... huh?"

"Yeah ... go back tomorrow."

"Caesar wants me to pick ya up and bring ya to him."

Elka caught her breath. What would she do now? She quickly asked, "Where's he?"

"He's in a roadhouse across the bay." A pause, "Midnight, okay?"

Caesar often met her sister late at night. "Why, sure, I'll be ready." She held back a giggle.

Elka's secret desire was to be an actress. She thought, now was her chance. She hurried to fill the cat's dish with food. The cat would eat after she left. She thought her sister's place was ugly with all that satin. Marlena's closet overflowed with clothes. She found the pink suit with the shiny glass buttons. A perfect fit. She scrambled to find the matching four-inch shoes. Marlena wore high heels all the time. Elka sat at the dressing table in the bedroom. The surface was a jumble of expensive crèmes, perfume, and pots of color. Elka studied her face. Marlena wore much more makeup. She began to draw heavier eyebrows with dark liner. Fluffing her hair, she added lipstick, lots of it. Satisfied, she looked through the drawers to find a pink and gray scarf to hide the birthmark on her neck. Thinking about her game, she trembled with excitement. She found the long scarf, wound it around her throat, and tied it, letting the silk ends swing loose.

She plotted. Jake always arrived early anywhere he went. She would offer him a drink and invite him to sit down. She remembered Marlena told her Jake liked to listen to her accent. He wanted to hear about Germany, especially about the walks in the park when she was a little girl. He said the people didn't sound too bad, for Germans.

It was fifteen minutes past midnight when the doorbell rang. Elka opened the door slowly, as she imagined Marlena would, and waited for Jake's comment. There was none. He barely glanced at her and entered the room.

"Get your coat. I'm runnin' late."

Elka shrugged. She found a black coat of Marlena's and put it on. "I'm ready." She hoped she wouldn't fall over in the shoes. How could Marlena wear them?

Jake was silent as he drove across the Bay Bridge to Oakland. Elka, busy with her own thoughts. The real test would come with Caesar. She would play the game as long as she could get by with it. Not too long, as she didn't want Caesar upset when he learned the truth. Hopefully, Marlena would be back by then.

She wondered why Jake drove so fast. They crossed the Bay Bridge and passed the curve leading to Oakland. He stayed on the highway headed north. Where could there be a roadhouse on this side of the bay? she thought. Maybe in Richmond?

Jake didn't reach Richmond. He turned off sooner before Golden Gate Fields Race Track onto a little road leading to the bay. The car bumped over railroad tracks. There was enough light to make out a narrow dock stretching into the bay surrounded by water.

"Jake, there's no roadhouse down this road. That's a dock. I can barely see it."

"I know where I'm goin'." He drove onto the dock, stopped the car, and turned off the headlights. "Get out." He didn't look at her. There was a strange sound in Jake's voice. She began to think her act wasn't such a good idea. Fear stabbed her like a sharp knife cut across the seam of her heart.

She got of the car and stumbled in her shoes trying to walk on the rough dock. On the highway far away she heard cars. Beneath her, the water lapped against the wood pilings. She began to smell her own fear and knew he planned to kill her.

"Keep goin'." He was behind her.

Elka's mind raced. This was going too far. He thinks I'm Marlena. Why would he want to kill Marlena? What had she done? Caesar must have ordered it. She had to tell Jake, let him know. "I'm not Marlena. It's just a game."

He shoved her forward and didn't hear her plea. It happened too fast. She felt the cord around her throat, shutting away her breath. It was too tight. She struggled to pull it from her neck. Then everything went black. Her body became limp.

Jake let her fall at his feet before he removed the cord. She hadn't resisted. Killing her had been too easy. He pulled her scarf away and felt her neck for a pulse. There was none. He went to the car and opened the trunk. The trunk light revealed an empty gray canvas sack. He went back, picked up her limp body, carried it to the rear of the car, and dumped it onto the trunk floor. She pitched forward, face down, her hair falling away from her neck. He saw the red birthmark behind her ear. "Jesus Christ! It was Elka!" Bile rose in his throat. Elka, sweet Elka. He loved Elka. He vomited.

Frightened and sweating, he closed the trunk lid and jumped back into the car. Starting the engine, he shifted into reverse, skidded, and backed off the dock. Where should he get rid of the body? His thoughts made him crazy. Why had he gone to the dock? Someone could have spotted him.

He drove onto the highway before turning on his headlights. Driving south, he decided to dump her body somewhere in Alameda. Starting through the tube to the island, he heard police sirens. Were they after him? Sweat slid down his forehead. He wiped it from his eyes. Damn him. Damn Caesar. Damn him.

If he had known it was Elka, he would not have killed her. He loved Elka. He began to sweat again. The palms of his hands were wet as he clenched the wheel. Shit, the heat in the car was on. He turned it off. Where would he take her? There was no place. He had planned to drop Marlena, in the bag, at the

Richmond dump. But not Elka. Caesar would find out it wasn't Marlena, then what would happen to him?

The siren was getting closer. Jake drove out of the tunnel and pulled to the side of the street. The squad car sped by. He heaved a sigh and turned back onto the almost empty street. Thank God there were few cars this late at night. He had to get rid of the body. Elka's body. Sweet Elka. He had to clear his mind. He remembered a road on the end of the island that led from a private club to a boathouse. He would put her in the canvas bag, fill it with rocks, tie it all to a boat, and push it out into the bay.

He found the narrow road to the private club. Shit, he almost missed the entrance; some kind of shit vines covered it. The lane leading to the boathouse was long. He turned off his headlights. The drive took more time, but it was safer. Thank God it was light enough to see.

When he reached the boathouse, he moved as if being pulled by wires. He put Elka in the bag. At least there's no blood. Beside a flowerbed, he found some rocks. He dug frantically at the dirt with his fingers. The earth was hard. When he had enough, he put them into the bag.

When he tried to lift the bag, it was too heavy. He would have to drag it. A century passed as he dragged the bag to the small boat. He managed to tie the cords of the canvas sack to a metal ring on the side of the boat. He shoved with all his strength to move the boat from the tiny dock. The waves would carry it away from the shore.

It never moved. He was exhausted and shaking. In desperation, he jumped into the icy water up to his neck and pushed the boat out into the bay. This time the boat was far enough from the shore for the tide to catch it. He watched it drift away with the canvas dragging in the water. He swam back to shore and knew the loosely tied bag would come undone and sink deep into the water. Jake trembled with the cold. Water filled his shoes and dripped from his suit. He climbed into car. The odor of Elka's perfume brought the return of nausea. Elka. What had he done? There was only one thing to do. He must find Marlena and get her to leave. Caesar must not know he killed the wrong woman.

He started back to San Francisco at breakneck speed. He made himself slow down. All he needed was for a cop to stop him.

He banged on Marlena's door. She was not home. He'd wait for her in his car on the dark street. Sleep was miles from him and his mind grabbed at plans. The money. He had the thirty thousand Caesar gave him. He would give it to her and demand she leave the city.

The dawn's first light came before he saw her arrive. A man was driving the car. What if the man goes inside with Marlena and stays? What then? Finally, Marlena got out of the car and went up the stairs to her doorway. The man drove away. For the first time in a very long time, Jake prayed. Would she listen to him? How would he tell her?

When Marlena saw Jake at her door she invited him in. Not waiting to be asked, he sat down in one of the chairs and faced her. She offered him a drink.

Jake watched her pour the bourbon. "Look at me, Marlena. Have you ever seen me like this?"

She handed him his drink, poured one for herself, and sat down across from him. "You look awful. What happened?"

Jake did not answer.

Her voice was soft. "I know Caesar sent you. What is it, Jake?" The cat came into the room and jumped into her lap.

"Please believe me, you must leave here. Disappear. Here, I have thirty thousand to give you. Take it, Marlena, and go."

"What? You're frightening me."

"I want to." She looked exactly like the girl he had killed.

Marlena leaned forward. "Jake, what's happened?"

"I can't tell you everything. If you value your life, just leave here as fast as you can. Take what you need. I have a car downstairs. I'll drive you to Oakland. You can get the train."

Malena was silent for a moment. "I think I understand. I didn't know Caesar felt so strongly about … Yes, Jake, I'll go with you. I have to tell my sister." She pushed the cat off her lap and stood up.

"No, no, just pack. I'll take care of it. I'll take care of everything. Just hurry."

She ran into the bedroom. "Oh, Jake," she called to him. "You're a good friend."

If she knew the truth, she wouldn't get in the car with him. "Grab a suitcase. Let's get outa here."

The cat mewed as he jumped into Jake's lap. Jake snarled as he knocked the animal away. "Damn cat. Get off me."

CHAPTER 69

It took Marlena only a minute to realize that because of the baby, he wanted to kill her.

Marlena took the thirty thousand dollars Jake gave her and fled to her old friend Hayward's ranch, Paradise. The ranch was twenty miles from Reno on a narrow back road. Hayward often said his ranch was a palace of comfort and delight. He provided the comfort. The girls were the delight. His girls were attractive and he took good care of them. Plenty of customers kept the place busy.

Marlena handed Hayward the keys to her apartment in San Francisco. "Just be sure you go in the morning after 2:00 a.m. Bring back my furs and jewels. I just got them out of the bank. They're in a silver box on the closet shelf. Oh! And bring the cat. If anyone asks, you're my Uncle Hayward from Germany." Marlena thought Hayward had to be at least sixty.

"Sure, I could pass for a short German Jew." Hayward was as tall as a pine tree. They laughed.

Marlena's baby boy was born in August under the sign of Leo. The girls at the Paradise called him King and said that with his fat cheeks and dark skin, he looked like a Buddha. Marlena thought he looked like his father and called him Little C. Sometimes an expression in his dark liquid eyes scared her. Because Little C was a good baby, the girls argued over who would take care of him. Marlena's time was her own.

Hayward was a big, raw-boned man who adored this blonde minx with a German accent. He gave her everything she asked for and more. The girls said they had no doubt he was King's father, with his swarthy skin and black eyes.

Hayward asked nothing of Marlena until she said she wanted to dye her hair black. He would not allow it. Her golden locks were to remain golden.

If there was a fly in Marlena's ointment, it was Sid, the twenty-eight-year-old adopted son of Hayward's dead wife. He helped Hayward around the ranch, helped himself to the cash, and stared at Marlena. When he found out she had been the nude swimmer at the 365 Club, he wanted to know whether she would perform for him if he bought a fish tank. He gave her the creeps. The girls hated him.

It was almost noon, but Marlena remained in bed with no desire to get up. The ranch had been quiet all Saturday morning. Usually there were the sounds of cars and trucks arriving and leaving. Now the only sounds came from the squeak of the windmill pumping water. And the wind, always the damned wind, moaning and blowing across the hot desert floor. She heard people went nuts listening to the wind.

Sometimes when she was alone like this, she thought of Elka. She knew something awful had happened to her sister and that Jake, that little rat, had something to do with it. She wondered if Caesar had had Elka killed?

Marlena hadn't loved Caesar, and she didn't love Hayward, but for the moment she'd lie low and stay at Paradise. One day she'd leave with Little C and find Caesar. She'd let him know he had a son and get what was coming to them. All in due time.

Someone pounded on the door. "Is this where you're going to stay all day?" The door opened and Hayward grinned at her.

He said, "I've got breakfast ready."

Her nightgown fell open and revealed rosy breasts. She took hold of his belt buckle and pulled him down beside her. "You're breakfast is right here."

CHAPTER 70

Carmel waited beside the pool at Laura's house. She'd come to get her friend only to find Scott there, too. She wished Laura and Scott would keep their voices down. Laura insisted she wait, telling her she'd be only a moment.

"Why do you have to go *this* morning?" Scott, waiting for an answer, glared at Laura. It was hot standing by the pool at Laura's house in the August sun. Laura kept trying to maneuver Scott into the shade under the arbor, but he wouldn't move.

"There's a dozen reasons. Your father can't drive to San Francisco. You know he's not strong enough to be driving and you're never around to drive. At harvest time he *always* sends fresh produce to your aunt and uncle. So Carmel will drive and I'm going with her. Besides, it'll do your sister good to get off the ranch." She knew her last remark would make him angry.

Carmel wished Laura wouldn't say that. She didn't want to cause trouble between them.

"You're not going to make me feel guilty for not driving the produce to the city," he said. "You don't *have* to go. I made plans for us this weekend to have dinner in Santa Cruz."

"You didn't tell me about your plans. How do *I* know what you plan? You can push me to start or stop to suit your time and convenience? Do you have any idea anymore how I feel? I promised Carmel I'd go with her. You might as well return home. I have to go. Please don't be mad at me." She pleaded, "I'll call you from San Francisco." She gave him a quick kiss and joined Carmel.

Scott yelled, "I don't feel happy about you going. I'm returning to Watsonville." The dogs, Bruno and Howard, had followed him to Laura's. "Come on, fellows, we've been turned down."

The two girls walked back to Carmel's in silence. Jose had filled the station wagon with boxes of strawberries, garden vegetables, and tomatoes. Andrew, his body rail thin, leaned on his cane and waited by the car. His speech had improved and strength was returning to his arm. He insisted on getting out of the wheelchair to tell the girls good-bye. "You gals tell my sister I'm coming along just fine and I'll see her soon." Andrew always sent more than enough produce for Lydia, who made a point of sending excess fruit and vegetables for church charities. "Will you be home, Monday?"

Carmel kissed him good-bye. "No, Dad, we're going to the Emporium and I Magnin's to shop. We'll be home Tuesday or Wednesday, I think."

Her father smiled. "Well, enjoy yourselves, but be careful. With two Japanese cities atom bombed by us, the world is waiting for the Japanese to surrender. When that happens, there's no telling how crazy San Francisco will be. Carmel, don't be picking up any hitchhikers. I don't care if they're in uniform."

"Oh, Dad, I know they're not allowed to hitchhike. Anyway, I couldn't slide a postage stamp in this car it's so full."

"I don't object to you driving to the city. You need a break from the ranch. I just want my girl safe." Andrew limped back to the house. He mumbled to himself, "I may just change my will. Scott has become a real devil."

Jerry had called two days before and asked Carmel to come to the city and have dinner with him on Monday. She asked if Laura might join them. Jerry gladly extended the invitation to Laura. Once Carmel decided to see Jerry, she allowed her enthusiasm for San Francisco to return. Until now, she had been successful in denying that she missed her music and the nightlife.

Bruno and Howard, barking and wagging their tails, followed the station wagon down the driveway. They stopped at the street. Carmel waved and pulled away. She drove the loaded station wagon across San Jose and onto the Bay Shore Highway. She turned on the radio, twisted the dial, and, getting nothing but static, turned it off. "I wish this thing worked. I'd like to know what's going on in the world. We'll have to find out from Uncle Russell." The highway ran along the edge of the bay. "Roll the windows down; feel the cool air blowing off the bay."

"I read it's so hot in New York, they turned firemen's hoses on the police department horses to cool them off." Laura rolled the window down.

"I hope the spray wasn't too hard. That could hurt. I can guarantee it'll be cool in the city, probably fog rolling in. It's August, you know. I hope you brought a dressy outfit for dinner tonight. Lydia and Russell enjoy dressing for dinner. We'll wear suits when we see Jerry tomorrow night."

"Yes, I brought a dress and a suit. By the way, we heard from Phillip. He's coming home."

Carmel's heart skipped a beat.

"I meant to tell you, but I was so excited about leaving for the city and Scott is so upsetting. In addition, I forgot to tell your father that Phillip saw your brother in the hospital. He said Grant's recovering from his burns and will be heading home when he's released."

When Laura said Phillip's name, Carmel's mind whirled. She wanted to ask when he would be back. Would he come to San Jose? She muttered she was glad Grant was coming home, but in her heart she dreaded her brother's return. Because of his big ego, she never knew what to expect from him.

It was late afternoon when they parked in front of the house. As expected, a dense fog was creeping in. Miles back, Carmel had turned the headlights on. Foghorns sounded from the bay.

Her aunt and uncle greeted Carmel and Laura with delight. They introduced their new Chinese houseman, Lyn Fu. He was very short and wore his house uniform, a white jacket, and black trousers. He smiled and bowed. "Most happy to meet ladies."

Carmel said, "Most happy to meet you. Auntie, we really brought you and Uncle Russell a carful. We had a large crop this year."

Lydia giggled like a schoolgirl. "Oh, Carmel, I love it. My brother is so good to me."

Lyn Fu began to unload the station wagon.

Lydia asked, "How's my brother?"

"I think he improves every day. He said to tell you he's fine. Uncle Russell, what is the news? The car radio is nothing but static."

"We haven't heard. We're still waiting."

They entered the large and cool entrance. A familiar smell of camphor greeted Carmel, reminding her of faraway places.

"Oh, Aunt Lydia, the house looks beautiful." She pointed to an enormous bronze Buddha that filled the alcove near the stairs. "That must be new. It looks five feet high."

"Thank you, Carmel. Isn't the Buddha wonderful? I talked Mr. Gump into selling it to me."

Mr. Gump owned a prominent store on Post Street. Customers came from all over the world to buy from his celebrated Oriental collections and his impressive assortment of ancient stones in the Jade Room.

Hilda and Heidi bumped and slid into each other on the polished floor, begging the girls to pet them. Laura giggled when she saw the dogs. "What darling little guys." She rubbed their wiggling bodies.

Carmel stooped down to pat each one and said, "Have you been good girls? I doubt it."

Lydia said, "You see, you both are *so* welcome. Come, Laura, I've put you next to Carmel's room. Andrew's concentrating on the news. I'm sure he'll have something to tell us soon." She climbed the stairs with Laura and Carmel close behind. "Join us for cocktails and dinner at eight, as always."

Carmel loved being in her old room. It had been her haven.

It was in this bedroom where she had plotted to be with Phillip. Oh, Phillip! The anguish was still there. Did he ever think of her? Now, at last, he was coming home. But she also remembered she had read his good-bye letter in this very room.

He wasn't coming back to *her*. Would he come to San Francisco or San Jose? He might return to Sylvia, the shimmering blonde. With a groan, she sat on her bed and stared out the window at a city covered with fog.

With so much going on in the world, both girls were impatient to know the news. They dressed early and joined Lydia and Russell for cocktails.

The fire in the living room fireplace added cheer to the room. Uncle Russell wore his black jacket, gray trousers, and a bright-orange bowtie. He made martinis and served the three women. He raised his glass. "Here's to General Eisenhower, to you beautiful ladies, and to my good luck to know it." The ladies accepted his gracious toast and sipped their martinis.

Lyn Fu offered delicious hot canapés.

Carmel said, "Auntie, with your beautiful hair, you are elegant in sea-green silk."

"Thank you, Carmel. I believe the lace on your blouse looks good enough to eat."

Carmel's white jabot blouse, with its luxuriant lace trim and heavy black satin skirt, emphasized her figure. Tiny diamond earrings sparkled in her ears. "Thank you, Auntie. It's fun to dress up again."

"Laura, we're glad you're here to brighten our evening. You look lovely." Lydia referred to Laura's raspberry crepe dress.

"Thank you, I feel marvelous to be in the city with you all. It must be a relief to remove all those heavy blackout curtains."

"I hope there's never a reason to hang them again. Did you girls notice my Capezio ballet slippers? They can be purchased without coupons." She stuck out her feet from under her long dress to show them her black slippers.

Andrew held his finger to his lips for the group to be quiet, leaned toward the radio, and listened to an announcer report, "Nothing confirmed."

Laura listened for a moment before she asked, "Carmel, is this what your father meant when he said the world's waiting for the Japanese to surrender?"

Russell asked, "Don't you listen to the radio? We dropped a massive bomb on Hiroshima and, two days after, on the Japanese city of Nagasaki. Yes, indeed, we're waiting for news of surrender."

Laura replied. "Mr. Bannister, I *read* the paper just like everyone else. I saw the pictures in the *Chronicle*. All I'm saying, we have a funny way of waiting. Admiral Halsey is still knocking down planes."

Russell took a sip of his martini. "Very likely it's the last big strike. Frankly, I thought when word got out that Truman, Churchill, and Stalin met at the Potsdam Conference and offered the Japanese an ultimatum, the Japanese would surrender then. Those Japs are a stubborn lot." He shook his head at the thought. "Perhaps we've learned our lesson. They can continue to deceive us, you know. I don't believe we can treat the situation differently. Now the cagey Russians have declared war against Japan." He sighed, "I suspect the Soviets will want a piece of the cake."

"I guess you mean when Japan begins its reconstruction," Lydia said. There was the sound of popping noises outside the house.

Laura laughed before she said, "When San Francisco does celebrate, there will probably be fireworks all night long."

"You can bet on it." Lydia said. "San Francisco can be pretty rowdy."

Lyn Fu announced dinner.

Lydia followed him. "Russell, let's have a nice dinner. Please, don't start jumping up and down from the table."

Hilda and Heidi scampered ahead to lead the group to the dining room. Lydia admonished them to sit quietly or be removed from the room. Carmel surveyed the yellow table linen, candles, and a center piece of golden lilies. "Oh, Aunt Lydia, you always make anything you do so worthwhile."

Lydia was obviously pleased. "Thank you, Carmel; I know how much you appreciate what I do." Once they were seated, Lyn Fu served an excellent dinner of braised lamb shanks with vegetables from the garden.

Carmel felt an undercurrent of excitement flowing around the conversation. News that the war was over was imminent, and all were in high spirits.

Laura was answering Lydia's questions. "Oh, yes, Phillip will be home sometime in August or September. He's bringing a picture of the *Solace* coming into Pearl Harbor and Admiral Nimitz coming aboard giving out awards."

Lydia questioned. "What about Grant? Isn't he in some hospital in Hawaii?"

"Phillip said Grant would be coming home, too. We all know he's been burned, but we don't know how much. Phillip didn't say. We hope it's not too serious."

"Were they in that terrible typhoon?" Lydia asked.

Laura shook her head. "He didn't mention it. I could barely hear him. The phone connection kept going in and out."

Russell changed the conversation. "Laura, are you still planning on being a nurse?"

"I sure am. Who knows, I may be in the same hospital with my brother someday."

Carmel took a deep breath. "Is Phillip returning to San Francisco?"

Laura shrugged. "You know as much as I do. We'll find out when he gets here." Carmel resisted asking Laura why she hadn't asked Phillip more questions when she had the chance. It could be weeks before he came home.

Lydia said, "Girls, save room for dessert. Carmel, I know how much you like peaches. Lyn Fu has made a peach pie especially for you."

Laura said. "Lyn Fu is a marvelous cook. This dinner is beyond delicious."

"I think my Aunt Lydia had a lot to do with it. By the way, do you hear from Helen?" Carmel asked.

"Yes, she's working at the Kaiser plant, I would think, making money. Madison has retired. I read in an advertisement if you can drive a car you can operate a machine. Helen could surely do that."

Russell suddenly intoned in a very flat voice, "Any war bonds today?"

"He thinks he's Mel Blanc." Lydia explained.

Laura laughed. "Well, he does sound like him."

Russell abruptly left the table to listen to the news. Upon returning, he reached for his wine glass and raised it before him. "Well, it's definite. The Japanese are submitting surrender terms. I guess the news is already in our headlines. They want their emperor to remain on the throne. Now all we have to do is wait for President Truman to announce the Japanese surrender."

Lydia hesitated. "I feel strange, Russell, drinking a toast. It's like toasting death. I can't imagine a single bomb wiping out a whole city. All those people and families just gone." A look of sadness spread over her face.

Russell insisted, "We're not toasting death. We're toasting the end of the war and the end of killing. It's over. Think of the men that won't have to die because they don't have to invade the Japanese coast. They estimated that a million men would be needed for the invasion."

Carmel shook her head. "I can't fathom how a single bomb can be built to kill so many."

"One of my old friends, a physicist, explained to me how the bomb works." Russell sat and pulled his chair to the table. "The bomb starts a chain reaction similar to a string of firecrackers. It seems when nature is out of balance, it will search for *home*. The atom bomb is purposely built out of balance, and in its search it moves with incredible energy. When it hits anything, a tree or a building, even cities, it causes total destruction. The city of Hiroshima, an arsenal city, was 60 percent destroyed."

Carmel wondered aloud, "Not to mention Nagasaki. What'll happen with a weapon that deadly? Will it be turned on us someday?" No one answered her. The silence in the room was heavy except for the chattering radio in the next room.

Lydia suggested they have cognac and coffee in the living room. Lyn Fu brought a service of coffee then returned with Armagnac brandy and glasses.

"I find the world changing too fast for me," Lydia said. "To think we're not likely to hear Winston Churchill's voice anymore. How I enjoyed his wit and rhetoric. The Labor party is *in* control and Winston is *out*." She sighed and poured coffee. "I'll always miss President Roosevelt. The newspaper mentioned we have already stopped work on the Army Ammunition depot in Marine County."

"Thank God. I used to think about those men at that awful job," Carmel said. "Uncle Russell, what finally happened to all those men at Port Chicago when they refused to return to the ship?"

"If I remember correctly, of the three hundred and twenty men killed, two hundred and two were black. Two hundred and fifty-eight refused to return to work. Fifty were convicted of mutiny and imprisoned. Nearly two hundred were court-martialed and dishonorably discharged. However, many others continued to work. Now there's talk of a memorial to be erected with the names of those who died."

"You mean they actually put the men in prison?"

"This is war, Carmel. They refused to follow orders. Now that the war is ending, they'll probably release them. Who knows?"

"Just think of all those men coming home," Laura said. "Future fathers. Shipbuilding will stop. Rosie the Riveter will become Rosie the Housewife."

Russell said, "It won't happen overnight. It'll take awhile to get the men home."

Lydia pondered, "How did a hundred thousand people working on the bomb keep it so hush-hush?"

Russell answered, "For one thing, they worked miles apart. One plant was in the state of Washington and the other in Oak Ridge, Tennessee."

Carmel wondered, "Who'll govern Japan?"

Russell said, "I imagine it'll be decided between General MacArthur, General Marshall, and Admiral Nimitz. For my money, MacArthur leads the race."

Lydia asked, "Are you girls ready for a game of Parcheesi?"

"Auntie, if you don't mind, I'll finish my drink and retreat upstairs to my wonderful four-poster. I think tomorrow will be an exciting day." She stood.

"I'll join you," Laura said. "This has been a lovely evening."

"Girls, sleep as long as you like in the morning," Lydia said.

In her bed, Carmel couldn't help smiling. Phillip was coming home. To the familiar and frequent sound of foghorns, she soon fell into sleep.

On Monday, August 13, 1945, the weather report in the newspaper read "High morning fog along the coast; otherwise, clear."

After a light lunch, Carmel and Laura left for downtown to shop and to meet Jerry.

Shopping was exhausting. The sidewalks and streets were crowded, and already confetti was being thrown from the windows of office buildings. People stopped strangers just to talk about the end of the war. Even though the congestion was everywhere, including inside the stores, the girls were determined to shop. Carmel bought an angora green sweater at I. Magnin's. Laura bought a wide leather belt.

It was a short walk to meet Jerry in the lobby of the Clift Hotel on Geary Street. The lobby was crowded with noisy celebrants, male and female, young and old, shrieking and laughing, waiting for the joyous news.

Jerry waited for them. He gave Carmel a chest-crushing hug, before he held her at arm's length. "Let me look at you. You're thinner. It just makes you more beautiful."

"Oh, Jerry, you do know how to make a gal feel wonderful." Carmel grinned. "I want you to meet my friend, Laura."

"Laura." Before he could shake her hand, he was knocked against Carmel by an exuberant stranger, who apologized immediately. "Let's get away from this din to the Redwood Room. I have a table."

The Redwood Room was only a little quieter. Someone at the bar gave a big whoop of laughter and heads turned. Once seated, Jerry said, "That thirty-foot bar is made of a single piece of redwood burl."

Carmel looked across the room. "I doubt if we'll see the bar with the crowd around it."

"I think we should have champagne and celebrate," Jerry said. "Laura, I've looked forward to meeting you."

Laura blushed at his words.

Carmel laughed. "We met in our playpens and have been together ever since."

"I've heard about the astounding help you have given Carmel," Laura said.

"Thank you. But, frankly, Carmel has so much talent she accomplished a great deal on her own."

"Hey, you two," Carmel interceded. "Stop talking about me as if I'm not here." She joined in their laughter.

The waiter brought champagne and Jerry offered a toast. "To the end of the war, and …" He looked at Carmel. "Perhaps you'll return to San Francisco and sing again."

"I … I can't answer that, Jerry." She asked, "What are the Japanese waiting for? Why won't they surrender?"

"Oh, I suppose they are squabbling among themselves in the Japanese cabinet and consulting their commanders. President Truman has asked Congress to cut vacations short and return to deal with the problems of re-conversion of the home front to peacetime."

Laura grinned. "Peacetime, what a wonderful word."

A waiter took their dinner order and the girls decided on Carmel's favorite, crab cakes. Jerry ordered sole dore.

"I really should call Elka," Carmel said. "I haven't seen her or heard from her since Christmas."

Jerry, astonished, said, "Then you don't *know*?"

"Know what, Jerry?"

"Elka disappeared."

"Doesn't her sister know where she is?"

"No, she's gone, too."

"What're you saying? What happened to their possessions?"

"They had an uncle who came and took their things. I don't know. The whole situation is very strange. I hear the police haven't any clues."

"What does Caesar say?" Carmel asked. "Wasn't he dating Marlena?"

"He's not around much; spends most of his time in Las Vegas. Do you know Caesar very well?"

Laura gave Carmel a quick glance and waited for her answer.

Carmel said, "Jerry, if you remember, Caesar was responsible for my meeting John Canepa, and I sang with his band several times."

Just then a loud explosion boomed outside the tall draped windows. There was silence for a moment. A waiter came to the table and said, "Servicemen are dropping flower pots off the roof. They make holes in the sidewalk."

Jerry asked, "Why? Has there been some news?"

"Yes, sir, the Japanese accepted our ultimatum." He scurried away. There was another explosion. They heard sirens coming.

"There'll be a lot of horseplay. The town's been waiting," Jerry said.

Sirens sounded nearer, horns blew, and something clanged that made a terrible discord above the rest of the noise. Voices in the room grew so loud they rose above the outside disturbances.

"Carmel, Count Basie is playing at the Golden Gate. I hear the band really rocks. Would you like to go tomorrow? There's a two o'clock show."

Laura asked, "Is there a movie?"

"Yes, as a matter of fact. I hear it's a good one, *Along Came Jones* with Gary Cooper and Loretta Young."

Delighted, Laura said, "I'd like to see the movie. I don't know enough about Count Basie."

A loud bang came from the lobby. Several women in the dining room screamed.

"Girls, I think it's time to get you both out of here and home. My car is parked on Levenworth. If you walk a couple of blocks, I'll take you home."

"I've finished. I'm ready to leave," Carmel suggested.

"Me too." Laura stood.

Before they left the table, a waiter came and told them someone had lit a firecracker in the lobby.

On the way to the car they passed ash cans turned over, leaving debris blowing in the streets. A bus missing its bumper went by. A street sign was uprooted from its concrete base. The uproar behind them seemed to be coming from Market Street.

Once in the car on the way home, they saw a large crowd gathered around the fountain on Van Ness. Something was happening in the pool surrounding the fountain.

Jerry kept on driving. He said that anything important would be in the newspaper the next day. Jerry dropped them off at home.

"I won't be able to pick you up tomorrow. My car is totally unreliable. I can't promise you a ride and have it quit on us. Why don't you meet me *inside* the lobby of the Golden Gate Theater at two o'clock? It's important to meet *inside* the lobby."

The girls thanked him and promised if they changed their minds, they would call him.

Carmel was in bed before she allowed herself to think of Elka. Elka loved San Francisco. Why would she leave? What about Marlena? Something terrible must have happened. She had an uneasy feeling Caesar knew where the girls were.

She *had* to be wrong, didn't she? Would she ever see Elka again? Elka was the only one she had confided in about her feelings for Phillip. She prayed, "Please, God, help me find out what happened to Elka."

CHAPTER 71

San Franciscans woke Monday morning to a typical August weather report: "High morning fog; otherwise, clear except near ocean."

Carmel and Laura came down stairs dressed in their suits. Carmel hurried Laura through their lunch. They intended to catch the Hyde Street cable car to Market Street and walk the short block to the Golden Gate Theater.

Russell came in through the open front door. "I must protest, Carmel. I wish you wouldn't go downtown again. We received news last night the Japanese people accepted our terms and their emperor will remain as the head of their government, but I feel our celebration is premature since the real news that the war is officially over hasn't come from President Truman. Only heaven knows what will happen when it does. Last night huge fires were built in the middle of Market Street. Some servicemen spun the cable car at Powell like a record turntable. Today the department stores are closed—liquor stores and bars, too. Maybe the banks will close."

"Uncle, we were there last night; it was basically harmless except for those silly girls bathing nude in the Van Ness fountain." Carmel wasn't accustomed to her uncle dramatizing. "Besides, we're meeting Jerry inside the Golden Gate Theater for an early stage show and will return home right afterwards."

Lydia entered the hall. "Russell's right. Why not stay home. We can ring a few bells when President Truman makes the announcement."

"No, Auntie, I really want to hear Count Basie. I promise we'll be home early. Besides, it's a great way to celebrate."

Lydia accepted it was hopeless to try to stop them.

Carmel and Laura arrived on time at the theater on the corner of Golden Gate Avenue and Taylor Street. A flood of people milled about on the sidewalks, waiting for news. Servicemen and civilians alike were already staggering in various stages of drunkenness.

Carmel found Jerry waiting inside the lobby. The theater was full of servicemen. Many of the women in the audience wore jeans and carried hardhats under their arms. Carmel suspected after the performance they would leave to work the swing shift. However, the end of the war meant jobs for the women working in defense plants would end, too.

Searching for their seats, Jerry said, "Look, there're three comfortable seats for us near the front of the stage." They followed his suggestion and seated themselves with Jerry between them. He said, "Sherman and Clay are selling Count Basie's Columbia recordings for fifty-two cents with his signature. If you like, after the band finishes, we could go there."

Laura heard him and replied, "I want to stay and see the movie."

Carmel said, "Laura, we're staying for the movie. Jerry, I'm sorry. I don't think we can go to Sherman and Clay. The movie should be over at about four o'clock, and we promised my aunt and uncle we'd be home early. I have to keep my promise."

Jerry smiled. "Okay. You're the boss."

Behind the closed curtain, they heard Count Basie's theme song, "One O'clock Jump." The audience clapped and yelled their approval. As the curtain slowly opened, the full band appeared on stage with Count Basie seated at the piano. Carmel suspected he was humming and singing as he played. It was his habit.

The theme song finished to deafening applause. A master of ceremonies came on stage and announced the featured acts. "Mr. Five by Five, with James Rushing; The Three Rockets, a dance team; Shorts Davis Doin' the famous Shorty George."

For one hour, the band beat, vibrated, and rocked with music, filling the huge theater. When a band played to a theater crowd, the customers stayed seated and listened.

Carmel was thrilled to hear Count Basie's band playing jazz. She beat the rhythm with her foot. The big band brought back memories of music and singing as well as the agony she had gone through waiting, hoping, to see Phillip. Now, she wondered about him coming home.

She didn't feel the least bit guilty thinking about Phillip while sitting next to Jerry. He had confessed his love and remained a good friend, but friends were all they could ever be.

The curtain closed and the stage show was over to thunderous applause. The movie screen dropped down and a "Felix the Cat" cartoon played before the movie started.

She didn't give a hoot about *Along Came Jones*, but she promised Laura they would stay for the picture show. She loved watching Gary Cooper. He fascinated her the way he barely moved his lips and his body. These simple actions had made him a star.

After the movie, as they walked up the aisle toward the lobby of the theater, they heard a crash and the sound of glass breaking.

Carmel asked, "My, Gosh, what was that?"

Again they heard glass breaking. The three pushed through the heavy glass doors of the theater onto the sidewalk. Two sailors were breaking the glass cases on the walls that held the placards advertising future movies.

Jerry started to stop them, and a sailor yelled, "I wouldn't do that if I were you." His fist slammed into Jerry's face. Jerry reeled away from the man.

A woman yelled, "It's over! Truman announced it's over!"

Unknown to them, when President Truman announced at four o'clock the official surrender of the Japanese, Rear Admiral Wright, USN, Commandant of the Twelfth Naval District, granted leave to one hundred thousand sailors, many just out of boot camp. They crowded the streets, ready to repeat the fun their shipmates had the previous night.

Jerry grasped an arm of each girl and steered them up Taylor Street away from the theater. He said, "Let's try to get to the Clift Hotel. It's only five blocks."

Carmel said, "Look!" Sailors had climbed a scaffold hanging on the side of a building. They had broken a window and entered the building. Clothes were flying out the broken window.

One block up Taylor Street, a sailor grabbed Laura and kissed her. Another sailor pushed him away and grabbed Laura, shouting, "It's my turn." Jerry and Carmel pulled Laura away from the sailors. Carmel saw tears on Laura's cheeks.

Carmel struggled with a sailor and heard cloth rip. Fear ran through her body like an electric shock. A sleeve of her suit was missing. Someone had pulled hard and torn it from her jacket. She searched for Laura. She saw three sailors lift Laura above their heads, somehow push her dress up, and pull off her underpants. Setting her down, a sailor walked away wearing her panties on his head. Laura was in hysterics.

Jerry and Carmel pushed through the gang, trying to get to Laura. Bottles were breaking around them. A man passed a liquor store with a closed sign and yelled, "Let's get our booze." Carmel saw other men join him and break the storefront windows, grabbing full liquor bottles and handing them out to waiting hands.

She heard men yelling Jerry was a draft dodger. He was trying to break away from them and get to her. Blood ran from a cut above one eye and the corner of his mouth.

Servicemen were rocking a car back and forth in the intersection and finally turned it over. The driver had managed to escape just as the car burst into flames. The noise was thunderous.

Carmel tried to crouch against the building. Sailors went by yelling the song, "Bell Bottom Trousers." She screamed at Jerry, "We've got to find Laura." Carmel saw several sailors crowded into a recessed doorway. She and Jerry approached the group and found Laura on her back, on the cement, her skirt up, legs bared, and a sailor on top of her, his bottom naked. Another sailor leaned over Laura, pinning her arms down on the cement.

Throughout the melee, Carmel had kept her purse. Adrenaline and rage moved through her body with the force of a steam engine. She swung at one of the men, hitting him in the eyes and forehead. He backed away from her, and when the other men saw this raging woman moving in to attack they backed away, leaving Laura and the sailor exposed. Carmel kicked the man on top of Laura hard in the ribs with the point of her shoe. He fell away from Laura and crawled, trying to grab his pants.

Jerry lifted Laura off the cement and held her against him. Carmel pulled Laura's skirt down and looked at her friend. Laura's eyes were filled with terror.

Jerry said, "We have one block to go and we'll be safe at the hotel." He shifted Laura to his shoulder. Carmel limped behind Jerry trying her best to shelter Laura's face. She must have kicked off her shoe attacking the sailor. Outcries of women and men filled the air. Smoke from fires being set grew thicker and the shriek of sirens grew louder. Now Carmel felt fright as well as anger. For the first time she was afraid a drunken stranger might kill her. She kept saying over and over, "Just a few more steps to the hotel and we'll be safe."

Carmel saw a woman shrieking with laughter being raised above the bulb fixtures of a light pole. There the woman ripped off all of her clothes while she continued laughing. Sounds of men running and glass shattering filled the air. Carmel and Jerry moved as rapidly as possible. The cut on Jerry's forehead was bleeding again. Blood dripped into his eye, and sometimes he staggered. People left him alone.

Carmel felt a surge of relief when they entered the Clift Hotel. The lobby was full of people, all talking at once.

Jerry shifted Laura to his arms and went to the desk clerk. "Matt, do you have a couch? Someplace quiet. Anywhere will do."

After taking one look at his friend with the crumpled woman in his arms and the pale-faced woman with blazing eyes beside him, Matt led them to a windowless office. The noise of sirens and screaming voices of the crowds outside was muffled. A large leather couch sat in the corner against the wall. Jerry very gently lowered Laura onto it.

"Thanks, Matt," Jerry said.

"You're welcome. Stay here as long as you like. I have to get back to the desk. I'm worried about our immense windows in the dining room. Don't want them broken."

Carmel sat on the floor beside her friend and held Laura's hands. Laura's face was pale and her eyes were closed. A dark bruise was beginning to show on her chin; to Carmel, she appeared dead. Suppose she died? Carmel rose and bent over Laura with her ear at Laura's mouth and listened until she heard Laura's soft breathing. She said aloud, "Thank you, God. She's alive."

Carmel's feelings and words were stuck together like glue. What had she done bringing Laura to San Francisco? She sat back down on the floor, her head resting against the couch. Tears rolled down her cheeks.

Jerry came back into the room. He had wiped the blood off his face. Carmel saw his shirt was ripped free of its buttons. He tucked the shirt into his trousers and asked, "How is she?"

"There's no change. She hasn't said anything."

"We should get a doctor."

"I asked her if she needed a doctor. She didn't answer. When can you get us home?"

"I called someone I know in the police department. He said most of the windows on Market have been broken. Looting has begun. The police can do nothing. It's a mob scene. He said they've called the Military Police and Shore Patrol. We'll be here for a while."

"Jerry, I'm so glad you're here." She got up from the floor. "I think I'd better call my aunt and uncle." She lowered her voice. "I don't want anyone—not anyone—to know what happened to Laura." This was supposed to be the end of the war, she thought, but tonight seemed like the beginning.

"I understand. I'm glad you feel better with me here, but there's little I can do but wait with you. You can use the phone in the next room. I'll stay with Laura."

She suggested, "In a few minutes, please come and speak to my aunt or uncle. It'll help." She went into the next room and found a phone on the desk. She planned to lie.

Aunt Lydia was beside herself with worry. Carmel asked them to call her father and say traffic was too heavy and they would be back in San Jose tomorrow. Her uncle and aunt felt even better when Jerry spoke to them, reassuring them everyone was safe.

Carmel returned to the office to find Laura curled into a fetal position, her knees pulled up to her chest. Sometimes she moaned, making sounds like a wounded animal. Jerry's friend in the police department said he wouldn't be able to drive anyone until ten or eleven that night. He said the bars and the liquor stores couldn't resist the chance to make money, so they'd opened for business. Servicemen turned into a mass mob, and civilians joined them. The local police were beaten if they tried to stop them. The police did not dare retaliate when their badges and hats were snatched away from them.

Jerry requested room service. He insisted Carmel at least have soup and toast. The service was a long time arriving, but to make Jerry happy, Carmel ate. Then managed to get Laura to sit up and swallow a little hot tea.

Finally, the long wait in the hotel was over.

Carmel was worried about getting Laura across the lobby and into the waiting police car, but she need not have worried; Laura made it on her own, docile as a child, her hand in Carmel's. Matt escorted them to the entrance. Carmel was relieved to see two Military Police standing silently at the entrance, their eyes wary like a grizzly bear's.

A dripping fog had rolled in. The sidewalk was wet and empty of people. Once outside, Carmel saw Geary Street littered with papers, bottles, shoes, and hats of servicemen. The air smelled of burning rubber and gunpowder. There was another odor Carmel didn't recognize, the strange smell of riot and rebellion.

Carmel and Jerry put Laura between them in the back seat of the police car. They left the downtown area. Arriving at a corner, they saw a large group of police officers and Marines holding rifles. Jerry asked the driver, a police officer, who the men were.

"I'll drop you after we take the girls home. We have orders to join other police cars on Market. The Marines are joining us with fixed bayonets. They are lined up to push the crowds down Market. San Francisco is under martial law. They're ordered to return home and the servicemen return to their ships, bases, and camps."

The three passengers were silent. Carmel thought there are no words for such news. She said a prayer under her breath, "Thank you, God, we escaped." Jerry heard her, took her hand, and squeezed it.

Uncle Russell had heard the slam of the police car door. He stood at the wide-open front door. He waited and glowered. When Aunt Lydia saw their torn and stained clothes, she became more frightened; she didn't grasp the look of stunned quiet on Laura's face.

Jerry started to apologize for the long delay, but Lydia stopped him. "This night will go down in history. You had no idea such total mayhem would result. It's only important that you and the girls are here in one piece."

Carmel said, "Thank you, Jerry. We'll leave early tomorrow for San Jose. I'll keep you posted." She hugged him hard.

Jerry held her close for a moment. "Good night." He went out the front door.

Carmel turned away. "I must get Laura to bed."

Her aunt started to speak but Russell interrupted, "Let them get into bed. You'll see everyone in the morning."

Both girls went into their separate bathrooms and took long showers before putting on their nightgowns.

Afterwards Laura came into Carmel's room and said, "I think I'll take that aspirin you offered me."

Carmel gave Laura her water and aspirin and watched her swallow the pill before she hugged her. "We'll be in San Jose tomorrow, away from all this. You'll be able to see Scott."

Laura started to cry. "I can't do that."

Carmel followed her friend into her room. "I'll tuck you in. Promise me, if you can't sleep come sleep with me."

Laura promised.

Carmel lay in the dark waiting for sleep. She asked herself what the dreaded dawn and next day would bring. The mournful wail of foghorns filled the night air. They reminded her of the long nights thinking about Phillip.

Finally, exhausted and close to sleep, she knew people in San Francisco would never forget the day the war ended.

Sometime during the night, Laura took another shower, put back on her nightgown, and crawled into bed with Carmel. She remained on her side curled into a ball and whimpered occasionally.

Carmel, though asleep, was aware of her friend and reached out to pat her.

CHAPTER 72

Carmel rose early. She had not heard Laura get up and return to her own room.

After Carmel showered, she pulled on slacks and a shirt, the familiar clothes she wore driving to the city. It was hard to believe Sunday was only two days ago.

The burgundy suit, soiled and torn, she left in a chair. She wanted to join her aunt and uncle at breakfast ahead of Laura, to speak to them in confidence to save Laura embarrassing questions. Before going downstairs, she tapped on Laura's door. A faint voice greeted her.

"Come in."

Laura was a tiny heap under the bedding. "I'll be up in a few minutes, Carmel. Please don't ask me to come downstairs." She had been crying.

Laura's efforts to be agreeable touched Carmel's heart. "I wasn't going to. I'll bring something light on a tray. Afterwards we'll head home. How does that sound?"

Laura nodded. Carmel had a dreadful feeling Laura was going to take a long time to heal.

She found Aunt Lydia and Uncle Russell seated with their coffee. Lydia greeted her. "Oh my, darling, what a night for you girls. Is Laura having breakfast?"

"No. If Lyn Fu has time and will fix a tray. I'll take some orange juice and toast to her. I'll just have juice and toast." She poured coffee and took a big gulp. "That's heaven."

"Carmel. Dear, please tell us what happened." Her aunt and uncle waited.

"The streets were filled with crazy people, and we kept losing each other. Laura was ahead of us, and when we found her …" Carmel's voice trailed off. She stared at her coffee cup. "Sailors were all around her, she was lying on the sidewalk, her panties gone, and a sailor was on top of her with his pants down. I really don't know how much …" She looked into their faces with tears in her eyes. "I could have killed him. Jerry and I managed to pull her away and escape."

Lydia was horrified. "It's lucky you girls weren't killed. Oh, I should never have let you go to the movie."

"Lydia, that's enough! No one is to blame for last night, except that fool, Rear Admiral Wright. He's the one to blame." Russell grunted.

Lydia asked wincing, "Shouldn't Laura see a doctor?"

"She refuses, says she won't let a man touch her."

Russell put his hand on Carmel. "You'll both be home soon. Her father will know what to do. He's a doctor, isn't he?"

Carmel wondered if Laura would tell her father. At this moment she couldn't say what she thought, but she was relieved her aunt and uncle took the news so calmly. She didn't know what she would have done if they hadn't.

The morning papers were spread over the table.

Carmel asked, "May I see the front page?"

"You won't like it. I believe Rear Admiral Wright should be treated as a war criminal. How dare he release all those sailors. We had to use Marines with fixed bayonets in front of six—I repeat, six—rows of police cars, fender to fender, curb to curb, to push that unholy bunch of humanity to the Embarcadero. San Francisco is declared 'out of bounds' for any armed forces within a hundred miles. The whole episode is beyond comprehension, absolutely disgraceful."

"Was anyone killed?" Carmel asked.

Russell impatient said, "Yes, eleven men. Most of them skull injures. Idiots in hotels and buildings were dropping wastebaskets full of water out of windows."

"Not one … rape was mentioned in the paper," Lydia said. Carmel shuddered. She didn't dare tell what she thought had happened.

Carmel ate her toast and read about the very scenes she witnessed the night before. A woman climbed a light pole, throwing her clothes away. There was an item about sailors lifting a woman above their heads and stealing her panties. She thought, thank goodness the reporter didn't know the girl.

Russell's voice rose. "Listen to this. They already have some totals of the damage. Three hundred windows on streetcars broken, seven hundred and seventy windows on Market broken, and one hundred and thirty-five parking signs destroyed. Most of the vandalism was on Mason, Ellis, and Market Streets."

Carmel realized Jerry, Laura, and she had been in the middle of the fray. She thanked her guardian angel for helping them escape with their lives.

Lyn Fu brought a tray with a glass of orange juice, cup and saucer, and a small pot of coffee on it. "There's toast under the warmer. It looks heavy, Carmel. Do you want Lyn Fu to take it up to Laura?"

"No, Auntie. I'll do it right now. We'll try to leave soon. I think Dad'll feel better when I'm home."

Carmel carried the tray upstairs and found Laura dressed in the clothes she wore Sunday. Laura drank a little juice, ate a bite of toast, and sipped the coffee without saying a word. Carmel, just as silent, packed her friend's small amount of toiletries and ignored her suit. They were ready to leave.

Uncle Russell volunteered to drive them back to San Jose. When Laura heard of his offer, she started to cry. Carmel realized her friend didn't want a man in the car. Again, Carmel was grateful to her aunt and uncle for not pursuing the matter.

Later Carmel wondered how she managed to drive home with Laura huddled in the corner, refusing to speak. She couldn't help feeling the fault was hers. If they had returned to San Jose on schedule, Laura would have been all right. Now Laura was practically comatose. She hoped Laura would say how she felt, but she saw her friend's fist clenched tight. Maybe it was better she didn't.

They arrived in San Jose by the early afternoon. Carmel drove the station wagon into Laura's driveway. The house was quiet. Carmel insisted on carrying Laura's few possessions upstairs to her bedroom. She said, "I'll find your father."

Laura said, "Please, Carmel, I don't want to talk to anyone. My life will never be the same. The life I wanted with Scott is over. Everything I saved for him is soiled. I don't want anyone to know." She sat on the edge of her bed looking down at the floor.

"I don't believe what you are saying. Do you think a doctor should look at you?"

"My God, no."

Someone yelled, "Laura." It was Scott. They heard him coming up the stairs.

"Laura, do you want me to tell my brother?"

Laura's voice was savage. "No, Carmel. Leave me alone. I'll do it."

Scott stood at the door. He appeared disheveled, unshaven, and his thick blond hair was uncombed. "Well, the gadabouts are finally home," he said sarcastically.

Carmel saw Laura's stricken expression. "Laura I'll see you later." Laura didn't answer.

Carmel drove home. Anna greeted her and told her Andrew was taking a nap.

"Were things crazy here, Anna, like they were in the city?"

Anna shook her head. "We heard church bells ringing. The Chinese shot off fireworks. That was about it. Your father listened to the radio this morning. News didn't sound too good to me."

"Anna, it's good to be home. I'm exhausted." Carmel hurried to her room, avoiding Anna's questioning eyes.

In a few minutes Carmel heard the front door slam and knew her brother was home. "Carmel!" He yelled up the stairs. "I want to talk to you. Get down here."

Slowly, she came down the stairs and walked into the living room. "Yelling will get you nowhere with me."

Scott's face was beet red. "What in the hell happened to Laura?"

"Exactly what you think happened. Didn't she tell you?"

"No. She said you both went downtown to a movie with someone called Jerry. How could you go downtown when you knew the end of the war was about to be announced? My God, I thought you had more sense." He limped to the portable bar and poured himself a stiff drink.

Carmel sat down. She realized there was no way to escape the truth. "If you'll sit down, I'll explain what happened to us."

He brought his drink and sat down beside her. "When we decided to go to the Count Basie show, we thought the celebration was pretty much over. We promised Lydia and Russell we would be home early. Jerry, my very dear friend and one of the sweetest men you could ever meet, was to wait for us inside the theater. He's the one, Scott, who got me started in this business of singing."

"You mean the one who got you a job in a strip joint?"

"If you're going to keep that attitude, I'm not going to spend *any* time talking to you."

"I'll stop. For God's sake, I'm out of my mind. Laura won't let me near her. She told me to stay away from her. Carmel, was she raped? I want to know, now."

Carmel was furious with her brother most of the time, but now she felt pity for him. She always suspected Laura was a virgin—now she was sure of it. "I couldn't see very well. There was a group of sailors around her when we finally found her."

"My God, Carmel! How could you let this happen?"

"How can you blame it on me? It was a mob! There was nothing anyone could do. The war was over and people just went nuts!"

"Well you had no business being downtown in the first place. You and your damn music! Look what it brought you."

"Now you listen to me, you holier than thou brother. This was nobody's fault. If you had been here to drive us like you were supposed to be instead of worrying about your damn cannery, none of this would have happened either. There is no one to blame, least of all Laura, and don't you dare accuse her of anything. She's been through enough."

Scott sank into a chair near him. He lowered his head into his hands and said in a muffled voice. "I don't know how to handle this. I honestly don't."

"I think you have to help Laura handle it."

"Her father was talking to her when I left."

"Aren't you going back to see her?"

"I have to get back to Watsonville. I've been back and forth waiting for you. There's no way I can stay here. We're running beans. They wait for no one."

Carmel felt her life was falling apart. She was willing to extend deep sympathy to her brother, but every word he spoke was full of accusation, reminding her she should have come home earlier. She held herself rigid.

Her father had rolled his wheelchair unnoticed into the doorway, Howard by his side. "I'll join you if you're celebrating. Carmel, are you and Laura all right?"

Carmel rose and kissed him. "Yes, father, come in. I'll get you something." Her father looked tried. She thought, Maybe we better avoid telling him the truth.

"The papers are full of the melee last night in the city. I'm glad you weren't in it." Andrew sighed.

Carmel crossed the room to mix his drink and caught Scott's eye. She pleaded with him not to say too much, trying to make her voice light. "Just like New Year's Eve. Only tripled, I guess."

Carmel brought him a drink and attempted to change the subject. "Father, how fast do you think the government will act to change rationing?"

"There was something in the papers this morning. Let's see if I can remember. Shoes and tires are on the same schedule for a while. Gasoline rationing will end in two or three weeks. Congress has to end the draft. My God, there are nearly eight million laborers in shipbuilding, munitions, aircraft, and ordinance. We've got all that labor to think about. Where will they go? What will they do?" He took a swallow of his drink. "I wouldn't want that job."

Carmel sipped her drink. "How soon before the men are released?"

Scott, impatient with the conversation, said, "What difference does it make how long? I read it may take a year or more."

Anna came to the door. "Carmel, Dr. Barron would like to talk to you."

"Thank you, Anna." Carmel held her breath as she walked to the phone. "Hello, Dr. Barron."

"Carmel, are you all right?"

"Yes, Dr. Barron, I'm fine."

"If you have a minute, I want to walk over and talk to you."

Carmel heard a warning in his voice. "It's all right, but please talk to me outside, on the terrace."

"Fine, I'll be right over."

When she came back into the room, her father asked, "What's that about?"

"Harold Barron is coming over. He wants to talk to me for a minute."

In a few minutes, the door bell rang and Harold Barron came through the front door. "Hello, everyone. Excuse my interruption. Have to speak to your daughter, Andrew. Come, Carmel."

Scott replenished his drink and remained standing, a sentry ready to pounce.

Andrew muttered, "I smell deceit in this room."

Carmel was petrified at the impending questions and answers she would have to give.

"I want you to tell me the truth, Carmel. Was my daughter raped?" Harold Barron didn't wait a minute. "Did you actually see her raped?"

Carmel shivered when she heard the word.

"I want the truth, Carmel."

"There were men around her when my friend Jerry and I found her. A sailor was on top of her—they both were exposed. I don't see how he would have had time to rape her, but we couldn't be sure. I only know I wanted to kill him. Dr.

Barron, she never said anything, just became very quiet and remained quiet after we got her to the hotel."

"Did you say rape?" Andrew was in the doorway.

Damn that quiet wheelchair. Carmel had no idea how long he had been there and what he had heard. Andrew, his voice fainter, repeated the question. He began to gasp for air. Then he slumped over the arm of the chair.

Harold immediately called, "Scott, come quick."

Scott and Anna appeared at the same time. Scott lifted his frail father from out of the wheelchair and carried him to the couch. Andrew struggled to speak: "Who was raped? You said everything was fine."

Harold said, "Andrew, quiet down or you'll be back in the hospital." He listened to Andrew's heart and found nothing seriously wrong. Finally, satisfied that Andrew was all right, he prepared to leave. "Andrew, I think you better take it easy. It won't do any good to carry on. Just take it easy for a few days and you'll be up walking again." He beckoned to Carmel to follow him outside. "Thank you for your honesty, Carmel. She won't see Scott. We have to give her some time."

"Should I come over?" Carmel dreaded his answer.

"Why don't you give it a few days? She's not herself. Whatever happened, Carmel, don't blame yourself. No one had any idea the events would cause such grief. You and Laura were in the wrong place at the wrong time." His eyes were sympathetic. He patted her shoulder and left. She stood and listened to his footsteps fade. She wondered whether this day would ever end.

Carmel went back into the house to find Anna waiting for her. She sat down and told Anna while Scott listened.

For the following week, Carmel hated staying away from Laura. As far as she knew, Scott did, too. He came home twice during the week. Once, Carmel found him standing on the vegetable garden path, kicking at the hard ground. He raised his head. She saw the torture in his eyes.

Carmel lifted her arms to him, and he put his head on her shoulder. She felt hot tears on her cheek. This brought her tears. She said in a broken voice, "I'm so sorry, Scott. I wish I could say something. I feel so guilty not being able to see Laura."

He raised his head, letting her go. "Don't, Carmel. She won't see *me*." He sighed. "I think about her every minute, all day long. I came back today to see if she was better. She isn't. I'll just go back to work." He walked away.

That afternoon, Carmel sat on a step halfway up the stairway. Anna sat down beside her. "You must tell me why you make yourself ill."

"It's my fault."

"Is that reason you mope around?"

Carmel broke into sobs that shook her body. Anna sat and waited for the tears to stop.

"Who blames you?"

"Everyone! Scott, Laura and her father, and now Phillip's coming home. He will blame me, too."

Anna pulled Carmel close. "I think Phillip coming home, reason for tears. Am I right?"

"What do you mean?" Her tears stopped when Anna mentioned Phillip. Carmel wondered what she knew.

"Carmel, I share your life for years. I see looks between you and Phillip Christmastime." She smiled at Carmel. "I think my girl in love for long time."

Carmel jumped up. "Yes, I love him."

"Is that why you stay in the city?"

"One of the reasons."

"I want to read to you." Anna left the room and returned with a small red book. She found the page and began to read:

"'Your pain is the breaking of the shell that encloses your understanding. Even as the stone of the fruit must break, that its heart may stand in the sun, so must you know pain.' Those words are from Kahlil Gibran, *The Prophet*. Carmel, we break the shell and reach understanding, for our heart to stand in sun—but first we know pain, *conchita*."

"I'm not sure I like to hear that before we can understand we have to be miserable."

"Pain inside comes different times in lives. Many share same feelings. It helps to understand, to forgive." Anna's black eyes watched for Carmel's reaction. "You give a lot to come home and keep home fires burn. I think you forgive Scott."

Carmel laughed. "Have I, Anna? Maybe someday I'll possess some of your wisdom." She hugged her. Carmel knew Anna was also referring to Phillip when she mentioned forgiveness. "I'm going to ask Laura to see Scott."

CHAPTER 73

Carmel did not want to think about the distressing trip to San Francisco. The unfortunate circumstances tore at her heart. She prayed nothing that tortuous would ever happen again.

She thought about Anna and the words of the Prophet. She didn't feel she was resisting pain; she felt she was in the thick of it. Her mind flashed with memories of Laura's face as Jerry carried her away from the sailors. She remembered the stricken look on Scott's face after he saw Laura, Dr. Barron's demanding questions concerning his daughter, and the collapse of her father when he heard the word rape.

Then there was Elka and Marlena. What happened? How could they disappear into thin air? She suspected Caesar knew the answers.

Carmel often reflected on the girl she had once been. A past buried forever. Although she had once felt driven to prove she could succeed, now that goal seemed less important, somehow distant. She must admit the truth. After receiving Phillip's good-bye letter, she needed desperately to feel important to someone, to feel she was essential. Discovering that the ranch couldn't manage without her satisfied that purpose. She had grown up with little regard for the dedication needed to run the ranch. This last year she found out it was a never-ending job, night and day, to keep ahead of the seasons.

A week and a half passed before Carmel reluctantly accepted the fact Laura was not coming out of her room anytime soon. Carmel went to see her old friend. Carmel did not bring flowers or a gift, because she knew doing so would be admitting to Laura she was a shut-in.

The house was deadly silent when she opened the back door. She felt strange climbing the stairs and passing Phillip's closed bedroom door. How long would it be before her heart stopped pounding at the familiarity of Phillip's surroundings?

Carmel tapped softly on Laura's closed door. When there was no answer, she opened the door and went in. The drapes were closed and the room dark. Carmel's eyes adjusted to the gloom before she saw Laura sitting up in bed, a tiny, lonely figure, trying to gather all the pain in the world and keep it for herself.

Carmel hesitated, and then blurted, "I could bring the horses around and we could ride around the ranch. You need fresh air." Laura didn't respond. "Are you returning to school?"

"No."

"Why not?"

"They would know."

"That's an irrational answer, Laura. They will not know anything. If you *don't* return, then there has to be a reason."

"There's one."

"What?"

"I could be pregnant." Laura began to cry.

Carmel wanted to hug her friend, say something to help, but words failed her. She couldn't imagine anything more horrible. Pregnant by a man you didn't know, would never see again. What could she say to a dear friend, tied by guilt and terror, quietly accepting defeat?

"If I can't get you out of the room, please don't sit here and mope. Laura, no matter what happens, we love you and we'll be here for you."

There was no reply. Carmel left the room and gently closed the door.

Andrew started his day early by listening to *Don McNiel's Breakfast Club*. The radio remained on all day. Often Carmel worked close to the house and heard the organ music swell at the beginning of each broadcast. *The Romance of Helen Trent* and *Young Doctor Malone*.

Evening programs began with the galloping hoof beats of the *Lone Ranger*, followed by "Hi ho, Silver." *Fibber McGee and Moll* was a favorite of Andrew's.

On Sunday evenings, Carmel and Anna joined him. They listened to *One Man's Family*. The show began when the announcer said, "The story of a San Francisco family and their problems."

Carmel asked Anna, "Why do we listen to the Barbours' difficulties?"

Anna laughed, "They always solve their problems."

With Andrew's health improving, Carmel was relieved to see Anna gaining back the weight she lost nursing her father. She was also delighted Andrew had returned to his Thursday night poker games. His pals came to the house and he joined them in his wheelchair. Someone shuffled and dealt the cards for him. His boisterous friends played on a round table set up in the living room. They filled the room with their raucous humor and cigar smoke.

Scott came by infrequently, remaining silent and looking worn. One late summer day, he joined Carmel in the orchard. The workers were elated and gathered around him. He enjoyed the welcome and even took the time to say so to Carmel.

"These trees are looking great. I knew you could do it. You have too much rancher in you.

"How's your work going in Watsonville?" she asked.

"Our machinery broke down for three days. Our equipment is so damn old. I hope we can begin to buy parts as soon as the government releases them." Scott was quiet for a moment before he said, "Dr. Barron has requested a psychiatrist see Laura. He feels there're some good ones around. What do you think?"

"I know she really needs help. Having her see a psychiatrist is worth a try." She sensed Scott's anger was dissolving.

She asked, "Did Anna tell you Grant's in California at Letterman Hospital? He'll be here sometime today."

"I didn't see her when I came in. So that's why Dad is dressed up. I saw him catching a nap in his wheelchair.

Carmel laughed. "You mean his Cecil De Mille clothes?" She felt good when he bothered to dress, even if his outfit was a bit outlandish. "Maybe he'll rally for Grant."

"Let's hope so. Sis, call me when he arrives. Gotta get back to you know what. Keep it going. I love you." He kissed the top of her head before he left the orchard.

Andrew wakened with a jerk. He was dreaming about Grant, his boy hero, the football star. The Mean Marine was finally coming home. The ranch would swarm with young men and women again. Their laughter would fill the empty rooms. People gravitated to a healthy, good-looking young man. The big family rooms had been quiet for too long. Andrew told himself he didn't care if the ranch wasn't Grant's primary interest. He would encourage Grant to get into selling. Develop a business, maybe become a food broker. Scott could introduce him around. Andrew laughed aloud thinking about Grant. He was a born salesman. With his charisma, he could sell fleas back to a circus.

Andrew heard a car door slam and voices. He wheeled his chair to the front door. In a moment he saw Grant coming toward the house, with the sun behind him, a silhouette crossing the terrace. He would know that body anywhere. He always led with his left shoulder when he walked. Thank the Lord his body looked normal. At least he wasn't limping.

Grant stood in front of him, his voice deeper than he remembered. "Hello, old man."

Andrew saw the outline of Grant as he stood in front of the doorway. He wore a large brimmed hat. Andrew searched for his son's vibrant, healthy, glow, but it wasn't there. Grant's face was a mask, the color of chalk. A red, ugly scar cut across his cheek from below his eye to his chin. His eyes were stark, without eyelashes or eyebrows. Grant grabbed his father's hand to shake it. Andrew shrank away and lifted his arm to ward him off.

At his father's rejection, Grant lifted his hat from his head and said. "You haven't seen it all."

Andrew saw streaks of tomato red running across his son's bald scalp. His left ear was missing. The man before him was a freak.

Andrew's face collapsed. Tears clouded his vision. For the moment he struggled to tell Grant he loved him. To tell him his plans for the future, about the voices in the house full of laughter, about crowds yelling for their football hero. Then the breath left his body. His heart quit beating, but he felt no pain. The long four years of waiting for his favorite son to come home were over.

Carmel remained numb. She could not accept her father's death. She performed all the tasks for the funeral in stony silence, unable to let the tears flow. Bitter because she had told herself her father was getting better. Grant's homecoming should have been a reunion, not a funeral.

It broke her heart to see her once handsome brother so complacent. She had expected rage from him. The old Grant would have been undisciplined, acerbic, and sarcastic. Instead, he was withdrawn. He didn't attend his father's funeral. Dr. Barron said his malaria had returned and immediately put him to bed. Later he admitted to Carmel the real cause of Grant's withdrawal. He was drunk.

There were two services for her father. The first service—for the family, household, and Harold and Cynthia Barron—Laura refused to attend.

They stood in the grotto formed by the pines Carmel's great-grandfather had planted. The grass was a lush green carpet under their feet, the sky a faint robin egg blue. The only sound was water falling from the fountain in its midst. Even the usual noisy birds in the trees above them seemed to sense the serious moment and were quiet. Bruno and Howard sat silent at Scott's feet. Andrew's ashes were interned in a large stone jar and sat inside the grotto by the pool.

The Presbyterian minister, Dr. Roare, had bright red hair and spoke with a burr. Andrew had attended his church from the time he arrived in the valley. Dr. Roare spoke of Andrew's strength, his steadfastness, his discipline, and his kindness to his neighbors and his animals. From Romans he read:

For I am convinced that neither death, nor life, nor angels, nor rulers … nor anything else in all creation, will be able to separate us from the love of God.

"Let us pray. 'Our father who art in Heaven …'"

The words blurred in Carmel's mind as she stared at his final resting place.

Immediately after the service, Harold Barron took Cynthia home. Carmel had heard the doctor tell someone that he didn't know when Phillip was coming home.

To Carmel, it seemed the entire valley came for her father's wake. The large group of relatives and friends met for the gathering in the finished part of the new barn. Three long tables were covered with red-and-white checkered tablecloths. Centerpieces were enormous bouquets of summer flowers in earthen jars. Neighbors brought baskets of food. Scott barbecued a lamb on the spit. Bottles of wine sat on the tables.

Anna was everywhere helping, quiet and not smiling. Carmel's heart reached out to her. Anna hadn't cried at the funeral, but Carmel knew the sorrow was bottled up inside her.

She was touched by how many friends gathered to remember her father. Scott put his arm across her shoulder. "This is more than a wake. It's a gathering of love," he said.

"That's right, Scott. You kids don't realize how many people are here because your father helped them in some way." The voice came from a burly neighbor Carmel met delivering seed.

The visitors stayed until dusk. They shared their feelings and stories about Andrew, but there was also a respectful undercurrent of excitement. The war was over. The gathering provided a chance to talk about husbands, brothers, and sons coming home.

Finally, Carmel and Scott had said good-bye to everyone. Aunt Lydia and Uncle Russell stayed at the house and would drive back to the city in the morning. "Is there anything you want of dad's?" Carmel asked her aunt.

"I'd like some pictures of our life here at the ranch when we were young." She started to cry but abruptly stopped. Scott followed them into the house for a nightcap.

Afterwards Carmel sat on a stone bench in the grotto feeling helpless and lonely. The grotto was her father's favorite place. Bruno and Howard came over to nuzzle her knees. She patted their heads.

She reasoned every person she loved was shut up in a cocoon of loneliness. Grant was in another world. No matter what the doctors did for him physically, they hadn't helped his mind. She was frightened to discover he was quiet because he was dead drunk. Will he ever again be his old self? The life of her brother, once so alive and promising, was slowly dying inside him.

Scott came home less and less often, as though he despaired ever seeing Laura.

Laura stayed shut up in darkness made no effort to come out.

As for herself, Carmel had not permitted herself to weep. It would be admitting he was really gone. Now the emptiness filled her. The tears and sobs she held back began to flow.

Through her weeping she swore she heard her father say, "Find Anna; she's lonely, too."

Carmel thought for a moment and then stood. Yes, she would find Anna—not as the young girl she once had been but as the woman who had survived fires and death. Now she was resolute. She would continue to save the people she loved, and Costalotta.

CHAPTER 74

The early August morning, bright with sunshine and fresh air, drew Carmel out to sit on the terrace. When she moved her office into the barn, she discovered a box of misfiled papers. Just as she settled herself on a green garden chair beside the glass topped table to examine them, she heard a large crash of breaking glass from the living room.

She hurried into the room to find Grant getting up off the floor. On the edge of the wheeled bar a large glass decanter of liquor had been knocked over. Liquor dripped onto a floor covered with broken glass.

"OOPS! I swear the floor moved."

"Oh, Grant, let me help you." Carmel took his arm. She winced from the strong smell of liquor. "Have you been sleeping in your clothes?"

Grant looked at himself in his wrinkled black pants and blue shirt. He saluted his sister. "Affirmative."

Grant turned to the bar, set a liquor bottle upright, and reached for a glass.

Carmel thought he looked hideous. He had put his wig on backwards. His beard appeared two days old and his face was flushed and swollen. The scar appeared as a dark crevice across his cheek. How, her mind screamed, could this be happening?

"Have you eaten today?"

"I don't remember. Anyway, I'm not hungry."

Carmel took the bottle and put it out of sight in the liquor cabinet.

He watched her, then grinned and nodded his head. "I'll find it when I'm ready." His hands searched his pockets for a cigarette.

"Will you come outside and sit with me? I'll find you a smoke."

He shuffled along in front of her. Carmel was amazed he could walk. She waited for him to sit before returning to the house to find a cigarette.

Anna was cleaning up the liquor and broken glass.

"We'll find Pedro and get Grant back into bed," Carmel said. She found the cigarette in a silver box on the coffee table and returned to find Grant slumped in his chair, asleep.

This was the first time she faced the weight of her brother's problems. She knew his bitterness was destroying him, and she dreaded to think of the unhappiness he would bring to himself and to her. Grant's healing could take a very long, long time, if ever.

Carmel's hopes for the world around her to return to the peaceful days before the war faded. Scott had made it clear he would not come back. She accepted the fact she could never leave the ranch even if she wanted to. Not that she wanted to, but she would have been grateful to have a choice.

Carmel reminded herself repeatedly the St. Johns had struggled hard for this land, and if she had one ounce of their blood in her body, she would solve the challenge of ranching. The same grit that got her jobs singing kept her learning.

The ancient art of pruning was one of the many tasks Carmel felt she ought to learn. However, she was grateful and relieved when Jose told her he found someone to help him. Her job was to keep the ranch accounts and drive the tractor. The long days spent on the tractor tired her to the bone. She often felt closer to a hundred than her twenty-four years. When the men began to return home, she'd find an overseer to manage the ranch and relieve her of the hardest work. But she intended to always keep the books.

After the second time Grant woke the household falling out of bed, Carmel told Anna, "Please go in that room when he goes downstairs and take everything off the tops of the dressers. I guess in the bathroom, too."

Anna looked sympathetic. "I have to remove the bedding. The room smells, Carmel."

Tears filled Carmel's eyes. She had to help him. There was no one else. "I guess I better speak to Laura's father. I don't know if the hospitals have any rehabilitation for burn victims and when … when they become drunks." Anger swelled in her. She went to find her brother.

She found Grant slumped in a chair at the dining table with a drink in his hand. He looked awful without his wig. His bald, scarred scalp and missing ear made her once handsome brother looked cockeyed. She could have cried.

"Hi, sis. Have a drink."

"No, I will not have a drink. I love you very much, Grant, and I worry about you, but I'm not going to watch you destroy yourself. You're not the only man that came back mutilated, as you call it. How about the men younger than you who came back with no legs or arms? They have to learn to use their whole bodies again, just like babies. Your unhappiness has settled around you like a black cloud. You're too damn comfortable in that damn black box you call your mind."

"Wait a minute, sis." He tried to get up and failed. He sat down hard in the chair.

"You'd better sit back down. I'm just getting warmed up." Carmel's eyes had narrowed, her face flushed. "Let me tell you about your black box. There's no sunshine in your black box. It's cold, unfeeling, and fearful. A familiar friend for you but not for the people that love you. You shut us out. Why don't you kick the little black box? Instead, you've made it so big you can crawl in it anytime. No one else wants to be there with you. You have become cutting, belittling, and destroying with words. They scream your unhappiness. Let me take you upstairs."

Carmel walked him to his room and left him sitting on the edge of his bed.

Grant tried to feel remorse. He had failed his sister, but she was right. He was ugly. Grant stood unsteady on his feet. He shuffled over to the dresser mirror and stared at his ruined face. She was right—he was a mess. Picking up a vase, he smashed it against the image. The mirror didn't break. The monster stared back at him, still there. So what was he going to do about it? Just wallow in a river of self-pity? Wasn't he made of stronger stuff that that?

There was a letter on his desk urging him to return to the hospital. Until now he had ignored it. With shaking hands, he picked up the letter and reread the message of hope. They wanted to do more surgeries. He would never be the handsome man he had once been, but maybe they could fix him so he didn't look like such a freak. He shuffled to the hall. He slowly dialed the number on the letter.

Andrew's prediction was right. The crops in '45 produced an abundance of apricots, cherries, and plums.

When it was harvest time, Jose took the truck to Tulare and brought back families of young women to work in the orchards. Only women were available to work the orchards. Often they brought small children and a grandmother to watch them. They had replaced the men serving their country. In the past, Carmel's grandfather planned for the extra help to harvest his crops and built two small houses on the ranch for his laborers.

Carmel found the women dependable, efficient, and strong. They carried ladders to the orchards to climb and pick the harvest. The women wore colorful dresses and scarves around their heads. She liked to hear their voices chattering and laughing. When they sat under the trees eating their lunch, they sang folk songs of their native Spanish and Portuguese. They showed delight when she made the effort to learn their names.

Afterwards, the picked fruit was placed in shallow trays to dry in the sun. Then Jose and Pedro helped pack the fruit into boxes and stack them on two trucks, to be driven to the cannery.

In July, Jose told her they would spray the walnuts for aphids. Then in August it would be time to spray Malathion, which would then be repeated in fourteen days. She realized he told her to make her feel she was important, but she was grateful he went ahead to see his instructions were followed.

The last days of August brought scorching heat. The winds dried the earth, making it necessary to deep soak the ground. She thanked God there were three wells on the property, controlled by pumps that released water into large pipes. Jose told her there was water all around, twenty-three feet straight down. A schedule for turning the pumps on and off was posted on the wall of her office.

Carmel climbed off the tractor. She took off her straw hat and rubbed her forehead. It was hot in the orchard and she needed a cool glass of water. She heard the squeak of the wheel on the pump. She knew Jose would be near it. She found him by the first irrigation ditch waiting for the water to pour from the pump into the huge pipe.

She picked up the tin cup hanging against the water faucet. First, she turned on the faucet and let the water run for a minute to let it cool.

Jose watched her.

Carmel poured water from the cup onto her cotton bandanna and wiped her face with the damp cloth. "Jose, I think you should tell me about harvesting the walnuts."

"We spray soon in August to keep the husk fly from dropping eggs into the hulls to hatch worms. I show you when time comes. We put hull in our hands and squeeze. If the green hull breaks, ready for harvest. I promise, when hull cracks, I find workers," Jose said. "They use twelve-foot pole with hook on end to grab trees and shake walnuts off. Pickers take forty-pound fruit boxes of walnuts to hauler machine. Wire brushes will take hull off. They dry in sun seven to ten days."

"How do you know when they're dry?"

He turned the pump off. "We check—crack open shell, and bite it. If shell wet, it's not ready to store."

Carmel listened and added, "This fall walnuts will *not* be stored too soon. We're going to wait as long as it's necessary."

Jose nodded. "It'll rain by Halloween. The rain and wind blows the walnuts off the trees. You riding the tractor today?"

"Guess so." She waited for the dogs to slurp water from a trough. "Come on, hounds, let's stir up some dust." She walked off into the orchard to climb back on the tractor. The dogs scampered beside her.

Since Andrew died, Bruno and Howard slept outside Carmel's bedroom door and spent every day with her. Every person on the ranch grew accustomed to Carmel and the dogs, sitting beside her high on the tractor, driving through the trees, dust billowing around her.

Jose understood operating the tractor was hard work for her, and he knew her arms and back ached at the end of the day, but he did not suggest taking the job away from her.

Handling the tractor allowed Carmel to escape from the pressures of the ranch. It helped her to quiet the pain in her heart from her father's death and Grant's return. She bumped into trees, backed up, and tried again. She had to pay attention and think only of driving the tractor. It helped fill the great hole in her spirit where her music had been. Sometimes she wondered if she would ever sing again. Carmel felt her thoughts were like sand sifting through a screen. Nothing would plug them up.

One day Jose confided to her she had grown from the little girl who charmed her father and brothers into a capable caring woman. He was not surprised, because she came from good stock and proved herself. Carmel thanked him for his kind words.

CHAPTER 75

Jerry Cassidy sat beside Carmel in San Jose at the circular bar of the Hawaiian Gardens. He ordered martinis while they waited to be called to dinner. He grinned. "I'm happy you were free for dinner. I came down the peninsula to see Mom and lucked out to find you home."

"I'm glad you called."

"I'm sorry to hear about your father."

"Thank you, Jerry. I miss him terribly."

"With the war over, will the workload at the ranch lighten up?"

"Not a bit. There's always something unexpected happening. A waterline broke yesterday. It still isn't fixed." She tasted her martini.

The Hawaiian Gardens was one of the few restaurants in San Jose where customers enjoyed dinner and dancing to a band. Sometimes there was a floorshow. The crowd around the circular bar was jolly, noisy, and well dressed. The air was laden with cigarette smoke and women's perfume. Loud laughter burst at the end of the bar.

Jerry made a face. "Someone must have told a joke. This group reminds me of the bars in San Francisco during the war."

"Sounds like New Year's Eve, but there are fewer uniforms." Carmel observed Jerry, handsome and lean in his suit. His blue eyes, the color of the sky, missed nothing. She felt comfortable with him. They fit like a pair of old shoes.

The waiter appeared. "Your table is ready, Mr. Cassidy. Please follow me."

Carmel turned heads in her peach linen dinner suit as they walked to their table. It was on the edge of the dance floor, with a wall of windows behind them. Through the windows lit by small garden lights, they saw grottos with water running over rocks and twisting paths trailing over bridges. Throughout the area, lush plants flourished.

Carmel said, "It's beautiful here, isn't it? If you like, we can walk through the grotto after dinner. There's even a wishing well."

"Yes, I would like." The waiter came and took their order for another martini. Jerry scanned the menu. "What do you recommend?"

"The restaurant is famous for its frog legs. They catch them here." The expression on his face made her laugh. "Want to give them a try?"

"Why not?"

A ten-piece band played "Darn That Dream."

"The band sounds great. Let's dance."

They finished a whole set. Carmel felt free as a bird dancing with him. It had been a long time since a man had held her in his arms.

The crowded dance floor didn't stop Jerry from doing some fancy footwork. They came back to the table exhilarated and laughing.

They both ordered frog legs. The waiter insisted their choice was a good one.

They danced again and Carmel felt comfortable resting her head on Jerry's chest.

Dinner arrived and Jerry ordered a bottle of wine.

"How's Laura?"

"She's beginning to make progress, I think. Her father is a doctor. He insisted she consult a psychiatrist, and she agreed. That was two weeks ago. I try to see her as often as I can."

"Did she stop blaming you for that trip to the city?'

"I'm not sure she blames me, or anyone."

"I know I had a responsibility to see you two women home safe and sound."

"You did. We reached home. Don't blame yourself for one minute, Jerry." She squeezed his hand.

The band took a break. Their dinner arrived and the waiter opened the wine and served them.

"Carmel, what happened with your brother Scott? Didn't he and Laura plan a future together?"

"Laura won't see him."

"I thought you told me she was improving?"

"She is. She doesn't want a man around her, especially Scott."

"How does he feel about that?"

"Heartbroken."

"Does he want to be with her?"

"Very much so. I'm trying to encourage Laura to see him."

"Didn't you and Scott have a falling out? I remember you told me something about arguments with Scott."

Carmel sighed. "Yes. I was furious with him because he wanted to leave the ranch and start his cannery business. He expected me to come home and assume his place."

"I remember."

"When the fire destroyed the barns and Dad had a heart attack I couldn't do anything but stay home."

"And now?"

"I'm not as angry and I'm trying to understand. Scott asked me to forgive him for being so hard on me. And he's asked me to help with Laura if I can. He wants to marry her and even sooner than they planned."

"Good for him. Does she know that?"

"Time will tell."

"How is Grant? You said he suffered severe burns in the Marines."

"Yes. When he's able, he has to endure a lot of plastic surgery. He suffers inside something terrible and shuts himself away. The Marine hospital is planning to start treatments."

"I had no intention of making you unhappy, Carmel. I wanted this evening to be fun, but I have a letter to give you. Jerry put his hand in his breast pocket, pulled out a wrinkled white envelope, and handed it to her. "It's from Jake Refugo."

Her name was written on the envelope. Her fingers trembled as she opened it. The words on the note were handwritten in an uneven scrawl.

I strangled Elka, I didn't mean to. I thought she was Marlena. I put her body in a bag and tied it to a boat and pushed her out into the bay. I took Marlena to the train depot.

Jake Refugo

Carmel handed the paper to Jerry.

He read it and gave it back to her. "Jake was killed the night the war was over. A wastebasket full of water was dropped from a hotel window on him,

reaking his neck. Two other men died the same way. Jake's sister found this
envelope in his bank box with instructions to give it to you."

"I saw the article but didn't make the connection. I didn't know Jake's last
name, and it said he was a bookkeeper."

"I'm sorry, Carmel. She was a nice gal."

"Poor Elka. What a horrible way to die. She deserved better than this. What
does he mean 'I didn't mean to'? This means Marlena is alive."

"I wonder where?"

"I have a hunch Caesar would know."

"Have you seen him?" Carmel wondered.

"No, he sold his two houses with the connecting bridge. The buyer has eight
children. The nannies and children live in one house, the parents in another.
They love the bridge. I believe Caesar spends most of his time in Vegas."

"How do you know all this?"

"San Francisco is a small town in some ways." He smiled.

The band, back from their break, began "Sentimental Journey." "I didn't
want to put a damper on your evening. Let's dance."

Carmel's heart was touched by Jerry's efforts to entertain her. "Yes, let's."

Returning to their table, Jerry asked, "Carmel, aren't you ready to return to
San Francisco and your singing?"

"I'll try to tell you honestly how I feel. Many times in the last few months, I
questioned whether I really miss the hullabaloo of wearing long dresses and
singing before a band. I enjoy singing with all my heart, and I know how lucky
I was to get jobs. In the beginning, you were a big help with that. At first, when
I came back to San Jose, the ranch wasn't that important to me. Now I feel a
great sense of pride in my accomplishments and I don't want anyone else to fill
my shoes. This ranch is home—I'm needed, and every crop that grows and
produces thrills me. Can you understand? I guess I'm just a dirt farmer after
all."

"I'm trying."

"Maybe I'll sing again someday—who knows? I remember what you told
me about the business changing. Has it?"

"Yes. Many fellows are back from the war and there's less demand for dance
bands. People are staying home more."

"I can't believe that the people who love bands will quit coming. I know
they have the feelings I have, Jerry. A good band leader is sort of a father figure.
He senses when to play a ballad, when a guy wants to hold a girl closer, and

when she wants to put her head close to his cheek—it's Christmas and the Fourth of July. I felt this too many times sitting on the bandstand."

Jerry sat stunned at Carmel's words. "Yes, there's magic about band music You described the feelings so well. Are you blushing?"

"Maybe. I didn't expect to say that." She finished her coffee.

"I hope you never quit singing, but I think I understand your reasoning." Dinner over, he said, "Let's see the grotto."

They went outside to the dimly lit grotto. He pushed open the iron gates. They stopped to look into the wishing well. Each was silent as they dropped pennies into it. Water flowed over rocks and spilled into pools alive with koi. The garden reminded Carmel of her father's small pools with koi flashing about.

Jerry found a secluded bench behind ferns and suggested they sit. The bench was still warm from the sun, and it felt comfortable. The only sound was water trickling over rocks. The frogs were quiet when Carmel and Jerry walked about. When they sat, the frogs began their serenade.

Carmel listened a minute. "Did you see their size? One of these guys won the frog jumping contest in Angels Camp."

"Really!" Then he turned to look at her. "Carmel, I promise, if ever you need me for anything, I'll be there for you."

Carmel saw the look of love in his eyes. "You've always been there, Jerry, whenever I needed you." She didn't want to hurt him. "How are things at NBC? Are you staying in San Francisco?"

"Yes, the musicians at the station are tops."

Carmel yawned. "Oh, good heavens, I'm sorry. It's not the company."

"I know, it's the hour. I'll take you home."

"Yes. I rise early these days."

In the car they talked about the people they knew and who had remained in San Francisco.

At her front door Carmel said, "Thank you, Jerry, for the evening, especially all the dances. I loved it."

"So did I." He pulled her to him and kissed her.

She didn't mind. "Good night, Jerry."

He crossed the terrace to his car.

The next morning Carmel went to see Laura. She was wearing her robe and sitting in the overstuffed chair by the window. "You look better every time I see you," Carmel said in her most cheerful voice.

Actually, Laura looked worn. There were dark smudges under her eyes. She looked as if a tiny breeze would topple her.

"You're lying, but thanks. My clothes hang on me."

"Do you like Dr. Radar?"

"Yes. He's very kind. He doesn't say much. He said I'd think better if I'd get out of the room and get some sun."

"Why don't you open your drapes wide? Let the sunshine in." Carmel pulled the drape open. For a moment the glare was blinding. "Better yet, the day is lovely. Come down to the patio and stretch out. The sun will feel good. I'll check again later today."

It was two days before Laura, wearing her robe, stretched out on the lounge in the patio. Carmel was right. The bright sunshine fell across her, warm and wonderful. She closed her eyes and slept. She heard a male voice say her name.

"Laura." He said it softly. "You're here." His body sheltered her from the sun. He sat beside her on a low chair.

"Yes. I'm here."

"Laura, I want you to listen to me. I know what happened wasn't your fault. I'm sorry I was so angry at first, and I did blame you. If you had come with me that day, none of this would have happened. But it did happen, and we all have to deal with it. The fact is I love you. I have always loved you, all of my life, and nothing can change that. I want you for my wife—no matter what. Please, Laura.

Still she would not look at him, but a single tear slid down her cheek and her small hand crept into his. Scott held it gently.

"I love you. I'll be back."

In September, Caesar got up from the desk in his office at the Royal Flush in Las Vegas. Something had caused him to look through his one-way window at the casino floor below.

He saw Big Red, his pit boss, talking to a short blonde. He couldn't see her face, as her back was to him. For a moment, he felt his pulse jump. "It's Marlena."

Seeing the blonde started him thinking. It was not Caesar's habit to solve a problem with booze, but he went to his office bar and poured himself a Scotch over ice. Then he went back to the window; the blonde was gone.

Why did he care? Too many things happened because of Marlena and the baby. When he sent Jake to get rid of Marlena, he meant scare her out of town, not kill her. The stupid bastard killed the wrong woman and kept the money Marlena was out there someplace with a kid.

Caesar had heard, the night the war ended, somebody dropped a wastebasket full of water from a hotel window onto Jake's head. It squashed him flat as a grape. It served him right. Jake was stupid.

Caesar sent for Big Red. "Who's the blonde?"

"I dunno, boss. Been around for a while—comes and goes."

Caesar's idea to book only class acts had been expensive since the beginning, but music was a big draw in Vegas. The war had been good to him. The black market and selling liquor brought him all the money he needed. After all those trips back and forth from San Francisco, he finally established a Nevada residence and received his Nevada State Gaming License. He put his brother John in charge of the books. Caesar started small. He planned to learn the casino business from the slots up.

The old timers on Fremont Street liked this good-looking man with the San Francisco manners. Old Doc taught him how to catch a thief playing blackjack and craps. A casino owner had to have the eyes of an eagle, and Caesar had them.

He intended to keep the mob out of his business. Bugsey Segal was building a huge club on the edge of town. Caesar knew it was mob money and only a matter of time until the Chicago boys would start to put the pressure on Segal.

He told his brother, "Listen to me, the war changed the way people live. People are searching for fun, and they'll come where the gambling and women are. They'll cross the United States right down Highway 91." The prospect excited him. His voice became louder. "It's the only highway through town. They'll have to drive down Highway 91, right by my front door."

Tony warned him, "Caesar, don't go too big. We won't be able to fill the rooms."

"Our club will stay small and the rooms inexpensive. We'll give the customers free booze when they're gambling. And good food—just like San Francisco. And music, lots of music. There's something else." He grinned at his brother. "Did you know we're Irish?"

Tony shook his head. He liked to see his brother happy.

Caesar said, "I'm beginning to recognize my Irish ancestors. Buy land in another name—and keep buying land. I don't want anybody, anybody, to know what I'm doing. Someday I want a club as big as Segal's, but it'll be mine."

He planned to send for Carmel, offer her a chance to sing. What the hell was he doing playing farmer on that ranch in California?

CHAPTER 76

Laura was certain she would find Scott behind the barn. She would be safe with Scott. Night was coming; she had to run fast. She passed under the arched gates of Costalotta, ran swiftly along the drive, and sped out across the pasture. She felt her lungs would burst, her heart spring from her body. The night air was laden with black smoke and smelled of burning tires. Behind the barn she found Scott gone. Instead a group of men in sailors' uniforms waited for her. She heard the guttural sounds of strange men's voices. The loud screams of women, sirens shrieking, and glass breaking filled the air. Arms reached for her, pulling her down, down. Hands held her as her clothes were stripped away. In the dark, fingers touched her bare legs, reached for her exposed thighs. She felt a man's naked body between her open thighs. He pushed himself against her skin. No one stopped him from twisting and ripping at her. Fear clamped her throat, smothered her breath. Laura screamed, "Scott, I'm going to die."

The nightmare woke her. She opened her eyes to her pitch-black bedroom and stared into the dark. Her nightclothes were wet with perspiration under the damp bed sheets. Awake, she huddled under the covers. When would it end? Dr. Radar said the dreams would stop. She didn't believe him. Her flesh still felt unclean. In the shower, she scrubbed and scrubbed her body. She lay in the dark and thought, No one can help. She will never feel any different. Tears slid down her cheeks. Finally, she slept.

Hours later, a man in uniform tapped lightly on Laura's bedroom door. He opened it, a tall figure framed in the doorway.

"Laura, it's your brother."

The bright morning sun crept along the edges of the heavy drapes.

"Oh, Phillip, Phillip, you're home." She struggled to push the bedclothes back and sit up. "When did you arrive? What time is it?"

"I arrived in the last hour. It's about seven o'clock. I hesitated to wake you. Do you want to sleep? We can talk later."

"Please stay." She began to cry.

"There, there, little gal. I'm going to open these drapes so I can see you."

He pulled the cord. The drapes opened. A square of bright sunlight bounced off the pine floors and filled the room.

Phillip wore his navy uniform without his cap. His hair was uncombed. He needed a shave.

He sat down beside her. She appeared to him as frail as a small child. "You are too thin and as white as a ghost. We must get you out of this room into some sunshine."

"I've been trying. It's hard for me."

"Why?"

"My life is over."

"When did you decide that?"

"The night the war was over. I got …" She sobbed.

"Yes, Dad told me. Were you hurt any other way?"

"No. Just bruises."

"Were you examined?"

"No."

"Did the man complete the action or spill semen on you?"

"Phillip, I don't want to talk about it."

"I believe your problem is you haven't faced what really happened." He thought maybe the shock of hearing the words might help. "Laura, it is possible you weren't actually raped, but close enough that you believed you were."

"I'm treated like I have a terrible disease. No one comes near me."

"Perhaps you make people feel they shouldn't come near you. They don't want to remind you."

"Don't they know I think about it all the time?"

"Laura, you were in the wrong place at the wrong time. You're allowing this awful mistake someone else made to affect your whole life. You're at war with yourself, feeling inferior because of human error." His voice was gentle and his words tender. "Laura, I just fought a war, but you must not."

"But I may be pregnant."

"How long has it been?"

"A long time." She faced him with doe eyes.

"Are your breasts sore?"

"No."

"Are you nauseated in the morning?"

"No."

"Are you late with your period?"

"Yes."

"Anxiety can cause body functions to change."

"I wanted to be perfect for Scott. Now I'm soiled."

"Have you stopped loving him?"

"No."

"I have a strong feeling he hasn't stopped loving you. None of us have."

Her sobs broke his heart. Phillip held her in his arms.

"Laura, our life on this Earth is so short. People, problems, and pain seem to be our burden. I want to read you the words of Abraham Lincoln."

"Lincoln's young son Willie died. To add to his pain, he had to continue sending men to face terrible battles. He knew many would die. Laura, I've read this message to several who felt life was not to be endured." Phillip took a little white card out of his breast pocket. He began to read.

"In this sad world of ours, sorrow comes to all ... it comes with bitterest agony ... Perfect relief is not possible, except with time. You cannot now realize that you will ever feel better ... And yet it is a mistake. You are sure to be happy again. To know this, which is certainly true, will make you some less miserable now. I have had experience enough to know what I say."

Laura remained quiet for a moment. She gave Phillip a hug and kissed his cheek. "Thank you."

"I hope it helps. Dad says you're seeing Doctor Radar."

"Yes I am."

"Good girl. I know he'll help you."

She leaned back on her pillows and pulled the covers up under her chin. "Are you out of the navy?"

"No. I have to return to Oak Knoll Navy Hospital."

Phillip stood. "I believe I'll get a shower and shave." He looked at his sister with her blonde hair in snarls, her brown eyes full of trust. "Will you have breakfast with me?"

"Yes, I will." She smiled for the first time.

"Good. I'll see you at breakfast." He kissed her forehead.

The days were long and golden in September. The leaves still green on the trees. The few flowering eucalyptus trees that survived the fire were loaded with red blossoms, which attracted thousands of orange and black monarch butterflies. Now was the time for the California brown pelicans, after following the migrating fish to Vancouver Island, to fly back over California on their return to Mexico.

When Carmel first climbed up to sit on the tractor a heavy mist had covered the ground. It was cold enough for her heavy wool sweater. Since early morning she toiled with the tractor, disking the soil under the cherry trees. Bruno and Howard sat beside her on the seat Pedro built for them. When the sun rose over the tops of the cherry trees and warmed the earth, she removed her sweater. She had grown to love this time of the morning, with the sight and smell of the rich dark earth as the disk turned it over. Sparrows and chickadees hopped behind her in the deep, freshly turned moist soil looking for worms. Two barn cats hoping for a full breakfast cautiously followed the birds. The dogs sat beside her wanting nothing more than to be allowed to chase the cats. They knew once they jumped off their perch they were not allowed back.

She took some measure of pride in cultivating such uniform rows. Intent on her work, the morning slipped by. Near noon she told herself, One more row up and back and I'll quit for the day, head for a shower. She stopped at the edge of the orchard to turn around. The dogs stood up to balance themselves and began to bark.

"Stop it, both of you. Do you want to break your necks? Stop barking." She noticed a lone figure walking toward her between the rows of cherry trees.

The dogs jumped off the tractor. With tails wagging, they ran to greet the visitor. She saw the figure was a man. He patted the dogs. She couldn't hear what he said to them. They followed the man walking toward her. Suddenly Carmel's breath left her body.

Phillip!

He continued until he reached her and stopped by the tractor. "Hello, Carmel." He smiled. Even white teeth gleamed in a tan face. He was spotless, in dark blue trousers and a white shirt, open at the neck.

Carmel thought, Mother of God, why does he always do this to me? Just pop out of nowhere?

She turned the motor off. "Hello, Phillip. Where did you come from?"

"From across the seas." He chuckled. "I left Pearl a couple of days ago. I'm stationed at Oak Knoll Navy Hospital. Be out soon. How've you been? You look well." His brown eyes held hers.

She could have easily killed him. "Can't you see I'm working?" Her voice was cool.

"I heard you really whip this tractor around."

"I'm only on the tractor once in a while. I'm usually in the office." Why did he make her feel as if she must defend herself? She must look like a ragamuffin. Her cut-off corduroys had been Scott's, and her old green shirt was torn. After all these months, this was not the way she planned to look when he came home. Carmel felt uncomfortable and defensive. She wasn't sure what to say and changed the subject. "Have you seen Laura?"

"I had breakfast with her."

"You mean she came downstairs?"

"Yes. We both had breakfast with Mom."

"Oh, Phillip, she'll be on the mend now."

"Yes, in time. She must realize she's still the wonderful girl she was before and stop blaming herself. I believe there's a strong possibility she was not actually raped. I hope she will accept that."

"Did you have a chance to tell your mom?"

"Mom and I talked before Laura came to breakfast. Afterwards I called Dad at the clinic and told him what I thought. He suspected the same but felt helpless approaching her. He thinks Dr. Radar will help her if anyone does. He and Mom have suffered so much standing by watching sis suffer."

"What about Scott?"

"That will take some time, too. They love each other. Let's hope time and love will heal their wounds." He was quiet a moment. "I'm sorry about your father. He was a grand man."

Tears came to her eyes. Phillip saw them and handed her a handkerchief. "Thank you." She sniffed and blew her nose. Here was this dear, beautiful man resting against the dusty tire, staring up at her. She was so glad he was there, she could easily touch him. He was the only man in her life who could throw her completely off her pins. She was trying very hard to stay in control, but she couldn't bring herself to ask him if he was home for good.

Phillip said, "I take it Grant's home."

"Yes. Oh … Phillip, he's such a muddle. I don't think I know what to do about him. He was so handsome and now he's so … I can see in his eyes when his mind shuts me away and he goes back into his black box. He knows the box is cold and lonely and no one wants to be with him. Yet he goes back to it. I guess because it's familiar and he feels safe. I was awful mad at him one day and told him so." She stopped. "I feel so helpless. I'm not sure what to do about

ny brother. I was hoping he would see Laura's doctor and the doctors at Let-
erman Hospital."

Phillip listened. "Maybe I'll be able to help. There are solutions and doctors
o help people like Grant. One of the worst things that can happen to any of us
s to watch someone in pain and not be able to do anything about it." He stared
at her. "Carmel, enough about the family, I want to talk about us … now."

She frowned. "I didn't expect to see you again after your *only* letter."

"I had to write that letter. I did not have the right to ask anything of you. I
might not have returned."

"Don't you think you should have let me make my own decisions?"

"I didn't feel I should ask anything of you. I'm not sure I'm the greatest
catch in the world. I have been accused of being arrogant and self-centered."

Phillips's words astonished Carmel. She looked intently at him to see if he
was taunting her and saw something new behind the well-known light that
shone in his eyes. She realized it had to be part of the hell he had been through
and the misery he had witnessed. Beyond the weariness that showed in his
face, she thought she saw both concern and compassion.

She scowled. "Yes, but you did come back. And you *never* told me you
cared." She wanted him to hold her, kiss her, and tell her he loved her.

"But I do care. I've loved you for a long time. Probably since that foggy
night I drove you to your aunt and uncle's home and on the porch steps, when
I held you and kissed you. You seemed so vulnerable starting your new life.
Being so brave and determined. I didn't want to admit to myself my need for
you or hold you to a commitment by telling you. I regret the pain I forced you
to endure because of me. He stared at her for a moment. "I love you, Carmel."

Was this what she had waited for all those days and weeks and months?
That he would stand before her and ask her to come to him? She began to
tremble.

"Are you going to come down off that tractor so I can kiss you?"

"Since you love me," she said with a twinkle in her eyes, "I'll climb down."

With strong hands, he lifted her high and swung her to the ground. He
chuckled deep in his throat as his arms went around her, pulling her close. She
was quiet, her head on his chest. She felt his heart beating and could smell him,
warm and clean. Finally, he tipped her chin up. His eyes, dark and searching,
stared deep into hers before he bent down to kiss her tenderly. His lips were
warm and moist.

"Oh, Phillip." At her insistence, his mouth and lips searched hers. He kissed
her deeply and long.

Phillip stopped first and held her away from him. "Carmel, we have to talk. Do you want to return to San Francisco? Could you give up your singing to marry a doctor?"

She wasn't sure she heard right. Marry? She looked up.

"I have a friend, Will Nickers, who's a doctor. We shared many hours on the ship, and we plan to set up a practice as partners here in San Jose. I have to speak to my father and see if he wants to enlarge his practice." He stopped. "Carmel, will you marry me?"

"Do you mean you'll be happy living here in San Jose and working? Giving up San Francisco?" She waited.

"I especially want to give up a large practice. I learned about myself and my needs on that hospital ship. But you have talent. Do you want to give that up? What about your music?"

"In some ways I've already given up my music." She grinned. "I'll sing for you. I don't need to sing in front of a crowd. Maybe someday I'll have musicales at the house like your mother used to. I don't ever want to go through auditioning again. But for now, I'm too wrapped up in keeping this ranch going." Then she said, "Phillip, I do have one request. I have to stay here until I know Grant is beginning to heal—inside and out."

"You've grown up, Carmel. You're putting the needs of others above your own. Then, for a time we'll live at Costalotta. Sometime ago, I bought ten acres in Saratoga with beautiful oak trees on it. If you like, we could build."

"Do you accept my terms?" she asked.

"Hey, who's proposing here?"

They both cried, "Me!" and laughed.

"Oh, kiss me again, Phillip," she said, crying now.

He kissed the salty tears on her lips.

They heard the dogs barking before they saw them. A large, wild brown rabbit ran across their path and disappeared into the orchard, the panting dogs close behind.

Phillip watched the chase. "The Chinese say, 'A rabbit crossing your path generates a long, happy life.'"

Carmel giggled. "Yes, and you know what rabbits do? They bring forth generations."

"By the way, I never asked, where did you get your name, Genevieve Carmel?"

"Genevieve was the name of my mother's best friend. Carmel is the city on Monterey Bay where Mom and Dad fell in love."

"Well, Genevieve Carmel St. John, we'll add only one name to the list. Bar-on." He chuckled and tucked her arm under his.

They left the orchard and headed toward the house. They would celebrate with champagne the beginning of their new life together.

My thanks to June Tressler, a dear friend, who encouraged me to finish the book. My editor, Carol Mann and Bob Hurlburt, my computer mentor.

The Stone Must Break is a tale of people who lived during WWII. It is as accurate as possible regarding factual people and events. The words of Charlie Low, Izzy Gomez, Shorty Roberts, and Tempest Storm are fictitious.

The events surrounding the *Solace*, the first hospital ship in the Pacific, are based on the actual recorded manifest. The captains, Steadman and Richardson, are real people. However, the typhoon actually happened in 1944.

Jean Lee Porter

978-0-595-45462
0-595-45462-3

Printed in the United States
97948LV00001B/234/A

9 780595 454624